Love Potion #9

Claire Cross

JOVE BOOKS, NEW YORK

MAGICAL LOVE is a trademark of Penguin Putnam Inc.

LOVE POTION #9

A Jove Book / published by arrangement with
the author

PRINTING HISTORY
Jove edition / July 1999

The Penguin Putnam Inc. World Wide Web site address is
http://www.penguinputnam.com

ISBN: 0-515-12529-6

A JOVE BOOK®
Jove Books are published by The Berkley Publishing Group,
a division of Penguin Putnam Inc.,
375 Hudson Street, New York, New York 10014.
JOVE and the "J" design
are trademarks belonging to Penguin Putnam Inc.

PRINTED IN THE UNITED STATES OF AMERICA

10 9 8 7 6 5 4 3 2 1

Love
Potion #9

0

THE FOOL

Northern Italy—August 1420

The gypsies slid into the town square as quietly as the dusk, gold on their earlobes glinting like starlight, women's voluminous skirts rustling like the wind. They clung to the twilight shadows, silent and watchful.

They came in silk and velvet, fabulous colors, gold and silver, gems aplenty, their tanned feet bare. To Lilith's eyes, her clan was like visiting royalty among the dour townspeople, a glimmer of something rich and fine that these peasants would otherwise never know.

She walked proudly in the midst of her *kumpania,* refusing to acknowledge the townspeople's watchful silence. There had been a time when the *Rom*'s arrival had been greeted with cheers in this town. But on this night, suspicion was in the air, a taint of danger that no one with a nose could miss.

Cards and palms, even the tang in the wind, told the *Rom* that something of import would happen here this night, something with dire consequences for their own fate. It was as clear as a summoning. A shiver raced over Lilith's flesh as she stepped into the square, but she ignored the whisper of her Gift.

In her secret heart, she admitted that she was afraid.

Lilith fingered the tarot card hidden beneath her shawl. It had been the last card Sebastian had drawn, the card that had seemed so inappropriate at the time.

Lilith could almost feel the warmth from Sebastian's fingers still lingering on the card; she ran her thumb across its painted surface as the crowd parted. She craned her neck, seeking a glimpse of him in the crowd, seeking an explanation, seeking reassurance that her uncle had called the matter wrong.

But Sebastian was not there.

As Lilith's heart sank and her uncle's expression turned grim, the town crier raised his voice. He was a portly man, obviously filled with self-importance. "As you know, a woman, a kind and gentle widow, has been killed in the sanctity of her own home."

The crowd stirred angrily and the gypsies exchanged glances of concern.

"We gather this evening to see justice served, for the guilty culprit is in our own hands."

The hangman stepped forward and the *Rom* instinctively shrank back against the walls. The peasants cheered in bloodthirsty anticipation as the hangman donned his black hood.

"We have the murderer!" the crier shouted. "We know his name and 'tis not unfamiliar to you all."

And Lilith's lover was led into the square.

She caught her breath, her fingers tightening over the card. Sebastian, so tall and straight, so handsome, his chestnut hair in disarray, his wondrous eyes flashing in displeasure. Lilith's heart thundered, her gaze greedily devoured the sight of him.

Three whole days she had endured without his beguiling touch, the echo of his laughter, the warm glint in his eye.

This was why he had not returned! Relief made Lilith's knees weaken. She had not granted her maidenhead in vain. She cast a triumphant glance to her uncle, but that man did not even look her way.

Lilith noted that Sebastian's fine linen shirt was soiled, as he would never have permitted, had he been given the choice. His hands were bound behind his back, yet he managed to retain his dignity. There was a confident swagger to his step.

"This man"—roared the crier—"this man is infected with the witchery of the Egyptians! He killed his own neighbor in a bloodthirsty rage, a rage unlike anything ever witnessed in him before. The man is enchanted! These wandering sorcerers have cast demons into his soul, they have made him other than what he is!''

It was only then that Lilith fully understood the import of the crier's words. Her eyes widened in shock.

''NO!'' Lilith called in her dismay. This must be a cruel jest! She would vouch for her love. ''No, Sebastian is innocent!''

''HUSH!'' elderly Dritta hissed in Lilith's ears, but Lilith ignored her council.

Sebastian's head snapped up, his gaze seeking the source of Lilith's voice. Lilith's heart leapt when he smiled. She waved madly, oblivious to the agitated crowd. He *did* love her, after all! He had not come before because he could not come.

And surely nothing could come between them now.

''Sebastian, Sebastian, I am here!'' The gypsies instinctively stepped back into protective shadows and closed ranks around Lilith.

''Lilith!'' he roared and struggled against his bonds for the first time.

''You see the truth of it,'' the crier declared, his voice filled with disgust. ''He is tainted by vagabonds.''

''We are not vagabonds!'' Lilith cried angrily, but Dritta drove an elbow into her ribs.

The councilman spared Sebastian a glance and raised his voice over the din. ''The priest demands you be burned,'' he declared with a cold determination that chilled Lilith's blood. ''But you are Giorgio's son.'' There was a heavy pause and it seemed everyone in the square held their breath.

Lilith bit her lip and clenched her fingers. They would release him. Surely they would set Sebastian free.

He was innocent, he had to be!

The crier's grim voice carried over the expectant crowd. ''So, in deference to your father, we choose to hang you.''

''NO!'' Lilith fought to be free of the gypsies encircling her, frantic to go to her beloved's side. ''This is wrong! It is unjust! Sebastian is innocent!'' Lilith managed to say no more in defense of her lover, for Dritta clamped an iron hand across her mouth.

"Fool!" the older woman muttered. "They will see you dead this very night!" Two cousins caught Lilith's arms from the back and held her powerless, despite her struggles.

And as Lilith watched helplessly, the hangman fitted the noose around Sebastian's neck.

Lilith's mouth went dry. They could not do it. She fought, she bit, but she was sorely outnumbered. Desperate tears stung her eyes, but there was nothing she could do.

The crier cleared his throat and glared pointedly to the *Rom*. "The burning," he declared ominously, "we will save for the gypsy harlot. We shall burn the *puttana* who bewitched and tainted one of our finest sons." The crowd hissed, the gypsies stiffened.

Sebastian had not been bewitched! They were in love!

"Lilith!" Sebastian bellowed as he twisted against the heavy rope that bound his hands. "I promised I would return to you and I will, I WILL! I swear it to you."

Lilith bit Dritta's hand. "Sebastian!" she managed to cry. "I love you!"

Any answering declaration had no chance to leave Sebastian's lips. The hangman tightened the noose and kicked away the stool beneath the younger man's feet. Sebastian writhed as he dangled. Lilith could not bear to watch, she could not bear to turn away. Every eye was riveted on his struggle, but not a soul stepped forward to aid him. Lilith chanted his name in her mind, her tears falling on her cheeks.

"*No!*" Lilith screamed into Dritta's hand. The *kumpania* beset her again and she fought against them. She wanted to be beside Sebastian, she wanted to touch him one last time, she wanted to whisper farewell.

Then suddenly, Sebastian was still.

And the townspeople turned as one, a thirst for vengeance bright in their eyes. A bevy of burning torches were lit one after the other in rapid succession. The square was suddenly flooded with blinking orange light. The firelight flickered off the malice etched into the peasants' faces and Lilith's eyes widened as she suddenly understood her own peril.

She realized that they meant to see the burning done this very night.

The burning of her.

When her family released her, Lilith needed no urging to run as fast as her feet could carry her. The *Rom* retreated like the wind in the trees, but the infuriated crowd lent chase.

Within a trio of heartbeats, Lilith and her *kumpania* were fleeing through the cobbled streets, racing toward the hills they knew so well, running for the forest that had sheltered them all these years.

They ran to the screams of those behind, they ran with their hearts pounding like thunder, they ran aching with betrayal and fear, they ran until they could no longer breathe. They caught old Dritta beneath the elbows when she stumbled, they swept children on to their shoulders.

And they ran for their lives.

It was only when the town that had welcomed them just a year past was a small orange glow in the distance, only when the villager's vengeful cries had faded to nothing, that they halted, panting beneath the protective shadows of the trees. Every gaze dragged back to the angry village, every ear strained for sounds of pursuit.

But none came.

For now.

Lilith found Dritta by her side once more, and she braced herself for the older woman's tirade. But Dritta, with eerie certainty, plucked the tarot card from beneath Lilith's shawl.

"Fool," she snorted and Lilith knew she did not refer to the card itself. Dritta's lip curled in disdain, the patina of moonlight on her features made her look older than she was. "You *knew* better."

"It was just a card!" Lilith protested.

Dritta's eyes flashed, her fingers curled around the card as she hissed. "You have the Gift, you can see beyond others. Your mother's talent courses through your veins! How *dare* you disregard what you have been told?"

"I did not know. . . ." Lilith blinked back her tears, still fighting to understand what had just happened.

Sebastian was dead.

Dead and lost to her for all time.

It seemed suddenly that the world was devoid of promise,

that nothing mattered any longer. A magickal summer of promise was over and there would never be another.

Sebastian, her lover true, dangled dead at the end of a hangman's noose. Lilith wanted only to seclude herself and weep, not answer Dritta's demanding questions.

But Dritta spat in the grass. "You *knew*, you had to know that the Fool brings change and choice, transformation and journey. I taught you as much."

Lilith folded her arms across her chest and took a shaking breath, knowing that no one would respect her showing the weakness of tears. "*Sebastian* drew the card," she said deliberately. "And clearly, Sebastian will journey no longer."

"No?" Dritta chuckled to herself, her response making Lilith look deeply into the older woman's eyes. She found a curious certainty there, as well as a twinkle of mischief. "Maybe not in the way that you will."

"What do you mean?"

"Use the Gift you have been granted, child," Dritta urged, her tone more gentle now. She arched a brow. "Have you never truly listened to the tales we share? Nor attended the cards you read so well? You read for him, you answered his query about love with your own heart hanging full as a pomegranate ready to be plucked and peeled."

Lilith blushed.

"I saw you watch him, all the days since we came, child. I saw your eyes when he came to you for his future, I saw the look that passed between you two when he came to our camp. I knew what would happen—as would you, had you cared to look." Dritta shook her head, and Lilith knew she had no secrets beneath this woman's astute glance.

Lilith looked away.

Dritta turned the card between them, the painting catching the moon's ethereal light. Her voice turned thoughtful. "This card, this card of his love, is your card as well, is it not? Are you this Sebastian's love?"

Lilith's tears welled. She bit her lip, unable to keep from looking back to the distant glow of the village. Her heart ached with the weight of knowing she would never hear him laugh again. "You know that I was," she whispered.

"And you think love is something that dies with the

flesh?'' Dritta snorted. She suddenly gripped Lilith's shoulder, her fingers digging into Lilith's skin. The younger woman did not dare step away. "You *are* his love, for better or worse. He has sworn to return to you, and a pledge made on the gallows is not readily dismissed."

Lilith frowned. "But . . . how?"

Dritta chuckled. "How indeed?" She handed the card back to Lilith with a courtly air that earned her much silver from the *gadje,* a mysterious smile lurking on her lips. Lilith stared at the card, willing it to give her an answer.

The Fool spoke of travels, of a journey beyond your current place, a new beginning, a shucking of an old skin.

A beginning like a new life.

Lilith's eyes widened in sudden understanding and she met Dritta's gaze with astonishment. "Sebastian will return as a babe!"

Dritta's smile softened. "As do we all." She tapped Lilith on the shoulder. "And you, you had best be ready, child."

Lilith frowned at the card. Because even if Sebastian was reborn this very day, she would be aged before he grew to be a man once more. And if it was not this very day . . . Lilith could not bear the thought.

She could not *die* before Sebastian returned!

Lilith's hand rose to her lips, an ancient rumor echoing in her ears. Could it be true? Dritta would know. She cleared her throat and gave the words voice while she dared. "It is whispered that there is a way to immortality."

Dritta nodded, her eyes bright. "I do not know it, child, or on your mother's memory I would tell it to you." She leaned closer, her brow nearly touching Lilith's own, her dark gaze boring into Lilith's eyes. "But there are others, others who know different secrets than we. With your Gift, you can find them, learn what they know, prepare yourself."

Lilith was shocked by the very suggestion. "But I cannot leave the *kumpania*!"

Dritta's expression saddened. "You cannot stay."

Lilith noticed only now that the rest of her *Rom* family lingered in the shadows behind Dritta, watchful, silent as birds. There was a new distance in their gazes, a wariness not unlike the way they regarded the *gadje*. They all shared now in her uncle's expression of the past few days.

Only now, Lilith understood that they had sheltered her only in defiance of the *gadje*. And in doing so, they had risked their very lives. Any affection Lilith had known here, any old obligation to her mother, was gone. As she looked into the fathomless shadows of countless dark eyes, Lilith knew she too had been judged.

She was *mahrime*. Polluted. Unclean. She had consorted with a man not of her own breed, not of the true blood, not *tacho rat*. She was tainted.

And through no fault of his own, he left her doubly shamed, for Sebastian had not rendered the bride price to Lilith's *kumpania* for taking her maidenhead.

It did not matter that Lilith had granted it willingly. Only now she saw that in doing so, she had lost the only family, the only life, she had ever known.

It was a high price to pay for love, but Lilith regretted nothing. She could never have denied the passionate touch of the man she loved. If nothing else, she had those golden moments to treasure until—if?—she and Sebastian found each other once more.

"You must leave," Dritta said resolutely. "You are of us no longer."

Lilith lifted her chin. Even knowing this was the way things had always been done did not steal the sting from the wound. Her own family denied her. They cast her out to the four winds, they left her open to all manner of dire fates. The very fact of their denial made Lilith deeply angry.

But she could deny them in return.

First, knowing how they loved a tale, she would give them no tale of her departure to savor for the years ahead. She would not weep or gnash her teeth, or beg forgiveness that could not be granted.

She would leave silently.

And she would continue to deny them, as they denied her, for every day that remained of her life. Lilith straightened stubbornly, knowing that she would never forget this rejection.

"You are right," she told Dritta proudly. "I will leave

the *kumpania*. From this moment, I am not *Rom*."

"You are yet *Rom*."

"No." Lilith met the older woman's gaze steadily. "I choose to be *Rom* no longer."

Dritta shook her head. "It is in your blood, child. Who you are will follow you."

"I will not let it." Lilith stared at the others for a long moment, noting the unmistakable distrust in those eyes. For one deed, they would forget everything that had been between them, all the things she had done for them, all the bonds that tied them together. Lilith did not care if it was the Way, it would be her way no longer. She raised her voice. "Do not fear my taint, you who have been my brothers and sisters. I will leave this very night."

The relief that sweep through the watchful group was nearly tangible.

Lilith's anger rose anew as she turned away, only the sight of a rare tear sliding down Dritta's wrinkled cheek giving her pause. Lilith hesitated, her love for this woman making her ache to see her weep.

Dritta's fingertips gently touched her cheek. "*Bahtalo drom*, child," she whispered unevenly.

Lucky road. There would be no forgiveness for Lilith here, no second chance, no opportunity to regain her place.

No. She had been cast out for all time.

Lilith took a deep breath and plucked the Fool card from Dritta's hand, then abruptly turned away. She did not know where she would go, where she would find shelter, what dangers would confront her, whether she even could discover the secret of immortality.

But Lilith would cut a new path, make a new life, find a haven for herself in some corner of the world. She would become something other than what she was, she would shed the identity that had cost her all like a second skin. She would wait for the reappearance of her one true love.

It seemed that Sebastian was not the only one who took a step toward new horizons this day.

1

~

THE MAGICIAN

Toronto—August 1999

It was hotter than Hades, the kind of sticky steamy summer day that most people consider more characteristic of New Orleans than the great white north. The humidity was oppressive and tempers throughout the city were wearing thin on that Saturday afternoon.

And Mitch Davison had the misfortune to be moving.

"I wanna go swimming!" three-year-old Jen wailed from the back seat of the much-abused Honda wagon. She kicked her feet against her car seat impatiently and Mitch caught a glimpse of her trembling lower lip in the rearview mirror. The treasured toys she refused to entrust to the professional movers filled most of the back of the car—at least what was available after the family wolfhound staked his turf.

"I'm hot," her older brother Jason agreed.

Both children looked expectantly to their father, as though he could solve everything.

Mitch tried, he really did.

"Well, you're just going to have to wait a little bit longer," he said with as much cheer as he could dredge up. "What kind of Kool-Aid should we make first?"

The dog nudged Mitch in the back of the neck with his wet nose, demanding an open window. Mitch rolled down his window and got a great furry head beside his ear as a bonus. Cooley panted like a blast furnace on his shoulder.

"Cherry! And I wanna swim *now*!" Jen declared as though volume could make it be so.

A restless night and an unsettled day was affecting the toddler's usual sunny disposition. It was a tough day for them, Mitch knew, but he wasn't having a lot of fun himself. The sweat was running down his back like a river, and not for the first time, he knew why parents naturally came in teams.

Not that Janice would have done any better with this day than Jen was doing. That thought did just about nothing to improve Mitch's mood.

Maybe, maybe, Andrea was already at the house. Mitch could really use her help this weekend.

Which virtually guaranteed that she *wouldn't* be there. The last characteristic Mitch would attribute to his stepmother was reliability.

"I'm working on it, Jen," he said. "Just hang with me. How about a song for our new house?"

Jason started "Old Macdonald" and much to Mitch's relief, Jen went for the diversion. He turned into the common driveway that ran behind the houses on their street. Ramshackle garages were interspersed with new ones, sunflowers and grapevines dangling over fences as though they would take over the lane given half a chance.

"Look at those sunflowers!" Mitch pointed out the flowers in an effort to distract the kids when their song ended.

"They're really big," Jason pronounced, with his usual quiet voice.

"Orange!" Jen declared in marked contrast. She shook her beloved Bun by the ear. "I wanna swim!"

"Any minute now." Mitch turned into the driveway behind their house and his heart sank.

The yard that was now his own was a chaotic mess of greenery. The dandelions certainly had been a little bit more manageable when he had looked at the house.

Well, Jen would have to make do. Mowing the weeds was hardly on the agenda today.

A striped gray cat sat on the fence between their yard and an artfully overgrown garden beyond. The cat was backed by a brilliant array of bobbing flowers. It eyed the Honda's occupants, then calmly licked its paw.

Cooley barked, the noise enough to deafen a normal man at such close range. Mitch opened the door and 140 pounds of wolfhound exploded across the yard, barking his brains out.

Well, no one would miss that they had arrived.

The cat gave Cooley the disdainful look that cats everywhere reserve for non-felines and proceeded to clean the other paw from the safety of its perch. Cooley was beside himself, running back and forth, but at least he was occupied.

And he *was* flattening some of the weeds.

Jen began to bellow for escape, Jason was out the door and off to explore—no doubt to look for bugs—and Mitch was left to manage all the details. Once he had broken trail through the yard and unlocked the kitchen door, he wasn't surprised to find no sign of Andrea.

And the movers were ringing the front bell.

It was going to be a long day.

Lilith was in a funk. She rattled through her house, picking listlessly at this crystal or that astrological chart. She was dimly aware of the moving van disgorging possessions next door, but wasn't really interested.

She was hot in more ways than one.

It was their 579th anniversary and—just like the last 578 times—Sebastian hadn't showed.

Yet, even given that, today Lilith couldn't evict Sebastian from her mind. The memory of the night they had spent together tormented her, the echo of his last pledge rang in her ears. She had dreamed of him the night before, relived that precious night they had together, was sure she could feel his hands on her when she awakened this morning.

But he wasn't there.

Maybe it was the heat.

Maybe it was a marathon run of celibacy that was getting on her nerves. Lilith had been patient, but immortality alone wasn't a lot of fun. She was tired of being tough, she was tired of being resilient, she was tired of being cheerful in solitude.

Lilith was done with waiting.

And Sebastian was late, by any means of calculation.

Tarot card reader, astrologist, and crystal therapist, Lilith had adopted all the conventional trappings of the occult to mask her Gift. She was reluctant to give any hint of the real nature of her talent, so, she blamed it on her tarot cards. People found it easier to believe that the cards held the secrets of the future than that Lilith could see the truth in their eyes.

For the fact was that the draught for immortality—when Lilith ultimately earned the right to a sip—had added an interesting twist to her innate Gift. After drinking that elixir, Lilith could see anyone's match right there in their eyes. Regardless of where that lovematch was in the world, she could set anyone on the path to connecting with his or her soulmate.

It was a bitter kind of irony to make her living consoling the lovelorn when she was so lonely herself. Lilith didn't even know how many weddings she'd been invited to attend, mostly because she had in some way been responsible for introducing the bride and groom.

Always a bridesmaid, as the saying went.

The experience was getting old. She'd stopped going stag to weddings five years ago, but it didn't make her feel any better. The invitations were bad enough.

Sebastian was taking his own sweet time returning to her, that much was for certain. Lilith remembered the way he had kissed her on that long-ago midsummer afternoon and her skin heated. She closed her eyes and leaned back in her favorite chair to remember one more time.

So much for promises made on the gallows.

Lilith scowled at the room and caught the knowing expression in D'Artagnan's eye. That cat saw too much, that was for sure, and it was a blessing that he couldn't talk. He had moved in with purpose two years before, characteristically disinterested in Lilith's opinion about the matter.

She wondered whether the cat knew that she only let him stay in deliberate defiance of *Rom* norms. Cats licked themselves, polluting inside with outside. Cats were dirty in *Rom* terms. Cats were *mahrime*.

But then, Lilith had been *mahrime* herself for a long time. Maybe there was a twisted kind of justice in

D'Artagnan's deliberate adoption of her. Maybe they belonged together.

There was a promising thought.

She wondered why she'd even had a flicker of concern about *mahrime* conventions. It wasn't as though they had anything to do with her. Nope, Lilith was just a witch who told fortunes, not a gypsy at all. She had studied *gadje* witchcraft, learned to mix potions and cast spells, draw circles for the moon and read astrological charts.

She was not *Rom.*

She refused to be *Rom.*

And that was that.

D'Artagnan started cleaning himself—always fastidious—and even the sight of his little darting tongue made Lilith fidget.

Oh, she had been alone far too long.

And what was keeping Sebastian?

Lilith picked up her deck of cards, shuffled and considered the riddle of what to do. She fanned the cards across the table and plucked one from their midst, her heart skipping a beat when she turned it over and saw what it was.

The Magician.

A card about making things happen, a card for the creative and the powerful, a card hinting that it was time things got done.

A card that demanded immediate action.

It seemed a rather apt card given the moment. Why *was* she just waiting for Sebastian? It certainty wasn't like Lilith to sit back and wait for anything when she could do something to make a difference. Although it would be a lot more romantic if Sebastian swept into her life again on his own.

He had *promised*, after all.

Lilith tapped her toe. She considered whether the cards were telling her to get off her butt. She had looked deeply into her own eyes reflected in the mirror, time and again, without catching the merest glimpse of Sebastian. So, Lilith knew her Gift didn't extend to herself.

But maybe some of the tricks she had learned over the centuries could be put to use.

The thought had no sooner crossed her mind than Lilith was on the way to the kitchen. She checked the calendar and discovered that both moon and sun were right for a love spell. That could only be a sign that this was the way to go.

She felt better already. Whether her actions provoked a response or not, it was good just to be *doing* something. Lilith turned on the radio and tuned into the oldies station that was her usual choice. The first song made Lilith smile and turn up the volume.

It was "Love Potion Number Nine."

Perfect. She'd take that as a sign. A potion it would be.

Lilith danced as she conjured, a reckless glee making her feel decidedly younger than her many years. Her cauldron was on the stove and the strongest love potion of all time was rapidly being assembled.

If Sebastian was anywhere within the galaxy, Lilith was going to make sure he'd get this message Special Delivery. And when he showed up, well, she had several hundred years of creative thinking to put to good use.

Lilith felt the warmth of desire heat to a fever pitch with every pinch of this and two petals of that cast into the brew.

Anticipation hummed beneath her skin and every passing second added to her conviction that this spell would work. The mixture began to boil and its earthy perfume rolled through the house.

And Lilith chanted softly before the simmering brew.

> *"Lover true, come to me,*
> *Through the air or across the sea.*
> *Once we loved through the night with style*
> *Come back NOW..."*

Lilith chuckled under her breath as she thought of the perfect ending.

"I'll make it worth your while."

She quickly ladled the bubbling green brew into her coffee cup. The last chorus of the song bounced off the kitchen walls, D'Artagnan lashed his tail in the doorway, his eyes bright. The potion smelled absolutely vile.

Lilith held her nose, she closed her eyes, she held her breath.

She took a sip.

• • •

Andrea sailed in at six, announcing that she had a massive chocolate cake, of all things. Jen and Jason were delighted, Mitch was not.

Junk food was an old issue between Andrea and Mitch.

"You have heard of the four food groups, haven't you?" he demanded by way of greeting, flicking the front door shut with his fingertips behind his guest.

"Of course!" Andrea grinned unrepentantly over her shoulder as she danced into the kitchen. "Chocolate, sugar, fat, and caffeine, right?" She wrinkled her nose. "I thought the kids were a bit young for coffee, you know, but otherwise I've got it covered."

Mitch shoved a hand through his hair, grimaced, and trudged back to the kitchen. Andrea had a heart of gold, even if she was chronically late and more than a little disorganized. Mitch's deceased father's second wife was the only family Mitch had left, besides his own children. Despite their ongoing differences of opinion, he *liked* Andrea.

Maybe because she was so completely different from him.

She was nearing sixty, her short hair uniformly silver, her blue eyes invariably twinkling. Andrea could afford to indulge herself, after outliving three comparatively successful men, and indulge herself she did. She dressed her short and slightly plump figure both expensively and exquisitely, she took lavish trips, and more often than not treated herself and her friends to fancy dinners.

And Andrea's generosity extended to include Mitch's kids. Never having had children of her own, she adored Jen and Jason. And the kids couldn't have had a more indulgent grandmother.

For whatever that was worth.

Jen clapped her hands in delight at first sight of the cake, Jason studied it solemnly. Both licked their lips. Mitch noticed that the icing was starting to melt.

To her credit, Jen was much happier since Mitch had taken an hour to hack down a circle of grass and inflate her pink wading pool. And the break he had had to take to watch both kids in the water hadn't been that hard to bear.

Never mind the cold beer he had treated himself to.

Of course, then, it had been back to the grind of moving. This day seemed as if it would never end. He returned philosophically to the box he had been unpacking and wondered how he had managed to accumulate such a lot of apparently useless kitchen junk.

Andrea considered the cake. "But I could get mocha fudge next time, if you'd rather."

"Andrea!" Mitch looked up and gave his stepmother the Eye. "They'll be up half the night with the sugar buzz, which is the last thing I need right now."

"Your problem is that you want everything nice and neat," the older woman informed him with a shake of her finger. "One of these days, Mitch, you're just going to have to admit that the world isn't always going to play by your rules."

"Yeah, *this* was definitely in my plan," Mitch grumbled. Raising his kids alone was a far cry from the 'until death do us part' that Mitch had always envisioned.

Andrea took a deep breath, immediately catching his meaning. "Mitch, the only decent thing that woman ever did for you is sitting right—"

"Hey!" Mitch straightened and glared.

Andrea bit her tongue and fell silent, though it was clear she had plenty more to say.

Mitch glanced pointedly at the kids, then met his stepmother's gaze again. "We agreed *not* to talk about that," he said silkily.

Andrea grimaced, then cleared a corner of the table and served up massive portions of cake. The kids dove in. Cooley circled, inhaling out errant crumbs, his sniffing nose on full throttle.

Mitch watched his kids carefully and finally decided they hadn't understood Andrea's reference. Fortunately, they were still too young to pay a lot of attention to adult innuendo, but that would change.

Mitch was dreading the day he couldn't protect them from everything nasty in the world, or make everything come right with a hug and a Band-Aid.

"You can't ignore the truth forever," Andrea said now.

"I can sure as hell try," Mitch growled, digging deter-

minedly for the coffeemaker. "And where does it say that
your interpretation is the truth, hmmm?"

Andrea rolled her eyes. "Let's just agree to disagree on
the subject of Janice, shall we?" She moved a box to the
floor and perched on a kitchen chair. "I like this place,"
she said brightly, then ran a fingertip across the counter and
grimaced. "Although it really could use a good cleaning."

Mitch cast her a significant glance. "There's a sponge in
the sink."

Andrea laughed. "I don't do windows." Before Mitch
could say anything to that, she leaned forward, her eyes
shining. "Have you met your neighbors?"

Mitch snorted a laugh and gestured to the chaos around
him. "Oh, yeah, you missed the big social tea this afternoon. I was up all night making watercress sandwiches.
Cutting off all those crusts was really a pain."

Andrea playfully threw a wad of packing paper at him.
"I never know when to believe you," she complained, then
pointed to the house with a cat and garden. "You have a
fortune-teller for a neighbor!"

Mitch slanted a glance to the window and back. "Go on.
Here I thought this was a good neighborhood."

"No, really! She has the most darling little neon sign out
front."

"Eenie meenie jelly beanie, the spirits are about to
speak." Mitch wiggled his eyebrows and the kids giggled,
recognizing the line from cartoon reruns.

"But are they friendly?" Jason demanded.

"Just listen!" the kids crowed together.

Jen took a chocolate hit on her chest and pulled up her
bathing suit to suck the icing off. Cooley sniffed with disappointment and she dropped her spoon for him, going after
the rest of her cake with both hands.

Mitch didn't have it in him to argue the point. He'd have
to dunk Jen right into the tub before bed.

Too bad they didn't make a spin cycle just for kids.

"Lilith's Lovematches is what it says," Andrea said with
a toss of her hair. "Isn't that lovely? So romantic!"

Mitch snorted. "Visa and Mastercard accepted." The
coffeemaker wasn't in this box so he set it aside and opened
the next. God knew he was going to need the sucker in the

morning. Might as well find it now and make life a little easier.

"Don't be silly, it's not really like that."

Mitch didn't bother to hide his skepticism. "She does it for free?"

"Of course not!"

"Uh-huh. Need I say more?"

Andrea leaned closer, undeterred by his attitude. "Do you think she'd do a reading for me?"

"Andrea!" Mitch spun to face his stepmother, wishing for the umpteenth time that she wasn't so trusting. "How many times have I told you that all of that stuff is garbage?"

"It's not!"

"It *is*." Mitch poked through the box, wondering why on earth he had saved half this stuff. "These people are all charlatans looking to make a quick buck."

"You don't even know her!"

Mitch's tone was grim. "I don't have to."

"Well! You certainly don't have a very open mind," his stepmother huffed.

"These things are just a cover for opportunism. I don't even know how many frauds have been uncovered. It's old news." Mitch eyed his stepmother pointedly. "You should be more careful about going to these places, let alone giving them your credit card number."

Andrea folded her arms across her chest, a sure sign that she was digging in her heels. "Nonsense! There's bad in every kind, but lots of these people have a genuine gift. You should go and meet this woman, just to prove yourself wrong."

"No way."

"She's your neighbor!"

"Cooley's going to eat her cat any day now, so even the most remote acquaintance is doomed."

Andrea leaned forward, eyes gleaming. "You're afraid that you could be wrong."

Mitch's head snapped up. "I am not!"

"Daddy's not afraid of nothing," Jen declared supportively. She tapped her besmirched hand on Andrea's wrist with a confidential air she had obviously copied from that woman. "Nana, we went swimming."

"Did you, dear?" Andrea's gaze never wavered from Mitch and he knew she wasn't distracted in the least from their conversation. "I'll bet you've never even talked to a psychic."

"There's a yawning hole in my life." Mitch spied his prey lurking in the bottom of the box beneath countless faded Tupperware tubs. "Ha!" He hauled out the coffeemaker and set it on the counter victoriously.

Now the filters. Could he possibly have been so organized as to have packed them in the same box?

Andrea arched a brow. "Some investigative reporter," she charged softly. "I thought journalists were supposed to base their conclusions on *facts*."

Whoa! That statement caught Mitch's attention as surely as it was meant to do. There was nothing he held more sacred than his journalistic integrity.

Except maybe his natural ability to hone in on the truth. Mitch was a damn good reporter and he knew it.

But Andrea had found a telling niche in his armor. He *knew* that all this paranormal stuff was bunk, but he had never actually proved it. And that was not a welcome realization.

"Are you insinuating that I'm making a biased judgement?" he asked quietly.

"No," Andrea retorted with a smile. "I'm *saying* you are." She paused, and smiled slowly. "Afraid to find out that you're wrong, Mr. Hotshot Reporter?"

"I'm not wrong," Mitch said in a low voice that should have warned Andrea that he was on dangerous ground.

If she understood the warning, she ignored it. Andrea shook her head with mock disparagement. "Your father always said you were too stubborn for your own good. *I* thought he was too hard on you, but . . ."

"That's it!" Mitch slammed the box closed and marched to the front door. He turned back to glare at his stepmother. "Watch the kids for a few minutes, would you?"

He would go and meet the flake, see that she was a charlatan, and be home within five minutes. Mission accomplished.

It wasn't exactly rocket science.

Mitch ignored Andrea's laughter as he strode down the steps and across the lawn. The neon sign blinked in candy-cane pink.

Lilith's Lovematches.

Right.

Lilith prowled through her house restlessly, noting how the light coming through the back windows had turned golden. Soon the twilight would creep over the sky, the time she found more and more difficult to bear, that moment when it seemed anything could happen.

She had first seen Sebastian in that strange light, the sun sinking on the horizon, the moon dawning opposite, the first stars scattered across the sky. And in that one moment, Lilith had been smitten.

And later, the night they had shared, he had come to the *Rom* camp in that same magickal time of day. Lilith hugged herself, remembering the heat in his eyes, the slow smile that was just for her. Her heart pounded in recollection and her mouth went dry.

The doorbell rang and Lilith's heart jumped.

Sebastian!

But a wink of neon from the corner of her eye killed her excitement. She had just left the sign on.

Lilith swore softly. The last thing she wanted to do to-night was provide advice when she was aching—and itch-ing—herself.

The doorbell rang again, more insistently this time.

Nuts! It wouldn't be right not to answer.

Lilith trudged to the door, her thoughts filled with the memories from a single night of passion. D'Artagnan wound around her ankles when she got to the front hall, but she ignored the cat and opened the door.

Lilith gasped and stared in disbelief.

Sebastian!

His chestnut hair still curled slightly, his eyes were still the same golden brown. He was taller than she remembered and more powerfully built than he had been before. He was a little older than he had been, but then, so was Lilith.

Neither of them were impetuous teenagers any more.

Sebastian wore a red T-shirt that clung damply to his chest and denim shorts that still hid too much of his muscled legs. His feet were shoved into faded running shoes, his hair looked like he had just pushed his fingers through it. Certainly the tinge of impatience in the set of his lips was new, but then Lilith was pretty much out of patience herself.

Obviously, he had had trouble finding her again.

But he was *here*! Just the sight of him—on her very own doorstep—sent a spark racing through Lilith's veins. He was all man, he was her man, he was her beloved.

And she had waited a long long *long* time. This was hardly the moment to waste making conversation.

She had, after all, pledged to make a return worth his while.

Lilith grabbed Sebastian's shirt and hauled him into the foyer. She slammed the door behind him, locked it with one hand as she curled the other one around his neck and kissed him hard.

Sebastian jumped in surprise—maybe he had forgotten how passionate Lilith could be!—but she backed him into the hallway and rolled her tongue into his mouth.

This man was going to know that he was missed.

He tasted so good, the scent of his skin a tantalizing mix of sun and wind and masculinity. Lilith ran her hands over his muscled shoulders and melted inside.

Sebastian made a sound of protest, but Lilith gobbled it up. She didn't care if this was too fast—she was burning with desire. Next time, they would take it slowly.

And the next time and the next time after that. They could spend all night reaffirming their love, a glorious repeat of the passion that had flamed between them once before.

Lilith pressed her breasts against Sebastian and felt the heat of his erection. Ha! She pressed her hips against him and loved how he caught his breath, though he was still obviously trying to tell her something.

She didn't care. They could talk later.

Lilith unzipped his fly, her fingers closing quickly around his erection. Sebastian moaned and caught his breath as she started to caress him. It might have been centuries, but Lilith hadn't forgotten everything her lover had taught her. Sebastian's hands landed on her shoulders as though he was going to push her away.

He muttered something, but Lilith slid her fingers into his hair, slanted her mouth even more demandingly across his. She lifted her dress and rubbed his erection against her bare belly as she kept stroking him. Sebastian sagged against the wall, his fingers slipped beneath her silky panties and clenched her buttocks.

In that moment, Lilith knew that he was all hers.

Lilith urged his fingers into the wetness waiting for him and his erection grew even more. His fingers moved against her, reluctantly, then with increasing vigor. His kiss turned ravenous and Lilith arched against him like a cat in heat.

He felt *so* good.

She pushed him down to the Persian rug, kissing him hungrily all the while. Lilith rolled on top of Sebastian as soon as he hit the floor, chucked her undies, and straddled him. She urged him into her heat without hesitation.

Sebastian was thicker and longer than Lilith remembered but the news was welcome. He gasped, apparently surprised by her as well. Lilith kissed him as though she would devour him whole and rode him hard. The heat rose inside her, demanding they climb further and faster.

When Sebastian clenched her hips, his strong fingers digging into her flesh, and bellowed, Lilith cried out in delight as the warmth of his release flooded her. Every fibre of her being sang in exaltation as she tumbled into the haven of his arms.

Sebastian was back.

And this time, Lilith wasn't going to lose him.

For any price.

2

THE HIGH PRIESTESS

Mitch was quite certain that he had never had a beautiful woman pounce on him before.

He definitely would have remembered that. He felt as though he had just tasted single malt scotch for the first time. Even his toes tingled.

But people didn't just do stuff like this.

Did they? Mitch leaned back against the hardwood floor and kept his eyes tightly closed. He moved his fingers and found the curve of a perfectly bare, luscious buttock beneath his hand. The woman's perfume—something warmly seductive and completely alien to Mitch's life—wound into his nostrils.

His mouth went dry.

Mitch frowned as he reviewed the course of events. He had knocked on the door, he remembered that. And an exotic woman had opened the door. She was dark-eyed and dark-haired, curvaceous, and wearing a dress as red as cherries. He'd never seen a woman like her, outside of Italian fashion magazines.

Mitch had gotten no further than that before her dark eyes flashed in welcome, she hauled him into her foyer, locked the door, and started kissing him like there was no tomorrow.

This neighborhood had one hell of a welcome wagon.

Mitch was unable to explain rationally what had just happened, yet for the moment, he didn't really care. After all, it had been a long, long, *long* three years since Janice had packed her bags, and even longer than that since she had slept with him.

She'd certainly never jumped on him.

Not even once.

Mitch exhaled unevenly, knowing there was no way he could have stopped what just happened, regardless of his usual chivalrous inclinations. Swearing off relationships and just not being a fling kind of guy could seriously impact a man's sex life.

It had certainly impacted Mitch's.

Until just now.

He hadn't had a chance. Mitch was unable to shake the sense that he had just stepped into one of his buddy Kurt's frequently recounted—and seldom believed, at least by Mitch—amorous adventures.

He couldn't exactly remember how things went from here.

"Wow," the lady purred. "You *were* worth waiting for."

She had an accent as exotic as her looks. Something European, maybe French or Italian. Her voice was low, just the sound of it making Mitch shiver in anticipation.

She sighed with obvious pleasure and ran her fingertips across his shoulder. Mitch slanted a glance her way, instinctively bracing himself for a reality check.

But she was smiling. At him.

Mitch stared as his first impression was vehemently reinforced. The lady was a stunner. Dark hair and creamy skin, thick lashes and lips almost as curvy as the rest of her. She was more unabashedly feminine than any woman he had ever seen before.

And her presence was so tranquil. She simply watched him study her, apparently not in a rush to go anywhere or say anything. Mitch had the definite sense that she'd be perfectly content to lay together here all day.

A hint of a smile curved her lips and something in those eyes made Mitch's blood quicken. Her eyes were dark, dark brown, so dark that he couldn't discern where the iris ended and the pupil began. They were remarkable eyes, even more remarkable than the rest of her, which was really saying something.

If the eyes were the window to the soul, this woman's eyes would open a portal into a whole other universe. A universe of secrets, wisdom, and things a man might not really want to know.

Before Mitch could wonder how that kind of whimsy had made its way into the relentless logic that he usually followed, she tapped a finger in the middle of his chest.

A twinkle glimmered in the depths of her eyes. "I told you I'd make coming back worth your while," she murmured, her unabashedly sensual tone making Mitch's heart pound again.

Mitch's good sense chose that moment to return with a vengeance. His eyes widened as realization finally hit. He had just had sex with a complete stranger!

WAS HE OUT OF HIS EVER-LOVING MIND?

For God's sake, he was a journalist! He wrote articles about STDs, he compounded stats about unsafe sex, he had done a series on AIDS. And he, as a matter of personal principle, had never *ever* been casual about intimacy!

Mitch was on his feet in a flash, his hands shaking as he fought against his unruly zipper.

She was still watching him, that bemused smile clinging to her ripe lips. Mitch couldn't even think straight, but he tried to talk his way through it.

"Look, I don't know what just happened here, but . . ."

The woman rolled to one hip and laughed unexpectedly. Her dark, wavy hair cascaded over her shoulder, her dress gaped open to reveal the luscious curves of her breasts. She was so at ease with her sensuality, in marked contrast to how uptight Janice had been, that Mitch had to fight his urge to have a good look.

"Whatever it was," she said, a thread of humor in her voice, "it was very, very good."

Her admiration was so open that Mitch felt the back of his neck heat. What was protocol here? A life without casual sex had left Mitch without a script, never mind a marriage with a woman who hated being touched. This woman's cheerful enjoyment was as puzzling as the situation itself.

Should Mitch apologize? Should he thank her? Should he try to explain?

Explain *what* exactly? Mitch didn't like being at a loss for words, but none popped into his mind to save him.

The woman stretched with leisurely satisfaction, then rose to her feet. Her red floral dress fluttered around her shapely calves, the bodice·draped open as though inviting Mitch to take a look at those creamy breasts.

She treated Mitch to a sultry smile as she flicked back her impossibly long hair, then she took a step closer. Those eyes smoldered and Mitch knew he was not nearly as immune to the lady as he would have liked to have been.

This was crazy. He knew nothing about her.

He was a father, Mitch reminded himself when she sidled closer and his heart began to pound. He was a responsible man. He was a journalist.

He was an *adult*, for God's sake!

"Was it worth your while?" she asked softly and Mitch felt a telltale response in his shorts.

This was not how things should be proceeding! Mitch frowned and tried to look suitably forbidding. He had to steer their conversation back to some rational course.

But the woman wasn't paying any attention to his best glower. Mitch stiffened as her fingertips trailed along the neck of his T-shirt. He fought to keep his mind out of the gutter and his gaze out of her cleavage.

It wasn't easy.

And the way she leaned against him to kiss his throat wasn't helping. "Maybe we should adjourn to the bedroom," she whispered, her words heating Mitch's very blood.

Wait a minute! Mitch cleared his throat deliberately. What he had to do was get to the root of the story.

Right! He'd ask the questions. Familiar ground, to be sure. He summoned his best reporter voice. "When exactly did you tell me that you'd make it worth my while?"

The lady chuckled, her breasts pressed against his chest as she backed Mitch into the door. Mitch's nostrils flooded with the scent of that wondrous perfume, his hands itched to close around her slender waist.

He stared at the ceiling and knew he was in big trouble.

"Well, I never told you directly," she admitted. "But it was in the spell I cast to summon you." She winked when he looked at her in astonishment, those fingertips sliding up his neck and into his hair. "You *must* have heard me."

A little bit too late, Mitch understood her words and remembered his neighbor's stock in trade. "What spell?" he managed to ask.

"The spell that brought you here." The woman chuckled under her breath. "I'm a witch now. I guess you didn't know." Her manner was easy, as though she was confiding something mundane, like a fondness for chocolate. It made it even harder for Mitch to make sense of what she was saying. "I make spells, read fortunes, all of that stuff." The tip of her tongue slid into Mitch's ear and he closed his eyes against a tidal wave of desire. "Right now, though, I'd rather make love."

Mitch grasped her upper arms, put as much space between them as he could, and seized on her claim. He was more than ready to set the record straight. "No, you see, you've got it all wrong. No spell summoned me," he informed her. "I just came to find out about your sign. . . ."

But her hearty laugh startled him into silence. "Sebastian! We've known each other long enough that we don't need to play games."

Mitch stared at her as his blood turned to ice.

Sebastian? Why did she call him Sebastian?

Because, obviously, she thought he was someone else! Suddenly the enthusiasm of her welcome made a whole lot more sense. Mitch had just made one hell of a mistake. She was going to slap him when she learned the truth.

Or worse.

He straightened, frowned, and cleared his throat. "I'm sorry, but I'm not Sebastian," he admitted. The woman blinked, her surprise obvious. "You must have me confused with someone else."

She said nothing at all.

As awkward moments went, this was a biggie. "Uh, Mitch Davison. Your new neighbor to the left." He released her shoulders and stuck out his hand, but she just stared at it and frowned.

And no wonder. She had just mistaken him for some other guy and ravished him as a result. No wonder she looked so stunned—she must be really embarrassed.

Well, she couldn't be any more embarrassed than Mitch was. He cleared his throat and wished he were anywhere else on the face of the earth.

Or that the floor would yawn open and swallow him whole.

No luck on either front, so Mitch shoved one hand through his hair and unlocked the dead bolt behind his back with the other. He took a deep breath. "Look, I'm sorry we got our wires crossed here. We've certainly gotten off to a rocky start and I can only apologize for my part in this."

The lady stared at him as though she didn't understand what he was saying. This conversation had died and was well beyond revival. Mitch tried for his most charming smile, without any noticeable result in her response.

Oh, he was batting a thousand here.

"Maybe it would be best if we just forgot this ever happened," he managed to suggest.

Then, her slender hand snapped out and abruptly gripped his chin. Mitch froze in surprise at the strength of her grip. Her perusal was so thorough, her gaze so cat-bright, that the hair on the back of Mitch's neck started to stand on end.

He had just concluded that things were definitely a little weird on this side of the property line, when the lady went one better.

"No," she concluded, the word barely more than a breath. It fanned against his lips and made Mitch's toes tingle again. "You *are* Sebastian. There's no doubt about it."

"No," Mitch said firmly. "I'm not."

"Yes," the lady said equally firmly. "You are."

Enough was enough. Mitch tried very hard to be polite. "I think," he said with surgical precision, "that I would know if I was this Sebastian person."

The lady's full lips quirked and she lifted one brow, her expression unexpectedly mischievous. "Really?"

Mitch frowned. "Really."

She obviously bit back a smile, as though he had said something particularly funny. Her response pushed Mitch too far. He had had quite enough of whatever flavor of bizarre was being served here.

It was bad enough that he had acted on impulse, it was bad enough that he hadn't been able to control himself, never mind that she was consistently driving his desire toward the sky again. There was something about the flick of her glance, the quirk of her smile, the low whisper of her voice that gave Mitch half a mind to accept her offer, to pretend that he was this Sebastian, and accept the lady's invitation to the bedroom.

That, in and of itself, was so out of character that Mitch could barely wrap his mind around his undeniable urge.

It was too much for her to turn him inside out *and* insist that he didn't even know who he was.

Mitch propped his hands on his hips and glared at the woman who was consistently tying his gut in knots. "Look, I don't know what your deal is or why you think I'm this Sebastian guy, but trust me, I *know* who I am!" His mood worsened when she still looked like she was going to laugh. "Look! I don't even know anybody named Sebastian!"

The lady folded her arms across her chest and regarded him. Her eyes danced. "You're very sure of yourself," she commented dryly.

"And that's a surprising accomplishment? To be sure of my own name?" Mitch rolled his eyes in exasperation. "Thank you very much."

She laughed aloud, the merry sound almost enough to dismiss Mitch's mood.

"You're welcome," she said, completely unrepentant, then tossed her hair. It wasn't quite fair that she kept smiling like that, that she kept looking so damn delighted to have him here in her foyer. Now, she smiled warmly at him. "But then, you always were so confident."

"Were?" Mitch echoed. "I've told you that I'm not who you think I am. And we've never met before. . . ."

The lady interrupted his argument. "So, Mr. Mitch Davison, why do you believe that you've come here?"

"Believe? I *know* why I've come here!" Mitch declared with exasperation. She won the award for infuriating, no doubt about it. "There's no question of believing or misleading myself." He jabbed a finger through the air toward his new house. "I just moved in next door!"

She shrugged easily. "Because you were summoned. I called you just a few hours ago."

Mitch's usual skepticism finally found firm ground. "Look, no spell of yours brought me here. I bought that house months ago! And it wasn't because anyone summoned me—it was because it was what I could afford!"

There was a galling little confession he would have preferred not to have made.

But the lady seemed delighted by this news.

"You bought it *months* ago? Really?" Her smile flashed briefly again and Mitch was confused to feel himself respond to her obvious pleasure. "So, you *were* already on your way! That's wonderful!" She clasped his jaw in her hands and kissed him so quickly that Mitch didn't have time to step away.

He stared down at her, hearing his heartbeat thunder in his ears. She must be a nutcase. There was no other possible explanation for her behavior.

Because Mitch knew that there was no such thing as witches, and certainly no such thing as spells that actually worked.

"I guess I didn't have enough faith, after all these years," she confessed with glowing eyes. "I'm so sorry I underestimated you."

Mitch pushed a hand through his hair, not quite certain where to start in untangling this woman's misconceptions. "Look. I don't actually know you," he said firmly but gently. To his relief, she didn't interrupt. "I can't apologize enough for my behavior—it was wrong."

"It was perfectly right," she breathed, then smiled again. "And that's why you couldn't stop yourself." She nestled closer and clasped his neck, stretching to kiss him again.

But Mitch evaded her touch as he frowned anew, disliking an intuitive sense that she had hit the nail on the head. "It couldn't have been right," he argued carefully. "Because I've never met you before in my life."

Her calm confidence didn't waver, much to Mitch's dismay. She arched one dark brow, as though amused by his protest. "Which particular life do you mean?"

"What was that?"

"Just because we haven't met in this life, doesn't mean we haven't met before." Her tone was surprisingly matter-of-fact. "You may not remember, but I certainly do."

She remembered all her past lives. Oh boy, loony tunes. Mitch worked hard to take her claim in stride but failed. He should have paid more attention to that sign. There was no way he would be able to argue his way free of this one.

"Look. Believe it, don't believe it. We all make our choices," he said lightly. "I'm your new neighbor and that's it as far as I'm concerned. No past lives, no previous scores to settle, or bad karma leading to lives as cockroaches. I don't do mumbo jumbo. One life is just plenty for me."

"So very practical," she teased with soft affection. "Why were you knocking on my door, then?"

Mitch wished that knowing little smile of hers didn't make him want to kiss her quite so badly.

"My stepmother has this idea that people who tell fortunes are perfectly sane," he confessed. "I came over here to prove her wrong." He didn't finish the argument—he didn't think he needed to and he didn't want to be rude.

But the lady didn't seem to get his inference, which surprised Mitch. There was something in those eyes that made him think she didn't miss much.

Mitch pointed in the direction of the neon sign. "You would be the Lilith of Lilith's Lovematches?"

Her sudden smile was dazzling, and she stuck out her hand in turn. "Lilith Romano: tarot card reader, matchmaker, small business owner, damn good cook." She quirked a brow. "And perfectly sane, by all accounts."

She was charming, Mitch had to concede that. "Except for one small kink in the belief system?" he dared to suggest.

Lilith laughed. The sound was rich and rippling, it made Mitch want to laugh along with her. "Speak for yourself," she retorted.

Mitch couldn't completely stop his unwilling smile at her stubborn consistency. Nor could he refuse to shake Lilith's proffered hand.

It would have just been rude.

But he wasn't expecting her touch to send an army of

little tingles over his flesh. The sweet recollection of Lilith's kiss flooded his mind once more, his gaze dropped to her lips in time to see her smile knowingly again.

It was as though she knew what he was thinking and that was a little bit too unsettling for Mitch.

Even if any red-blooded guy would be thinking pretty much the same thing in the same circumstance. He liked to think of himself as somewhat more ethical than the average bear.

Mitch ended their handshake quickly, hauled open the door and stepped out onto her porch. A big sunflower bobbed to one side, its yellow petals seeming to have snared the sunlight.

"Well, I guess it's a question of perspective," he declared, having no real idea what the heck he meant. He had to say *something*.

To Mitch's surprise, Lilith laughed easily again. She leaned in the doorframe, her bare feet on the threshold, her hair wild curls behind her. The gray cat Cooley had chased twined around her ankles, but she ignored it. God, she was sexy.

And very engaging, if wound a bit loose. Mitch felt like an idiot for what he had done.

For what he hadn't been able to *not* do. For a guy who prided himself on his self-control, it was a pretty pathetic showing.

Mitch shoved his hands in his pockets, ashamed at his own behavior and feeling guilty as hell. "Look, Lilith. About what just happened . . ."

"Forget it," Lilith interrupted softly. "It was an honest mistake."

Mitch flicked a glance her way, astounded by this concession. But she appeared to mean it.

"Sorry you got me confused with someone else," he said in a low voice.

Her smile flashed. "Sorry you don't remember."

At least she stuck to her story. Mitch was suddenly reluctant to hurry home and hose down the chocolate cake that must be smeared all over his kitchen by now.

So, she believed in all that New Age gunk. She wasn't the only one, by any means. And if Mitch ignored that,

Lilith was far and away the most intriguing woman he had met in a quite a while.

Maybe ever.

"So, when did you know this Sebastian guy?" he asked impulsively.

Lilith's full lips quirked. "Oh, you and I were together six hundred years ago." She wrinkled her nose playfully. "Give or take."

Mitch stomped hard on his skepticism and told himself he was just being polite. "That would be in a past life?" he asked as mildly as he could.

"Oh, no." Lilith shook her head and frowned, much to Mitch's surprise. "Well, speak for yourself, at least."

Just for himself? Their supposed meeting six hundred years ago wasn't her past life? That could only mean one thing. Mitch felt his brows shoot skyward as he stared back at her.

Lilith's gaze never wavered, the intelligence he saw there never flickered.

Mitch cleared his throat and came up with his best reporter voice. "Are you implying that you're six *hundred* years old?"

"No, I'm saying it." Lilith winked. "Frankly, I don't think I look a day over thirty."

Mitch stared as the words sank in. That was crazy, plain and simple. Trust him to find a wacko so attractive—it fit perfectly with every other incident in his romantic history!

Mitch was out of there.

"Right!" he called with false cheer from the safety of his own porch. He waved, then ducked inside the door, feeling decidedly at odds.

His gorgeous, passionate, clever neighbor thought she was an immortal. She was completely nuts—and he liked her.

Oh, Mitch could pick 'em, that was for sure.

"Tell your stepmother to drop over for a free reading anytime," Lilith called. "I'd be delighted!"

"I'll just bet," Mitch muttered and stormed toward the kitchen without answering.

He reminded himself that he didn't approve of people— like fortune-tellers—who preyed on others. It wasn't right.

It wasn't fair. But even knowing that, his gut response to Lilith wasn't readily dismissed.

He *liked* her, strange assertions and all. He was tempted to believe her.

Which was almost as insane as Lilith thinking she was six hundred years old. Mitch's gut instinct was always right, it had been honed to a fine edge of journalistic integrity.

But obviously, it had just been fooled.

Mitch felt all jumbled up inside: guilty over losing his self-control, confused by Lilith's easy acceptance of what had happened, frustrated by her crazy claims, and itching with a desire that had been safely in cold storage for years.

Women. He hadn't missed them at all.

Mitch growled at the chocolate icing adorning the kitchen. He could hear the kids' voices upstairs, but needed a minute to collect himself. Andrea trotted down the stairs, and trailed him into the kitchen.

Mitch rummaged in the fridge and ignored her. He needed a beer. He *deserved* a beer.

And he wasn't going to even consider that some guy named Sebastian had Lilith waiting for him. Mitch certainly wasn't going to wish on any level that he could have been this Sebastian. Now or ever. It was all a bunch of baloney.

The beer, to his delight, was wonderfully cold.

"Did she say a *free* reading?" Andrea demanded with evident excitement. Mitch turned to find her hands clasped together like a child's on Christmas morning.

"I don't want to talk about it," Mitch retorted. He shook a heavy finger at Andrea. "And don't even *think* about going over there. Don't you go over there. Don't let the kids go over there. Period."

"Why not?"

Mitch indicated the window facing Lilith's house with his beer bottle. "Because she's *nuts.*"

And that, to Mitch Davison's mind, was that.

He should have known better, of course.

Lilith shut her front door and leaned against it with a frown. It certainly wasn't very convenient that Sebastian had forgotten everything about her, no less his pledge to return.

It was going to make living happily ever after a little bit more difficult than Lilith had planned.

But they were destined to be together. Surely everything would work itself out?

Leaving such important matters to the whim of the Fates wasn't a very encouraging possibility after what they'd endured before. But what should she do?

Lilith stepped away from the door and remembered that her sign was still on. She grimaced, headed for the switch in the living room, then froze halfway at the sight of something on the floor.

It was one of her tarot cards. It lay on the floor, facedown, the rest of the deck still wrapped in silk on the table where she had left it.

She couldn't have dropped it. Lilith was not careless with her cards. They could taste disrespect and they would punish anyone who treated them poorly. The cards were vengeful and mischievous.

Mischievous. Lilith shivered suddenly as she stared at the card. It couldn't have pulled itself from the deck.

Could it? She frowned and stepped closer, her eyes widening as she picked up the card.

The High Priestess. A card of intuition, of trusting your gut, of going with what you know. A card counselling belief in your own convictions. A card that opened the path between conscious knowledge and unconscious belief.

Lilith turned the card in her hands thoughtfully, well aware of her instincts in the matter of Sebastian. So what if Mitch just didn't remember his past life? It would hardly be a first. In fact, some people insisted that reincarnation routinely wiped away all past life memories.

Lilith remembered an ancient priestess telling her that the indent between the nose and the upper lip was the mark of an archangel's kiss, a kiss that swept memory of all but this world and this life from a babe's mind.

And if Mitch didn't remember everything that had happened between them, then that would explain why it had taken him so long to find her. Lilith should be encouraged that he had reincarnated and found his way to her door, even if he didn't remember exactly why.

And he had admitted that he had bought the house *right next to her own* months ago.

Lilith smiled, immensely reassured. Some part of Mitch did remember Sebastian! Something buried in a corner of his mind had forced him to reincarnate, had compelled him to come here, had urged him to seek her out when he was the right chronological age—even though Mitch himself didn't know it! He was trusting his own instincts, without knowing why.

Sako peskero charo dikhel. Dritta's voice echoed in Lilith's ears unexpectedly. But the words were apt enough. "Everyone sees only his own dish." Lilith had been so focused on Sebastian returning, that she hadn't considered events from his perspective.

The High Priestess seemed to shimmer slightly at Lilith's conclusion. It was all so perfectly obvious that Lilith couldn't believe she hadn't thought of it before. The world truly did work in wondrous and mysterious ways!

She and Mitch/Sebastian were going to be very happy together, once they worked out a few technical complications. Lilith kissed the card, silently thanking it for reminding her of the power of faith, and slid it back into the deck. She wrapped the silk around the ancient deck and put it on top of the highest shelf in the room.

Lilith flicked off her neon sign thoughtfully. The only question now was how to proceed. She had never imagined that she would have to deal with such issues, but then, the course of love did not always run true.

How could she prompt Mitch's memory of the past?

Should she conjure up a little something, or give him some time?

D'Artagnan meowed, clearly indignant at the state of his dish, whether empty or full. Lilith, puzzling over her choice, followed him to the kitchen.

D'Artagnan bounded to the counter and flicked his tail at Lilith in evident annoyance. He howled, indignant that he was being ignored, and Lilith immediately brushed him off the counter.

"We have a deal. You know better," she charged.

D'Artagnan bared his teeth, as though to say "so do

you.'' He sniffed his empty dish with disdain, then sat down beside it, regal and expectant.

Lilith opened a can, her mind working busily all the while. Mitch seemed to be very much a man who put value in the tangible, and he seemed to find her attractive, even after all this time.

Lilith smiled. Maybe her personal magick would do just fine.

The Annex is a neighborhood in Toronto roughly sandwiched between the downtown campus of the university and the posh urban residences of Forest Hill village, that village long ago swallowed by the spreading city.

It's a warren of one-way streets and narrow lots, its houses pressed cheek to jowl. The area hosts an eclectic mix of artists, actors, flower children, activists, and young professionals. It also boasts the distinction of having both the highest concentration of writers in any neighborhood in Canada and the highest rate of bicycle theft in the country.

The two statistics are not believed to be related.

Mitch Davison's house was fairly typical of the area. It was about a hundred years old, made of reddish brick and nestled between two remarkably similar houses. There was a skinny walkway between his house and Lilith's, while the house shared a common walk with the house on the other side.

There was a tiny front yard, long abandoned to the weeds, and a rickety wooden front porch that might have been original. The lot allowed for a bigger backyard, with a garage in one corner. The garage was accessed by a common lane which ran between the lots facing Mitch's street and those that faced the street behind.

The house was two stories high, with a high gingerbread-ornamented gable over the front second floor window. Similar trim—in an equal state of disrepair—graced the roofline of the front porch.

There was a living room, dining room, and eat-in kitchen on the main floor, a back door leading from the kitchen to the backyard. Upstairs were four bedrooms—two quite small—and a bathroom. The basement had been made into a perfectly hideous apartment some thirty years before, though Mitch had plans to gut it and make the kids a play-room.

In his spare time.

Such as it was.

Mitch liked that the house appeared to be structurally sound, if in dire need of some repairs. He liked that it was close to the subway. He liked that the kids would have a yard to play in and he appreciated the friendly atmosphere of the neighborhood. Although the Annex was funky and urban, there was a vestige of small-town concern between its residents.

And Mitch liked that. He also appreciated that he could afford the place, no small feat for a single-income family in a city of high-priced real estate.

The realtor said the house had Potential.

Mitch wasn't thinking about any of this at five the next morning, when a wet nose poked his ear in silent demand. He grimaced and feigned sleep, but Cooley wasn't fooled.

The damn dog could tell when his breathing changed.

Cooley took off like a shot at the first sign of life, his nails clicking on the hardwood floor, his weight thumping down the stairs to the kitchen. Mitch rolled to his back, managed to open one eye and survey the ceiling.

At least it was light out.

But it was already hot.

And Mitch had aches where he had forgotten he had muscles. He'd been up half the night, sorting, unpacking, and moving furniture as quietly as he could while the kids slept. Andrea had retired at midnight, leaving Mitch to his work.

He surveyed the room, less than impressed with his pro-gress. There were still boxes crowding the room on every side. A sheet was tacked over the window and Mitch's sleeping bag was cast over the mattress on the floor.

He would not think about families having two adult play-ers.

It was the moment in the midst of a move when everyone is exhausted and it seems that the chaos will never be set into any kind of order. Mitch decided right then and there that he really hated moving.

Maybe he would die in this house, a good sixty years

downstream, so he'd never have to move again. It was a cheering thought.

Mitch considered the wobbly line where the avocado green paint ran out and the chartreuse began. The previous owner must have shopped in the odd lots section of the paint store. All those colors mixed wrong that no one wanted. His gaze wandered to the miscellaneous Slavic blessings written over the door in red crayon.

Mitch thought somewhat more critically about Potential.

Cooley howled plaintively from the kitchen.

"All right, all right." Mitch rolled out of bed and hauled on his shorts.

He peeked in on the kids, making Cooley wait, his heart contracting to find them sleeping like little cherubs. Jen had a death grip on Bun, her cherished toy of the moment. Jason frowned as though concentrating on sleeping very well.

The door to the guest room was closed but he knew better than to look in on Andrea before she declared herself ready to face the morning. Mutual respect was based on understanding the Rules.

Cooley barked, his low woof resonating through the house. Mitch took the stairs two at a time, not wanting the dog to wake anyone. As soon as Mitch set foot in the kitchen, Cooley wagged his tail and nosed the back door with rare impatience.

"Really gotta go, eh?" Mitch unlocked the door and grinned at the dog. "Don't let the dandelions get you. They're pretty big." He barely opened the screen door before Cooley shoved it open and took off.

Barking all the way across the yard.

Dammit! It was five o'clock on a Sunday morning!

"Cooley! Give it a rest!" Mitch called *sotto voce*, but the dog was oblivious to his command.

He muttered a curse and lunged out the back door, just in time to see a cat's silvery tail flick amidst the dew-encrusted sunflowers.

Having everything make sense was little consolation right now.

"Cooley! Be quiet!" Mitch darted barefoot across the yard. He quickly discovered that the dandelions were mixed with a healthy crop of thistles. Mitch cursed and picked a thorn out of his toe, hopping closer to the barking dog.

He'd certainly had better mornings.

The cat watched Mitch from its perch on the fence, its tail waving as though it taunted him to come and shoo it away. Something in its expression was eerily assessing. Then the cat looked down at Cooley and hissed in open antagonism.

The dog went wild.

Cooley barked and jumped on the fence, thoroughly ignoring Mitch's commands for silence and sitting. The wolfhound's considerable weight made the fence wobble dangerously. Mitch realized with horror just how old that fence was and saw what was going to happen.

Right before it did.

"Cooley! *No!* Get down!" he roared, forgetting his own demands for quiet in the heat of the moment. He sprinted across the remaining distance and got one hand on the dog's collar.

But it was too late.

The rotten fence posts gave out with a moan and a creak. The fence went down with a bang—right into Lilith's crop of sunflowers. The cat yowled in astonishment, then ran like hell.

Cooley shook off Mitch's grip, bounded over the debris and gave chase, barking all the while. The pair cut a swath of destruction through Lilith's yard, the dog clearly trying to gobble up the cat, the cat running for its life.

In a heartbeat, they had wrought havoc.

One glance was enough to tell Mitch that Lilith treasured this garden. It was all gardens and blooms, little pathways lined with nodding flowers Mitch couldn't name, a horticultural haven like the ones in glossy magazines.

And his dog was trashing it.

Mitch wasn't doing a very good job of stopping him. He bellowed, but to no avail. He darted after the pair but couldn't get a grip on Cooley.

Suddenly, the cat scrambled up a trellis. It perched on the roof, looking daggers at the dog, as its tail lashed angrily.

Cooley had his front paws up on the house, his back

paws planted in flattened flowers, while he barked fit to beat the band.

"*Cooley!*" Mitch shouted, certain every single one of his neighbors were all awake by now.

Maybe they were entertained.

Either way, it was a hell of an entry into the neighborhood.

The dog, his prey clearly out of range, stopped barking. He looked at Mitch and seemed suddenly to understand that he was in deep trouble. The wolfhound sat back on his haunches, right in the middle of something with a lot of crushed orange flowers, and looked as sheepish as a big hairy dog can look.

Mitch surveyed the damage and felt sick. Flowers were broken, tomatoes lay bleeding on the pathways, sunflower stalks were broken. He didn't know a lot about gardens, but he guessed that this one wouldn't recover this summer.

Mitch met the dog's gaze, snapped his fingers, and pointed imperatively to his own yard. Cooley skulked across Lilith's garden, steering a wide path from Mitch. The huge dog was trying so hard to make himself small that Mitch might have laughed under other circumstances.

But there was nothing funny about this. Mitch owed his neighbor another apology, however nutty she might be. Another biggie.

"Well done," he commented to Cooley, who lay down in the furthest corner of the yard, sulking. "We're making a great impression here. Thanks a lot for doing your part."

The wolfhound dropped his nose to his paws—no doubt a bid to look pathetic—but Mitch wasn't interested in making up just yet.

He shook a warning finger at the dog. "Cat or no cat, don't even *think* about crossing that fenceline again."

Cooley inched further back into the corner, as though acknowledging the command, his big brown eyes so sad that he looked like he might weep.

Mitch heaved a sigh and winced as he looked at the damage one more time. It was too damn early for this kind of stuff. Even the birds were still quiet. Lilith would be asleep and Mitch wasn't going to wake her up early for this.

How was he going to set this right? He shook his head and went back in the house. At least Mitch knew where the coffeemaker was. He'd treat himself to a cup of brew. Maybe that would help him come up with a brilliant solution by the time Lilith woke up.

What a way to start the day.

THE EMPRESS

Lilith awakened to the sound of hammering.

D'Artagnan was at the foot of the bed, looking smug. Lilith sat up, eyeing the cat warily.

"We have a deal," she reminded him. "No jumping on the counters, no sneaking onto my bed."

The cat didn't even blink.

Nor did he move. Honestly, he was getting too cocky for his own good! Lilith moved her foot under the sheets and he bounded away, his nose in the air as though he was insulted.

That was hardly anything new.

Lilith took a deep breath, not liking the humidity in the air. The sun was streaming through her sheer draperies, but not a whisper of breeze lifted them away from the open window. It was stuffy and still, even so early in the day.

So much for hoping it would rain and clear the air. Lilith rubbed her eyes and knew she hadn't slept that well. She reached for the deck of tarot cards beside her bed and drew a card, as she often did in the morning, to give her counsel for the day.

The Empress. Lilith rolled her eyes. A card of productivity, of getting things done, of harvesting what has been sown, of finding a glimmer of the divine in the mundane through simple labor.

Well, someone was being productive, there was no doubt about that, despite the hour. That hammering sounded close. And it just didn't quit. Lilith frowned in irritation, wondering who would be building something so early in the morning.

Couldn't they give it a rest?

Lilith's window faced the back of the house and she loved to look out at her garden in the morning. It delighted her to see the sunlight glint off the dew, to watch the bumblebees meander through the flowers. It would ease her irritation this morning. She rose with a smile of anticipation, tugged back the drapes, and gasped.

Because this morning, her perfect garden was a perfect disaster.

Lilith stared in horror at the damage. Everything along the fenceline was smashed flat. Her sunflowers were broken, her columbines were trodden down, several zucchinis were pureed on the garden path. Leaves and petals from the roses had been cast on the ground, and several beds were crushed beyond recognition.

A very grim Mitch was hammering a section of their common fence back into place. His shirt was off, and a glimmer of sweat shone on his tanned skin. The other three sections of the fence lay on the ground in Mitch's yard, obviously having been moved off Lilith's plants.

Mitch's massive dog cowered guiltily against the garage in the far corner of his yard and Lilith recognized a prime mover when she saw it.

But big dogs didn't just suddenly take it into their heads to be destructive. The dog's current manner indicated that he had forgotten himself in the heat of the moment.

Lilith made a very good guess as to what exactly that particular moment had been.

"D'Artagnan!" She dropped the curtain and turned to confront the cat. D'Artagnan strove to look innocent, as sure a sign as there could be of his guilt. "You had something to do with this. Don't think I don't know it."

The cat bolted so fast that he was no more than a silver blur in the hall. Lilith rolled her eyes, knowing she had all the answers she needed.

But her garden!

She turned back and found herself watching Mitch instead of looking at her once vigorous flowers. There was something about the sight of a handsome man out fixing things in her yard that made Lilith catch her breath.

Not just any handsome man either. Her one true love.

Whether he knew it or not.

Although this was hardly the kind of interaction she had hoped for the night before, Lilith had learned long ago that the great forces could be playful. A can-do kind of witch worked with what she had.

What Lilith had was a half-naked, grumpy Mitch fixing her fence.

She'd have to make that work.

Later, she'd deal with the darned cat.

Jason was feeling pretty important. He liked helping his dad just about best of all, even better than catching tadpoles. Dad had said they'd have lots to fix in this new house and he'd been right.

They were fixing the fence already.

Dad put out his hand for a nail. Jason picked one out of the old olive jar in Dad's toolbox. He liked Dad's toolbox. It was kind of a mess, but there were lots of interesting things in there, if you looked close. All sorts of bits and ends, things that Dad could put together to fix just about anything.

Like the fence.

Dad winked as he took the nail. "Thanks, sport. Don't know how I'd get this done without you." Jason grinned as his dad hammered that nail into the old fence.

Jason was getting another nail out of the jar when the lady came out of her house next door. She saw where the fence had landed on her plants and looked really sad. Jason felt bad that her flowers got smushed and felt a bit guilty that he had been so excited to see her yard when he got up today.

He'd been peeking through the fence the day before. Jason just knew she had better bugs over there and he had kind of been hoping to have a chance to look at them.

His dad stopped hammering. "Lilith, I thought you'd still be asleep." It sounded as though Dad felt really bad too.

The lady looked at Dad. "Some hammering woke me up," she said quietly. She had a nice voice, kind of low. And she was really pretty. She had her hair in a ponytail, but it was all dark and curly. It looked soft. She had a long dress on, like a princess, and it was blue like Jen's Bun.

"I was hoping to get it fixed before you got up." Dad's ears got red. "I'm really sorry about the fence, Lilith, especially about your garden."

She looked at the flowers, and Dad fidgeted, which he didn't usually do. "I don't know a lot about gardens," Dad said quietly. He was looking really hard at the lady. "So, Lilith, please tell me what to do to make this come right."

The lady stepped off her porch into the garden. She wandered along, touching a sunflower, then dropped to one knee beside Jason. She picked up a red flower that was broken right off and looked like she might cry.

Dad looked really worried.

Jason wanted to help. "That's pretty," he said.

The lady looked up at him, then very slowly she smiled. Jason smiled back. "And who are you?" she asked quietly.

"Jason."

"My son," Dad said.

The lady looked at Dad. "I didn't know you were married."

Dad got That Look, the one he got whenever Nana started talking about stuff that made Dad go *shhh!* "I'm not. Not anymore."

"Oh." The lady smiled at Jason again. "Hello, Jason. I'm Lilith."

"Hi."

"Do you have any brothers and sisters?"

"Just Jen. She's little."

"How little?"

"Only three."

Lilith smiled, then wrinkled her nose. Jason felt like she understood him. "Much littler than you." She looked down at the flower again and her smile went away.

It was like the sun going behind a cloud. Jason wanted to make her smile again.

Good thing he had an idea.

"We could put it back on the plant," he suggested. "We've got nails and duck tape and everything. Dad can fix anything."

She did smile, but she shook her head. "That won't

work, Jason. You see, plants are different from fences. They're more like people.''

"Oh." Jason didn't know what to do.

He didn't think his dad did either.

The lady turned the flower in her hand. Suddenly, something fluttered through the air. Jason couldn't see what it was, at least not until it paused in the air right in front of Lilith.

Then, she smiled, really smiled, for the first time.

"Hello, Ralph," she said softly.

It was a little bird, Jason realized, but its wings moved so fast that he could hardly see them. He thought he could hear a hum coming from its wings. It was gray or dark green with a white tummy and a little red mark at its throat. The bird seemed to hang in the air, its long beak just a bit away from the flower Lilith held.

She looked at Jason and winked. "He wouldn't tell me his name, so I gave him one."

That made perfect sense to Jason. The bird moved forward and put his beak into the end of the red flower. Jason saw that it was actually a bunch of little red flowers all growing together. They were long and skinny, but the bird's beak fit right into one.

Ralph moved to the next flower and the next, and Lilith held the flower very still.

"He comes every day," Lilith whispered.

Jason was awed. "For the flowers?"

"For the nectar that's in them. It's like juice. That's what Ralph eats and he knows he can find them here."

Jason thought about that and wished he could see the little bird better. He didn't want to move and scare it, though.

As though she knew what he was thinking, Lilith beckoned with her free hand. "Bring the honeysuckle," she whispered and pointed to an orange and yellow flower on the ground beside him. It had the same kind of pointy shape as the ones she held. "And move very slowly."

Jason looked up and his dad nodded. He picked up the flower and moved closer to Lilith, watching Ralph carefully. The sun sparkled on the bird's red throat like it did on some cars.

Ralph suddenly darted back and seemed to face him for a long moment. Jason understood that the bird was checking him out. He offered the flower very slowly, just like Lilith said.

He held his breath.

In the blink of an eye, Ralph zoomed closer. He was right there! Jason could have touched him, but he was afraid even to move. Ralph stuck his beak into the flower, then pulled back.

"Breakfast!" Nana called, slamming the kitchen door behind herself. "Who's up for chocolate cake?"

Ralph zipped skyward.

Jason spun to face his grandmother and yelled as he almost never did. "Nana! You scared Ralph!"

Nana looked confused. "What?"

"Jason was feeding a hummingbird," Dad told Nana and she bit her lip.

"Oh, honey, I'm sorry . . ." and then Nana gasped. She jumped back and Jason almost laughed.

Because Ralph was hovering beside Nana's shoulder, giving her the same look he had given Jason.

"It's the flowers on her shirt," Lilith whispered with a smile. "He's not sure if they're real."

And it seemed he wasn't. Nana was wearing one of her bright shirts from Hawaii, this one covered with big pink flowers. Ralph took only a moment to decide they weren't worth the trouble, then zinged over the house and disappeared.

"That was neat!" Jason declared.

Lilith smiled. "Yes, I like Ralph."

"Does he really come all the time?"

Lilith nodded. "Every day."

"Can I come see him again?"

"Jason!" Dad objected, but Lilith just nodded.

"Of course you can!" She leaned closer. "But you know what you might like even better?" Jason shook his head. "What if Ralph came to your yard too?"

Jason looked at their yard and didn't see anything like the long pointy flowers Ralph liked. "But we don't have any flowers for him."

"Not yet." Lilith turned the red flower. "This is called

beebalm. Ralph looks for bright flowers and ones that are long with nectar at the bottom.'' She handed it to Jason. ''If you put this in water, it will probably root. Then you'll have a whole new plant for your garden.''

''What about yours?''

Lilith touched the spot where the plant came out of the ground. ''Beebalm is a perennial. That means the top dies but the root lives through the winter and it grows again every spring. It just gets a little bigger every year. My beebalm will come back.''

Jason frowned. ''But it wouldn't be fair if Ralph stopped coming to your flowers.''

Lilith smiled. ''I don't have enough flowers for Ralph. He needs to eat a lot of nectar, so that he can keep flying so fast.'' She touched Jason's arm with one fingertip. ''You can help make sure that he gets enough to eat.''

Jason liked the idea of that. He decided it would be pretty neat if Ralph came to his yard every day. He turned the plant in his hands and it smelled a bit sweet.

No wonder Ralph liked it.

''Do you like birds?'' Lilith asked.

''I like Ralph.'' Jason nodded. ''And I like bugs. A lot.''

''Well, bumblebees like a lot of the same things that Ralph likes. What do you say we get your garden started?'' She looked at Dad. ''If that's okay with you?''

Dad grinned. ''That would be more than okay.''

''Well, then, that's that. Jason, if you go back there''— Lilith pointed to the end of her yard—''you'll find some plastic buckets. We'll put some water in them, then some of these flowers.''

This was so neat! He was going to have bugs and Ralph and everything, right in his own backyard! Jason set out for the back of Lilith's lot with purpose.

''But please don't step on the toad!'' she called after him.

Toad? She had a *toad*?

Wow!

Beebalm clenched in his fist, Jason inched toward the back of Lilith's yard. He frowned at the path, determined not to miss the toad or anything else of interest.

He liked their new house already.

• • •

Mitch cleared his throat. Here he was supposed to be apologizing to Lilith, and he was expecting her to be furious with him, yet she was being nice to his son.

"Look, Lilith, it's really nice, but you don't have to do this."

She smiled at Mitch and his heart did a little flip-flop. The sapphire dress she wore swirled around her ankles as she stepped closer. Her hair was in a ponytail—the way she had it tied up revealed the graceful curve of her nape.

The woman was so lethally sexy that Mitch just wanted to eat her up with a spoon. A night's sleep had done nothing to diminish her appeal.

"But I want to show him!" she protested with a smooth smile. "He's so interested and it's nice to share what you know with someone who wants to learn."

Mitch couldn't argue with that. "Well, yeah. Jason will listen to you for as long as you keep talking to him." He grinned at her. "Forewarned is forearmed. Just send him home if you get done with it."

"He's just like a little sponge!" Andrea interjected pertly. Mitch blinked, having forgotten his stepmother's presence. Andrea peeked around the end of the fence that Mitch was fixing and smiled sunnily at Lilith.

Lilith smiled back. "Well, hello."

"Andrea Davison. Mitch is my stepson." She shook Lilith's hand and practically bounced in anticipation.

"Pleased to meet you." Lilith's gaze slid to Mitch and her eyes danced with mischief. "You must be the one interested in having your fortune told."

Mitch opened his mouth to interrupt, but neither woman was listening to him.

"Oh, yes! Tarot cards, tea leaves, it doesn't matter to me." Andrea giggled, then leaned closer to Lilith. "Can you really predict lovematches?"

"Of course."

Mitch stifled his snort of disdain. Of course?

The women ignored him.

Andrea bounced with impatience. "Do you think you might have time to do a reading for me this weekend?"

That was enough.

"Andrea! Cooley has just trashed Lilith's fence and Jason is moving into her yard." Mitch threw out his hands in exasperation. "I think we're wearing out our welcome."

But Lilith laughed. Her low laughter coaxed that ember lingering in Mitch's belly back to a flame. Had he ever met a more attractive woman?

That thought led naturally to the recollection of their first meeting and Mitch had a hard time keeping his thoughts straight after that. It didn't help that Lilith was watching him as though she knew what he was thinking.

And smiling that seductive, secretive smile that made his ears feel hot.

"It wouldn't be any problem at all," she conceded. "How about this afternoon?"

"Oh! That would be perfect!" Andrea playfully punched Mitch in the shoulder. "See? I *told* you." She rolled her eyes and smiled back at Lilith. "He worries so much about everything. I'll just pop over when the kids have their nap."

"I'll look forward to seeing you."

A plaintive cry came from the second floor and Mitch suddenly realized that Jen was not only awake but confused.

He stepped away from the fence, but Andrea was on the porch in record time. "I'll get her," she said quickly. "I shouldn't have even left her, but I just—well, I just had to meet you." Andrea beamed. "Well, I'll see you this afternoon."

As Jen began to wail, Andrea ran.

Mitch had a hard time staying put, even knowing that Andrea could manage. He really didn't like hearing his little girl cry. He fidgeted and glanced anxiously to the house.

"Two kids?" Lilith asked softly. She was beside him again, her eyes impossibly wide and dark.

"Yeah. Five and three." Mitch managed to smile. "Busy, busy, busy."

Jen stopped crying and Andrea's dulcet tones carried through the open upstairs window. Mitch felt relief flood through him just as Lilith leaned against the restored fence. "I'll bet."

To Mitch's relief, she seemed uninterested in the whole sordid story of how he had ended up with kids but no wife.

Lilith's gaze ran over the chunks of fence scattered across his yard, then paused on the banished Cooley.

She glanced back to Mitch, her eyes dancing. "Am I right to guess your dog finally coaxed these old fence posts to break?"

"Oh, yeah." Mitch lined up a final nail and hammered it home, welcoming the change of subject. He tested the fence. The shims around the rotten posts seemed to be holding well enough.

At least for the short term.

"He's like a freight train once he gets moving," Mitch acknowledged.

"And probably just as hard to stop."

They looked to the dog in unison, who lifted his head hopefully. "Cooley the wolfhound," Mitch said by way of introduction. "Seldom bites and never very hard."

Lilith chuckled. "He looks very friendly." Cooley's tail thumped against the ground.

"You stay there," Mitch advised the dog. "You're still in trouble."

"In the doghouse," Lilith corrected, a smile lurking in her voice.

Mitch chuckled, met her dancing gaze, and was snared for a long, hot moment. When he realized what he was doing, he deliberately turned to frown at the remnants of the fence. "Well, I've got a buddy who's a real carpenter. He's coming up next weekend to help me decide where to start inside, but we'll replace this fence first."

"You don't have to do that."

"But I want to." Mitch was suddenly very serious. "I'm really sorry, Lilith. Again."

Lilith folded her arms across her chest, a smile playing over her full lips. "The fence was bound to go sooner or later. The posts were really getting rotten."

"But I wish it hadn't fallen on your plants."

Lilith shrugged philosophically. "Well, cut flowers all around. I'll give you some for your kitchen."

The woman was just too nice to be believed! "Lilith, you don't have to do that."

"We might as well enjoy them. When life gives you lemons, make lemonade, right? And at least some of the cuttings can start your garden.'' She wrinkled her nose, her dark gaze fixing intently on Mitch and making him feel hotter than he was. ''Are you sure you don't mind about Jason starting a garden? It's a lot of work.''

Mitch gave her his best smile, immensely relieved that she had accepted his apology. ''I'd kind of like to have a garden. Grow some vegetables that aren't doused in pesticides, you know?'' Lilith nodded in agreement. ''But I don't know how to start.''

''I'd be glad to help.'' They shared a smile so warm that it curled Mitch's toes.

Then Lilith waved a hand at the fence. ''But why bother to fix the fence now? You could just leave it down until the weekend.''

Mitch granted his dog a significant glance. ''We'll all sleep better with a fence around him.'' He dared to meet Lilith's gaze again. ''I'll pay for the whole thing, so don't worry about that.''

''Mitch! That's not fair.''

''It sure is.'' Mitch cleared his throat, unwilling to name the precise reason he felt so guilty. ''Look, Lilith, we haven't started out on the right foot here.'' He couldn't hold her gaze, so frowned and stared at the nail in his hand. ''I, uh, I'm not proud of how I behaved yesterday. I usually have more self-control.''

She took a step closer, the curve of her shoulder in his peripheral vision. Mitch didn't look up.

''Do you regret what happened?'' she asked, her voice low and sweet.

Mitch closed his eyes, certain the temperature in the yard had just doubled.

Maybe trebled.

But he couldn't lie to Lilith. He'd never guessed that sex could be so hot and impetuous. He'd never imagined that he could want a woman so desperately—or that a woman could want him the same way. Just thinking about it made his shorts tight again.

But that didn't mean he could accept his own behavior. Mitch forced himself to meet her gaze steadily. ''No,'' he admitted. ''But that doesn't change anything. We're probably going to be neighbors for a while and I want to make this right. I *want* to do this, Lilith. Let me.''

She bit her lip and seemed suddenly very young. A flush rose over her cheeks, a feminine blush that made everything inside Mitch go tight. She looked away and he took advantage of the opportunity to study the soft sweep of her jawline, the lush thickness of her ebony lashes. She then turned and captured him with a bright glance, those lips quirking in a smile once more.

"I shouldn't let you," she said softly, a mischievous glint in her eye. "But it's just too tempting. That would be really nice, Mitch.''

His name sounded impossibly exotic on her tongue. Mitch felt his neck heat, but told himself it was just the sun. "To have a new fence?" he asked as evenly as he could manage. He lined up another nail, fully expecting her agreement.

She grinned impishly. "Well, that too. I was thinking about having a handsome man toiling in the yard," she teased. Mitch nearly missed the nail when her fingertips fluttered unexpectedly against his shoulder. "Promise me," she whispered wickedly, "that you won't wear a shirt this weekend either."

Mitch caught his breath in surprise. Lilith laughed, then she stepped away as Jason reappeared, lugging a pair of pails. Her feet flashed under the hem of her skirt, the bare soles slightly dirty.

She had called him handsome.

Mitch concentrated on hammering that nail home, telling himself her comment just didn't matter. It didn't matter that she really wanted him, it didn't matter that she was so sweet and helpful, it didn't matter that her eyes twinkled in a way that made him want to stare into them forever.

Lilith was a New Age nut, after all.

Although it was awfully hard to remember that right now.

"Well, consider it done," Mitch concluded in his most businesslike voice, unwilling to examine why he wanted to snare Lilith's attention again. "If you want it different from the last one, just say the word. Taller, shorter, lattice on top, whatever."

"Whatever you want to do." She grinned over her shoulder. "You know better what will stop that freight train special of yours."

Mitch grimaced. "Sinking the posts into concrete, for a start."

"Are you sure you should start this weekend? You have so much to do at your place."

Mitch arched a skeptical brow and feigned astonishment. "Is it that obvious?"

Lilith laughed aloud, the hearty sound coaxing Mitch's own grin. "Uh-huh."

"Well, it'll wait. Righting wrongs is always first on the agenda." Mitch picked up the next section of fence and set it into position. He looked around for his assistant, but Jason appeared to have found the toad. The boy was hunkered down, the pots abandoned, his concentration fixed on a dark shadow.

Mitch looked at Lilith. "Would you mind holding that for a minute? I've just got to get a couple of nails and I seem to have lost my helper." He inclined his head toward Jason and Lilith smiled.

She gripped the fence where he told her, their hands brushing in the transaction. Mitch tingled, knowing he didn't imagine the luscious scent of her perfume.

Or the sweet undertone that had to be the scent of Lilith's own skin. Mitch was well aware of her gaze following him as he bent over.

He really, really hoped he didn't have plumber's butt.

"We're *nothing* compared to toads," Lilith commented drily just as Mitch got a pair of nails between his teeth. He nearly spit them into the grass at her unexpected comment, and glanced back to find her grinning.

His heart skipped a beat. Mitch let himself forget for the moment that Lilith was bananas. Instead, he stood beside her, nailing the fence into place, and let himself enjoy the moment. The thing was, Mitch had a weakness for funny, clever, sexy women and it wasn't nearly often enough that one crossed his path.

Even one who was convinced she was a real, live witch.

The section of fence stood on its own and Mitch was trying to think of something clever to say when Jen's howl from the kitchen effectively ended the moment.

"Daddy!"

And there was nothing else in Mitch's world. He dropped his hammer and bounded to the porch at one glimpse of Jen's tear-streaked face. Even Andrea looked alarmed, as well as incapable of settling her tiny stricken charge.

Mitch scooped Jen into his arms, Bun and all, and bounced her on his hip as he murmured to her. "It's okay, I'm right here." Jen's plump arms locked around his neck and she sobbed as though her heart had been ripped in two. Her fair hair curled against Mitch's chin like soft down, her weeping made him cringe.

"It's okay, we're all right here. See? There's nothing to worry about." Mitch sat on the step and cuddled his daughter close, intent on consoling her. He should never have left her sleeping. He should have guessed that she would be frightened. Jen was always afraid of being left alone, left behind, and Mitch knew exactly why.

Knowing it was all his fault never made him feel any better.

"We were right here," Jason said with five-year-old scorn. Jen ignored him as she sniffled and peeked, taking silent inventory of everyone in attendance. Mitch gently stroked her blond curls back from her brow. Meanwhile, Andrea skillfully steered the little boy over to the buckets he had dropped and the fallen plants, leaving Mitch to make everything better.

As usual. Fortunately, he'd gotten pretty good at it.

"See? Everything's just fine." Mitch tickled Jen under the chin. She squirmed and wiped her tears with Bun's blue ear. "Guess what I did this morning?"

Jen flicked a glance at him and sniffed.

Mitch took that tiny hint of curiosity as encouragement. "I made fruit salad," he tapped the end of her nose, "just for you."

Jen's eyes lit up at mention of one of her favorite foods—and the only one Mitch approved of—but she pursed her lips. Negotiation was a good sign, to Mitch's way of thinking. "With grapes?"

"Extra grapes," Mitch confirmed.

Her little lips pursed thoughtfully as she considered him. "*Green* grapes?"

Mitch smiled, knowing how she loved the green ones. "Lots of them." He tickled her tummy. "Didn't I say it was special for you?"

The little girl's expression turned coy in a way that made Mitch dread the day she would become a teenager. Jen tapped Bun on Mitch's shoulder. "Can I have some? Now? And Bun too?" she asked, then granted her daddy the gift of a smile.

"Well, I don't know," Mitch teased. "I thought you were going to sleep in this morning."

"Woody Woodpecker woke me up," Jen confided cheerfully, then tapped her finger on Mitch's chest. "Bang, bang, bang."

Mitch mimicked the cartoon character's laugh and Jen giggled right on cue. He grinned with relief. "That's not the first time I've heard that complaint this morning," he said, then stood, intending to share the joke with Lilith.

But Lilith was gone. The screen door to her kitchen swung slowly but there was absolutely no sign of the lady.

Mitch was honest enough with himself to admit that he was disappointed.

Lilith had never experienced such a sense of being desperately alone. But when Mitch scooped up his daughter, his features drawn with concern, and the little girl clung to him for solace, Lilith had fully understood, perhaps for the first time, just how alone she was.

Immortal and alone. Lilith was effectively frozen in time, locked forever in the moment when the elixir slid through her veins. She would always be thirty-three years old.

Lilith stood still while time swirled around her.

For the first time, Lilith didn't think that was such a good thing. She had lived in solitude for almost six centuries. Even D'Artagnan was a recent concession. There had just been her plants and countless houses and thousands upon thousands of strangers with secrets of love hidden in their eyes. They went on to find their lovers true, to have children, to grow old in the circle of their love.

But Lilith stayed alone. Always alone. The sight of Mitch and his daughter had made that point painfully clear.

It had made Lilith suddenly want to cry.

So she had run, as much from the sight of the closeness of Mitch's family as from her realization. But inside her house lurked the memory of the Empress card she had drawn this very morning.

The *pregnant* Empress who governed fertility and parenthood.

Lilith saw the card still lying on her nightstand, and she dropped to her bed and wept. It was not exactly a reminder she needed right now. Lilith thought about little babies and faded assumptions that she would rock untold numbers of her own children in her arms.

Because Lilith could never have a child of her own— her monthly cycles had ceased when she drank the potion. That naive expectation now destined to remain unfulfilled left Lilith feeling barren and empty, cold despite the heat. She cried, certain her womb had shriveled like an old piece of fruit.

Even though she had never let herself cry since she had walked away from the *Rom kumpania*.

It must be the weather that was finally getting to her. Or the anticipation of having Sebastian on the periphery of her life again.

But Mitch had his own children. Although she hadn't expected them, maybe Lilith could live vicariously. She certainly had enjoyed her first encounter with Jason.

That made her feel better. Lilith sniffed and wiped away her foolish tears, determined to put this unwanted emotion behind her. She wrapped her arms around herself and paced. Lilith certainly had never been bothered by any of this before.

But no matter how fast she walked, Lilith just couldn't erase the image of Mitch's daughter's tears from her mind. Even that tiny girl had someone to turn to when everything seemed wrong.

Lilith had only herself and she would have only herself until Mitch remembered their entwined destiny. It had been that way for so long that she had almost forgotten life could be any other way.

Almost, but not quite.

•   •   •

Lilith jumped hours later when there was a rap on her kitchen door.

"Hellooooooo!" Someone called from the back porch and Lilith recognized Andrea's voice with relief. She was more than ready for a bit of company.

Lilith stepped quickly through the kitchen and summoned a smile. "Hello, Andrea. Come on in!"

Andrea did as she was bidden, her gaze quickly trailing over Lilith's spotless red-and-white kitchen. "Oh, this is lovely! We'll have to show Mitch—he's been muttering about potential and cursing realtors all day long." Her eyes twinkled. "I honestly don't think the man knows where to start."

Lilith's smile broadened. "You have to have a vision of what you want the house to be."

"Well!" Andrea heaved a sigh and glanced over the kitchen once more. "You clearly have an eye for such things."

Lilith warmed to the older woman, not because of her praise but simply because she said what she thought. She shrugged. "I enjoy it."

Andrea smiled. "I can tell."

Lilith bit her lip in sudden recollection and had to ask. "Is your granddaughter all right? She seemed quite upset this morning."

Andrea sobered immediately. "Oh, Jen. She's such a sweetie but she really doesn't handle change well at all. Mitch worries so much about her."

Lilith's heart contracted for both father and daughter. "What about her mother?"

Andrea snorted. "There's a story and a half there, that's for certain." She dropped her voice to a conspiratorial whisper. "Mitch has sworn that he'll hunt me down and hurt me if I ever breathe a word of what happened to anyone. Unfortunately"—she winked, a disclaimer if ever there was one—"I *believe* him."

"Surely it can't be that bad."

Andrea waved off the comment. "Mitch just doesn't want those two little angels ever to hear anything bad about their mom. I can't blame him for a little over-protectiveness." Andrea shrugged and a wicked twinkle glinted in her eye. "Even if there isn't much good to say about her."

Lilith was so shocked by this comment that she didn't have time to hide her response. "Andrea!"

"It's true," the older woman declared unrepentantly. "She never knew what she had—God bless us for small mercies—otherwise, she'd still be here." Andrea rolled her eyes in silent assessment of that. "Suffice to say, the man blames himself, but then he was always too quick to take responsibility for the woes of this world."

Andrea straightened with sudden primness, as though she had just realized she'd said too much. "But that's all I have to say about that."

Andrea's words were certainly consistent with Mitch's tight-lipped response about not being married anymore. Something nasty had happened, unless Lilith missed her guess.

"Well, I'm glad your granddaughter is all right."

Andrea smiled again. "More than all right, although Mitch is fretting up a storm. He's a regular old mother hen. He's asked me to stay a few days so Jen doesn't have to go to a new day care tomorrow."

"That might be a good idea," Lilith conceded, touched by his concern for the little girl's fears.

Andrea grinned. "Oh, it is. I think Mitch's exact words were that it could be a seriously ugly proposition." She arched a brow. "But just because he's right doesn't mean I won't tease him about being such a worrywart."

The two women shared a warm smile and Lilith decided it was time for a change of subject. "Why don't you come into the front room?" she suggested. "That's where I usually read."

Andrea turned in the direction Lilith gestured. "Oh, this is so exciting! I just can't wait. You know, I have the strongest feeling about you, Lilith. As soon as I saw your sign, I knew you would have something to tell me." She flicked a pert glance over her shoulder. "Do you think that's crazy?"

Lilith shook her head. "No."

She didn't think it was crazy quite simply because it was true. The portent of Andrea's future love was right there in her eyes. Lilith had seen it immediately. A person just had to know where and how to look.

Too late, Lilith wished she'd had a better look into Mitch's eyes.

A reassured Andrea danced ahead, anticipation in every line of her figure. Her gaze roved openly over the furnishings of the front room. Lilith trailed behind her, granting her the opportunity to look.

If there was one place where Lilith most actively and obviously denied her *Rom* roots, it was in her place of business, her fortune-telling parlor. The room was furnished in mission-style furniture, the clean lines of the oak and warm finish of the oxblood leather emanating a definite sense of *this* world.

There were Persian rugs cast on the gleaming hardwood floor and Turkish kilims woven in earth tones cast over the backs of chairs. A particularly spectacular batik from Indonesia of two traditional dancers was framed without a backing and hung over the window so that the light shone through it.

Bookcases stood on either side of the fireplace, their leaded glass doors gleaming. It was there that the evidence of Lilith's livelihood could be found in the wide array of occult titles. There were mineral samples and seashells scattered unobtrusively around the room and fat beeswax candles on many of the tables.

"It's not what I expected," Andrea declared finally. "But it's very nice."

Lilith smiled. "What did you expect?"

"You know, red velvet and crystal balls. The usual tacky mishmash." Andrea took the chair Lilith indicated and practically bounced in place. "But I like this." She wrinkled her nose. "It seems *real*."

"Thank you." Lilith retrieved her cards from their high vantage point and unfolded the silk that surrounded them. She had never been able to resist different tarot decks and had at least half a dozen decks in the house. This current "working" deck had lovely paintings which patrons seemed to like.

Andrea's eyes widened at the sight. "What an odd place to keep your cards."

"They have to be respected," Lilith confided easily. "And granted the honor of the highest point in the room." She shuffled the deck. "There are those who insist the cards watch over the home of those who treat them well."

"Really?" Andrea breathed.

"That's what they say. I certainly have no complaints." Lilith set the cards on the coffee table, then retrieved a small crystal ball. She took the seat opposite the older woman and smiled. "Would you like to ask a specific question, or shall I just read?"

Andrea's smile shone. "Would you just read?"

Her enthusiasm was infectious, especially as Lilith knew Andrea wouldn't be disappointed by what she heard today.

"Of course." When Lilith spared the crystal ball a glance as she put it down, a fleeting image there caught her eye. She straightened in shocked recognition.

It was Dritta!

It couldn't be! Lilith blinked and carefully looked again, trying to hide her gesture from Andrea.

But the ball was clear once more.

Lilith must have imagined the image. It couldn't have been Dritta. No, she had left all of that behind, centuries ago, outside an Italian village.

She was upset. She was thinking too much of old *Rom* expectations for her future, expectations that had nothing to do with her life. She was just lonely.

It was nothing more than that.

Lilith deliberately smiled for Andrea, then cupped the woman's left hand within both of hers. The older woman's skin was soft and warm, and there were a thousand lines in her palm.

Impressionable, Dritta whispered in Lilith's ear. Lilith frowned and chose to ignore the source. But she would have to be particularly careful about what she said. Andrea caught her breath in anticipation as Lilith leaned closer to read the omens hidden there.

"You're right-handed?"

Andrea nodded.

"Then this is what you were born with," Lilith said softly, with a gentle squeeze of Andrea's left hand before reaching to take her right. "And this is what you have made of it."

Though there were just the two of them in the room—even D'Artagnan had not deigned to join them—Lilith had a definite sense that they two were not alone. In fact, she looked over her shoulder more than once in the following minutes, but there was no one there.

Yet when she read, Lilith heard an echo from the past in her choice of words, though she never intended any such thing. She knew it was no accident she heard Dritta's wisdom echo in her own voice that afternoon.

Although she wondered at the change.

The room had fallen into darkness when the reading was done. What Lilith had seen in Andrea's eyes had been echoed and reinforced in her palm and in the cards. By the end, they both had a very clear answer of where Andrea's next love would be found.

It was a really good reading, one loaded with specific details, one of the best readings Lilith had given in a long time. It left Lilith bone tired. She waved to a thrilled Andrea from the porch and leaned against the doorjamb in exhaustion.

Perhaps it was because she was so tired that the unexpected words fell from her lips.

"Te sav ka to biav!" Lilith called, though she had no intention of doing any such thing. She blinked in surprise to hear the first *Rom* words cross her lips in nearly six centuries.

Andrea spun around. "What language is that?"

"Rom," Lilith admitted, then clarified. "Gypsy."

Andrea gasped and her eyes went round with wonder once more. "Are you a Gypsy?"

Oddly enough, Lilith couldn't manage to utter her usual rejection of her roots. It didn't seem right after this day, after this reading.

She really *was* tired.

"I was," she conceded quietly.

Andrea snorted, an unconscious reminder of Dritta's dismissiveness. "And so you still are."

Lilith's heart skipped at the declaration, then she gave

her head a shake. But Andrea didn't know anything about being *mahrime*. Andrea didn't know what she was talking about.

Lilith was not *Rom*, not any more.

"What does it mean?"

Lilith grinned and held the screen door open with her toe, feeling suddenly playful. "May I eat at your wedding."

Andrea laughed with delight. "You will! I just know it! Wait until I tell Mitch about this." She chuckled impishly as she darted up his porch steps. "He'll be *livid*!"

But Lilith had already turned back, old words echoing in her ears despite the silence of her house.

"It is in your blood, child. Who you are will follow you."

No. Lilith frowned and locked the door. Nothing had followed her. They had cast her out, they had denied her and she would deny them.

Lilith was *Rom* no longer.

And that was that.

4

THE EMPEROR

"She told you *what*?"

Livid was apparently a woeful miscalculation of Mitch's response. He was incredulous, skeptical, and mad as hops. Andrea tried to find another way to share the good news.

Because it *was* good news.

If only Mitch would *listen*.

"There's nothing to get excited about, Mitch," she said flatly. "I'm going on a cruise. And I'm going to meet the man of my dreams." Andrea waved her hand airily. "It's perfectly simple. Lilith said so."

"Lilith said so." Mitch echoed in a low growl and paced the kitchen. He was clearly fighting his urge to bellow like a boar. "You know, Andrea, that's not exactly how love is supposed to work."

"So now you're an authority on matters of the heart," Andrea snorted. "What were those credentials again?"

"Ouch," Mitch said flatly.

Andrea tossed her hair. "I've at least got experience."

"Ouch again." Her stepson took a deep breath, then deliberately sat backwards on a chair. Mitch was clearly exasperated, and just as clearly bent on convincing her to change her mind.

In a way, Andrea liked it better when he ranted. When Mitch got all cold and logical, it was harder to refute his points. Andrea braced her feet against the ground, folded her arms across her chest, and dug in her heels.

She was going on that cruise.

"Andrea, think about what you're saying."

Danger, danger. He was very cool and decisive. Andrea knew Mitch would have her agreeing with him but quick if she didn't stick to her guns.

She was going. "I have!"

Mitch arched a brow. "Then consider the source."

"What does that mean?"

Mitch frowned. "Lilith told me that she's a witch."

"Pshaw! Wiccans are as thick on the ground as bicycle thieves in this neighborhood. So what?"

Mitch's eyes flashed. "She says that she's six hundred years old. Six *hundred* years, Andrea." He arched an eloquent brow. "Is this the kind of clear thinking you want in an advisor?"

Andrea blinked, surprised by this information. "She did?"

Mitch nodded solemnly. "She's nuts."

But Andrea shook her head. "I don't think so. She's certainly lonely, but she's far too nice to be nuts."

Mitch exhaled and rubbed one hand across his brow. "So, now you're a psychologist. Who says crazy people can't be nice?"

"Mitch! Anyone can see that Lilith's a sweet girl!"

"Which proves nothing." Mitch's lips drew to a thin line. "Think about what you're saying!"

"I know what I'm saying!" Andrea took a deep breath. "You know, you really should go and have a look at Lilith's place. It's so cute and it must be exactly the same layout as this house. I mean, you'd never believe it, but clearly Lilith has more than one gift. . . ."

"I am not going over there to compare decorating notes!" Mitch abandoned the chair and cast it aside, his annoyance front and center once more as he glowered at Andrea.

When he continued, his voice was tight and low once more. "Will you please stay on the subject?"

"Well, it was just a suggestion," Andrea huffed.

Mitch muttered something that Andrea was glad she hadn't clearly heard, then propped his hands on his hips. His eyes glinted dangerously, like gold in candlelight, his lips were taut.

The man could seethe, there was no doubt about it.

Then, Mitch took another deep breath and when he spoke, his words were even. "Andrea," he said with careful control, "It's not unreasonable that I worry about you. Now, I want you to listen to me for just two minutes."

He really wanted to make his point. And he was really trying not to blow his stack. Andrea supposed that should earn him an audience.

But she wasn't going to make it easy on him.

And she wasn't going to change her mind.

Andrea heaved a sigh of apparent reluctance, then perched on a chair, knowing full well what she was going to hear. "Fine. You have to promise not to take any longer than that, because I know what you're going to say and you could say it in half that time."

"Look." Mitch squatted down in front of Andrea, so concerned for her safety and future that her heart wrenched a little. He was such a good son, even if he wasn't exactly her son.

Mitch's voice was intent, his gaze was steady. "Andrea, I want you to really think about what you're saying here. A fortune-teller—"

"Not just any fortune-teller!" she corrected. *"Lilith!"* Andrea leaned down and patted Mitch on the shoulder. If only he worried half as much about himself as he did about everyone else! She had to find him a nice young woman who would appreciate him.

Andrea straightened at the realization that there was one very good candidate right next door. "She seems like a very nice girl, you know, Mitch, and it's about time you started thinking about dating again. You can't beat yourself up over Janice forever. . . ."

"Andrea!" Mitch roared.

Andrea decided to shut up.

Mitch took a Herculean breath, stared at the floor for a long moment, then impaled her with a glance. "I get two minutes," he reminded her.

Andrea folded her arms across her chest. "Well, time's wasting."

"A fortune-teller," Mitch repeated with a stern look her way, "told you to go on a specific cruise at a specific time, that you would meet a specific kind of man there, and that this man—your own true love—would sweep you off your feet.'' Mitch arched a brow. ''Doesn't that sound a teeny bit suspicious to you?''

''It sounds like destiny,'' Andrea retorted haughtily. ''It sounds like Lilith is reading the future.''

Mitch snorted. ''Come on, Andrea, this is how cons are arranged! Keep in mind that you are in very comfortable financial circumstances.''

''Lilith couldn't know that.''

''*Anyone* could know that,'' Mitch retorted so crisply that Andrea wondered. ''The real estate records show my acquisition of the house, a little digging in the marriage registry and the birth files could come up with my association with you. It's *easy* to find people, Andrea, and to find out a lot about them. The Internet is a positive minefield of personal information.''

He looked so serious that Andrea believed him. She bit her lip. ''Really?''

''Trust me, I know. I'm a *journalist*, Andrea. We dig up stuff on people all the time.''

''Oh.''

Mitch inched closer, his words persuasive. ''Of course, you're going to meet some guy on this cruise, some guy who knows in advance''—he counted off on his fingers— ''one, that you'll be there; two, that you'll be looking for him, courtesy of Lilith; three, just exactly what your net worth would be; and four, that he and Lilith have a deal to split the profits of any ensuing match. Fifty-fifty at divorce court, that's the law. Even splitting it between your Romeo and Lilith will leave them both with a nice chunk of change.''

Andrea bounded to her feet in horror. ''Mitch Davison! How could you think something so perfectly awful about your new neighbor? How could you think that Lilith is so calculating as that? That she'd take advantage of *me*? That's just horrible!''

Mitch spread out his hands, unapologetic. ''We don't really know her, Andrea, or very much about her. These people thrive on establishing quick trust. They're very, very good at it.''

''*These* people.'' Andrea straightened with disdain. Oh!

She knew Lilith wasn't trying to swindle her! "Lilith isn't that kind of person! Just look at how nice she's been to you and Jason already. And she gave me that reading for free!" She shook a finger at her stepson. "You're not behaving as graciously as I know you are. What's gotten into you? And where are your manners?"

Mitch, to his credit, looked a little shamefaced by this. And so he should, to Andrea's way of thinking. A lot of people would have been really nasty about that fence.

"Maybe she has a partner who does the dirty work," he suggested quietly. "The details really aren't important."

"*Mitch Davison!!* The details *are* important!" Andrea cried. "I don't know what's gotten into you. You never used to be so suspicious of people." She poked him in the chest and he didn't even flinch. "Maybe you just don't know what to do when a pretty woman is *nice* to you."

"Ouch one more time," Mitch retorted grimly.

Andrea lifted her chin defiantly. "Mitch, I don't care how suspicious you are or even why. I trust Lilith and because of that, I'm going on that cruise." She waved her finger beneath his nose. "And when I marry the wonderful man I'm going to meet there, *you* are going to be the first to toast the happy couple."

"Andrea!" Mitch's exasperation was more than clear. He was in hot pursuit when she swept regally from the room. "You can't do this!"

"I most certainly can. And I'm going to." Andrea let her eyes narrow as she glared at the most stubborn and protective man alive. "Just watch me."

Andrea knew Mitch wouldn't stop her when she turned to march up the stairs. Just as she knew that he wouldn't stop her from going on that cruise. And he would gradually, grudgingly accept any man she married, provided that man was good to her.

And how could the man of her destiny be anything else?

Of course, that didn't mean that Mitch would give up very easily.

"Well, don't sign any prenuptial agreements before your lawyer reads them!" he called behind her and Andrea smiled as she climbed the stairs.

He was just a protective old bear, that was Mitch's problem. Trying to save the world from itself, just like she told Lilith. It was endearing in a way.

When it wasn't downright irritating.

She pivoted at the top of the stairs and eyed her disgruntled stepson saucily. "Tsk-tsk. If you'd been nice to me, I might have volunteered to do your grocery shopping tomorrow."

Mitch snorted, but Andrea could hear his usual even temper already being restored. "Right. Cheetos and Popsicles all around. Don't do me any favors."

Andrea grinned. "I was thinking more of chocolate bars and bubble gum."

Mitch groaned in mock agony and she laughed.

"What if I make you a list?" he suggested.

"Oh, all those boring nutritious foods. Fruits and vegetables, whole-grain bread. I know how you are." Andrea wrinkled her nose and sighed in mock concession. "But I *suppose* I could be convinced to follow a list. With just a few embellishments. There really is a tragic shortage of frozen burritos in this house."

Mitch grinned. "That would be great, Andrea. If you think you can manage with the kids."

"It's no problem at all. I'd be glad to do it."

The pair smiled at each other with mutual affection. "Have I thanked you enough recently for everything you've done?"

Andrea shrugged, her smile turning loving. "Probably not, but I know when I'm appreciated."

Mitch suddenly sobered. "Just promise me you'll really think about the wisdom of going on this cruise, Andrea. You're too smart of a lady to get conned."

Andrea's heart melted, but she pointed a finger at him playfully. "Now, why didn't you remember that two minutes ago?"

Mitch chuckled and raised a hand in concession. "Just promise me you'll think about it."

Andrea smiled, having no intention of doing any such thing, and her stepson turned back to the task of wringing order from chaos in the kitchen. Mitch had made great progress in setting things right—the house already looked half-civilized.

And time would prove his worries about this cruise wrong. Time and a big diamond rockeroo on Andrea's left hand. After all, Mitch didn't know much about love and how good it could be, thanks to Janice. No, it really wasn't Mitch's fault that he couldn't trust in the concept of love.

He'd learn.

Eventually.

What Mitch needed was a woman to tie a big bow around his heart and drag him around behind her for the rest of his life. A woman like Lilith. That would keep him busy! And give him a much more appropriate focus for all that protectiveness.

Hmm. She'd have to think of a way to get those two together somehow.

Andrea's smile widened as she thought about someone tying a bow around her own heart. Oh, she hoped the man of her dreams would be a really good dancer, as Lilith predicted. Three trips to the altar and she'd never yet married a man who could dance worth a hoot. Andrea dearly loved to dance.

Especially waltzes.

She would dream tonight of a captain's black-tie dinner and dancing, dancing, swirling around an elegant room, locked in a perfectly eligible man's arms. Andrea made a mental note to find a lovely swingy dress for that cruise.

You had to dress for success, after all.

The calls of "bye-bye" brought Lilith to her front window Monday morning. She peeked through the blinds, feeling a bit guilty for spying, but unable to miss witnessing Mitch saying good-bye to his kids. Little Jen gave him a big hug, that well-loved blue bunny right in the middle of the transaction.

Lilith's heart clenched and she bit her lip, those tears threatening to rise one more time. But she was never going to have children and she might as well get over it. Why on earth had it just started to bother her now?

Maybe because her true love was back?

Lilith wouldn't have believed it, but Mitch looked even better dressed for work than he had on the weekend. His khaki chinos were pleated to perfection, his plaid short-sleeved shirt emphasized the breadth of his shoulders and his muscled forearms. Her heart twisted when he winked at Andrea and Lilith was certain he'd at least glance toward her house.

She braced herself for that look.

But Mitch just pivoted and walked toward Bloor Street and the subway. Lilith nibbled her lip and turned away, avoiding D'Artagnan's perceptive glance.

She had the very definite sense that it wasn't a coincidence that Mitch hadn't looked her way. No, Lilith knew that he was irked with her.

But why?

Lilith's gaze landed on the tarot cards she used for her readings, but for the first time in a long time, they just wouldn't do. Neither would the stack on her night table. Lilith impulsively raced upstairs, rummaged in her cedar chest and brought an ancient treasure to light.

The tarot cards Dritta had given her. The tarot cards she had learned with. The tarot cards Lilith had not used since Sebastian drew The Fool.

Since she left the *Rom kumpania*.

They were heavy in Lilith's hands, heavier than she remembered. Just holding them prompted a wealth of memories—she imagined the deck smelled faintly of patchouli. She cradled them in her hands, for they were frail after so many years, even with Lilith's careful storage. She carried them down to the living room and eased them from their protective cocoon of silk.

It had been so long since she had even revealed them to the light. Lilith held her breath as she unwound the last layer of silk, half expecting that the cards would have disintegrated.

But they hadn't; they were still whole, even though their edges were frayed and feathered. They were so thick! The colors of the paintings had faded—she supposed it was tempura paint or something equally perishable that had been used all those years ago.

The images made her smile in recollection. Lilith went slowly through the cards, Dritta's voice echoing in her ears with the sight of each one. When she reached The Fool, she paused, her fingertips easing over the painting, then lingering on the zero above his head.

The first card. The null. Nothing on its own, The Fool increases everything it joins tenfold. It is magical number, a mystical number, a card to be reckoned with.

A card of journeys, follies, adventures.

Lilith suddenly remembered an assertion Dritta had once made when they sat together late one night, a claim the other woman had never repeated. Lilith had never been able to coax Dritta to acknowledge again that she had even made the claim.

But she had, and Lilith remembered. Dritta had said that the high cards—those twenty-one numbered individually—marked the path of a journey or a transformation, a coming to wisdom.

Lilith shuffled through the old deck with shaking fingers, unable to deny her sudden sense that she had remembered something very important.

Sebastian had drawn The Fool, the zero card.

On Saturday, Lilith had drawn The Magician, the one card.

After Mitch left Saturday night The High Priestess had separated herself from the deck. Her number was two.

Yesterday, Lilith had drawn The Empress, number three.

She spread the four cards out on the table and looked at them carefully. It couldn't be a coincidence that they had been coming to her in order. Just to test her belief that there was no such thing as coincidence, Lilith drew another card randomly from the deck.

It was The Emperor. Number five.

Lilith's heart skipped a beat and she was instantly reassured at the state of matters between herself and Mitch. The Emperor signified an audience with authority, with the man in charge, with a charismatic and decisive man. A man who valued logic and tangible evidence, a man who could be relied upon to do what is right.

Lilith had a pretty good idea who that man was.

Mitch was coming to see her.

But when?

Lilith had a sense that the cards were telling her something, just as they did in every consultation. She studied the six cards more carefully, the horizontal figure eight hanging in the air over The Magician's head reminding her of something Dritta had done that night. She had lain out the court cards in a strange way, a way that represented the journey upon which they were guideposts.

Lilith quickly separated the rest of the court cards from her old deck and laid them out in her best recollection of how they should be. A few adjustments, some lip nibbling and concentration, and she was certain she had it right.

Immediately in front of herself, Lilith had laid The Fool, followed to his left by the next ten cards. They made a circle—or the left half of the sideways figure eight—each card facing outwards, their toes into the circle. Closing the circle was the eleventh card, number ten, The Wheel of Fortune, at what could be called three o'clock.

From there, Lilith had echoed the composition to the right, making the right half of the figure eight with the remaining cards. These ones, though, she had faced inwards, with their heads into the circle and their toes out. The twenty-second card—The World, number twenty-one— lay on top of the The Wheel of Fortune.

The result was a figure eight turned sideways.

The symbol of infinity.

Lilith traced the curve with one fingertip, beginning with The Fool and ending with The World. Then she did it again. Dritta had talked that night about the endless cycle of re-incarnation, the cycle of renewal and transformation. The path of the lower cards she had called sunwise, outward, male; the path of the higher cards being moonwise, inward, female.

Lilith understood instinctively that Sebastian had been reborn as Mitch, that he was on this journey, and some-where, somehow, the course of his travels would mesh with Lilith's. She supposed the cards were telling her that it al-ready had.

The Fool was the beginning of it all, the new threshold that Sebastian had crossed, and, Lilith supposed, the one that she had crossed when she was declared *mahrime*.

The Magician defined the moment she had chosen herself to have some influence on events, the moment Lilith had decided to act and create a spell. Perhaps it also represented the moment Mitch had chosen to buy his house, to make a home out of a neglected property, to conjure gold from dross.

The High Priestess whispered of intuition. It had been she who told Lilith to have faith in her conviction that Mitch was truly Sebastian, even if he didn't remember. And maybe she had given Mitch a similar message, for he had been charming to Lilith when they had next met.

Of course, his dog had trashed her garden in the interim.

Lilith ran her fingertips across The Empress card. Productivity was her realm, not just in terms of work but in terms of the earth itself. The Empress knew of gardens, of fruit and harvest. Lilith's smile faded. And The Empress advised on parenting. Hadn't yesterday shown what a protective parent Mitch was?

And reminded Lilith of the parent she would never be?

Lilith forced herself to consider the next card in their mutual adventure. A decisive man demanding an audience, that was The Emperor, which no doubt hinted at what Mitch would do sometime soon. But The Emperor was also concerned with the balance of power, with domination and submission, with defining who was in charge.

Lilith sat back and chewed her lip thoughtfully, unable to dismiss her sense that she didn't like the import of that.

Eventually, Lilith inverted the successive cards, leaving only those leading up to The Emperor faceup. With one last glance over them, she left the cards where they lay and went to make herself a pot of chamomile tea to help her ponder Mitch's next move.

The newsroom was a familiar cacophony of sound and Mitch welcomed the evidence of organization after his muddled weekend.

"Get moved all right?" Isabel demanded cheerfully. Their current intern, she was young and idealistic, too thin to be healthy to Mitch's way of thinking, and a whiz with both her camera and their antiquated filing system. Today she wore black, despite the heat, her lips a decidedly Gothic burgundy.

"Pretty much," Mitch admitted. He gave her clothing a significant glance. "You look like you've been hanging out with those Edwardian vampires on Queen West.''

"New guy,'' Isabel conceded. ''So, what's going on to-day?''

"I don't know yet.'' Mitch noted that his boss was beck-oning him into their morning meeting. He grabbed a coffee and decided to take a chance. ''But maybe you could do me a favor in the interim.''

"Anything for the star reporter.'' Isabel grinned. ''Might as well learn from the best.''

Mitch took the compliment in stride, knowing an inves-tigative reporter was only as good as his latest scoop. ''Have a look through the files and see if you can find anything about cons done by fortune tellers. Maybe in teams. And whenever there's a woman involved, try to get me a description.''

Isabel whistled. ''Sounds like a juicy lead. We gonna bust somebody?''

Mitch shrugged, striving to look more casual than he felt about this. ''You never know. You can only follow them up.''

"Okay. I'll see what I can get.''

"Thanks.'' Mitch nodded, then headed into the meeting, scalding his lip on the coffee. It wasn't even worth it, the stuff tasted so bad. All the same, he felt a grim satisfaction with both his idea and Isabel's agreement to help.

Because cons weren't the only ones who could retrieve information and use it to their own advantage. A harmless wacko next door was one thing—but a scam being run on his stepmother by that neighbor was quite another. Mitch was markedly less well disposed to his beguiling neighbor. By the end of the day, he was certain he'd have the goods on Lilith Romano.

Or whoever she really was.

By Monday afternoon, Lilith knew she had a serious prob-lem.

She hadn't thought much of it when a trio of cable re-pairmen came to her door that morning, insisting that they had to have access to her yard to fix the main line. She didn't have cable herself, but she knew the line ran across the end of the backyard, along with the telephone wires.

It *had* been a bit strange that the trio lingered on the porch grinning goofily at her, especially after she told them where the gate was.

Even after she shut the door, they still stood there.

And when they turned up in the backyard, they seemed to spend a lot more time looking for her than fixing the cable line. One waved so hard when he glimpsed her in the kitchen that he nearly fell off his ladder.

Lilith decided they had just been compelled to sit through a seminar on improving consumer relations or some non-sense and didn't think too much more about it.

Monday lunch brought the paperboy, whom Lilith hadn't even known still came to collect personally. And she didn't even have the paper delivered—she bought it at the corner every day. An earnest twelve-year-old, he stood in her foyer and gaped at her like a fish out of water.

It was more than a bit uncomfortable, especially as the boy stammered and flushed and couldn't manage to tell her why he was there.

Then he comped her for a month of newspapers, blushed scarlet, and ran.

Lilith watched him go in puzzlement. She checked her blouse and skirt but found nothing odd about what she was wearing. Everything was done up as it should be, the foyer was orderly and there was no obvious indication of what could have made the boy respond that way.

Maybe it was something in the wind. Or the stars. Lilith checked her charts, but there was nothing adverse there.

She might have forgotten it all, if cranky Mr. Lewison next door hadn't gone out of his way to be friendly when she was leaving to run errands. He even gave Lilith a bloom from his prize Austen rose, the one he guarded jealously from the most fleeting glance of admiration. He bowed, before her astonished eyes, and surrendered the rose with a romantic flourish.

"Beauty to beauty," he declared gallantly.

Lilith put the rose in water and wondered if Mr. Lewison had gone back to drinking gin for breakfast again.

The boy at the grocery store insisted on carrying her box of acquisitions all the way to the house, flatly refusing a tip. He just grinned and said carrying her groceries was enough of a bonus for him.

Lilith was starting to think that things were definitely odd by the time she rode her ancient bike down to the occult bookstore for her afternoon session of readings. A startling number of car accidents seemed to occur right behind her.

She supposed the roads were getting really dangerous.

But she had never noticed so many men idling around, apparently with nothing better to do than whistle appreciatively at women on bicycles.

At least, not until she got to the bookstore. Oddly enough, there was a whole line of people waiting for her to read their cards. That was a bit disconcerting. Usually there were one or two anxious older women, or a few giggling teenage girls, but Lilith had never been confronted by fifty men who looked like they probably had real jobs.

Fifty men with their tongues hanging out.

She frowned and entered the bookstore, just as the first two started a shoving match as to who was actually at the front of the line. The argument quickly escalated into a fist fight, even though the proprietor—a reedy man of the gentle, daisies-in-guns variety—tried desperately to intervene.

One last punch resolved the matter and the loser went down. As Lilith watched in astonishment, the victor clutched his bloody nose and lunged into the chair opposite Lilith, a very familiar gleam in his eye.

"Hey, baby, what's your sign?" he murmured, a wolfish grin at his own cleverness curving over his lips. "Maybe you and me could, like, make a *love* connection."

And Lilith suddenly understood. These men were all in lust.

For *her.*

And it was all because of her spell.

She sat back in her chair and regarded the line of agitated men with dawning horror, the lines she had chanted trailing through her mind.

> *"Lover true, come to me,*
> *Through the air or across the sea;*
> *Once we loved through the night with style—*
> *Come back NOW! I'll make it worth your while."*

Oops.

Lilith checked the state of all the pants she could see and swallowed hard. Oops, oops, oops. She had concocted a love potion, drunk it, and flat out forgotten to make it specific to Mitch.

These men: the paperboy, the cable guys, the grocery clerk, they all hoped to seduce her. They were all expecting her to make it worth their while.

They didn't even know why they were attracted to her—they were just like dogs following a bitch in heat.

And Lilith had done this to herself. Just like the song said.

She really had made Love Potion Number Nine and was apparently irresistible to the male sex as a result.

Yet the one man at whom the spell was supposed to be targeted seemed to be remarkably immune. Didn't that just figure? It was really too bad, because Lilith could have used a staunch defender of her honor just about now. She wasn't entirely sure she could escape this bookstore unscathed otherwise.

It was doubly annoying to realize that defending a woman's honor was probably something Mitch Davison did quite well.

So Mitch wasn't in the best mood of his life. There seemed to be a lot of that going around. No doubt about it—when the facts didn't come up the way he expected them to, the journalist in Mitch got cranky.

He climbed out of the subway station to the street and swung his briefcase into his other hand. Sweat trickled down his back as he trudged up his street.

He noted ruefully that his house was readily identifiable. Not only was it the worst-maintained dump on the block, the fastidiously kept house directly past it made the contrast unavoidable.

Lilith's house. Mitch growled at the unwelcome reminder of the woman who was tormenting him. Not only had Isabel come up with a big fat zip on con teams in her foray through the files today, but they had discovered that Lilith Romano didn't actually exist. Mitch had double-checked everything himself. But there it was.

It was as though she had never been.

Mitch smelled a story. But without anything in the files, he didn't know where he'd find a lead.

Because people had to exist. They had to have social insurance numbers, they had to have immigration papers, they had to have bank accounts and various other numbers assigned to them.

Except Lilith didn't.

Oh, she had bought the house ten years before all right, paid cash, which said something about the financial power of fortune telling that Mitch had never considered before. She had used a bogus social insurance number on the transaction, but it didn't trace anywhere.

And before that property title, there was no record of Lilith Romano anywhere at all. She hadn't been born here, she hadn't immigrated here, she hadn't ever been to the hospital, or passed a driver's license test. She hadn't had a run-in with the cops, she hadn't filed a complaint with anybody anywhere.

She didn't have a bank account. She didn't have a phone. She didn't answer surveys or buy investments or get on mailing lists. Somebody paid her property taxes in cash.

As far as Mitch could discern, she didn't even pay income tax. That was a hell of a trick and one he wouldn't mind learning himself. He eyed the winking neon sign in her window and resolved to check the business registry.

But Mitch was quite certain he wouldn't find anything there either. He grimaced, pushed his way through the crowd of men on the sidewalk, and made his way up his own walkway.

The big question was *why* Lilith didn't exist. Because people didn't "disappear" by accident. No, Lilith had spent a lot of money making sure she couldn't be found.

And honest people didn't need to do that.

Mitch wasn't going to consider that finding indications of Lilith's nefarious intent was at the root of his bad mood. He wasn't going to admit on any level that he'd been hoping that a little research would prove him overprotective and maybe even wrong.

He couldn't be grumpy just because that hadn't happened. After all, Mitch didn't like being wrong, so being pleased by being proven wrong would have made no logical sense.

Mitch opened the front door and called as cheerful a greeting as he could manage. He had a policy of not bringing work—or its emotional fallout—home.

Jen squealed as she ran down the hall, the faithful Bun in tow, and threw herself into his arms. Mitch grinned and swung her high, very glad to see her giggling again.

"Daddy, we went swimming again. And we went to the store and Nana bought *blue* Jell-O and . . ."

Mitch shook his head with mock solemnity. "They don't make blue Jell-O."

"They do! Daddy, they do! We had some. It's *booberry*."

Mitch bounced his daughter on his hip as he headed for the kitchen, her litany of news running in one ear and out the other. Cooley nudged his knee, demanding his ears be scratched, his jowls dripping water.

Jason proudly displayed a mayonnaise jar. Its lid had been punctured, no doubt with one of Mitch's better screwdrivers.

"I caught a cicada," he declared and Mitch bent to squint into the jumble of grass.

"It's a big one."

Jen bounced Bun on her dad's shoulder. "Nana made stir-fry and we helped and it took forever!"

Mitch looked up at that incredible bit of news. "Nana made a stir-fry?"

Jen and Jason nodded in unison.

Something *was* up. Mitch slanted a glance to Andrea who stirred honest-to-goodness vegetables a little too quickly to be entirely innocent.

What had happened while he was at work? Mitch wasn't sure he wanted to know, the very presence of a healthy dinner hinting that it was something really bad.

Jen unwittingly spilled the beans. "And Daddy, Nana is going on a boat! A big white boat like on television!"

Mitch straightened with a snap. Andrea cast a tentative smile over her shoulder and stirred more quickly.

"Are you?" he asked, a decided frost in his tone.

His stepmother tossed her hair. "Love is in the gentle

Caribbean breezes, Mitch," she said casually. "I *told* you I was going."

Mitch put Jen down as his temper came to a simmer. "I thought we had decided about this," he said grimly.

"We did." Andrea plunked a jug of grape Kool-Aid on the table with so much defiance that it sloshed high. "We just decided differently."

Mitch kept his mouth shut while he counted to three.

It didn't help a whole lot.

But then, Andrea didn't know the whole story. Mitch cleared his throat and frowned. "Look, Andrea, I found out some stuff today. *Someone*"—he punctuated that word with a heavy glance—"has spent a lot of money to make sure she doesn't have a paper trail. It's like she doesn't exist. . . ."

Andrea dropped the spoon and spun in horror. "You snooped!"

"I did what I do best," Mitch retorted. "And I did it for you."

"Ha!" Andrea snatched up her wooden spoon and stirred with vigor. "You did it to prove that you were right. What is it with men? Why do you all have to be right, all the time, even when you're *wrong*?"

"Andrea, what I found is not the mark of an honest citizen. . . ."

"Oh, Mitch, give it a rest!" the older woman snapped. She threw the spoon into the skillet and turned a frustrated look on him. "I'm going on the cruise, and that's that. Just let it go."

"You should cancel it," Mitch argued stubbornly. "Go on a cruise, any cruise, anywhere, just not that one. Book another."

"It's nonrefundable," Andrea enunciated carefully. She banged a couple of pots. "And I'm glad. Now, sit down, the chicken's getting cold."

But Mitch wasn't ready to let this go just yet.

Clearly, he wasn't going to get through to Andrea now. She had that come-hell-or-high-water look that he knew better than to fight.

The argument had moved next door.

Because if Andrea was going to rely on Lilith's advice,

then Lilith had to be persuaded to abandon this con game.

Mitch knew he was the very man for the job.

"You go ahead," he said tightly. "I'll be right back."

Andrea glanced up, no doubt hearing the resolve in his tone, but Mitch didn't care. He strode down the hall, kicked open the storm door and stalked toward his neighbor's porch.

It was only now that he noticed the collection of men and boys lingering on the sidewalk in front of Lilith's house. There was even a cable television repair crew, their truck parked illegally, all three of them staring at Lilith's house as though they couldn't look away. Mitch followed their gazes and couldn't see anything that would prompt such an expression of moonstruck wonder.

Mitch scowled and pushed his way through the small crowd, heading decisively for Lilith's porch.

A lanky man stepped suddenly into Mitch's path, holding a massive box of chocolates. "Are you going to talk to Lilith?" he whispered with obvious awe.

"Yeah. Why?" Mitch knew he didn't imagine the wonder that swept through the ranks in the wake of his simple agreement.

The man's voice trembled when he spoke. "Then could you give this to her? Please?" He licked his lips nervously, his gaze darting to Lilith's door and back to Mitch, his words tumbling forth. "It's for today, at the bookstore. I hope she'll understand that it wasn't my fault, that I feel just awful about everything. I hope, I hope, I hope she isn't mad at me."

Before Mitch could make sense of that, the man pressed the box insistently into Mitch's hands. To keep it from falling, Mitch ended up taking it.

And the man darted away.

"But, wait!" Mitch called. "You should take this to her yourself! Make your own apology!" But the man was running down the street as though the hounds of hell were after him.

It had to be the biggest damn box of chocolates Mitch had ever seen. And here he had thought they only packaged them like this at Valentine's Day. The smell of warm chocolate wafted through the cardboard and Mitch's belly growled.

A teenage boy stepped forward then, offering a pink envelope, his eyes hopeful. "It's a card for her. Chicks like cards, don't they? Don't they?"

Mitch didn't know what to say, his experience in such matters fairly limited and not incredibly successful. "I guess."

But Mitch's acceptance of this token seemed to turn him into the official envoy. He didn't know what else to do. He certainly wasn't expecting to get loaded up. Every guy there had something for Lilith, some affectionate gift or another, and Mitch ended up carrying them all.

This was really weird.

Mitch wasn't quite sure what to do to get out of this. He almost forgot that he was mad at Lilith, because this whole situation was so very strange. The men and boys stepped back as one, their tokens entrusted to Mitch, their expressions hesitant and hopeful.

And horny.

Oh, yeah, Mitch knew that look. Been there, done that. He frowned, not liking his role here at all. Mitch eyed the chocolates, perfume, stuffed toys, and balloons, but before he could figure out what exactly to say, a throat cleared portentously.

Mitch looked up into the rheumy old eyes of the man who must be Lilith's other neighbor. That man offered a bouquet of roses, evidently cut from the plants surrounding his house. His gnarled hand shook as he handed it over the short hedge.

"These, too," he said hoarsely. "Tell her Joe sends them." He smiled crookedly. "Joe next door." He nodded sagely. "It's good just to know they'll be close to her."

There was definitely something wrong with the drinking water in this neighborhood. Mitch would have to start buying the bottled stuff for the kids.

All the same, Mitch couldn't bring himself to be rude. He juggled his load and made his way to the door, more than aware of his expectant audience. Before he rang the bell, Mitch struggled to remember why he was here.

Right! He was *mad*. Lilith was a crook, she was trying

to swindle Andrea. Right. And Mitch wasn't going to let his stepmother be ripped off.

That was it. Mitch took a deep breath as he rang the bell and tried to look forbidding. It was pretty hard to summon indignation with an armload of romantic gifts, but Mitch did his best.

He rang the bell again, then again, then knocked on the door. Lilith might have hidden herself away from the world, but she wasn't hidden from him. Nope, Mitch was on to her, he smelled a story and his instincts were never wrong.

They were going to get this straightened out right now.

5

THE POPE

"I'm coming!" Lilith called as the doorbell rang and rang and rang. The person was even knocking at the door, as if she could *miss* all that noise!

What could be so important? Lilith was rattled, having escaped the bookstore by a narrow margin and come home to find a growing legion of men on the sidewalk.

But everything was wrong in the stars for a counter-spell. So, Lilith barricaded herself in the house to wait it out. She distrusted the fact that her bell rang now.

It was probably one of Those Men.

Well, Lilith was ready to tell them what she thought of their behavior. She'd been trapped in her house long enough and was done with it. Yes! She would give them a piece of her mind—and if they were looking to win her affections, that would finish that!

"Well? Where's the fire?" Lilith demanded as she hauled open the door, then her mouth fell open in shock.

Because it seemed that Mitch wasn't as immune to her spell as he'd insisted, after all. Gifts of a most romantic sort cascaded from his arms, and he even clutched roses. He looked mildly startled by her greeting, but Lilith was delighted.

He *remembered*!

That alone made every trial of the day fade out of Lilith's mind. Everything was finally falling into place. Lilith lunged out the door and cast herself into Mitch's arms.

Actually, she landed in the midst of his packages and Mitch couldn't do much about it. Lilith didn't care. She

landed a seriously yummy kiss on Mitch and embraced him
with all the ardor she'd been saving just for him.

He made a little growl of protest, but much less than he
had the first time, and maybe only because he was going
to drop that great big box of chocolates. They'd probably
cost a fortune, but Lilith didn't care about the box. She
wasn't much for chocolate anyhow.

There was another kind of sweet treat she had in mind.

The box fell, the chocolates rolled, Lilith framed Mitch's
face with her hands and kissed him harder.

Mitch swore under his breath, shivered, and nearly lost
his balance. Then he abruptly dropped everything else and
caught Lilith up against him. His hands cradled the back
of her waist possessively and he pulled her right to her toes.
His lips slanted across hers with purpose and Lilith's heart
began to thunder.

He *remembered*!

This time would be even better than the last. Lilith joy-
ously pressed her breasts against Mitch's chest and took a
deep breath of the warm masculine scent of him. She
twined her fingers into the thickness of his hair and ran one
bare toe up the back of his leg. He was so strong, so muscled, so perfectly delicious.

And he was really back.

Lilith slid her tongue between his teeth and Mitch
groaned. She felt the evidence that their thinking was as
one in this and arched herself against him. Mitch gripped
the back of her waist even tighter, he plundered her mouth
with his. Sunlight danced in Lilith's veins, she rubbed her
belly against his raging erection.

This was more like it! She had known that her one true
love would be irresistible when he put his mind to seduction.

But just when everything seemed to be going exactly
right for a change, Mitch suddenly gripped Lilith's shoulders in his hands. He pushed her away from him, a steely
glint of determination in his amber eyes.

"Not again," he declared, his voice so low and gritty
that it made Lilith tremble in anticipation. "Not like that
again."

Lilith blinked in alarm before she understood. No. Not

on the porch. Or even in the foyer. Of course not. The house presented myriad, more private options.

What a marvel of practicality her man was!

Lilith snared Mitch's collar and dragged him into the house. "Don't worry. We can be very creative. Where should we start? In the living room? The bedroom? The kitchen?"

He frowned and planted his feet resolutely against the floor. "No. That's not what I mean."

Lilith was puzzled by his change of attitude. "You want to do it on the porch?"

At that suggestion, Mitch looked decidedly agitated. "No!"

"In the foyer again?"

Mitch looked at the carpet and swallowed, obviously remembering their first passionate encounter. When he looked back to her, the heat smouldering in his eyes made Lilith's heart skip a beat. "Yes," he said silkily, and reached out one hand to her before he suddenly checked his response.

"Wait a minute, wait a minute!" Mitch shook his head as though he was remembering something, or trying to shake something loose. "No!" He took a step back. "This isn't what's supposed to be happening here. This isn't why I came!"

"It isn't?" Lilith knew her confusion showed. "But I thought everything was going according to plan."

Mitch quickly looked up at that. "Not *my* plan." He shoved a hand through his hair and eyed Lilith with obvious exasperation. "What do you do to me, anyhow? How do you manage to make me forget the point, just like that?" He snapped his fingers, not looking too pleased about the situation.

But Lilith laughed. The answer was so perfectly obvious. "We're destined to be together," she said easily. "Of course, we have a powerful effect on each other."

"Destiny," Mitch muttered. "And here I thought you were going to blame it on a spell."

Lilith smiled. "Well, maybe that didn't hurt."

Mitch took a deep and deliberate breath, then granted her a quelling glance. "Whatever it is, I wish you'd stop."

Lilith blinked in surprise. "You do?" Then she smiled

again, seeing his teasing for what it was. "You could have fooled me," she purred, backing Mitch into the wall as she closed in for another kiss.

But Lilith never connected.

Mitch stepped quickly away, leaving her in mid-pucker. "Lilith!"

He flung out his hands. "This has to stop! And it has to stop right now!"

"You're the one who came bearing romantic gifts," she felt compelled to observe.

But Mitch jabbed a finger toward the debris on the porch. "That stuff isn't from me, so don't go leaping to conclusions. I didn't come to bring it either." Lilith watched him, mystified as to what was his problem. He certainly was wound up. "It's from *them*, so your gratitude is misplaced."

Lilith looked to find that the army of men camped out in front of her house had grown. She winced. "Oh, no. I was hoping they were gone."

"Well, they're not." Mitch sounded quite disgruntled about the whole thing, and rightly so, to Lilith's way of thinking. "And they made me into their official envoy since I was coming here anyway."

Lilith felt her lips quirk at this admission. Suddenly everything made perfect sense. Trust Mitch to be worried about only taking credit where it was due! So, he had remembered and come to tell her so, but he didn't want her misunderstanding the source of these gifts. He certainly had developed some noble traits in his character over the centuries.

She tried not to tease him, but she couldn't resist. He was so serious about doing the Right Thing.

"And you only accept kisses that you think you've earned?" Lilith heard the laughter lurking in her voice, but Mitch didn't smile. Lilith was undeterred. "So, do I have to wait until you bring me something to give you another kiss?" She playfully ran a fingertip up his bare forearm. "Or should we think of some other ways for you to earn a kiss?"

This time her lips brushed against his before Mitch caught his breath and took another step away.

"You've got to stop doing that!"

"Why?"

"Well, just because." Mitch lifted a hand as though he would wipe away her kiss, but his fingers lingered against his lips. Lilith liked when he looked disheveled, surprised, and slightly uncertain of himself. It was very sexy to know that she could rattle this man's cage.

Because he definitely rattled hers.

Mitch's gaze slid to meet Lilith's, then narrowed thoughtfully. "Do you do that to everybody who comes to your door?"

Lilith laughed. So that was what was bothering him! "No, of course not." She wrinkled her nose. "Just you." She walked her fingers up his chest and smiled up at him. "I only have one absolutely perfect soulmate, after all."

Mitch's eyes flashed golden, a markedly good sign to Lilith's way of thinking, before he cleared his throat portentously. She leaned closer, but he gripped her shoulders and stared into her eyes. "I don't really think we're talking about the same thing here," he began, but Lilith wasn't interested in any further disclaimer.

This was silly. Mitch had remembered and that was no small thing. It called for a celebration! And Lilith was more than ready to get down to the business of celebrating.

Their future could begin right now.

"The reason I came . . ." Mitch would have continued, but Lilith landed a fingertip firmly against his lips. He swallowed and stared at her, as though he was helpless to step away.

"Enough talk," Lilith whispered. "This calls for a celebration and I can think of the perfect one." Mitch's eyes flashed as Lilith pressed herself against him. She replaced her fingertip with her lips and felt Mitch shiver right to the core.

Oh, yes, they could try out every single room in the house tonight. Their reunion was a little later than she had expected, but better late than never. Lilith's heart sang. Mitch was so much more than she remembered him being as Sebastian. Now that he had remembered, well, Lilith wanted to share everything that had happened in the many years they'd been apart. She lifted her lips from his and felt his heartbeat under her fingertips.

It was racing just as fast as her own.

"We just have to talk," she assured him with a slow smile.

But Mitch took a deep breath, gripped her shoulders and set her an arm's length away from himself. The distance he put between them seemed to restore his solemnity.

"Oh, yeah," he said grimly. "We sure do."

No doubt he had lots of things to share with her too. Lilith was very glad that they were finally remembering the same thing. She danced down the hall to the kitchen and beckoned to Mitch.

"Come on, let's have a glass of wine and toast the moment first." Lilith snatched up a bottle of Valpolicella and twisted the corkscrew into the cork. She'd waited so long for this! "The celebrating could take all night!"

"Funny," Mitch commented, his footsteps falling heavily in the hall behind her. "I don't think it's going to take very long at all."

There was a resolve lurking in his tone that made Lilith pause in the act of tugging out the cork. For a man who had just found his one true love, Mitch didn't sound very excited.

Something wasn't right.

Lilith pivoted and studied Mitch for a long moment, noticing only now the tightness of his lips and the determination in every line of his figure.

Her heart fluttered. He looked very male amidst the bright cheerfulness of her kitchen, maybe because men seldom entered it.

And now, Lilith realized, Mitch looked very annoyed.

But that wasn't how he should be looking right now.

What was going on? Lilith bit her lip. Mitch certainly didn't look smitten, or even very pleased to be welcomed into the haven of her kitchen. Belatedly, she realized that he had said that he didn't think they were talking about the same thing.

Uh-oh.

Lilith cleared her throat. "What exactly," she asked softly, "is going on?"

Mitch's brows rose and he folded his arms across his chest, the move making him fill her doorframe. "That

would be my question,'' he said wryly and cocked a brow.
"What in the hell are you trying to pull?''

Lilith felt suddenly that the conversation had taken a
sharp left without signalling. She looked down at the bottle
of wine and knew he wasn't referring to the cork. In fact,
she had a funny feeling that there might not be anything to
celebrate at all.

Lilith put the bottle deliberately back on the counter and
straightened. She tried to keep her disappointment out of
her voice. "Are you saying that you don't remember being
Sebastian, being with me? Isn't that why you're here?''

Mitch regarded her for a long moment and when he answered, his tone turned gentle. "I don't remember that,
Lilith. I told you before, we've never met.''

Lilith spun and put the length of the kitchen between
them, unable to halt the unruly tide of emotion within her.
Only in the face of disappointment did she realize how
much she had been hoping. . . .

But that didn't matter. Mitch didn't remember.

Which left the question of why he had come.

Lilith took a deep breath and spun to face Mitch again.
He hadn't moved, although his gaze was locked on her. His
eyes glowed, the way old amber did in sunlight, and Lilith
was certain that she was the complete focus of his attention.
"Then why *did* you come here tonight?''

"I want to know who you are.''

"But you know that already!''

"Nope.'' Mitch shook his head. "I know what you told
me, but other than that, there's no hint that you even exist.''

Lilith frowned, not understanding this assertion at all.
"Of course I exist. I'm standing right here!''

Mitch's brows rose and fell. "Correction: there's no sign
that anyone named Lilith Romano exists. No birth record,
no immigration record, no marriage record, no telephone
bill or bank accounts.'' Mitch surveyed her, his eyes bright
with intelligence. "Where did you come from, Lilith? Who
are you *really*?''

Lilith had been very careful over the years to make sure
she didn't arouse any suspicion wherever she lived. She
was never going to be chased out of a village again for

being different—and immortals were fundamentally different from everybody else.

It wasn't very reassuring to find doubt glistening in the eyes of her beloved. She had a definite sense that mysteries didn't survive very long once they'd attracted Mitch's attention.

Lilith took an unwilling step backwards, fear rising once more in her chest. She fought to keep her voice level, even as her heart pounded in the recollection of running from *gadje* flames.

"I'm Lilith Romano," she said, her words falling in haste. "I don't have a bank account because I don't want one. Same for the phone. I don't know what those other records even are."

Mitch shook his head. "That can't be the truth."

Lilith gasped. "Of course it is!"

"You must have spent a lot of money becoming invisible, Lilith," Mitch explained, his voice low with conviction. "It wouldn't matter, except that I want to know who's sending my stepmother on a specific cruise. Mostly I want to know *why*."

"Why?" Lilith frowned. "But you know that Andrea's going on that cruise to meet her one true love."

Mitch settled into the doorframe, looking markedly less certain of that. His gaze was relentlessly steady. "Understand that I don't want her to be disappointed."

Lilith's confusion melted away at this sign of Mitch's concern. He was being protective of Andrea, a regular old bear, just as that woman had said he would be. He really did take responsibility for everyone around him.

Lilith smiled in mingled relief and admiration. "But you don't need to worry about this, Mitch. She's going to meet the man of her dreams and be perfectly happy."

"Lilith, that doesn't make any sense." Mitch did not look reassured. "How could you possibly know such a thing?"

"I *do* tell fortunes for a living, you know."

Mitch arched a skeptical brow. "And I sniff out swindles for mine."

Lilith's smile disappeared with a snap. She bounded

across the kitchen in her indignation. No one, but *no one*, insulted the merit of her Gift. It was real!

"I'm not swindling anyone! How could you even think such a thing?"

"Lilith, how could I think otherwise? Nothing else makes sense. No one can read the future. . . ."

"I can read the future!" Lilith poked herself in the chest. "I have a precious Gift! And I told Andrea what I saw in her future."

Mitch didn't even blink. "How could you know such a thing?"

"She brought it with her, it's right there in her eyes for anyone who cares to look."

"Right." Mitch's skepticism was clear. "Isn't it odd that you're the only one who can see it there? Come on, Lilith, at least tell me the truth."

"I am telling the truth! Look at this!" Lilith snatched up dozens of wedding invitations when he looked unimpressed—the haul of the previous week—and tossed them at Mitch. "I send people to meet their one true love all the time! It's what I *do*!"

Mitch caught the cards, then turned them over in his hands, no doubt noting all the grateful messages scrawled inside. He read them, one after the other, and his expression grew more drawn.

Lilith had hoped to persuade him, but instead she saw a sadness dawn in his eyes. When Mitch eventually spoke, his words came low and flat, as though he was disappointed in her. "You really fool them, don't you?" He glanced up suddenly and Lilith was shaken by the disillusion she saw there. "I was hoping that you'd prove me wrong, Lilith."

"You are wrong!"

Mitch shook his head and fingered the cards. "You really get them hooked. How long until your associates pull the rug out from under your starstruck victims?"

"Mitch!" Lilith gasped. "They're not victims! They're *happy*!"

Mitch grimaced and handed her back the cards. "For how long, Lilith?"

"Forever! Love is *forever*!"

"Read that book and saw that movie." Mitch shook his

head and looked away. "That wasn't the ending I recall."

An awkward silence descended in the kitchen and Lilith wished she knew what had happened in his marriage to so disillusion him.

"I help people," she maintained quietly, not knowing how to persuade him of her good intentions if he couldn't believe in her Gift. "I really do."

Mitch smiled wryly and heaved a sigh. "I guess I'm wasting everyone's time here." He turned to leave, obviously thinking little good of Lilith.

She shouldn't have been surprised. The Emperor only believed in the tangible, after all.

Lilith felt sick.

"No, Mitch, wait. Please, let me try to explain." Lilith had to try one last time. "I can look into people's eyes and see their one true love. I can tell them where to find their soulmate. It's not logical, it's not sensible, but it's what I do. I can't even explain it myself. It's the Gift that was entrusted to me. It's my responsibility to use it."

Mitch paused in her hallway and glanced over his shoulder. He must have seen something that persuaded him to give her another chance, because he suddenly pivoted.

"All right." Mitch stepped forward, his hands braced on his hips. Lilith instinctively distrusted the challenge she heard in his tone. "Prove it. Go ahead and look. Tell me where to find my one true love."

It was a brilliant idea. This would persuade him! Lilith immediately looked into Mitch's eyes. She looked hard.

Then, she looked again, just to make sure.

But there was absolutely nothing lurking in the deep gold of his eyes.

It couldn't be. Lilith's heart began to pound. She looked one last time into Mitch's eyes, studied him carefully, then took a slow step backward.

Something wasn't right.

"There's nothing there," she admitted softly.

"See?" Mitch shrugged, his manner less triumphant than Lilith might have expected.

She didn't know what else to say, didn't know what to do other than watch him go.

But Mitch paused on the front threshold, suddenly very

still. His head was bowed and he didn't look back. "Lilith, I want you to tell Andrea not to go on the cruise."

Lilith was appalled at the very suggestion. "Mitch, I can't do that! She'll miss a chance for love! Don't you want her to be happy?"

He turned as his lips tightened. "Of course I do." His eyes glittered. "And I don't want anyone taking advantage of her. That's why I'm here."

Their gazes held for a charged moment and Lilith saw that she hadn't come close to convincing him of anything. She didn't know how to change his mind.

She didn't know how to make him remember.

Lilith felt suddenly very small and very alone. She folded her arms around herself and held her ground. "I'm not taking advantage of her."

"A very wise choice," Mitch murmured.

And with that, he was gone.

Lilith looked down at the invitations scattered on the counter and shook her head in bewilderment. Why couldn't Mitch just believe in love, like everyone else did?

Why wasn't there any portent of love in his eyes?

A lump rose in Lilith's throat at the prospect of Mitch not even having a true love. She'd never seen anything like that before. How could it be so?

Andrea's earlier assertions rang in Lilith's ears once more. She stared unseeingly at the invitations with the gold script and pearly roses, promises of fidelity and eternal love. Mitch had had these once, he must have believed once that he would be as happy as these couples were destined to be.

Lilith wondered what kind of a woman could destroy those idealistic convictions so very quickly. She wondered what kind of woman could leave two little children alone.

Lilith bit her lip. She had a feeling it was the same kind of woman who could steal a man's heart away and leave a cold hollow in its place. Obviously, Mitch didn't believe in love because he had loved his wife, and she had treated him badly.

This really hadn't worked out the way she had always imagined it. Lilith sighed and fingered the cards, noticing only now that her hands were shaking. She had never anticipated that finding Sebastian again would prove to be so difficult. Fortunately, Lilith was not one to give up easily.

She'd think of something.

Maybe Mitch would change his mind when Andrea found her love on the cruise. Maybe time would melt the frost around his heart. Maybe then, something would change in his eyes.

Maybe.

Or maybe not. Lilith's fingers trembled. Because either way, one thing couldn't be denied.

Lilith Romano was not lurking in Mitch Davison's eyes. And even knowing that the decisions of every passing moment affected the course of the future didn't make that news any less troubling.

Not in the least.

It wasn't supposed to be this way.

But then, that seemed to be becoming Mitch's theme song. He wasn't supposed to prove his instincts right and then feel like garbage. But he had and he did.

Mitch wasn't supposed to charge into battle to defend someone he cared about, win the battle, and wish he'd lost. He wasn't supposed to forget every logical thought in his mind when he looked into his neighbor's dark eyes, especially when he knew all sorts of suspicious things about her.

But he had.

At least, he didn't have to like it.

Mitch ate cold chicken stir-fry with stoic resolve and ignored Andrea's worried frown. He smiled at Jen's nonsensical stories and answered Jason's endless questions about how everything worked, but Mitch's heart wasn't really in it.

His heart was still next door.

He wasn't supposed to have lost control again, he wasn't supposed to have kissed Lilith as though his life depended on it. She wasn't supposed to taste so good, she wasn't supposed to be the most attractive and delightful woman he'd ever met, she wasn't supposed to make him want to believe all sorts of wacky nonsense.

She wasn't supposed to tangle him up inside and make

him feel as though he was sliding into quicksand, with no chance of resisting her charms.

He wasn't supposed to wonder why he was resisting at all. His hormones were supposed to be in cold storage, not running the show.

They certainly shouldn't have been interfering with his thinking, much less his ability to get the job done. Mitch's gut told him that Lilith was a fraud, his mind told him there was something fishy about the business next door, but his heart—a heart that hadn't had much to say for a good, long time—told him to get his sorry butt back next door and apologize to the lady.

Because his heart had never been a very trustworthy judge of matters, Mitch decided to sleep on its advice.

And double-check those files in the morning. Mitch was going to get to the bottom of this, and Lilith's allure wasn't going to shake a seasoned reporter like him off the trail.

It sounded like a good strategy, but Mitch's heart—in league with his hormones—kept him awake all night long in the sticky August heat. It was as though, having finally found its voice, his heart intended to be heard.

Or that it intended to make Mitch realize that in his concern for right and wrong, he had just made a big mistake.

Lilith didn't imagine the flash of bright blue in her backyard Tuesday morning. She groaned silently and pulled open the kitchen door, half expecting to find one of Those Men in her yard trying to peep through the window.

But it was Jason who spun guiltily at the sound of the door opening. He clasped his hands behind his back and bit his lip, clearly certain he had been caught at some crime. He was more fair than Mitch, though he had his father's eyes. He would be a handsome boy when he grew up, Lilith acknowledged.

"Well, hello," she said easily.

"I was looking for Ralph," the boy admitted hopefully.

Lilith smiled. "I didn't see him yesterday because I was out, but maybe he'll come today. He usually comes in the morning."

The little boy's eyes lit up. "Like right now?"

"Pretty much." She smiled as he scanned the garden

anxiously. "Does your nana know you're here?"

Jason shook his head. "She thinks I'm playing in our yard." He grimaced comically. "But you have better bugs."

"Well, I don't mind you coming to see them, as long as everyone at your house knows where you are." Lilith indicated the gate. "Go tell your nana, then let's see if we can find Balthasar."

"Who's Balthasar?"

"The praying mantis. He likes it around the compost for some reason. He'll sit on your finger if you're still because he likes how warm it is."

"Cool!"

And the little boy ran for the gate as fast as his legs could carry him. Lilith smiled, more than looking forward to sharing her knowledge of her garden.

Especially with such a curious pupil.

In the end, Ralph did come, delighting Jason once more as he sipped nectar from a flower the boy held. Balthasar sat on Jason's finger for an eternity, warming his body in the sunlight, before finally bounding away. They explored the toad's favorite hiding places and found him lurking in a damp back corner.

Lilith invited Jason to give the toad a name and, inexplicably, the toad became Millie.

It was a wonderful morning. They laughed together and watched dragonflies and bumblebees. They tied the tops of the hollyhocks together and made a teepee that seemed to have flowers for walls. Monarchs came when the phlox released their heady perfume in the late morning and Jason watched wide-eyed as they sipped nectar in their turn.

When Andrea called for lunch, Jason folded his hands in front of him and stood before Lilith. Lilith bit back her smile as he politely and formally thanked her for letting him see her garden and her bugs. He looked like a miniature version of Mitch, solemnly doing what he knew was right.

Abruptly, Jason was five years old again, running for the gate and calling to his nana, all boundless enthusiasm, dirty fingers, and scraped knees.

Lilith watched him go, thinking all the while that Mitch

was a very, very lucky man. Her doorbell rang and she reluctantly abandoned her sunny garden.

It was Andrea, bouncing Jen on her hip.

"Oh, Jason just went home, around the back."

"He'll be fine for a moment." The older woman glanced quickly toward Mitch's house. "That's not exactly why I'm here. I'm sorry to bother you, dear, I know you're busy, but I was wondering whether you could do me a little favor."

"Certainly."

Andrea grinned. "Don't agree too quickly, Lilith! I'm usually the one to leap before I look."

Lilith smiled in turn, then sobered at Andrea's next words.

"It's about the cruise. I forgot that I promised to watch the children on the weekend that's right in the middle. Mitch is going to a conference and if I don't find someone else, then I'll have to cancel."

Oh.

Lilith looked at Jen. The little girl smiled tentatively, just as D'Artagnan wound his way out to the porch.

Her shyness was immediately banished.

"Kitty!" Jen squealed. "Nana! I want to pet the kitty!"

She squirmed and reached out. Lilith winced, expecting nothing good from her live-in companion. The cat stiffened, then haughtily sniffed the little girl's outstretched hand. He sat back on his haunches, like a king ready to receive his subjects, and shook his head with disdainful tolerance of humans.

He gave Jen the Ol' Fish Eye and Lilith breathed a silent sigh of relief.

"It's okay," she confirmed, then lowered her voice to Jen. "Pet him behind his ears, he likes that."

Jen bit her lip and edged closer, her eyes shining. The cat visibly braced himself, but the little girl was surprisingly tentative when she reached out her hand. D'Artagnan averted his gaze as though unaware of her presence, though his ears moved tellingly. She patted him gently, hitting his special spot, and the cat leaned back into her touch as though he was powerless to do anything else.

And he purred.

Jen was enchanted. She hunkered down to lavish attention upon the cat, whispering little stories to him as he purred like an outboard motor.

Andrea smiled, then her eyes widened in appeal as she leaned closer. Belatedly, Lilith recalled the issue at hand and wondered at her role.

She wasn't destined to wonder for long.

"Lilith, you're the only one who understands how important this is. I couldn't help noticing how good you were with Jason this morning. Do you think you might be able to manage the children for those few days?"

Watch Mitch's children? After their last encounter, Lilith couldn't imagine that he'd take well to the idea.

But on the other hand, the only way for Lilith to get herself into Mitch's eyes where she rightly belonged was to work her way into his life. Things had to be set to rights and Lilith knew she was the woman for the job.

After all, she and Mitch were destined to be together. Fortunately, Lilith wasn't one to be shy about taking chances. And winning her one true love back again was a prize well worth putting herself on the line. She was going to make Mitch remember and acknowledge their entwined destiny if it was the last thing she did.

Love, after all, was worth fighting for.

But before she spoke, Lilith's gaze fell on the little girl. She suddenly remembered Jen's upset of the other morning. "Andrea, I don't even know Jen. . . ."

Andrea waved dismissively. "It's not for almost three weeks!"

Lilith dropped her voice. "Doesn't she get frightened when she's alone?"

"Sometimes, but Lilith, I'll make sure they both get to know you well enough that there won't be any problems. And she'll be settled into the house by then. Please?" She smiled tentatively. "So the course of true love can run smooth?"

Lilith looked to Jen and considered. She just couldn't say no. She couldn't make Andrea miss this cruise. Lilith knew how happy this new love was going to make Andrea.

And if Andrea thought there was time for both children to get used to her, then she must be right.

Mitch would come around.

"I'll do it."

"Thank you! You won't regret this, dear!" Andrea squeezed Lilith's hand, then kissed her suddenly on the cheek. Then Andrea straightened and offered her granddaughter a hand. "Come on, Jen, Jason is waiting for his lunch."

The little girl shook her head. "I'll stay with the kitty."

It was as good a time as any to start forging familiarity. Lilith squatted down beside Jen and scratched D'Artagnan's ears too, well aware that Jen watched her. "His name is D'Artagnan," she confided quietly, immensely relieved that the cat tolerated this attention. "And you can come to see him anytime you like."

"Dartaggin." Jen smiled and Lilith didn't have the heart to correct her. The cat looked mildly insulted by this variant of his name. "Nana! I can come pet the kitty!"

Her delight, or perhaps her mispronunciation, seemed to persuade D'Artagnan that it was time to leave. He leapt to the windowsill and proceeded to clean himself as though unaware they all watched him.

Andrea captured the little girl's hand when she might have given chase. "Isn't that nice of Lilith? Now, let's leave the kitty alone for a few moments and have lunch. You thank Lilith."

Jen grinned and waved to Lilith, before turning her attention to the stairs. "Thank you, Lillit."

The mangling of her own name made Lilith smile. "You're welcome, Jen."

Two kids for a weekend. Oh, she would be running!

Lilith grinned at the prospect. She felt suddenly much younger than her six hundred or so years. D'Artagnan bounded past her and stalked into the house, his tail straight as though he was proud of his own role in this.

He might come to regret it, if Jen chased him for a whole weekend. In fact, they both might sleep well after a few days with two children underfoot.

Lilith could hardly wait.

It seemed that every day of the week was hotter than the day before. The mercury inched higher and Mitch's temper wore thinner. He couldn't stop thinking about Lilith. He blamed it on guilt over his less-than-chivalrous behavior.

Just to make matters worse, Mitch wasn't sleeping at night, but he blamed that on the heat. He deliberately ignored the cluster of men on the sidewalk in front of Lilith's house, refused to so much as glance in the direction of her house.

Mitch settled Jen and Jason into a friendly day care at the end of the street by midweek and waved Andrea on her way home that same morning. He walked the children home every night, and unpacked with merciless persistence. One night, he drove over to the lumberyard to get materials for the fence. He bent his not-inconsiderable will on getting Andrea to change her mind—without any noticeable signs of success.

And he thought about Lilith every moment of every day.

He noticed that Lilith had cleaned up her garden so that it didn't look so bad. He found himself listening closely to Jason's stories about Balthasar, the praying mantis near Lilith's compost, and was startled to feel envious of his son for the chance to enjoy Lilith's company.

Mitch tore apart the files at the office, and found nothing more about his neighbor than he had the first time. He looked again and again, he tried to dig deeper, but without success. Even Isabel was starting to think he had lost it.

On Thursday night, as Mitch lay staring at the duo-green ceiling, he resolved to spend any Christmas bonus on installing air-conditioning before the next summer. It was only the heat keeping him awake, after all. Mitch was not going to admit—even to himself—that he was thinking of Lilith's soft curves tangled in her sheets not that far away.

It was a matter of principle, though, that kept Mitch from Lilith's door—as much as a certainty that she would land another one of those kisses on him and his control would melt like butter in the sun.

She probably used that technique all the time. No wonder it worked so damn well.

Mitch hated that he was even susceptible.

Because it was wrong to swindle people. Criminal. The issue was perfectly simple and clear. Mitch was right and he knew it.

So why did being apart from Lilith feel so wrong? She was nuts, or a manipulative con artist, or a witch, or some combination platter of the above.

But Mitch wanted her in ways he had never wanted a woman before. It was more than her luscious kisses, it was that mischievous twinkle in her eye, her cleverness, the way she surprised him, the way she kept him guessing. Mitch wanted to know more about Lilith, and what he wanted to know wasn't going to be lurking in any dusty office files or government databases.

Mitch was starting to wonder about his own sanity. Because the fact was, even knowing everything he knew, he was really looking forward to the possibility of crossing paths with Lilith this weekend.

Accidentally, of course.

It made absolutely no sense. And—remarkably—it had nothing to do with being right or being wrong. Mitch would be rebuilding a fence on the property line. It was only natural that they would see each other, that Lilith might come out to see their progress or make a suggestion.

The prospect of seeing her again was enough to make Mitch anxious for Saturday morning to begin. He told himself that his anticipation was a natural part of his quest for the truth about Andrea's cruise.

But even Mitch noticed that the thought lacked a ring of truth. He scowled at the ceiling as the clock struck three and he faced an uncomfortable reality.

What he was looking forward to was, plain and simple, a glimpse of Lilith's smile. Just the acknowledgement tightened everything within him. Mitch's hormones were winning the field, despite his perfectly reasonable suspicions.

It wasn't like him to lose his professional detachment when he chased a story, it wasn't like him to lose track of the point, it was like him to be . . . beguiled.

Maybe Lilith *had* cast a spell on him.

That prospect was so troubling that Mitch couldn't sleep at all.

6

≈

THE LOVERS

By Saturday morning, Lilith was done with it.

She had had more than enough of Those Men mooning around in front of her porch and she wasn't going to take it anymore. She had been hoping that time would do its thing on wearing down the spell, but no such luck. The calendar was wrong for her spell, but it didn't matter. Lilith couldn't wait any longer.

Besides, she had a sneaking feeling that their presence was affecting the reestablishment of her relationship with Mitch. And that simply wouldn't do.

Lilith put her cauldron on the stove and set to work. An unbeguiling spell took a lot of concentration. It was a delicate balance to persuade a smitten man to simply *not* love a woman anymore, at least without pushing the man into actively disliking or even hating the woman in question.

Do whatsoever you will but harm none. The old oath was tough to hold in this circumstance. Lilith was determined not to mess up.

She peeked through the front curtains and counted Those Men. If anything, their ranks had increased over the week. Lilith might have been pleased to have concocted such an effective potion—at least, if it had worked as it was supposed to.

She would not think about Mitch or the argument they had had the other night. And she certainly wouldn't think any more about him having no one lurking in his eyes— let alone what she could do about it.

Lilith had lain awake enough nights over that already.

She was going to fix all of that, first things first.

Lilith frowned and considered the problem at hand. A potion gone wrong should definitely be countered with another potion, although Lilith winced as she guesstimated the quantity of elixir she would need.

This concocting could take all day.

And it would clean out her supplies.

But there was no other choice. She had to make this come right. In fact, righting this unexpected wrinkle in her magick could put her back in Mitch's eyes where she belonged. You never knew. At that promising thought, Lilith pushed up her sleeves and went to work.

With luck, by late afternoon, she'd be able to offer Those Men a quenchingly cool "herbal drink." And then, provided they each only had a precise measure, one of Lilith's troubles would be solved. She turned on the radio and grinned as the chorus of the Supremes' "Where Did Our Love Go?" filled the kitchen.

Lilith danced barefoot across the cool tiles and opened her cupboards with purpose, as her cauldron came to a boil.

She even sang along.

Saturday went better than expected. Not only did Kurt declare Mitch's house basically sound, he set to work with a vengeance that Mitch found hard to match. Cooley and both kids defied expectation by staying out of the drying concrete in the fence postholes.

In fact, they all played so amiably together that Mitch tried not to look surprised. The fence took shape with surprising speed and Mitch could have called the day a great success.

Except for one critical detail. Lilith didn't make an appearance. Mitch peeled off his shirt in the afternoon sun and couldn't help thinking of her comment.

Instead, it was Andrea who appeared, lugging a great big box emblazoned with the logo of a fancy clothier. It looked as though she'd been indulging herself again.

Mitch smiled and shook his head. The kids called delighted greetings, while Andrea waved to the two men. "Hello, Kurt! How are you?"

"Great, Andrea." Kurt paused to rub a hand over his

perspiration-drenched brow and grinned his most charming grin. He whistled low at the sight of her and Andrea preened playfully. "How do you manage to look younger every time I see you?" he demanded.

Andrea shook a finger at Kurt and laughed. "And how do you get smoother and smoother every time I see you? Still breaking all those hearts?"

"As many as I can."

"And not getting any younger while you're at it." Andrea sniffed disapprovingly. "What you need is a nice steady girlfriend."

"Bah! A man needs variety. I'm a dyed-in-the-wool bachelor, Andrea, and don't even imagine that I'll change. Gonna die with my boots on." Kurt winked devilishly at Mitch, then nailed a board in place. "You'll never catch me committing to one flavor of ice cream for the rest of my life."

"Ice cream!" Jen echoed, picking up on a key word with her characteristic selective hearing. "Who has ice cream?"

"Are we having ice cream?" Jason asked, poking his head out from behind the massive thistle that had claimed the back corner of the yard.

Mitch rolled his eyes good-naturedly. "Now, see what you've started?"

Kurt chuckled, then began to whistle as he worked.

"Ice cream in a minute," Andrea declared.

"Funny," Mitch mused as though he hadn't already guessed what Andrea had brought. "We don't even have any ice cream."

Jen pouted, Jason sniffed and went back to his current investigation.

But Andrea grinned. "Now, how did I know that? You know, I just happened to bring a gallon of my favorite double chocolate chip. It jumped right into my basket at the quickie mart."

Both kids cheered and Mitch shook his head. He pointed his hammer at Andrea. "Then, this afternoon, *you* can scrape them off the ceiling with a spatula," he informed his unrepentant stepmother. "It would serve you right for filling them up with refined sugar."

Andrea stuck out her tongue, then waved the big box.

"First, you all have to be suitably dazzled by what I bought!" She hauled out an armload of blue chiffon and held it up to herself, swirling on the steps. It was a great color for her and Mitch had a sinking feeling that he knew exactly why she had bought the dress.

His smile disappeared in record time.

"Nana, let me see!" Jen launched herself across the yard, muddy fingers outstretched for this feminine delight, but Andrea whisked the dress out of harm's way in the nick of time.

"It's for Nana's trip," she said sweetly. "For *dancing*." And she punctuated that last word with a glance at Mitch.

Though he'd fought the good fight, Mitch was smart enough to know that he had lost this one—big time. No doubt Andrea would come to him to do damage control—and knowing himself, Mitch knew he wouldn't even have the heart to say he'd told her so.

He tried not to growl. "Nobody says you'll find anyone who can dance well enough for you."

Andrea snorted. "Lilith says and Lilith knows."

At the sound of a woman's name—any woman's name—Kurt looked up with interest. "Lilith? Who's Lilith?" He nudged Mitch hard and grinned. "Got a new girlfriend I can steal?"

"You should have stolen the last one," Andrea commented dryly.

"Hey!" Mitch shook a finger at her.

Andrea rolled her eyes, then held up a hand in surrender. "Okay, I know, I know. That topic's off limits."

Mitch checked but the kids weren't listening.

"Where's the ice cream, Nana?" Jen asked as Jason listened avidly for the answer.

"Lilith's just our neighbor," he said firmly, concentrating on hammering a nail home.

"Lilith is the most lovely person," Andrea confirmed.

"Lillit has a kitty," Jen contributed.

"And really neat bugs," Jason amended.

"And she tells fortunes for a living!" Andrea concluded. "She can tell you how to find your one true love." References apparently completed, Andrea herded the children toward the kitchen. "Now, who wants ice cream?"

The clamor was enough to deafen anyone unprepared for it. Cooley barked and bounded after the trio, pressing his nose hopefully against the screen door when Andrea firmly shut him out.

The dog whimpered, to no avail.

"A fortune-teller? No kidding." Kurt glanced to Mitch and Mitch saw a familiar gleam in his buddy's eye. "The ditzy ones are a lot less trouble. This Lilith have a true love of her own?"

"She's single," Mitch supplied tersely, not at all liking the smile that curved Kurt's lips. It suddenly seemed like a critical error to have forgotten Kurt's seducing ways. "Look, Kurt, leave her alone. She's a nut anyway."

"What do you mean?"

Mitch instinctively decided to make things sound worse than they were. He would not consider why. "I mean she thinks she's a six-hundred-year-old witch and that she casts spells on people that work. Nutty as a fruitcake." Mitch rolled his eyes, trying to convey the ridiculousness of that.

But Kurt was unpersuaded. "A witch!" Kurt eyed Lilith's house pointedly. "Wow. That would be something different." He slanted a glance at Mitch. "What do you think it's like? Being with a witch? You think it's freaky?"

It really mattered to Mitch that he keep Kurt from going next door. "Isn't there an old story that witches make things shrivel and fall off?" he asked idly as he hammered home a nail.

"Things?"

Mitch looked Kurt dead in the eye. "One particular *thing*."

Kurt whistled low, his speculative gaze drifting back to Lilith's house. "Yeah, but what would you know about it? You're too much the family man, ol' buddy."

Mitch concentrated on hammering that nail and ignored the heat on the back of his neck. Sunburn. Plain and simple.

Kurt exhaled through his teeth, his attention fixed again on Lilith's house. "I think that a little witchy action might be just what the doctor ordered today."

"What?" Panic rolled through Mitch. "Look, Kurt, leave it be. She's my neighbor, after all!"

"Yeah, so? I'm not expecting *you* to do the mogambo with her."

That sunburn was hotter than hot. Mitch tried to sound as grim as he could, though why he imagined he'd win this battle, he didn't know. "Kurt, don't. It would be more than awkward. She's just a fortune-teller. . . ."

"What's she look like?"

Mitch might have lied—his own astonishment over that uncharacteristic urge was the only reason the words didn't jump out in time—but Lilith chose that moment to make an appearance on her back step. She let her cat out, glanced up, and granted Mitch a warm smile.

His heart thumped in a way he was quite sure it wasn't supposed to. And he couldn't catch his breath. She was every bit as gorgeous as Mitch recalled, her smile every bit as breathtaking as he remembered. Maybe even more so.

She really made it hard to keep all the dastardly things he knew about her straight in his mind, never mind the way she took advantage of people. That sweet, slow smile made it hard to believe that she was a master criminal who had somehow ensured that her identity had been erased from all files. Maybe it was those dark eyes with that twinkle lurking in their depths that did Mitch in.

Mitch was surprised to realize that he didn't really care. He just wanted to smile back at Lilith all day long.

But the lady had other ideas. She waved and ducked back inside, her cat curled into a watchful ball on the back step. In fact, she was already back in the house by the time Kurt whistled in low admiration.

"Wow! You didn't tell me she was *gorgeous!*"

"Well . . ."

"Trying to keep her for yourself, huh? Can't say I blame you." Kurt put his hammer down and scooped up his T-shirt. "But hey, I'm on to you now. Open field. All's fair in love and war, right?"

"Wait a minute! Where are you going? It's too early to quit." Mitch gestured impatiently to the nearly finished fence. "Let's get finished. We're almost done."

Kurt sighed theatrically and put a hand over his heart. "But I suddenly feel this burning desire to have my fortune told." And with a wink, Kurt swaggered through the gate and headed for Lilith's front porch.

Mitch had to stop Kurt from going in there! "But she's an opportunist!" he called.

Kurt's grin flashed in the shadows between the houses. "And you don't think I am?" he joked.

Mitch hated with newfound passion that Kurt was both so classically good-looking and so successful in pursuing women. The guy looked like some kind of love god! And he spread his affections around as though he had invented sex.

Why, if Lilith pounced on Kurt the way she had pounced on Mitch, the pair of them wouldn't come up for air until Tuesday.

And that bothered Mitch a whole lot more than he knew it should.

"But she's a witch!" he hissed, making the only other protest he could think of.

"Hey, I'll let you know if anything falls off!" Kurt chuckled, then vaulted onto Lilith's porch without a backward glance.

No, this wasn't how things were supposed to go. Not at all. It wasn't in Mitch's script—and he sure as hell didn't like the revision.

His hormones had plenty to say about it, but Mitch deliberately listened to his logic. Maybe he was right about Lilith's interest in Andrea's money, maybe he was wrong. Maybe there was some other explanation for her not being in any of the files she should have been in.

Either way, he wasn't going to find out the truth by his usual means. Conventional research had yielded a big fat zero.

But Mitch was by no means out of options. The sudden idea that popped into his head was just too good to ignore. He put aside his own hammer and scooped up his T-shirt, tugging it quickly over his head. Of course, he was only doing this for Andrea's good, and for the sake of uncovering a story, maybe of exposing a fraud.

But as Mitch stalked down the alley between the houses, he wasn't thinking about any of those things. He was thinking of stopping Kurt from making Lilith another notch in his well-adorned bedpost.

It didn't make any damn sense to worry about protecting a woman who seemed to prey on others for a living, but Mitch didn't have time to think about it too much right now.

He had to do something. And he had to do it now.

And pretending to remember being Sebastian was the best plan Mitch could come up with in such short order. Lilith would certainly buy it, given her consistency with that concept.

Yep. Mitch was going Under Cover to get the truth. He was definitely on familiar ground.

For the moment, at least.

Cooley eventually realized that he was alone in the yard. He whimpered and pressed his nose to the screen—nosing it distinctly inward as he watched more than one glop of ice cream drop to the floor uncontested.

He sniffled to general disinterest.

No one was letting him in. Andrea finally glanced his way and shook her head sternly, dishing out more ice cream, all of it tantalizingly out of range.

Cooley's ears drooped. He turned, then sprawled across the porch, practically covering its surface, and whimpered when he dropped his nose to his paws. Thoroughly ignored, he looked across his new haunt dejectedly.

A certain gray cat tiptoed across the back fence.

Cooley straightened, his nose twitched.

The cat turned to look at him, then flicked its tail in a silent dare.

"Go ahead," that tail declared. "Make my day."

The wolfhound exploded off the porch in a frenzy of barking. He landed hard, but bolted for the back fence. The cat took one look and ran like greased lightning to the neighbor's yard.

But the fence in between wasn't done. And Cooley was through the gap in record time.

He was going to get that cat, once and for all.

• • •

Lilith almost immediately regretted opening the door. She had only done so because she had seen that it was Mitch's friend knocking and she wondered whether something was wrong.

Something *was* wrong—but it was having this amorous wolf in her house when she was alone.

Even D'Artagnan, a fairly indifferent champion at the best of times, had gone out into the yard. Lilith's potion for Those Men was cooling in the sink and she was too tired in the wake of concocting it to deal with this challenge.

Because it was clear that this man intended to launch a full assault, frontal or otherwise.

"Hi! I'm Kurt, Mitch's friend. We're working next door, you know." He folded his arms across his chest and flexed a few muscles Lilith couldn't name. His eyes twinkled in what was doubtless his interpretation of an engaging way. "Mitch tells me you read fortunes."

Lilith retreated from the hungry gleam in Kurt's eye and found herself in the foyer. He shut the door and smiled at her in a way that made her feel like the Special of the Day.

And that Kurt hadn't eaten in a while.

From one glimpse, it was more than clear that Mitch's friend thought he was Goddess's gift to women everywhere. He was blond and tanned, his physique an obvious result of countless hours spent in the gym. His hair was boyishly ruffled to perfection and Lilith was certain he took longer to get ready for anything than any six women she could name.

"I do, but not today. I'm sorry." Lilith smiled with pert professionalism. She waved her hand as though she was a bit dotty and said the first silly thing that hopped into her head. "Venus in Taurus, you know. My crystals are out at the cleaners. Not a good time." She reached to open the door to boot this man out, but he unexpectedly captured her hand.

"Hey, I'm just looking for a little inside scoop, you know?" He winked, in no doubt of his own allure. "Maybe you could help me out. You know, point me in the direction of Grand Amour."

Lilith took one look into Kurt's eyes, an instinctive reaction to his request, and wasn't surprised in the least by what she found. None other that Kurt himself smiled winningly back at her and she smiled slightly at this confirmation that the man could never love anyone as much as he loved himself.

Unfortunately, Kurt took that tiny smile as encouragement.

"Or maybe we could just chat for a couple of minutes, you and me," he murmured in a confidentially low tone. "Maybe over a quiet dinner somewhere." Kurt smiled what Lilith knew he considered his winning smile and ran his thumb over the back of her hand.

And Lilith suddenly had a very good idea.

It was the best opportunity she was likely to have, after all.

"You must be terribly thirsty," Lilith said with feigned concern. "You two have been working so hard out there." Kurt flexed his muscles once more, no doubt to impress her with his masculinity. "How about some iced tea?"

His face brightened. "Hey, that would be great."

"It's herbal, so it might taste a bit odd," Lilith said airily and headed for the kitchen. She wasn't surprised when Kurt followed hot on her heels. She whispered a silent entreaty that her potion would work, because otherwise she didn't know how she'd get rid of him.

And that could mean serious trouble.

Lilith refused to think about that. Once an optimist, always an optimist. The potion *would* work. She ladled ice into a glass and tried to sound casual. "I try to avoid caffeine, so I drink a lot of herbal brews instead."

"Oh, yeah. You gotta watch that stuff." He frowned at her cauldron. "That's some kind of pot you've got there."

"Oh!" Lilith smiled and lied as fast as she could. "Family piece, you know. Good luck."

Kurt harumphed, his gaze fixed assessingly on her as he sipped. He grimaced and Lilith cursed the bitter taste of the stuff. She hadn't thought of that! She should have put some honey in it.

Because if Kurt didn't drink it, the potion couldn't work. And if the potion didn't work, well, Lilith didn't want to

think too much about having to evict him from her house
by herself.

He was big, really big. A good eight inches taller than
Lilith, even though she was tall. He clearly worked out, a
lot, and might have a good eighty pounds on her.

When Kurt fingered the glass and hesitated after drinking
only the barest sip, Lilith did the only thing she could under
the circumstances. She stepped closer and opened her eyes
wide in what she hoped was a hopeful expression.

"Do you like it? It's my own very special mixture." She
pouted as though her teeny tiny heart would be fatally
wounded by any rejection of her tea. "You wouldn't hurt
my feelings by not liking it, would you?"

"Of course, I like it." Kurt smiled a slow sensual smile
of intent, kept his gaze fixed on her and pointedly drained
his glass.

When he set it deliberately on the counter, Lilith caught
her breath and prayed.

Mitch didn't trust the way Lilith's door was closed tight.
He knew she was home, he knew Kurt was in there, and it
wasn't a good sign that the heavy wooden door was closed
on such a hot day.

Nope, Mitch did not have a good feeling about this. Remembering how quickly Lilith had gotten into his shorts
was not reassuring in the least. He spared a glance for the
vigilant crew on the sidewalk, frowned, then knocked.

To Mitch's astonishment, he heard running footsteps.
Lilith opened the door almost immediately.

To his further amazement, she didn't look as though he
had interrupted anything. Her dress didn't appear in the
least bit rumpled and she seemed safely unravished.

It was then he noticed that those incredible eyes glowed
with pleasure. Mitch nearly dropped his teeth when he realized it was because she was glad to see *him*.

And Kurt, Mr. Seduction Central, was already here.

Or was he?

"Hi. I uh, I just thought I'd check up on Kurt," Mitch
managed to say. "Is he here?"

Lilith grimaced and Mitch almost laughed at the expression on her face when she nodded. She met his gaze and

her smile dawned like a sunrise, her voice low and warm. "I'm so glad you stopped by. I'm not sure I can get rid of him!"

Mitch barely had time to feel good about her certainty he would help her before Lilith hauled him into her foyer. She linked her arm deliberately through his as she turned around, making the two of them seem like a team.

Mitch could smell that damned perfume of hers again. The tangle of her hair was soft against his upper arm and he felt his blood start to boil. He struggled to keep his mind on the reason why he had come and pretty much failed.

It was then he noticed that Kurt was standing in the doorway to Lilith's kitchen, looking a little dazed. Kurt squinted at Lilith, then shook his head, then eyed her again. He leaned in the doorframe as though his balance was off.

Either that or he was drunk. But there hadn't been nearly enough elapsed time for that.

What had happened? A cold hand clenched Mitch's gut and he wondered whether he had been too slow in following his buddy. Certainly, Lilith's linking arms with him seemed to hint at presenting a united front, and one against his old pal.

Had Kurt already come on to her?

Had she decked him or broken something over his head? It took that much to get Kurt's attention sometimes when he was fixed on doing something.

Like seducing a beautiful woman.

"Hey, is he bothering you?" Mitch asked in a low voice.

"Not anymore." Lilith shook her head, then flicked a warm glance at Mitch.

He felt a sense of relief that seemed decidedly inappropriate given the circumstances. Or at least, given the identity of the lady so determinedly pressing the soft curve of her breast against his arm.

Mitch cleared his throat deliberately. "Hey, Kurt, are you making trouble with the ladies again?"

"Me?" Kurt straightened with a grimace and shook his head once more. He reached back and fingered a glass on the kitchen countertop as though it confused him, too. He really was in bad shape. He even sounded groggy. "Nah. Just had a little iced tea and am heading on my way."

Kurt lumbered right past Lilith without so much as a glance in her direction. Mitch couldn't understand that, but he could almost feel the laughter bubbling up inside Lilith.

On the threshold, Kurt frowned, rubbed his forehead, and looked at Lilith as though he couldn't quite see her straight. He squinted, then rubbed his temples. "Hey Mitch, I'm just going to finish that fence, then I'll be on my way. See you next Saturday?"

Mitch glanced sidelong at the lady beside him. She was biting back a smile. It seemed she had somehow persuaded Kurt to abandon his pursuit.

Which was saying something. Kurt was nothing if not determined when he was, as he called it, "on the hunt."

Mitch cleared his throat and frowned. "I thought you were staying for dinner."

"Nope. A man's got to run wild on a Saturday night." Kurt winked with a vestige of his characteristic nonchalance and Mitch was slightly reassured. Then he swaggered out the door. Kurt waved, without so much as another peek at Lilith, and strolled between the houses, his whistle carrying back to Mitch's ears.

Kurt seemed to be all right, Lilith seemed to be all right, but something strange was definitely going on.

Mitch looked at the lady and reassured himself that she was every bit as lovely as she always had been. That wasn't the problem. But the devilish twinkle that was dancing in her eyes hinted that she knew more than she was telling. "What exactly happened here?"

Lilith grinned. "What do you mean?"

"I mean, he came waltzing over here determined to seduce you. It's not like Kurt to just walk away."

Lilith fought to look innocent and didn't even come close to pulling it off. "Maybe I told him I wasn't interested."

Mitch rolled his eyes. "That wouldn't have made any difference. Kurt always says he likes a challenge."

"Well, maybe I was too much of a challenge for him," she declared.

"Color me skeptical," Mitch murmured. "I don't think there's a beautiful woman alive who's too much of a challenge for Kurt."

Lilith smiled sunnily. "Well, thank you."

Mitch felt the back of his neck heat again as he realized what he had said. "Well, you know—"

"Shh!" Her fingertips landed against his lips. "Don't spoil a compliment with an explanation," she whispered. Lilith's eyes danced and she wrinkled her nose playfully before her smile flashed once more. "Maybe I just cast a spell on him."

And Mitch chuckled. He couldn't help it. The glow in Lilith's eyes and the softness of her fingertips against his skin made Mitch wonder why the hell he was worried about Kurt. The guy could take care of himself.

And besides, wasn't he *glad* that Kurt hadn't hit on Lilith with any success?

"Let's talk about something much more interesting," Lilith whispered. She leaned against Mitch's chest, her curvy lips well within range. "Why did you leap in to protect me from his wiles?"

Mitch tried to shrug off the question. "Kurt doesn't treat women well. I wouldn't want him to hurt you or anyone else."

Lilith smiled. "You'd champion me, even though you're worried I'm trying to con Andrea?"

She had him there. Despite himself, Mitch felt an admiration for the lady's clear thinking. She was doing better than he was, come to think of it.

And maybe that was why Mitch found it a lot harder to use his cover story than he had expected. Or maybe it was just that strange sense that she could read his thoughts.

Either way, Mitch didn't say exactly what he had planned to say.

"Maybe I was wrong," he admitted softly.

Lilith's eyes widened with delight and she stretched to her toes, as though so anxious to hear his words that she had to be closer to his lips. Her eyes were wide and bright with anticipation. "Do you remember, then?" she asked breathlessly.

Mitch's heart began to pound in his ears. He stared down into Lilith's eyes and knew what she was hoping his answer would be. And he knew what he should say, at least if he was going to follow his plan of "going inside" to get the real story.

But there was something about this woman that made Mitch loathe to lie to her. It had seemed like such a good idea, but now, when he stood before her, Mitch couldn't summon that lie to his lips.

"I'd like to," was the best he could do.

Much to Mitch's own surprise, as soon as he uttered the words, he knew they were true. In this moment, in this place, he wanted to remember that this woman and he had once been together, had once been in love, had once trusted each other completely.

It was crazy and it made no sense at all, but for once in his life, Mitch didn't care. Standing in Lilith's foyer, with her almost in his arms, being with her seemed to be the only thing that *did* make sense.

And when she looked deeply into his eyes, then flushed slightly and smiled, Mitch knew she was the most irresistible woman he'd ever met.

He didn't want her to ask him any more questions. He didn't want to lie to her. He just wanted to get past this moment. He told himself that it was for lack of any better options that he gave in to temptation.

Mitch captured Lilith's fingers in his hand and pressed a kiss into her palm. She caught her breath, their gazes locked, then slowly, feeling like a fish being towed in on a lure, Mitch bent and touched her lips with his. He felt the barest twinge of guilt before Lilith cast her arms around his neck with undisguised delight.

And once she started kissing him back, well, anything other than the taste of her just seemed a petty technicality. Mitch braced his feet against the floor, leaned back against the wall, and gathered the lady into his arms with purpose.

Her kiss was so sweet, so warm and welcoming, so downright wonderful that Mitch very quickly forgot everything else but the woman in his arms. He didn't care about getting to the bottom of a story, he didn't care about the truth, he didn't even care how Lilith managed to evade every kind of record-keeping there was.

He only cared that she kissed like a goddess. Mitch might have taken a wrong turn at Albuquerque, but he wasn't going to stop and ask for directions now.

Unfortunately, the moment wasn't destined to last long at all.

Lilith was so relieved that she barely noticed the agitated barking from the backyard. She abandoned herself to Mitch's kiss with a vengeance. Something had happened, something had broken free inside him.

Because when he admitted he'd like to remember, Lilith had found a teeny tiny mirror image of herself waving back from the depths of his eyes.

Whatever obstacle had stood between them was banished and Lilith wasn't holding anything back.

Everything was going to be fine.

The volume of the barking grew louder. Mitch lifted his head, muttered a curse that told Lilith just whose dog was responsible, then gave her a crooked smile.

"He is a great dog, really, and not usually so noisy."

Lilith shrugged, but a very feline yowl echoed from the back of the house before she could admit her own cat's almost certain role in this. "D'Artagnan!"

"Cooley!" Mitch muttered.

They turned as one for the kitchen just as the cat rocketed through his cat door and flung himself into the kitchen. It seemed every hair of fur D'Artagnan had was standing on end as he skated down the expanse of tile. Cooley barked from the yard, then Lilith heard the dog's nails on the porch. Through the kitchen window, she saw a huge shadow lunge against the back door.

"Oh no!" Mitch seemed to know what was going to happen right before it did.

Right after it was too late to do anything about it.

Even knowing it was too late, he still ran. The door creaked, the dog barked, and with a resounding screech, the screen surrendered to Cooley's weight and popped from its frame. Cooley landed in the kitchen with a thump, amidst a tangled pile of screen. He was on his feet in a heartbeat, his gaze fixed on D'Artagnan. He growled and fought for traction on the tile.

"Cooley, *sit*!" Mitch raced the length of the room, bellowing in a most authoritative tone, but the dog was oblivious to anything other than his prey.

Cooley's nose quivered, his ears stood up, his bark resonated through the house when D'Artagnan leapt to the counter.

Lilith knew that things were rapidly going to get worse.

"No!" Mitch dove for the dog's collar but he didn't have a chance.

"No!" Lilith cried when the cat raced down the countertop. It was so disgusting when he did that! All her little pots and canisters wobbled dangerously, several teetered and broke.

But to Lilith's horror, that was only the beginning. The dog leapt and made it up onto the counter, as well. Everything scattered in the wake of a decidedly flawed landing. Chaos reigned briefly, both Lilith and Mitch shouted to no avail.

Until Cooley reached the sink.

The dog froze, sniffed, and appeared to forget all about the cat. He hunkered down and proceeded to vacuum up Lilith's potion.

"Cooley! No!" Lilith cried. D'Artagnan quietly slid out the door and headed for safety in some dog-proof zone.

"Cooley! Off!" Mitch roared.

The dog evidently knew he'd be challenged on this, because he gulped the contents of the pot with record speed. His gaze tracked how close the two humans were, his tongue moved like it was jet-powered.

It was Lilith who reached him first, but half of the liquid was already gone.

"Cooley, no!" Lilith repeated as she drew near the dog. She reached out her hand to grab the cauldron.

But the wolfhound lifted his head and snarled at her.

Lilith snatched back her hand. "I thought you said he seldom bit."

"My mistake." Mitch groaned. "This is just getting better and better," he muttered under his breath.

But Lilith suddenly guessed what the problem was. She took a step closer, just to be sure, and the dog showed her his teeth.

Lilith was delighted. Her potion did work! She hadn't been positive when Kurt left whether the change in his manner was due to Mitch's presence or her "tea."

Now there could be no doubt.

"That's it!" Mitch bellowed. "*Cooley!* Down! Out!"

The dog straightened suddenly, as though surprised at what he had done, then turned a mortified expression on his master.

"Get off that counter and out of this house," Mitch told the beast grimly. "Right *now*."

The dog had the wits to do as he was told. Or at least, if he didn't literally understand the command, he knew he was in trouble and would be better off elsewhere.

Cooley almost fell off the counter, he was so busy trying to keep a low profile, and skulked to the back door. Mitch opened what was left of the door and pointed imperiously to his own yard.

"You know where to go," he informed the dog, who returned guiltily to his corner of exile from the week before.

Mitch exhaled slowly, winced at the damage to the door, then turned toward Lilith. It seemed he couldn't look her in the eye.

"Looks like I owe you another apology," he said quietly. He nudged the remains of the screen with his toe and Lilith knew it would never go back in place. In fact, the door had bent beneath the dog's weight and didn't even shut right anymore. Mitch swung it back and forth, eyeing the damage with a wince. "And a new storm door, too."

Lilith folded her arms across her chest, secretly too thrilled that her potion was effective to fret over details. She knew Mitch would do the right thing, and she didn't really care very much about the door.

Everything, after all, was right back on track between them and that made Lilith feel all bubbly inside.

What she did care about was how upset Mitch was about his dog's deeds.

"I had no idea dogs were so expensive," she mused, keeping her tone deliberately light. Mitch's head snapped up and he blinked at her smile as though he didn't know quite what to do about it.

"I should have cast that spell years ago." Lilith grinned outright and leaned one hip against the counter. "Just think of all the home repairs that would have been done. I could have been living in the lap of luxury all this time."

Mitch grinned despite himself, then sobered. "It's really not funny," he insisted solemnly.

Lilith sobered in turn. "No, of course not. I was very attached to that ancient, warped, and extremely well-painted storm door. I could have gotten, oh, a dollar in a garage sale for it. On a good day." She scowled with mock ferocity. "No. Losing it is not funny at all."

Their eyes met.

Their lips twitched.

They chuckled.

"I don't think I've ever seen a cat move so fast," Mitch said under his breath.

Lilith laughed. "Did you see D'Artagnan's fur?"

Mitch snorted. "He looked like he'd caught the wrong end of an electrical wire."

"Or fell into the dryer without fabric softener."

Mitch leaned against the wall and chuckled. The smile tugging his lips made Lilith want to jump on him again. The light of concern that invaded his warm gaze was icing on the cake. "You think he's all right?"

"Insulted horribly, I'm sure, but that's hardly lethal." Lilith held a hand to her lips as she remembered something else. "And the look on Cooley's face when he was trying to drain that pot before we reached him. It was priceless!"

Mitch grinned. "Even though he knew he would be dead meat for it. Talk about stubborn! That must be something you've cooked up there."

Lilith smiled. "Oh, it's a wicked brew. You know, a witch always has to have a little something on the boil."

The words seemed to erase any trace of humor in Mitch's expression. He frowned thoughtfully at the door, his gaze trailing to the repentant dog. When he spoke, his words were low with conviction. "Lilith, my dog growled at you. That's not funny." His frown deepened. "It's not like him to do something like that."

But Lilith didn't want Mitch blaming the dog. "Maybe it wasn't his fault."

"What do you mean? Of course it was. He's smart enough to know what he's doing." Mitch's lips drew to a taut line and he cast a glance over the fence. "And he's trained well enough to know better than that."

"It's not his fault." Lilith shook her head and pointed to the half-empty pot in her sink. "No joke, that *is* a magickal brew, Mitch. Cooley drank half of a potion intended for forty men. It's no wonder it had such an effect on him."

Mitch folded his arms across his chest. One chestnut brow arched high. "Another love potion?"

Lilith laughed. "No, a love *antidote*."

Mitch didn't smile. "I don't understand."

Lilith was more than ready to explain. After all, there was no reason to keep secrets from her one true love. "It's for those men out there. You see, they were caught up in the web of the love spell I cast for you. It seems to have worked really well on them, for whatever that's worth, but I just can't have them standing out there forever."

Mitch's expression was blank and Lilith had no doubt that was deliberate. She just couldn't guess why.

But then, it was going to take time for them to learn all of each other's secrets. Lilith was more than prepared to make the investment.

"So, you mixed up an antidote," he said casually.

"Well, what else could I do? At least we know it works."

Mitch shook his head. "We don't know anything of the kind."

"Of course we do. I gave some to Kurt and he changed his mind about pursuing me."

Mitch peered at the green contents of the pot. "Kurt drank this willingly?"

Lilith smiled. "I told him it was my own special brew." She fluttered her eyelashes tellingly and Mitch shook his head.

His eyes twinkled, then eyed the concoction dubiously. "It is amazing what he'll do. Will it hurt him?"

"No." Lilith tapped a fingertip on Mitch's arm. "Of course, if I had known you were coming to save me," she murmured, "I wouldn't have had to even give him any."

"I wasn't . . ." Mitch started to protest, then fell silent. He frowned, looked at Lilith, then turned his attention back to the cauldron.

The back of his neck turned red. Lilith smiled, liking very much that Mitch was hesitant to name his own noble urges. Actions were the proof of good intent, after all, not just words.

"Kurt's a good guy, but he has kind of a one-track mind," he said gruffly.

"It's okay," Lilith whispered and sidled up beside him. "Feel free to come to my rescue any time you like."

Mitch's eyes flashed, but Lilith reached past him for the cauldron. He stepped back as she hefted it over to the stove.

His tone was contemplative when he finally spoke. "And you're saying this potion is why Cooley growled at you?"

"Of course! It's clearly not in his nature. Kurt and Cooley—that's proof enough for me." Lilith gave Mitch a stern glance. "Two points do make a line, you know, at least last I heard. Honestly, Mitch, you just have to think these things through logically to see what perfect sense they make. It's not hard."

Mitch blinked and didn't seem to have much to say about that.

Lilith frowned at the pot, intent on getting things back on schedule. "Maybe if I pick out the dog hairs and bring it back up to a boil, it will still be okay."

Mitch grimaced comically. "After Cooley's had his jowls in it? Remind me never to eat at this restaurant."

Lilith threw back her head and laughed at his teasing. "You don't have to drink it! Besides I don't have enough ingredients to make up another batch." She considered the pot and decided. "It's just going to have to do."

Lilith turned on the element, then glanced pointedly to Mitch. "So, will you pour for the first hour or should I?"

7

THE CHARIOT

If anyone had told Mitch two weeks before that he would be offering a green brew in mismatched bone china cups and saucers to an unlikely gathering of men on the sidewalk in front of his new neighbor's house, he wouldn't have believed it.

And even a few minutes before, he wouldn't have believed that those same men would have willingly drunk Lilith's brew. The stuff had a wicked smell, even after she ladled a big glob of honey into it.

But it seemed that just her endorsement was enough to have all those starstruck men sipping like obedient puppies. They lifted their pinkies in the air as they held the delicate cups, and their gazes locked on Lilith as though they couldn't bear to look anywhere else.

Mitch certainly didn't imagine that the "potion" would work, even after Cooley's and Kurt's responses. He wasn't nearly as ready as Lilith to draw a line between those points.

But he was curious. It was the mark of a good journalist, Mitch told himself, refusing to acknowledge that he had any interest in seeing these guys out of here.

He watched them drink, not a word from any of them, and felt as though he had stepped into a foreign film with incomprehensible subtitles. The scary thing was that this wasn't the first Truly Weird thing Mitch had witnessed since he moved. Or even the first Truly Weird thing he had done in Lilith's company.

He tried not to think about that.

He tried not to think about Lilith's new certainty that he was her champion, much less the warm feeling that that gave him inside.

He tried not to think about the way she kissed him, or the scent of her perfume, or even to notice the contrast of her bare feet against the grass.

He really tried not to be charmed by a woman who chided him for not using good solid logic to make conclusions, even if her assumptions were a bit out of this world.

And most of all, Mitch tried not to worry about any of these men responding to Lilith's potion the way Cooley supposedly had. Lilith had refused to hear anything about the possibility, but Mitch watched them sip dutifully and wondered.

Of course, what Mitch should have been doing was trying to find out about Lilith's nefarious schemes. He should have been ferreting out the truth about Andrea's cruise. He should have been focused and diligent and concentrating on the job he had made his own.

But instead, after the men had drained their teacups, he stood with Lilith, holding the empty tray and his breath. And Mitch watched as, one at a time, they each got that look of confusion, as though they had just awakened from a long dream and weren't quite sure where they were.

They looked at Lilith.

In obvious uncertainty, they looked at Mitch, the house, each other, then back at Lilith again. They looked down to the cups in their hands, then at Lilith one more time. Several checked their watches, one looked at the sky as though unable to fathom where the hours had gone. The cable guys frowned at the parking tickets clustered on the windshield of their truck.

Then, without a single word, the men turned and left as one.

They dumped their cups back on Mitch's tray, studiously avoided his gaze, and stepped away without a backward glance. It was incomprehensible, it was illogical, it was whimsical.

But it seemed that Lilith's potion was working.

And even more oddly, Mitch couldn't quell his relief when the last of them rubbed his brow and wandered away.

When Lilith hooted with delight and threw herself into his arms, Mitch decided it would be rude to not catch her.

And even more rude to not kiss her.

Although he suspected that he invited her for dinner for an entirely different reason than he should, Mitch did it anyway. And even though his heart made that strange double-skip when Lilith accepted the invitation, he knew that couldn't mean anything at all.

It wouldn't have been logical, after all.

When Mitch ushered Lilith into the house and announced with no small measure of triumph that she was staying for dinner, Andrea was certain she couldn't have planned things better herself. Mitch didn't look nearly as grim as he had recently, which could only be a good sign. And Lilith was flushed like a girl in love.

Perfect.

"About time you showed up," Andrea chided, having no intention of revealing how much this development pleased her. "Dinner's going to be burned to a crisp."

"Cooley had an altercation with Lilith's storm door," Mitch supplied amiably.

Lilith's eyes twinkled. "The door lost."

Andrea smiled. She could just imagine. And from the look of these two, there were no hard feelings over the matter.

. "Lillit, where's your kitty?" Jen demanded, her fair brow tight with concern. "Is he all alone?"

"No, Jen, he's okay." Lilith crouched down beside the little girl and shared that smile. "He's just asleep."

"In the furthest corner of the attic," Mitch muttered. "It'll probably be days before he"—Mitch paused and looked at Jen—"uh, before he wakes up."

Jen bit her lip with consternation. "Is Dartaggin sick?"

"No, no." Lilith shook her head. She seemed to exude a soothing calm and Andrea noted with approval that Jen was not immune to its effect. The little girl visibly relaxed. "He's just tired." Lilith's lips quirked as though she couldn't stop them. "He had a busy, busy day."

"Lots of running around," Mitch contributed. The pair looked at each other for the first time since they had walked in the door and started to chuckle.

Andrea didn't understand why and she didn't much care. It was good to see Mitch smiling in a woman's company again.

The timer went off and Andrea flicked on the oven light, trying to discern without opening the door whether the frozen french fries were cooked or not.

"Well, my bug *is* sick," Jason piped up.

Lilith immediately looked as though this was the mightiest problem confronting the free world. Andrea smiled to herself, then decided to leave those fries just a few minutes longer. She hated when they were mushy inside.

"Oh, what's wrong with him?"

"I dunno." Jason entrusted Lilith with his mayonnaise jar and they peered through the fogged glass together. "He hasn't moved much since I caught him."

"Mmm. Do you know what kind of bug it is?"

"A cicada. His name is Bob."

"Bob the Cicada?" Lilith echoed.

Mitch cleared his throat suddenly and Andrea caught the glint in his eye. "Bob," he mouthed silently as he came to Andrea's side, then shook his head as he bit back his laughter. Andrea was very relieved to see his eyes sparkle like that. Mitch reached into the fridge for the hamburger patties. "Is the grill on?"

"Yes, it's ready," Andrea confided. "So are the fries, just about."

"Fries?" Mitch grimaced. "What happened to salad?"

"Oh, we won't waste your nice salad. Now, shoo. And hurry up." Andrea flicked her hands and Mitch shooed, both of them content to leave the kids talking to Lilith.

"There's Bob!" Jen cried.

Jason tapped a finger on the jar. "See? Right there."

Lilith frowned with concern. "He's awfully still, Jason."

"What's the matter with him?"

Lilith pursed her lips in thought. "Do you know what cicadas do when they're happy?"

Jason shrugged, Jen watched Lilith with wide eyes.

"Well, they're not so different from us," Lilith confided and dropped to sit cross-legged on the floor between the children. "They like to sing."

Jason shook his head, daddy's little skeptic. "Bugs don't sing!"

"Not really. But they can rub their wings together and make a sound that we call singing. Crickets do it, too."

"I thought that was when they wanted to find a lady cricket and make babies."

"See? Just like us." Lilith smiled. "People sing when they're courting, too. And they court when they're happy. Has Bob been singing?"

"No." Jason was solemn.

"Then maybe he isn't very happy."

"But why not? I put lots of grass and stuff in the jar for him!"

"Maybe it's too hot. Or maybe he just doesn't like being stuck in the jar." Lilith made a face. "Do you like when you have to stay in your room?"

"No."

"It's kind of the same, isn't it?"

Jason shuffled his feet as he considered that.

Mitch strode back into the kitchen and put the dirty plate in the sink. "Five minutes a side."

"Can't I have mine rare?" Andrea asked.

One look from Mitch answered her question. "You do remember our microscopic friend E. coli bacteria? And that article I did about all those people who were so sick last summer?"

Andrea rolled her eyes and soundly cursed little invisible things that took the fun out of life. But Mitch had already begun listening intently to Lilith's conversation with Jason.

"But if I let Bob go," Jason reasoned carefully, a tiny version of his father chasing down a solution, "then I won't be able to look at him anymore."

Lilith smiled sadly. "If you don't let him go, Bob will stay sad. He might get so sad that he dies." Jason frowned, but Lilith leaned closer to him. "You know, a long time ago, I knew a very wise woman and she told me a magic rule that just might help you decide what to do."

Jason immediately brightened. "What kind of magic rule?"

"Is it a secret?" Jen asked in a hushed voice.

Lilith smiled. "Kind of a secret," she acknowledged.

"It's a rule to make sure you live a good life. *Do whatsoever you will, but harm none.*"

Jason's brow furrowed. "What does that mean?"

"It means that you can do whatever you want as long as it doesn't hurt anybody else."

That sounded like fine thinking to Andrea. In fact, it sounded like a variant of Mitch's own code of ethics. She slanted a glance to her stepson and found his gaze fixed on their neighbor. He looked a bit surprised by Lilith's rule.

It was about time the man had a surprise or two!

"Is this hurting Bob?" Jason asked, his little brow furrowed.

Lilith looked at the jar and wrinkled her nose. "What do you think?"

Jason bit his lip as he considered the matter. "Maybe I should let Bob go."

Lilith watched him carefully. "It's up to you."

Jason's face brightened. "Maybe I'll be able to hear Bob sing again if I let him go."

Lilith smiled. "Maybe." Andrea admired how she exerted no pressure on Jason, just expressed her point of view and let him make up his own mind.

Which Jason quickly did. He took his jar back from Lilith and marched purposefully to the back door. "Come on, Bob," he said, as though Bob had much choice in the matter. "It's time to let you go. Maybe you can sing and find a wife. Then, you can bring lots of baby cicadas to see us."

"Will Bob fly out of the jar?" Jen asked in excitement.

Lilith shrugged. "Let's go see."

They followed Jason, hand in hand, Bun dragging behind. Mitch blinked and shook his head. A gasp of delight from the back porch a moment later revealed that Bob had, in fact, taken flight. The children began to chatter, Lilith's low laughter underscoring their tones.

"It's amazing," Mitch murmured. "Jen never takes to anyone that fast."

Andrea swung the spatula at him and decided not to push her luck by talking about kismet. "I told you she was a nice girl," she hissed. "Even your kids can see the truth." She pretended to chase Mitch across the kitchen. "Now, go get those burgers before we starve!"

He grinned and bowed low. "Yes, ma'am. Right away, ma'am."

Andrea rolled her eyes as he ducked out to the porch and the kids clamored for his attention. She reached for the oven mitts and eyed the french fries again. They were never as good this way as when they were deep-fried, but she supposed it didn't hurt to compromise with Mitch.

Once in a while.

Then, Andrea's lips curved with the realization that there was one teeny detail about her trip she had forgotten to tell Mitch.

Well, this was as good a time as any.

She marched to the back door and peered through the screen. "Mitch?"

"Uh-huh." He barely looked up from the grill. Andrea could hear the children chattering away to Lilith from further away in the backyard. They were speculating on whether one of the cicadas currently singing could be Bob. Lilith's manner with them confirmed Andrea's suspicions that her plan was a good one.

"There's something I should tell you, about the cruise." That got her stepson's attention, as Andrea had thought it would. She smiled broadly when his head snapped up. "Don't fret, worrywart. It's just that the weekend in the middle of my cruise is the same weekend that you have that conference in Kansas City."

An expression of exasperation just had time to work its way across Mitch's features before Andrea continued. "But you promised . . ."

"I know, I know, and I've solved it, so you have nothing to be concerned about." Andrea gave Mitch a smile that was supposed to be reassuring.

But Mitch treated Andrea to one of Those Looks. "Why doesn't that inspire great confidence in me?" he asked wryly. "I suppose it's too much to hope you've bitten the bullet and cancelled?"

"What a thought!" Andrea rolled her eyes. "Of course not! Lilith is going to watch the kids that weekend."

"Lilith!" Mitch's lips tightened, he glanced over his shoulder to the silhouette of the lady in question, then leaned closer to Andrea. His voice was low, his gaze bored right through the screen mesh to lock with hers.

"Didn't it occur to you that we might be imposing? This woman is just our neighbor, Andrea. We've only known her for a week, Cooley keeps trashing her house. Did you ever think that she might not want to be swept into our chaotic household?"

Andrea hadn't. She frowned. "But she said she'd be delighted . . ."

"What else was she going to say?" Mitch demanded in frustration. "Andrea, I think you've really put Lilith on the spot here. It's not fair."

Andrea smiled slowly as she realized just what Mitch was doing. She folded her arms across her chest and leaned against the counter to eye him.

"What?" he asked impatiently. "Is it so bizarre not to want to impose on people?"

"No, but it is bizarre that you're suddenly worried about protecting Lilith from the rest of us," Andrea retorted, not bothering to disguise her triumph. "I thought *she* was supposed to be the one with the evil plans for me."

Mitch tellingly looked away. "I don't really know what's going on," he said gruffly.

"Uh-huh. But the funny thing is, you're not worried about leaving those two little ones in her care."

Mitch inhaled sharply and fired a bright glance at his stepmother.

Andrea grinned, then tapped him on the screen between them. "I think you like her," she whispered knowingly. "And I think that's a very good thing. It's about time you put the past where it belongs."

Mitch covered his surprise quickly, but not quickly enough that Andrea didn't see it. He snorted, as though indifferent to Andrea's claim, although that lady knew better. "Right. I think you've got love on the brain, Andrea. You're only seeing what you want to see."

"And what are you seeing, eligible single father of two?"

Mitch's lips twisted wryly. "I'm seeing a woman's life seriously affected by our moving in here and probably being changed against her will. A woman who's probably too nice to argue about it."

"Ha! See? You do like her. That's the only reason you care about imposing on her."

Mitch flashed his Death Glare but he was wasting it on Andrea. She didn't even flinch.

"I care about imposing on *anyone*," he insisted. "Do unto others and all that jazz."

Andrea let her skepticism show.

Mitch shook the barbeque spatula at her. "And I'm going to talk to her about this tonight. If you can't watch the kids, I'll find someone else, or I'll cancel my conference."

"I thought you couldn't do that."

"It would not be a good career move." Mitch headed back to the grill again, his expression grim when he glanced back at Andrea. "But you've got to have principles, and you've got to live by them."

Andrea couldn't think of a thing to say to that, so she just grinned back at Mitch. She could always count on Mitch to do the right thing and to take the high road, no matter what the cost to himself. As much as his career meant to him, it was nothing compared to those kids.

Before she could think any further than that, the new smoke alarm started to screech.

Mitch looked back through the storm door and lifted one brow. "Is that the french fry timer?" he teased and Andrea wished she had something to throw at him.

But then he'd have two storm doors to fix, and the man had more than enough on his plate these days.

Andrea had hauled her dress box out to a taxi after dinner and waved madly as she went on her way. Mitch had asked Lilith whether they could talk after he put the kids to bed, and she quite contentedly sat on his back porch waiting for him.

Jen and Jason had given her unexpected goodnight hugs before they were herded upstairs, the sweetness of their trust tugging at Lilith's heartstrings. She stared at the sky, listening to the rumble of Mitch's voice between childish squeals and giggles, splashes, and noisy kisses. Lilith was well aware of the wolfhound keeping a vigilant eye on her from the far corner of the yard, but she'd figure out how to solve that problem later.

For now, she savored the twinge of the twilight capturing the azure of the sky and the silence descending in the house behind her. It was still hot, still clear, and she watched the first stars appear.

She heard Mitch's footsteps in the kitchen but didn't turn around, smiling to herself as he came to her, once more, in the twilight.

"Could I interest you in some sangria?" he asked. "House brew?"

Lilith cast that smile over her shoulder. "That sounds nice."

A moment later, Mitch joined her, two glasses filled with ice in one hand and a pitcher filled with red wine and bobbing fruit in the other. He sat down beside Lilith on the top step, stretching out his long, tanned legs and leaning his back against the pillar of the porch.

Lilith accepted a glass, he poured, and they clinked glasses. "To new fences," Mitch said.

"And good neighbors," Lilith added. They shared a smile and Lilith sipped. The sangria was cool and fruity, rich on her tongue. "It's lovely. Very refreshing."

"Hmmm. Just the thing after a day of chasing dogs and kids." Mitch swirled the drink around his tongue, then nodded approval.

They sipped in companionable silence for several relaxing moments. Lilith was quite certain there was nowhere else she'd rather be. The faint calls of parents summoning children carried through the air, there was a murmur of conversation and the clink of glasses in the distance, the cicadas were singing.

Maybe even Bob joined the chorus.

Slowly, indigo claimed the sky, the smear of orange over the opposite rooftops fading to darkness with every passing moment.

"Did you get enough to eat for dinner?" Mitch asked.

Lilith glanced to him. "Of course. Why?"

He shrugged. "Well, I didn't know you were a vegetarian and burgers were kind of the main deal."

"The salad was great," Lilith said graciously. "And I haven't had french fries in a long time."

Mitch shook his head. "I try to keep them infrequent

around here too." He narrowed his eyes with mock suspicion. "But there are subversive elements at work."

Lilith laughed lightly, then Mitch's gaze suddenly sharpened. She had a distinct sense that his next words would be important and braced herself for a tough question.

"So, why did you become a vegetarian?"

Lilith blinked. It was a pretty pedestrian question to have him be so interested in her answer. "When I pledged to that witch's creed."

Mitch frowned into his glass. "The 'harm none' one?"

Lilith nodded and smiled. "After all, becoming burgers isn't a really good experience for the cow."

"No, I guess not." His expression turned thoughtful. "How do you make sure your nutrition is adequate?"

"It's a different kind of cooking, certainly, but after a while, you get used to pairing your proteins. It's really not hard." Lilith sipped her sangria. "If you're interested in eating less meat, I can give you some recipes."

Mitch's slow smile made her heart pick up its pace. "You've been very helpful, you know, and very nice."

Lilith felt herself flush. "Just being neighborly."

Mitch's gaze never wavered from hers. "I don't see too many other neighbors offering to help with gardens or teach vegetarian cooking. . . ."

"Or mend my back door."

Mitch chuckled. "There was a prime mover there."

They glanced as one to the wolfhound, the glimmer of his eyes barely visible in the shadows. Lilith heard his license tags jingle as he lifted his head.

"I'd forgive and forget, but I don't want a repeat of what he did this afternoon," Mitch said softly.

"I really don't think it was his fault."

"Either way, I don't care for the change." Mitch flicked a glance to Lilith's storm door, just the top of it visible over the new fence, and winced. "One job down, six million to go. I'll measure your door tomorrow—maybe we'll be lucky and the hardware store will stock the size."

"You don't have to fix it right away."

Mitch nodded. "You can't be without it in this heat. You won't have any circulation in your house. Besides, it's only right."

Lilith smiled at him, not remembering this facet of his character but liking it very much. "You're quite concerned with doing what's right, aren't you?"

Mitch seemed slightly surprised by her question. "Well, sure. I mean, the alternative isn't very attractive, is it?"

Lilith laughed lightly at the truth of that. It was so good to be sitting with him like this, just talking, just enjoying each other's company. "No, I suppose not."

Mitch turned his glass in his hands and frowned as though he was looking for the right words. "Look, Lilith, Andrea told me that she asked you to watch the kids. It's nice of you to agree, but . . ."

Lilith straightened. "You don't want me to watch them?"

Mitch glanced up, his gaze bright. "I don't want you to feel *obligated* to do anything you don't want to do. I mean, you must have plans. I'm sure Andrea didn't bother to ask."

Lilith shook her head. "No plans. Just fortune-telling and I can always turn off the sign."

"Well, I don't want you to feel that you have to do this just because you were asked." He smiled ruefully. "Andrea is a freight train in her own way, sometimes. I can find someone else, or cancel my trip."

Lilith put her hand on Mitch's and savored the heat of his skin beneath her own. He flicked a very gold glance at her, then looked down at her hand upon his. "But I *don't* mind," Lilith insisted. She leaned slightly closer. "Although it sounds as though you do."

Mitch stared at her hand resting on his for a long moment. Slowly, his turned over, as though he couldn't stop it from doing so, and his fingers closed warmly over her own. Lilith's heart skipped a beat, then another when she looked up and found Mitch's concerned gaze fixed on her.

It had been a long time since anyone had worried about Lilith.

"It seems very unfair to you," he admitted quietly.

"I don't think so."

Mitch shook his head ruefully. "Lilith, they're at the age when they're into everything. I swear that when one goes one way, the other goes in the opposite direction just to keep me on my toes.''

Lilith smiled. ''It sounds like fun.''

Mitch looked at her with mock sternness. ''Aha, the certainty of the uninitiated.''

Lilith knew he was trying to make her laugh. All the same, the unwitting reminder that she was without children of her own made her smile fade to nothing. She frowned and looked across the yard, fighting the return of that lonely ache.

Mitch eased closer, his voice low with concern. He squeezed her fingers. ''Hey, did I hit a sore point? I'm sorry.''

Lilith forced a smile and glanced to him, not expecting to be snared by the concern shining in his eyes. ''I always wanted kids,'' she confessed quietly.

Mitch winced. ''Oh, I am sorry. I didn't mean it that way. It's really just the luck of the draw, isn't it?''

''I think it takes a little more than luck,'' Lilith said softly.

Mitch took a sip of his drink, his gaze assessing. Lilith had the sense that she didn't have to tell him she couldn't have kids, that he already understood. He smiled wryly and gave her fingers a little squeeze. ''Fair enough, but these things still don't always work out according to plan.''

Lilith stared at their entangled fingers and dared to ask the question. ''Is that what happened to you?''

Mitch frowned at the garden, his thumb slowly moving across the back of Lilith's hand in an unconscious caress. She didn't say anything, just let him work through whatever he was thinking.

From the crease in his brow, she guessed that whatever Mitch was remembering hadn't been pleasant.

Mitch straightened suddenly, as though he had just realized she was waiting for an answer. He looked suddenly down at Lilith's hand, then carefully extracted his fingers from hers. He folded his hands resolutely around his glass and forced a smile that didn't reach his eyes.

''Yes, I guess it did.'' He looked ready to change the subject, but Lilith wanted to know more.

''What was your plan?''

Mitch froze for a moment, then he shrugged with a non-chalance she knew was feigned. "Oh, I wanted all that old-fashioned stuff. Kids and a house and a dog, summer vacations up north and the occasional visit to Disneyland." He seemed to be looking for an answer in the depths of his sangria. "Cooking together and sitting on the porch, laughing and making love for a lifetime. All that good stuff. Nothing particularly earth-shattering."

When Mitch's words halted, Lilith understood he hadn't found much of that in his marriage. The divorce wasn't his fault alone—Lilith knew it as well as she knew that Mitch blamed himself thoroughly. It took two to tango—two to make a marriage and two to break it.

Maybe divorce was what happened when people weren't destined to be together. Lilith was suddenly very glad that she knew beyond the shadow of a doubt that Mitch was the man for her. She now understood the reluctance she had already seen in him. On some level, he recognized Lilith and couldn't fight his instinctive attraction. But on another, his ex-wife had left him wary of pursuing women and re-lationships.

Lilith couldn't blame Mitch for a little healthy caution. What she had to do was win his trust and prompt his memory further. Just the fact that they were sitting like this had to be a sign of progress.

Never mind that he had invited her into his home.

Lilith deliberately guided the conversation back to more neutral territory. "I'd really like to watch the children that weekend. Jason and I have had a lot of fun in the garden. They're such sweet children. . . ."

Mitch straightened and forced a teasing smile. "Don't be fooled. They're not nearly perfect."

Lilith smiled and nodded. "I know, I know, but they're good kids, Mitch. You should be proud of them. The only thing that worries me is that Jen might be afraid."

Mitch's gaze clung to Lilith's for a heady moment, then he smiled warmly as though he wanted to reassure her. "Jen's very selective with her hugs. It's quite an honor that you've already had one." He leaned closer, his expression solemn. "But, Lilith, are you *sure* about this?"

"You have no idea how much I'm looking forward to

being needed,'' Lilith confessed. It was supposed to be a
joke, but her breath caught tellingly. She glanced at Mitch
and knew he hadn't missed the inadvertent sign of how
much this meant to her.

Lilith bit her lip, feeling that a little more explanation
was necessary. She tried to keep her tone light. ''You
know, I've been alone for so long. Five and a half centuries.
Even D'Artagnan doesn't need me—if I forgot to feed him,
he'd just go somewhere else to bum a meal.''

The silence stretched between them, although Lilith
wasn't sure what exactly prompted Mitch's quiet. She wondered whether she had spoiled the mood by confessing a
vulnerability and wished she could take the words back.

Then Mitch leaned closer, his eyes gleaming. ''Hey,'' he
said quietly, the thread of humor in his voice telling Lilith
that he was going to try to make her smile. Her heart
warmed at the sign of his concern.

''Are you trying to give me a run for my money on this
worrying front?'' Mitch winked. ''You ought to know
you're taking on a champ.''

It worked.

Lilith grinned. ''I know.'' Mitch *was* a champion, and
in more ways than he even guessed. And he would be hers
for all eternity.

The very thought made Lilith's smile broaden.

Mitch eyed the pitcher. ''Do you want some more of this
sangria? It's a pretty wicked batch, if I do say so myself.''

Lilith chuckled. ''A regular witch's brew.''

Mitch joined her laughter. ''It takes one to know one?''

Lilith nodded, then sobered. ''I'll take good care of
them.''

Mitch frowned. His gaze flicked away, then met Lilith's
again. ''Yes, I know,'' he said quietly, as though surprised
by his own certainty in that. He studied Lilith's features as
though he sought the key to some puzzle there, then
reached for the pitcher.

''This stuff just seems to evaporate,'' he murmured with
a wink, then topped up their glasses.

''It's very, very warm tonight,'' Lilith concurred solemnly.

''So, why don't you prompt my memory a bit?'' Mitch

said with a casualness that didn't ring quite true. He flicked an intent glance Lilith's way. "Why don't you tell me how we met?"

Lilith felt a little surge of disappointment. "You still don't remember?"

Mitch looked away. "Not enough."

Clearly he was embarrassed by his own inability to recall all the important details. But Lilith was more than happy to help this man remember.

She wrapped her arms around her knees. In her mind's eye, the events of all those centuries ago were as clear as if they had only just occurred.

Maybe if she gave her memories voice, a word or an image would prompt Mitch's memory. And there was no reason to keep all her secrets safely locked away any longer. Mitch was her love returned to her, Mitch she could trust with her life and her history.

"I was born among the *Rom*," Lilith began softly, well aware of how intently Mitch listened. "That's what we called ourselves. Others called us Egyptians—later shortened to "Gypsies"—although we never came from Egypt, as far as I knew. We did travel constantly, spending a month here and another there. We were entertainers, fortune-tellers, acrobats, as well as merchants of gold and horses and baskets woven by our menfolk."

"So you are a Gypsy. That's what Andrea said."

"I was," Lilith corrected firmly.

Mitch arched a brow as he sipped. "Not anymore?"

Again Lilith found the denial didn't come easily to her lips, so she just shook her head. "But I'll get to that. It was the spring of 1420—although I knew nothing of dates in those days—when we came to a village in what is now northern Italy. It was there, in the twilight of a spring evening, that I first glimpsed the man who would hold my heart for all time."

Lilith bit back her smile of recollection. "He was unlike any man I had ever seen before, his hair not black but the shade of ripe chestnuts, his eyes not dark but as fiery as the sun. And in that twilight, he was chopping wood in the forest near where we made our camp. He heard me running—a remarkable thing for a *gadjo*—"

"A what?"

"*Gadjo*. A man not of the *Rom*," Lilith explained softly. "It is said that the *Rom* move as silently as the wind through the grass, and I was held to be more quiet than most." She shook her head, still marvelling at the truth of it. "But he heard me."

Lilith turned and looked deeply into Mitch's eyes, golden eyes like sunlight snared in a bottomless pond. "*You* heard me, when you were Sebastian. It was just the first sign of many that we were destined to be together."

If Mitch looked slightly discomfited by this, Lilith didn't notice. She looked back to the changing sky and hugged her knees closer.

"It was a wonderful summer, a year when everything seemed possible to me, a year of unspeakable magick. I was twenty-one years of age, well past the age when the *Rom* would have seen me wed, but I knew there was something special in my future. And I was indulged because I had the Gift."

"What gift?"

"The one I told you about. I could always see the future, I could see what would come to pass, with greater clarity than anyone else within our *kumpania*. There were those who said it was because I was born on the night of a blue moon, those who insisted it was the kiss of a goddess on my brow, but old Dritta said it was my mother's talent that coursed through my veins. She said it passed thus from mother to daughter."

Lilith paused. It felt so good to be able to share these precious memories. It felt so good to have Mitch/Sebastian back by her side, with the unexpected bonus that he was even more wonderful than she remembered.

"You sound fond of this Dritta."

Lilith smiled in reminiscence. "She was a total tyrant. Some said she was my grandmother—I never knew the truth."

"Didn't your mother tell you?"

Lilith sobered and shook her head. "My mother died when I was an infant, I don't remember her. But Dritta took me in as her own. She always said she only did it because she could discern the power of my Gift. Dritta was a true *shuvani.*'' The *Rom* word fell easily from Lilith's tongue.

''What's that?''

''A wise woman, maybe a sorceress. It doesn't translate perfectly well.'' Lilith considered that for a moment and realized suddenly how much *Rom* had crossed her lips since Mitch moved in next door to her. It was strange, but she shrugged it off as coincidence.

''At any rate, she had a rare ability to see beyond this world, through the veil to the possibilities of the future. Dritta taught me to read the cards, and to read customers, too.''

''I don't understand.'' Mitch's voice sharpened in his interest. ''What do you mean by reading customers?''

Lilith glanced at him. ''Most people only come to have their fortune told for a reason, although there are some, particularly now, who indulge their curiosity regularly. In those days, though, it was risky to visit the *Rom*, you could be charged for consorting with heretics and burned.''

Lilith paused, then decided to state the worst. It might prompt Mitch's memory, although she had made it a matter of principle not to recall the events of a certain night.

''You could be hanged,'' she said deliberately, then looked to him.

Mitch didn't say anything. He held her gaze without blinking and she wondered whether her words had stirred an uneasy recollection within him.

She swallowed the lump in her throat that that short sentence had prompted and pulled her mind away from the dark abyss of that night's memories. She never dwelt upon that.

Lilith forced herself to continue in an even tone. ''So, those who came, usually had a good reason to come. And an astute observer like Dritta could often guess the reason before a word was uttered.''

''That doesn't sound very honest.''

''On the contrary, it saves a lot of time. The reading has a focus, a focus derived from the seeker as surely as the lay of the cards themselves. Keen observation makes for better readings.'' Lilith smiled. ''And greater customer satisfaction.'' She looked steadily at Mitch. ''When your presence is barely tolerated by the locals, it is wise to ensure that they have no complaints about services rendered."

Mitch slowly lifted one brow. "What kind of observations?" he asked.

Lilith frowned. These were secrets whispered to her by Dritta and not readily given voice, even to someone she knew she could trust more than herself.

But the time for hugging all her secrets to herself was passed.

"Generalizations. Young women often consult a fortune-teller about love. Either they have an affection for someone they know casually, or they want to know what the future will bring in terms of love. Older married women often come because they believe their husband is unfaithful and they don't know who else to ask for advice."

"In case they're wrong," Mitch contributed. "In a small community, that kind of accusation could have made a lot of trouble."

"Exactly. One wants to be certain, or one wants to be reassured that such suspicions are foolish."

"And men?"

"Younger men can come for much the same reason as younger women, or they may be concerned about their trade and financial future. Older men, particularly established ones, only come to fortune-tellers when they have a secret."

"A mistress?"

"Or shady business dealings, or something from the past that they fear could return to jeopardize their position in the community. An illegitimate child, a forsaken fiancée, a deal made in the shadows. There must be a good deal at stake for a man of influence and prestige to risk being seen visiting a fortune-teller."

"Sounds like a study of human nature."

"I suppose it is, in a way." Lilith shrugged. "And there are the obvious signs, of course. Missing wedding bands that have left their mark indicate unfaithfulness, people who play nervously with their wedding band have come about marital problems. That sort of thing." Lilith smiled at Mitch. "It has become much more complicated in these days than it once was."

"You make it sound so innocuous."

"It is! These observations don't change what I see—they just confirm which part of what I see the seeker most wants to know about." Lilith flicked a playful glance at her companion. "I guess they'd call it target marketing now."

Mitch shook his head. They sipped sangria in silence and she watched him, loving the play of shadows on his features. He glanced up suddenly, and their gazes locked and held. The warmth of an unstated compliment shone in the depths of Mitch's eyes, and made Lilith's heart pound.

She felt admired and respected beneath his gaze, feminine yet appreciated for more than her appearance. He really listened to her. He had become so much more over the time they had been apart.

Lilith loved Mitch's protectiveness, she loved his sense of duty, she loved that he did what was right regardless of the price. She loved how he adored his kids, she loved how he talked and listened to her, how he frowned when he reasoned things through.

Lilith realized suddenly that she loved Mitch Davison with an intensity that she had never felt when she loved him as Sebastian. She decided right then and there that Mitch's ideas about "all that old-fashioned stuff" sounded like a perfect way to spend the rest of her life. In fact, she would give anything to begin as soon as possible.

Remarkably enough, her Gift gave her no inkling of how much Mitch would ask from her in just a moment's time. He would ask for no less than the tale of the most painful night of her life.

And Lilith would give it to him, willingly paying the postage due on that glorious future. She would not consider how it might shred her heart to step into that abyss, to explore dark memories that she had declared off-limits for nearly six centuries.

She would do it because she loved him.

JUSTICE

She was doing it to him again.

But this time, Lilith wasn't seducing Mitch with her eyes or her perfume or even her kisses. It was her clear thinking, her understanding of human nature, the flash of compassion in her eyes when she spoke of troubled people coming for advice that prompted his admiration. Her low voice with its exotic accent made him want to listen to her all night long.

She could lull him to sleep with that voice, dispatch him on a journey from which he would never return. It was so low and musical, so rich and evocative. When she lingered over a word, or saw humor in some small thing, Mitch had to fight the sense that she truly had experienced the better part of six centuries.

Lilith was unlike anyone he had ever known.

And the fact that she made good sense was no small thing to a man who prized reason as Mitch did. The acknowledgement that there were other factors at play besides her so-called gift for seeing the future was an interesting one. That Lilith clung tenaciously to a faith in her ability, even conceding as much as she had, was doubly intriguing.

On this night, when the conversation flowed so readily between them, Mitch could smell the truth he sought, lingering just out of reach.

"So what happened that summer in 1420?" he invited conversationally as he topped up their sangria. "Remind me."

Lilith froze.

Then she carefully set down her glass and took a deep breath. "I've never spoken of the end," she said so evenly that Mitch knew she was trying to veil her feelings. "I don't even think about it, as a rule."

If she had wanted to prompt Mitch's curiosity, Lilith had just done a really good job. "Why not?"

She glanced across the yard, frowned, then shook her head. "I suppose, like all tales, there is good and bad in it," she murmured. "It is the extremes that make it so painful."

And then she fell silent so long that Mitch was sure he had crossed an invisible line.

"I don't mean to pry," he said quietly. "Let's talk about something else."

"No." Lilith shook her head with unexpected resolve. She turned to meet his gaze and studied him for a moment. "You really don't remember that night?"

Mitch shook his head.

"Then you have a right to know," she concluded crisply.

Lilith turned away before Mitch could say anything. "My first glimpse of you wasn't the last, by any means." She smiled with sudden mischievousness and shook a finger at Mitch. "You surprised me quite often, in fact, and you *gadjo* types shouldn't be able to do that."

"Maybe I was a sorcerer myself." Mitch grinned. She had spooked him for a minute there, but this didn't sound so bad. The edge of skepticism in his next words was surprisingly slight. "Or was it just another sign of destiny?"

"Destiny," Lilith said with conviction. "We knew each other from first sight and your actions showed that our minds were as one. I'd find flowers on the path in front of me in the forest—flowers obviously left for me—and no sign of anyone until I heard your whistling in the distance. And there were ribbons left in pretty bundles on the path I took to town, always in colors that I particularly liked. You knew instinctively how to woo me because we were destined to be soulmates."

Lilith smiled and wrapped her arms around her knees again. Her delighted expression and pose made her look young and trusting. Mitch relaxed against the post and enjoyed the luxury of watching her. "There was a great sense of anticipation in me that summer, that something wonderful was about to happen, and each gift made it feel closer and closer. It was very romantic of you."

Lilith cast a smile at Mitch, but he anticipated her move and examined the bottom of his glass instead of holding her gaze. He felt a funny pang of jealousy, hearing how terrific this Sebastian guy had been, how deliberate he had been about cultivating Lilith's attention.

It must just be his conscience tweaking him. After all, it was one thing for Mitch to let Lilith think he was some other guy, at least for the purpose of seeing Andrea safe, but quite another to accept credit for anything that guy had done.

To his relief, Lilith seemed to take his silence as a sign of modesty, for she soon continued on. "At any rate, one August twilight, you came to have your fortune read." Her eyes shone as though they were filled with stardust. "I can still see you stepping into our camp, so proud and strong, so determined that only I could read for you. Our gazes met and held across the fire—in that moment, it was as though there was a tangible realization of all the great forces that linked us together."

Mitch didn't have the heart to question her assertion. It would have interrupted the flow of her story, after all, and he knew how irritating it was when people did that to him.

"A cord snapped tight between us," Lilith whispered, her ripe lips curved in a smile of recollection. "I know the others felt it too. I couldn't have stayed away from you. There was nowhere else to be but by your side. I remember coming to you and taking your hand, I remember leading you to my tent without a single word, pulling back the flap and secreting us two inside."

Mitch had a sudden definite sense that he really didn't want to know what had happened. He didn't want to think about Lilith pouncing on another guy, even if she thought that guy was him, even if she thought it had all happened some six hundred years ago.

Lilith leaned closer, her fingertips landed on his arm and Mitch opened his mouth to confess his deception right that minute.

But Lilith's intent whisper cut off whatever he might have said. "Do you remember anything of that evening? Do you remember the shadows that clung like velvet to the corners inside the tent?"

Her hand slid up his arm, her fingertips danced along the line of his jaw like butterflies. She was so close, her eyes flashed with a thousand recollections, her perfume surrounded him.

She was making him forget everything else in the world except her. Again. Lilith traced the line of his lips with one fingertip and Mitch didn't even think he could feel any other part of his body.

Well, maybe one.

He stared into her dark, dark eyes, he thought about love antidotes, he thought about love spells, and he wondered.

"Do you remember the flickering gold of the oil lamp, the distant singing of the *kumpania*, the wind whistling through the trees overhead?" Lilith whispered, her lips a fingers-breadth from his own. Mitch was transfixed. He couldn't have moved away to save his life. "I swore the very starlight shone through the roof of the tent as we sat together, I thought your flesh glowed with its own light."

Mitch stared. Lilith was so persuasive. She couldn't be pretending this, no one could act this well. He looked again into those eyes, but there wasn't a glimmer of doubt in their magnificent depths. Lilith was clearly convinced that everything she told him not only had happened, but that it had happened to her.

And to him.

In the blink of an eye, Mitch's entire universe did a 180. Her conviction was the key to the solution. Mitch felt as though he'd been hit in the head with a two-by-four. Lilith *believed* this mumbo jumbo with all her heart and soul.

Which explained everything.

He'd been bothered since dinner over that creed she had told Jason she followed. Because harming no one didn't mesh very well with running cons as a business. Mitch couldn't imagine that a woman who believed cicadas shouldn't die in mayonnaise jars could really hurt anything or anyone. Which hadn't made a lick of sense until this very minute, because Mitch had already noticed that Lilith was nothing if not consistent.

But Lilith *could* reconcile her creed of hurting no one with her profession if she *wasn't* a con artist.

It was so simple that Mitch wanted to smack himself. Lilith wasn't a crook—she was just a flake who believed she could see the future and remember the distant past.

It was a bit scary how very reassuring Mitch found that particular conclusion.

Because he did. The surge of relief that rolled through him had the irresistible force of a tsunami. He didn't have to brace himself against Lilith's allure. Andrea wasn't at any kind of risk. Mitch didn't have to protect his family from her, he didn't have to deny his instinctive attraction to her.

Mitch had been wrong. And for once, he was very, very glad about that. In the wake of that realization, the barriers he had hastily erected against Lilith tumbled like dominos. The most intriguing woman who had ever waltzed through Mitch's life might be a little bit muddled up, but she was very much available.

And Mitch was delighted at the news.

Lilith seemed markedly less delighted. In fact, she seemed quite concerned. Belatedly, Mitch realized that he hadn't been following everything she said.

She looked upset.

Lilith's voice quivered slightly as she reached up and framed his face in her hands. Mitch's heart started to two-step at the press of her fingertips against his skin. She was close enough that he could see each thick eyelash, close enough to kiss.

"Do you remember shuffling the cards?" she asked, her voice wavering slightly.

He couldn't lie to her.

Especially now. Mitch shook his head.

Disappointment flitted across her brow. Lilith glanced down, giving Mitch the chance to study her elegant profile as she dropped her hand and traced the length of his fingers with her fingertip. Her hair spilled over his arm and Mitch felt heat spread over his skin from her touch.

"The cards looked so fragile in your hands," she murmured. "I can still see how nimbly you shuffled them although you said you had never done the like. I can still see you separating The Fool from the deck like a conjuror, still hear your laughter, still see you shake your head." She swallowed. "It is as though it happened only moments ago, not hundreds of years ago."

Lilith looked up at Mitch with wide eyes. She was very serious. His mouth went dry as he wondered where this story was going—obviously it was very important to her, whether it was true or not.

"And I have never forgotten what you said." Lilith paused, then whispered something in a foreign tongue.

Mitch shook his head in incomprehension. "What does it mean?"

Lilith held his gaze. *"I came for love,"* she murmured, *"but had hoped for a different answer than this."*

Love. That was at the root of all of this.

Maybe Lilith's worst crime was convincing those who came to visit her that they were lovable, that there *was* a lovematch out there somewhere for each and every one of them. Maybe Lilith's faith was all they needed to have the confidence not only to find love but to believe in it themselves.

As flaws went, that wasn't a bad one.

Maybe it was time that Mitch believed a little bit more in love than he had for the last couple of years.

"I asked you not to go," Lilith confessed in a heated whisper. "You asked why you should stay. Do you remember my response?"

Mitch shook his head slowly, glad he could be honest about that.

Lilith licked her lips, she edged closer, she lifted one hand to his jaw. Mitch couldn't find it within himself to move away, to remove her hand, to tell her that he really wasn't this Sebastian guy.

"There was only one answer I could give," she murmured. Her gaze flicked to his, Mitch's heart skipped a beat in anticipation, then Lilith reached to brush her lips across his.

It was a tentative and cautious embrace, as sweet as a young girl's first offering, as different as night and day from the first kiss Lilith had given Mitch. Mitch tasted Lilith's vulnerability, and knew he couldn't take advantage of her dismay.

Obviously, the telling of this story was not easy for her, even if Mitch wasn't sure why. He tipped Lilith's chin with gentle fingers and kissed her lightly, wanting only to ease her distress. Mitch savored the sangria-tinged taste of her lips for the barest moment, then lifted his mouth slowly from hers.

Lilith's breathing was rapid, her eyes were luminous. Her lips were slightly reddened from Mitch's kiss, her hand rested against his chest. She looked puzzled, despite the flame in her eyes. "Why did you stop? You didn't then."

If nothing else, she was honest about her desire.

Mitch's certainty that Lilith wanted him—again—was all he needed to be ready to repeat their first meeting, with ease. But Mitch didn't want to do that.

There was something too precious at stake.

Mitch caught Lilith's hand in his and ran his thumb across her palm as he watched its course. He wondered how he could explain to her that he wouldn't surrender his self-control again.

The task might kill him, but Mitch was not an impulsive kind of guy. He wasn't like Kurt, he didn't love 'em and leave 'em, he deeply believed that lovemaking was an expression of commitment between two people.

If he and Lilith ever made love again—and Mitch was starting to think it was a serious possibility—it wasn't going to be on impulse. It wasn't going to be a one-night fling or a one-time deal, it was going to be for all the right reasons. It was going to be for good. If Mitch ventured back onto the field of love, he was going to get it right.

Lilith deserved as much.

He wanted to know her, he wanted to love her, he wanted to believe as ardently as she did that they were destined to be together.

It was kind of a weird certainty she had, and an illogical one, but now that he knew it was harmless, it was starting to grow on Mitch. He smiled down at her. "Because you didn't finish the story. What happened?"

To Mitch's surprise, Lilith's eyes clouded and she bit her

lip. He frowned, having expected roses and sunshine from this point forward.

"We made love," Lilith admitted softly, her voice breaking over the words. "All the night long."

She traced a little circle on Mitch's T-shirt with her fingertip and he watched her tears inexplicably well up, even though he couldn't imagine what had made her so sad.

"One of my uncles saw you leaving my tent in the morning. He demanded the truth and I didn't lie." Lilith swallowed. "He went to the town to demand a bride price."

That sounded pretty medieval. "A bride price?"

Lilith lifted her chin. "You had taken my virginity. I had given it to you willingly, and I refused to lie about it. I didn't care who knew we loved each other. My uncle declared that you owed compensation to the *kumpania*, whether you wed me or not." Lilith inhaled sharply and Mitch was surprised by the obvious strength of her feelings. "I knew that you would marry me, because you had pledged to return to my side."

Mitch had a definite sense that things hadn't gone well from this point. Lilith's tearful defiance was not a good sign. "And?"

"You did not come." Lilith frowned and pursed her lips. "Not the next night or the next. My uncle could not find you, and all in the *kumpania* shunned me. They were certain that a *gadjo* had used me for his pleasure and cast me aside."

Mitch watched her, more than a little troubled by the toll her story obviously took from her, yet not knowing quite what to do about it.

"Then, suddenly, we were summoned to a hearing in the town square. All the cards and signs in the wind declared that the meeting would be one of great import." She straightened and squared her shoulders, but her voice was small. "We went."

Lilith licked her lips and stared resolutely at the middle of Mitch's chest. He felt her tremble. "It had been three days since we laid together, three days and nights that you had not kept your pledge. I was so worried, half-afraid something had happened to you, half-afraid that my uncle was right and that you did not love me after all."

Mitch felt a lump rise in his throat for this trusting young girl. He was half-afraid himself that she was right about her Romeo's motives.

He wondered suddenly whether this story was a way she dealt with a painful, but much more recent memory. That would make an awful lot of sense.

Mitch wondered how he could find out for sure.

"In the square, they said a widow had been murdered, that the culprit was found and would be punished." Lilith lifted her gaze to meet Mitch's and he saw pain shining there.

No doubt about it, Lilith was hurting.

Mitch's protectiveness surged to the fore and he instinctively put a hand on her shoulder. She leaned against him in a way that seemed markedly out of character. Mitch had already seen how independent and strong Lilith could be.

But this story cut deep. He wished belatedly that he hadn't asked her for it. Mitch's gut told him that it was only going to get worse. He pulled Lilith into his arms without another thought.

She was shivering, as though it wasn't hot enough to fry eggs on the sidewalk, and she clutched two fistfuls of his shirt.

"It was you," Lilith whispered unevenly. Mitch blinked, then he realized that she meant him as Sebastian.

Lilith's words suddenly gained momentum. "They said you had been possessed by demons, tainted by laying with a Gypsy whore, they said you were a criminal. I knew it wasn't true, I knew it was a lie, I knew that you would never hurt another, but they would not listen to me."

Her voice dropped low and for the first time, Mitch heard bitterness in her voice. "I was just the Gypsy whore, after all." Lilith halted and swallowed awkwardly, her fingers tapping restlessly on Mitch's chest. She caught her breath, she trembled, and the words tumbled out of her.

"And then, before all of us, they hanged you until you were dead."

That startled Mitch, no less than the way Lilith's tears began to fall in earnest. They fell like scattering jewels, splashing on his skin in an endless torrent.

This had gone far enough.

Mitch closed his arms tightly around Lilith, his voice dropped with low urgency. There were psychologists who specialized in treating emotional trauma, all sorts of experts who could help Lilith deal with whatever had happened to her and put it securely in the past.

And Mitch decided right then and there that he would ensure she got that help.

"But, Lilith, that can't be . . ." he began, but got no further before she laid a firm finger across his lips. One look into the intensity of her eyes silenced him, at least for the moment.

"You don't know the rest of it," she declared. "You *can't*. They said it was my fault, they said they would burn the Gypsy whore who had poisoned one of their own sons. They chased us from the town with flames, all of us, and set fire to the woods behind us. We fled with the speed of the wind and they could not catch us."

As delusions went, this one was pretty thorough. Mitch tried to find something good in all of this drama. "But, in the end, your *kumpania* sheltered you, right? You all stuck together?"

Lilith's lips twisted and her tears welled again. "Of course not! They could not. They cast me out."

"What?"

"I was declared *mahrime*. Unclean." Lilith's words were flat, although Mitch guessed her tone hid a wealth of emotion. "It was bad enough that I had lost my maidenhead to a *gadjo*, but the fact that he did not pay the bride price was an insult that could not be endured. No *Rom* man would have me, then. A *mahrime* person can infect others with their pollution. I could not be permitted to remain. My presence was a risk to the cleanliness of all."

Okay, things had gotten even more medieval in her mind.

But the truth was clear to see, at least to anyone who looked. Mitch heartily disapproved of what he perceived Lilith's family had done. So, she had been caught as a teenager in a compromising position—her family had no right chucking her out into the world.

Suddenly, a lot of puzzle pieces surrounding Lilith fell into place—Mitch would bet that all those missing records were registered in her real name, whatever that might be.

And she had simply taken another name for the purposes of day-to-day living—Lilith for the Old Testament woman who could not control her passions. That would be a result of whatever nonsense her parents had dumped on her. And Romano, perfectly fitting with this whole Gypsy thing she had concocted as an alternative to the truth and now ardently believed *was* the truth.

It wasn't that Lilith didn't exist—it was that Mitch had been looking for her in the wrong places.

Mitch didn't really care about such practicalities right now. It made him damned mad to think of what Lilith had endured at her family's behest. He couldn't imagine that either of his kids could do anything bad enough that he would just toss them out the door to fend for themselves. It was wrong. It was unfair.

It was not in the parental job description.

Mitch didn't want to frighten Lilith with his anger, but he couldn't just say nothing at all. He wanted her to know that he was on her side. Mitch forcibly kept his tone even. "It's pretty cruel to leave a young girl alone like that," he confined himself to saying.

To Mitch's surprise, Lilith smiled thinly. "I wasn't destined to be alone. You swore to return to me and repeated your vow on the gallows. I knew you would find me." Her eyes saddened again. "Even though I never imagined it would take so long."

Mitch saw the full weight of the loneliness he had only glimpsed in Lilith earlier. She seemed to be wrung out emotionally by sharing this story, even in its disguised version, though Mitch supposed that made sense. It hadn't been easy for her, and she had said she refused even to think about it anymore.

He was humbled that she trusted him enough to share this with him. Lilith leaned against Mitch, her cheek against his heartbeat, and Mitch felt her tears dampen his T-shirt again. This time, though, they ran silently.

"I'm so glad," she whispered softly and unevenly, "that you're finally here."

There was an ache in Lilith's voice that made Mitch want to make everything come right in her lopsided little world.

Someone was hurting, someone expected him to make it
all better, someone was counting on him.

Mitch was securely back on familiar ground.

He wanted to apologize for taking so long, even though
he knew Lilith wasn't talking about him or maybe even
aware of the truth anymore. But he wouldn't lie to her, at
any cost. So, the only way to reassure her without uttering
a lie was with his touch. It seemed the most natural thing
in the world to do, the one thing his heart had urged him
to do all along.

The difference was that Mitch had finally decided to listen to its urgings. Whatever the cause, whether it was the
lady's own allure, her vulnerability, or her concoction,
Mitch was completely enchanted by his neighbor.

And he couldn't bear her tears. Mitch gathered Lilith into
his arms, cupped her chin, and gently touched his lips to
hers. He gave her plenty of latitude to pull away, but she
immediately parted her lips beneath his own.

She still wanted him. Mitch's heart thumped. But that
wasn't what this was about. He wanted to reassure her, to
ease away her fears, to make sure she slept without night-
mares tonight.

Mitch tilted Lilith's face upward, then brushed away her
tears with his fingertips. He kissed her brow, her temple,
her eyelids, he tasted the salt on her flesh. He nuzzled her
earlobe, he swallowed every last tear as though he would
take her hurt into himself and wipe it away forever. Lilith
sighed and leaned against Mitch; her fingers found their
way into his hair.

She caught the back of his neck and deepened their kiss,
her need firing Mitch's desire. He let his hand slide down
her throat, and cradled the ripe curve of her breast in his
palm. His thumb moved surely across her breast and her
nipple tightened beneath his touch in silent demand. Lilith
made a tiny cry of surrender and Mitch knew then that mere
kisses wouldn't do.

She needed more reassurance than that—and Mitch knew
just what that would be. He scooped the lady up and headed
into the house, having no desire to entertain his new neighbors more than he already had.

• • •

Lilith's heart sang when Mitch swept her into his arms and strode into the kitchen. His gentleness was more than re-assuring, his touch made the pain of recollection fade to nothing. Everything had been so vivid in her mind, Lilith felt as though she was standing in that square again. She could smell the flames, she had seen Sebastian go limp and felt the wave of loss roll through her.

It was wonderful to be able to cling to the solid strength of his shoulders, to know that they were together again, to be certain that all had come right in the end.

Mitch kissed her and Lilith forgot everything except the feel and the taste of him, the here-and-now of him. She locked her arms around Mitch's neck and kissed him back, willing him to understand her fear and her relief. Lilith couldn't wait, she wanted to make love with him here and now, again and again and again.

They had waited long enough.

She had waited too long. She needed his touch this night the way a fish needed water and a bird needed air. Lilith needed her one true love.

Mitch's arms tightened around her and he halted beside the kitchen counter. When he put her down there, Lilith was delighted that their thoughts were as one. She shivered when his hand roamed down her back. She twisted to face him, wrapped her legs around his hips, and found that the height of the counter was absolutely perfect.

Lilith pressed herself against Mitch's chest, snuggled herself closer to his erection, and tangled her fingers in his hair. He was warm and muscular, solid and strong. His skin was smooth, she ran her toes through the hair on his legs. Mitch groaned, then slanted his mouth possessively over her own. His hands slid beneath her skirt and clenched her buttocks. He lifted her closer as he kissed her deeply.

Perfect bliss. Lilith closed her eyes and enjoyed the heat of his kiss.

When his fingers slid into her underwear, Lilith caught her breath. She reached for the fly of his shorts, but Mitch caught at her hand. He lifted his lips away from hers, his eyes blazing like stars, and kissed her errant fingertips.

"Not that," he said with quiet assurance and put her hand back on his shoulder. Lilith would have protested her confusion, but Mitch brushed his thumb across her lips to silence her.

"Not tonight," he murmured, then held her gaze resolutely. His eyes seemed to glow with an inner light of conviction. "If we ever make love again, Lilith, it'll be because we've both decided that that's what we want, not because one of us is hurting, not because we make a choice in the heat of the moment. It will be *right*, and we'll both be sure of that before anything happens."

Lilith frowned. "Aren't you sure now?"

Mitch smiled crookedly. "I'm sure I want you more than I've ever wanted a woman before," he confessed and her heart skipped a beat. "But that's not nearly good enough. I'm not like Kurt. I never wanted to just 'get lucky.'" Mitch leaned down to touch the tip of his nose to hers, his gaze intent. "I only ever wanted to make love."

And his somber expression told Lilith that Mitch wasn't certain he had ever had the good fortune to make love with a partner who was making love to him.

Her heart twisted in sympathy at the evidence of his wife's doings, whatever they were. Despite her own raging desire, her own need to feel his strength within her, Lilith wanted to give Mitch the certainty he craved.

She wanted the next time they made love to be everything he ever imagined lovemaking could be. She wanted it to be as magickal as that night they had once shared. If he could wait, then so could she.

Even if it wasn't going to be easy.

Lilith wriggled a little, but Mitch didn't loosen his hold on her. "I should go home, then," she whispered.

Mitch's slow smile caught her off-guard, although the way her belly tingled in response to the sight didn't. "Not yet." Lilith knew her surprise showed, because his grin widened.

"There's something I have to do first," Mitch said mysteriously. There was a twinkle in his eyes that Lilith was quite sure she shouldn't trust, but she was suitably intrigued.

Mitch brushed his lips across the tip of her nose, her cheekbone, then he placed a gentle kiss in her ear. Lilith shivered at his murmured words. "I want to make sure you have sweet dreams tonight."

Lilith felt a tingle of anticipation, but that was nothing compared to the thrill Mitch's kisses left as he blazed a trail down her neck. Lilith sighed and surrendered to whatever scheme he had in mind. Mitch turned her as though she weighed no more than a feather and cradled her against his chest. His warm fingers worked the buttons open at the front of her dress and his kisses slipped over the curve of her breast.

Lilith gasped when his mouth closed over her nipple. Her back arched with pleasure when Mitch's fingers slid inside her panties. He touched her with a persuasiveness that made her dizzy, he flicked his tongue against that nipple until it throbbed. He ran his teeth gently across the peak, even as his fingers caressed her without cease. As the desire already simmering within Lilith came rapidly to a boil, she clutched Mitch's shoulders, certain she would explode at any moment.

But he kept her just shy of the summit, teasing and touching, tempting a little more, then a little less. Lilith writhed in his embrace. She was certain she could stand the tension no longer, and whispered his name urgently.

Suddenly Mitch claimed Lilith's lips in a kiss so triumphant that she arched against him. His tongue tangled with hers, his scent surrounded her. His arm held her fast against his chest, his fingers dove and danced. Lilith felt a tremor begin in her belly, she twisted but Mitch granted her no quarter. If anything, he intensified his kiss, his fingers grew more demanding, until suddenly, they slid deep inside Lilith's heat.

And the earthquake erupted within her. Lilith trembled and shook right to her toes with the force of her orgasm. Mitch urged her on and on long past the moment Lilith thought there could be no more.

Finally, she sagged bonelessly against him, languid and sated as she had never been before. Lilith closed her eyes, more exhausted than she was after mixing the most demanding brew. She was ready to curl up in a little ball and sleep in the sun for a week.

"Okay?"

Lilith opened her eyes and met Mitch's questioning gaze. She smiled sleepily. "More than okay, thank you." She looped her arms around his neck and leaned her cheek against his chest. His heart thundered beneath her ear, the sound making her smile.

Lilith sighed with contentment.

"Good." Mitch rubbed the back of her neck. "Now, you can safely go home to bed." He wrapped his hands around Lilith's waist and lifted her off the counter, kissing the tip of her nose just before setting her on her feet.

She yawned and leaned against him as he buttoned her dress again. They strolled the length of his hall wrapped around each other, out the front door, and over to her own porch.

Lilith supposed it was sensible for them not to sleep together, at least until the children were used to her, although she would have been perfectly willing to do so. She smiled to herself in recollection of Mitch's old-fashioned goals, then sobered when she recalled the woman who had made him less likely to believe in them.

On her own porch, Lilith pivoted to face Mitch. The newly rising moon cast its silvery light over his features, making him look resolute, yet mysterious. There was so much of him that she didn't yet know. Mitch's eyes, though, gleamed warmly, and his firm lips curved in an affectionate smile. Lilith wanted to know everything about him, all his secrets, all his woes, all the tests he had endured.

"What happened to the mother of your children?" Lilith asked before she could reconsider the wisdom of the question.

Mitch's smile was wiped away as cleanly as if it had ever been. "Janice left," he said flatly. "Right after Jen was born." He paused and frowned at his feet. "She never wanted kids."

That brought Lilith wide awake again. It seemed to her that this Janice had a funny way of showing any such conviction. How did anyone in a world chockful of birth control devices and methods end up with *two* kids they didn't want?

Not to mention that Lilith knew Mitch would have listened to any concerns his partner voiced. It was just the way he did business.

It was one of those things she loved about him.

"I'm sorry."

"Don't be." Mitch shook his head. "It was bad news all around." He tipped his head back and looked at the stars for a long moment. Lilith knew he had many thoughts on the matter. She was by no means sure he would give them voice.

But Mitch did.

"Do you know why Jen is afraid to be alone?" he finally asked, his question so low that Lilith barely heard the words.

"No."

Mitch met Lilith's gaze abruptly, his own dark with intent. "Janice left when Jen was two weeks old." He swallowed and averted his gaze, a thread of wonder in his next words. "She just walked right out of the apartment."

"No!" Lilith was incredulous. It was incomprehensible to her that anyone could leave their own child in such circumstances. "She left a baby alone?"

Mitch nodded, the memory obviously still troubling to him. And no wonder! "She left a note, said she'd planned it so that I'd be home from work in less than five minutes."

Mitch looked to his feet and propped his hands on his hips. Lilith felt a tremor of premonition before he spoke. "But I was an hour late that night, Lilith. Some story broke, I don't remember what and it doesn't matter. What *does* matter is that Jen was crying, alone in that apartment, for a whole hour."

Lilith laid a hand on his arm, guessing who he was going to blame for this situation. "But where was Jason?"

Mitch frowned. "Andrea had taken him for a couple of weeks, to give Janice some time with the new baby." He heaved a ragged sigh. "But clearly she didn't want time with the baby."

His lips tightened and Lilith knew she didn't imagine the shimmer of tears in his eyes. She didn't know what to say, but Mitch continued heatedly.

"She was just a baby, Lilith! And all alone." His frustration shone in his eyes. "Jen was so red, so upset that she was nearly choking with fear when I finally got there and lifted her out of her cradle."

"Oh, Mitch, that's just horrible."

"Yeah." Mitch's face suddenly looked drawn. "And it was my fault."

"What do you mean? Don't say that!" Lilith wanted to give this big, caring man a shake. "How could it have been your fault? *She* left!"

"I shouldn't have been late," Mitch said grimly. "I should *never* have been late. I should have known better. I should have skipped that meeting. I should have guessed that Janice needed someone to talk to, that she didn't want to be home alone." His lips thinned. "I should have taken more time off right after Jen was born. I should have *known*."

Lilith's heart clenched that Mitch blamed himself for not being able to guess his wife's intentions. "Did she ever talk to you about it? Or ask for help?"

Mitch snorted. "Janice? No. She never talked to me, she never had. Whenever I asked her anything, she just clammed right up." He heaved a sigh and managed to summon a weak smile that didn't fool Lilith. "Maybe I never asked the right questions. Or maybe I wasn't persistent enough." His gaze flicked to hers. "Or maybe I'm just not any good at relationships."

Lilith folded her arms across her chest, more than ready to argue that point. "Then why are you so good with your children?"

Mitch shrugged. "Kids are easy. You pick them up and dust them off, kiss it better and pretend you know what's best. They believe you, they trust you, they don't ask hard questions."

"Baloney," Lilith declared with resolve. "You're not giving credit where it's due. Look around you—how many other people are parenting with your kind of determination? Those kids are crazy about you, and they know they can count on you. It's not your fault, Mitch, that Janice made a mistake."

He studied her for a long moment and Lilith had a definite sense that he wanted to believe her.

But then Mitch shook his head and smiled apologetically.

"This really isn't the ending to this evening that I had hoped for." He met her gaze and arched a brow. "Are you still going to have pleasant dreams?"

Lilith smiled. "Of course." She stepped into the circle of Mitch's arms and tapped a fingertip on his chest. "I'm going to dream about the wonderful man who captured my heart, then came galloping back to claim it again." She reached up and kissed Mitch's jaw. "And then I'm going to figure out a way to convince my champion that he's a pretty rare find."

Mitch grinned crookedly. "Now I'm in trouble," he teased, not looking too upset by the prospect.

Lilith smiled back at him, having no doubt that she would see the job done. She had a lot of practice with spells, after all.

"How about we dig some garden beds tomorrow?" he suggested, seeming reluctant to leave.

"That would be great. I'll supervise."

Mitch chuckled, then bent and kissed Lilith gently. He returned to his own porch, pausing there until Lilith went inside and closed the door. When Lilith turned the lock, the sound of Mitch's door opening and closing made her smile.

He was such a protective bear—even wanting to make sure she had good dreams. Lilith leaned back against the wood and smiled to herself, knowing she was living the very best dream of all.

9

THE HERMIT

The cards she had left on the table days before seemed to be shimmering in the starlight, even though that light couldn't have managed to slant through the window and shine on them. Lilith knew well enough to pay attention to such things. She slipped into the living room and stared down at the old tarot cards.

They were not as she had left them.

Ten cards lay face up now, almost the entire left circle on display. Without turning on a light, Lilith sat down and touched them with her fingertips.

The Pope was number five, Mitch in his fury over Andrea's cruise. He is the upholder of a code of acceptable behavior, a man unafraid to speak out for what he knows is right.

Even when he's wrong. Lilith smiled with affection and touched the next card.

The Lovers, card number six. A card of the choice between lingering in the past and stepping onto the yellow brick road to the future. A card marking the threshold that everyone crosses between the security of parents and the potential of partners. A card indicating a realization that any choice bears a cost as well as a prize, that something must be lost in order for something else to be gained.

Something had changed the day that Kurt came knocking, not just Lilith's choice to evict the men in front of her house, but Mitch had clearly come to a realization as well.

Lilith's smile broadened with the understanding of what that was. Mitch had begun to remember. Mitch had decided he wanted to remember more. Mitch had come to talk to her, not to mention protect her from his friend's seductive plans.

And she and Mitch had very nearly become lovers themselves in the process.

The next card was one of Lilith's favorites—The Chariot, number seven. A card of partnership and pairing, of two different steeds pulling together toward a single goal. A card that also represents the harnessing of animal desires, the act of putting them to work for the individual's own good instead of his detriment.

Mitch had certainly shackled their passion. Lilith traced the silhouette of the charioteer and decided it was not such a bad thing. She rather liked his determination that they should be lovers on every level when they came together again. It would make the moment a truly special one, a threshold to their future together. Lilith admired the strength of character and discipline he had developed over the years.

Because Lilith knew that when they did make love, it would be magickal in every way. She and Mitch had their own personalities, their own views of the world and ways of doing things, but like the two different steeds on the card, their objective was one.

And lifelong partnership was a pretty good goal.

Number eight, Justice, was next. The voice of conscience and morality, it was clearly the voice of Mitch. It was also, incidentally, the card of Lilith's creed, of living as blamelessly as possible.

But Justice rested upon the presence of laws. In addition to the written laws of society, the world of men was governed by another unwritten law, that of morality. And morality rose from conscience.

Conscience, the voice within one's own mind that governs choices, right or wrong. Lilith recalled that the first circle laid on the table represented external challenges, the second of those invisible hurdles that had to be conquered before the quest was done. The seated lady of Justice on the card, then, was the first glimpse through the portal from the world of the physical to the world of the spiritual. She provided a hint of the second half of the journey.

Lilith thought about Mitch's certainty of his own responsibility for Janice's departure and knew this was something he would have to resolve to see his own journey complete.

She'd have to consider how to help him with that when the opportunity arose.

Lilith touched the final card facing up. The Hermit held his beacon before the darkness and Lilith knew it represented the next step on Mitch's voyage. Another seeker, like The Fool, The Hermit has the wisdom of experience, though he shuns material aid. He sets out alone, to plan, to think, to unravel mysteries. The Hermit represents contemplation and a coming to understand one's own past and one's own self.

Lilith sat back in her chair and frowned at the card, unable to understand what it meant for Mitch. Was he going to disappear on his own for a while? Had it been closer to his conference, that possibility might have made more sense than it did.

Something flickered in her crystal ball like a beacon, but when Lilith frowned at it, there was nothing really there.

How strange.

But she was really tired, after all. Lilith smiled at the reason for her exhaustion. She yawned finally and stretched, knowing she wasn't going to see this solved tonight. At least not without some sleep.

And as Lilith climbed the stairs, she smiled once more at the prospect of her pleasant dreams.

But unbeknownst to Lilith, as she slumbered contentedly through that night, her very first gray hair unfurled like a silver thread in her dark tresses. It was a stark statement that things had not remained as once they were, that something had changed, that perhaps the elixir she had sipped so long ago was finally losing its grip.

Lilith, though, had such an abundance of hair that she would not immediately notice this herald of change.

Mitch strolled into the newsroom Monday morning, quite certain that the world was a good place. He and Lilith and the kids had had a great time the day before, all working together in the garden. Mitch had managed to more or less mow the lawn—even if most of what was growing there wasn't grass, the yard looked green. Jen's pool had a permanent location for the rest of the summer, and Jason and Lilith had managed to get one bed in place and plant some beans before the skies burst open.

It had been a great thunderstorm and they had watched its show from the shelter of the back porch. Much to Jason's delight, the power went off, and they ate Lilith's vegetarian quiche cold, by candlelight.

And the more Mitch talked to Lilith, the more he became convinced that one little kink in her system could be put to rights.

Mitch didn't even blink when Isabel bounced up to his desk in neon pink biker shorts. Her hair was woven into a thick ponytail. She had sunglasses perched on her head, and what looked like a butterfly tattoo on her upper arm. Mitch thought she had a few more earrings than she used to.

"New guy?" he guessed.

Isabel grinned. "Bike courier." She whistled under her breath and rolled her eyes appreciatively. "Legs like you wouldn't believe. And *stamina*." Isabel giggled, then blushed.

Mitch grinned and shook his head. "Hey, can you do something for me?"

"You know it."

"Try to dig me up some stuff on selective amnesia, repressed memories, basically whatever the brain does to protect someone from reliving a nasty experience. And if you run across the names of any clinics or psychologists who are particularly good at treating this kind of thing, jot them down."

"Another juicy lead?"

"No, no." Mitch got waved into the editorial meeting, so he scooped up his notepad. He dropped his voice. "This is personal, so don't spend the company dime on it. I'd just appreciate any quick pointers you could give me."

He'd figure out how he was going to run this by Lilith later.

"Sure." Isabel shrugged, her expression immediately serious. "Anything I can do to help?"

Mitch smiled. She was a good-hearted kid. "Not so far. I'll let you know what comes out of this meeting." He waved, sipped the horrible excuse for coffee, and headed into the morning meeting.

An Irish Wolfhound is a large dog, a *very* large dog. In fact, many books cite the wolfhound as the Largest Dog. It is not uncommon for a male wolfhound to tip the scales at 140 pounds of lean strength, as Cooley did. Jen wasn't even tall enough to look Cooley straight in the eye.

Like most dogs, wolfhounds eat their weight in dogfood every month. Mitch had never even considered joining a gym: the weekly adventure of hauling kibble home and daily task of doling it out for a very interested Cooley— never mind walking the amiable beast—was more than enough aerobics for him.

Characteristically placid, wolfhounds are often referred to as "gentle giants." Loyal and protective, they keep an eye on everyone they consider to be their personal responsibility. Cooley was great with the kids, more than tolerant of Jen's tail-tugging. He lumbered after Jason on the little boy's many adventures and Mitch often felt that the dog was the best sitter they could ever have.

But on this particular Monday morning, Cooley was uncharacteristically riled. It was more than a general sense that his "pack" was in jeopardy—he could smell trouble. With canine certainty, the wolfhound knew that the neighbor with the sunflowers posed a dangerous threat to his family.

He paced the length of the new fence, restless at his confinement in the yard. Cooley shoved his nose into the small gaps in the fence and could barely wedge it through, let alone the rest of him. He pawed at the fence and jumped on it a few times, but this time the fence seemed inclined to stay put.

But there was more than one way to get next door. He couldn't go through the fence or around it, he couldn't jump over the six-foot height, but with some diligence he could go *under* it.

So, determined to save his household, Cooley settled in to dig at the back corner of the lot. Unbeknownst to the dog, he was hidden from view by a particularly large and dangerously prickly thistle.

It would take a long time for such a large dog to dig a tunnel big enough to accommodate his size, but the thistle would ensure that days passed before the time anyone guessed what the dog was up to.

And by then it would be too late.

Much to Lilith's relief, there was no line of panting men at the bookstore that Monday afternoon. A pair of teenagers giggled as they waited for her and an older woman with sad eyes fiddled with her wedding ring.

And a very serious-looking young man waited quietly. He was so different from her usual customers that Lilith thought at first he must not be waiting for her.

He was dressed simply but neatly, in jeans and a white shirt, a black leather backpack at his feet, a sheaf that looked to have been torn out of the yellow pages in his hand. His hair was dark, his skin was fair. He was handsome but unaware of it. He looked about the age to be in university, although he dressed with the somber and well-pressed style of someone older. He sat quietly, barely moving, something about the fathomless darkness—and the steadiness—of his gaze making dread rise in Lilith's throat.

The bookstore owner was delighted to see her. Ryan had decked her little table with fresh flowers and kept saying how he hoped she enjoyed the chocolates. Lilith smiled and thanked him, then beckoned to the teenager first in line. She shuffled her cards, feeling the young man watch her and refusing to consider why he was here.

She knew without doubt that he was *Rom*, the first *Rom* she had faced since all those years ago. The first *Rom* who had ever sought her out. That couldn't be a good thing. Lilith had actively avoided her kind, refusing to consider herself among their ranks.

Because she was not. It was decided and done.

But the young man's presence made her nervous all the same.

Mitch came out of his meeting, buoyed by praise for his final copy on a recycling materials scam, to find crisis ready and waiting.

Isabel waved a phone at him. "Hey, you know that source you hung your story on?"

Mitch's heart sank as he guessed what she was going to say. "Don't tell me."

"He called. He's rescinding. His lawyer says he'll sue." Isabel grimaced. "Mitch, he sounds scared."

Well, that wasn't too improbable. Mitch had sniffed out organized crime connections to this scam, but hadn't been able to substantiate them.

The managing editor spoke from behind Mitch. "Davison, don't lose this one. I've cleared the front page for this." He looked grim. "I want that story, one way or the other."

"Yeah, me too." Mitch turned back to Isabel. "See if you can get him on the phone again. Let me talk to him—we'll try to set up a meeting."

Isabel chewed her lip. "What if he says no?"

"Then I'll find what I need somewhere else," Mitch affirmed, rummaging through the files on his desk. "The story's there and I'm not the only one who knows it. That forensic accountant knew more than he told us, I knew it at the time. I've got his card in here. And the security guard at the plant wasn't surprised. I'll revisit everybody and go over it again."

Isabel's eyes shone. "Wow! Can I tag along?"

"It'll be a long haul."

"But the closest I've been to real reporting yet." Isabel leaned both hands on his desk in her appeal. "Please, Mitch, get me out of the goddamned files."

Mitch considered her for a moment and could understand her frustration. And she could be a great help to him if things were heating up. He looked to the managing editor, who nodded subtle approval.

Mitch flicked the forensic accountant's card at Isabel. "Sweet-talk him into a lunch meeting, just the three of us. Tell him you'll make it look like a date, he was worried before and might be more worried now." Mitch eyed her funky clothing wryly. "But to make it look plausible, Isabel, you're going to have to change."

•   •   •

Even though she sensed the truth, Lilith was still shocked at his first words when he finally took the seat opposite her.

"Rom san?" he asked earnestly, his gaze searching, his pronunciation meticulous.

Are you Rom?

Lilith caught her breath at the question, her gaze flew to meet those eyes so like her own. She licked her lips, then shook her head. "I don't understand," she said flatly, disliking the taste of the lie on her tongue.

But she had made her choice and she would stick with it.

The boy heaved a sigh and frowned. "Neither do I," he confessed quietly and leaned back in his chair, "but my grandmother told me to ask fortune-tellers that until one answered me." He shoved a hand through his hair and looked suddenly very young and burdened. He smoothed the yellow page listings on the table and Lilith saw that he had torn out the section on occult bookstores.

They were crossed out in succession, Ryan's—with its declaration of "Real Fortune-telling on Mondays!" being the one he took a pencil to now.

Lilith couldn't stop her question, although she was certain it was just normal curiosity. "What's wrong?"

He shook his head and summoned a half-hearted smile. "It's really not your problem."

Lilith smiled. "But it might make you feel better to talk about it."

"You're busy."

Lilith indicated the lack of line behind him, her curiosity getting the better of her. "Not now. Tell me."

He looked steadily into her eyes as though considering whether he should do so, then abruptly nodded and leaned closer. "It's my grandmother."

He swallowed and Lilith saw how deeply he was troubled. She guessed the pair were close, that perhaps the grandmother was not well, and felt sorry for the boy opposite her. She wondered if there was anyone else left in his family, and he almost immediately answered her unspoken question.

"She raised me since my parents died and we used to talk all the time. But since she's been in the hospital, she seems to be forgetting English. She's stubborn, though, so maybe she just *refuses* to speak it.''

Lilith watched his fingers tap nervously and thought of another stubborn *Rom* grandmother she had known. ''What does she speak?'' she asked, already fairly certain of the answer.

''*Rom,*'' he declared, and Lilith's heart skipped a beat. ''Gypsy. She's a Gypsy, I guess I am, too. But now, I can't even understand her,'' he confessed with rising frustration. ''No one ever taught me the language. It's like she's pulled away to a place where I can't reach her anymore. I can't help her, or explain what's happening, what the doctors are doing. She has to be scared.''

Lilith's sympathetic heart twisted a little. ''But she must have told you something, otherwise you wouldn't be here.''

''Yeah. She taught me that question last weekend, told me to look for dark-haired, dark-eyed fortune-tellers.'' He smiled sadly. ''She sent me on a search for a Gypsy fortune-teller who could speak *Rom* to her. It's the only English she's spoken in a month and she refused to understand anything after that. The whole thing is nuts, it's never going to work, but I have to try.'' He frowned and heaved a sigh in frustration, his gaze flicking back to Lilith. ''What else am I going to do?''

Lilith studied him and saw more than he probably wanted her to see. ''She's very ill.''

His lips tightened, and he looked down at his hands. ''Yeah. Yeah, she is.'' He shrugged and straightened, deliberately looking at the torn pages once more. ''But like I said, it's not your problem. Thanks for letting me dump a bit. Hey, do you know where Mirvell Street is?''

''It's just west of here. It runs south.''

But he wouldn't find any *Rom* at the occult store there, Lilith knew. Her conviction wavered ever so slightly when she considered the difficulty of the task he had taken on, no less his determination to chase down every lead.

''Why don't you give me your name and a way to reach you?'' she suggested, without ever intending to do so. The boy looked up hopefully, but Lilith tried to keep her words light. ''You never know how things might come together— the world works in mysterious ways.''

He smiled suddenly, then delved in his backpack for a pen and paper. "Now you sound like my grandmother," he commented. He bent to write out an address in a precise hand and probably missed Lilith's quick intake of breath.

Then he thanked her and was gone, his footsteps turning west when he left Ryan's store.

Unfortunately Lilith couldn't wipe the exchange from her mind as easily as that. And she knew it wasn't her imagination that his sheet of paper seemed to generate an insistent heat of its own from the depths of her pocket.

Obviously, she was just jangled from sharing the story of his earlier demise with Mitch on Saturday night. That must be the only explanation for any uncertainty that had crept into her mind.

Because Lilith *knew* she could not do this. There was no question of it. In her mind's eye, Lilith saw again the condemnation in a dozen pairs of dark eyes, etched in the features of those she thought cared for her. The memory was painfully vivid, now that she had dredged it up, and the ache of rejection burned in her chest as though she had just been knifed. Lilith had been judged, found unacceptable, and cast out by those she loved.

She was *mahrime*, after all.

Time had not erased that. No doubt, this old *Rom* woman would reject her, too. To visit her would be inviting a replay of that painful experience.

Lilith just couldn't do it.

The Hermit card, though, separated itself from the deck as she absently shuffled, and Lilith's fingers hovered over it. The man pictured there was elderly, like a guardian in a fairy tale or a pilgrim seeking penitence.

Or like a wise teacher pointing out the thread of meaning that might otherwise be missed in the great tapestry of life.

Lilith thought of Dritta, she thought of a stubborn *Rom* grandmother dying in the alien world of a *gadje* hospital. The prevalence of white alone would make her crazy, white being considered a fiercely unlucky color by the *Rom*.

Lilith frowned when compassion coursed through her and defiantly shuffled The Hermit back into the deck. She even managed to smile for the next person who stepped up to her table.

∙   ∙   ∙

The whole story fell apart in Mitch's hands. Someone had been busy doing some major intimidation. He didn't much care where the leak was, he just wanted to get to the truth and get it on the front page.

His source had not only clammed up, but disappeared.

The longer it took to confirm his story through other sources, the greater the chance that the competition would catch a whiff of what was going on. Mitch met with the managing editor at close of business and that man made the call.

"We don't have enough to run on, not for our reputation," he said with a frown. "You've got another day, Davison. But at four tomorrow, I don't want to be disappointed." He shook a finger at Mitch. "This is good stuff. I want it."

Mitch nodded and ducked out of his boss's office. He eyed his watch, knew he had to pick up the kids. He stuffed every file he could imagine was remotely pertinent into his briefcase and closed up his laptop.

Isabel looked on enquiringly.

"I've got one more day and it's in here somewhere," Mitch informed her grimly. "I'll find another way to get this story, if it takes me all goddamned night."

But when Mitch got into the office the next morning, desperately short of clues and REM sleep, the managing editor was waiting for him.

Not a good sign.

"What was the name of that source who rescinded on you?"

Mitch told him and his boss grimaced. "What's wrong?" Mitch asked.

"He's dead, and not of old age. Maybe it really is a suicide—either way, the story just got bigger." The managing editor looked Mitch right in the eye, handing him a piece of paper. Mitch scanned the notes. "We picked it up on police frequencies—they're down there right now. Get your ass down there, take another day, but get the *whole* story."

Isabel was practically bouncing in her chair in anticipation as the managing editor walked away. She looked positively conservative, the funky color rinsed out of her hair, her floral dress decidedly feminine. "Can I come?"

"Nope, there won't be much there," Mitch declared, pulling out his keys again without even making it to his desk. Thank goodness he had driven in today.

There might not be much to see, but either way, he wasn't going to take Isabel to a crime scene. She really didn't need to be exposed to that kind of gritty reality just yet. "Call that accountant again and hit him hard at lunch. Someone's dead and he can save the world, something like that."

Isabel pouted. "Bill will spout professional standards again."

Bill? Well, she had laid it on. "Then, let him be an anonymous source. He likes you, Isabel, go get him."

Isabel suddenly showed great interest in the papers on her desk, her change of manner catching Mitch's attention. "What?" she demanded when he didn't leave. "Bill's kind of cute."

"What about your bike courier? The one with the legs?"

Isabel waved dismissively. "He was way too much trouble."

Mitch shook his head in amazement. "And you're done with him"—he snapped his fingers—"just like that."

"Well, yeah. It's not a crime to know what you want."

Mitch marveled that there should be two people in his life who thought members of the other sex were disposable accessories. He could have argued whether Isabel really did know what she wanted, but had had that argument too many times with Kurt not to know the ending.

"Nice choice of dress, by the way," he teased instead, guessing the reason for the intern's choice.

Isabel turned scarlet, then wadded up a sheet of computer paper and flung it at Mitch. "So, I was going to call Bill anyway."

Mitch ducked and ran.

"Davison, you be careful out there!"

Oh, yeah, he was going to be. Mitch had an awful lot to live for these days.

On Wednesday afternoon, Lilith was in her yard. The sunlight was golden, the butterflies were flitting, the humidity that had filled the air for all of August was gone. She could smell the tang of autumn in the air, and already see the change in the shade of green in every leaf. The nights had become suddenly cool and sleep was easier.

Everything should have been perfect. But Lilith edged her beds and weeded the garden, oblivious to the peace around her. She hadn't seen Mitch since Sunday and acknowledged that his absence was disappointing. With that stubborn grandmother persistently poking her nose into Lilith's thoughts—and Lilith shoving her out again—the few weeds in the garden didn't have a chance.

Quite suddenly, Lilith heard a scraping. It wasn't a sound that belonged in her yard. When she heard a sniffling, she looked for D'Artagnan, but he was nowhere in sight.

And neither was anything else. The garden suddenly seemed to be oddly still.

Then came the unmistakable sound of scratching. Something was digging in the dirt.

Something was digging a hole in *her* garden!

Lilith turned slowly, looking for the rodent responsible and determined to take action. Her survey was half complete when a whole lot of dog wriggled under the fence, bounded into her yard, and shook several buckets worth of topsoil out of his fur.

Cooley froze when he spotted Lilith.

She stared back at him, realizing a little too late the mission she had forgotten.

The wolfhound's nose and paws were encrusted with dirt, his gaze locked on Lilith. She suddenly had a very bad feeling and took a cautious step back. Cooley's lip curled, and Lilith saw just how very big his canine teeth were. The hair on the back of his neck stood up.

He snarled.

Oh, her antidote had worked very well. Maybe too well.

At this inopportune moment, Lilith remembered reading somewhere that a wolfhound's jaw was strong enough to snap a man's neck.

The dog growled.

Lilith backed away carefully, trying desperately to hide her fear but not coming anywhere near to doing so.

Cooley took a step forward, and Lilith took one back.

The dog took another, he hunkered low as though preparing to lunge and Lilith didn't care whether he saw her fear or not.

She turned and ran. Cooley barked and pounced after her, covering the length of the yard more quickly than she would have believed possible. Lilith made the porch, but her muddy boots slipped and she grabbed the door handle. Cooley barked wildly—he sounded like he was going to gobble her right up.

It seemed his breath was hot on her heels.

And Lilith was afraid. That was a lot of dog. She raced into the house and slammed the inner door just as the dog made the porch with a bound and a skitter of toenails. Lilith leaned her back against the door in relief. Her breath came in hasty puffs; her heart was hammering.

She locked the door, even though she knew it was dumb. D'Artagnan watched her with cool amusement from his perch on the dining room table.

Before Lilith could chide him, Cooley landed against the door with a resounding thump. His bark made the wood vibrate, and the impact of his weight against the door was enough to bounce Lilith off it. She backed across the room, half-afraid the dog would come right through the wood. At the proximity of his nemesis, D'Artagnan disappeared with lightning speed.

But the inner door was made of sterner stuff than the storm door had been.

Cooley barked in a frenzy, scratching at the door as if he would dig his way through it, too. He was snarling and growling. It was as though he couldn't stop himself, as though he couldn't get the idea of attacking her out of his doggy mind.

When it became clear that he couldn't force his way through the door, Lilith let out a shaking breath. She pushed up her sleeves, shed her muddy boots, and turned to her cauldron, determined to see this solved.

And the sooner the better.

10

THE WHEEL OF FORTUNE

It wasn't the most satisfying chase of Cooley's life.

His prey, after all, had gotten away.

Cooley barked and scratched at the door, but made absolutely no progress in getting inside the house. And eventually, in the notable absence of his quarry, his enthusiasm waned.

But that didn't mean that he couldn't make a point. Cooley stalked away from the house, then gave the garden a thorough sniff just in case the woman was hiding there somewhere. He didn't find her, so he marked everything of any size, staking the yard out as an extension of his own territory.

Nature called after all his activity and Cooley hunkered down to make a deposit in the middle of the garden.

"Cooley!" the woman called sweetly before he could really begin.

Cooley's head shot up. There was a porch directly over the door where she had disappeared and she was leaning over the rail.

The temptation was too much.

Cooley ran for the house, barking so that everyone would know the danger she posed to his family. He couldn't get to the balcony, but he lunged against the house and braced his front paws against the brick. He was so busy barking and snarling that he didn't notice her tipping something over the rail.

Until the chilly contents of the pot doused him from head to tail.

Cooley yelped in shock; he jumped away from the house. The liquid was icy cold, whatever it was, and smelled like nothing any respectable dog could stand to smell like. He shook himself, desperately trying to get rid of that stink, wondering whether he could find a dead fish somewhere to roll in. He shivered as cold trickled through to his flesh.

At the touch of the solution on Cooley's skin, everything seemed to brighten for just a moment. Then it faded abruptly back to its usual look, as though nothing had happened at all.

But suddenly, the dog wasn't quite sure what he was doing in the neighbor's yard. He just couldn't remember anything other than his sense of urgency.

A sense of urgency that now seemed inexplicable, even to Cooley.

Cooley blinked. He looked at the garden, but there was no cat in sight. None of his people was here and it seemed there wasn't a very good reason why he had needed to get into this yard so badly.

There was only a great big hole under the fence, and Cooley quite clearly remembered how it had gotten there.

The wolfhound had a sinking feeling that in particular, one of his people wasn't going to like the look of that at all.

He skulked across the yard guiltily and slipped through the hole. He had no sooner begun to roll in the shorn dandelions of his own yard, in an effort to get that smell out of his fur, than the garage opened into the alleyway behind.

Cooley bounded to his feet. The familiar sound of a car hummed a moment later, doors slammed, and a resolute step echoed inside the garage. Before the door of the garage opened, Cooley knew exactly who had come home. He sat up straight and tried to look innocent, the tentative thump of his tail a dead giveaway that he was anything but.

It was Wednesday night and real life was calling. Mitch's feature was safely in production, after that mad last-minute rush that had brought everything into question. Isabel had done a great job worming the lead they needed—albeit anonymously—out of the accountant. They hadn't been able to link the suicide and the scam with definite proof, but

Mitch had found a Mountie he knew and trusted at the scene Tuesday morning.

Clearly, Mitch wasn't the only one who smelled things in the wind—the federal officer was awfully senior to be taking an interest. This morning, Mitch had faxed his notes to the Mountie, knowing dots would be connected and justice would be done.

And his article would be on the front of tomorrow's morning edition. He'd put Isabel's name on the byline and smiled in anticipation of her excitement. It would be her first, and she deserved it.

In a way, he enjoyed when things really hit the fan. He enjoyed the adrenalin rush of having to find another solution while the clock was ticking. But now it was done and gone—another story put to bed—and Mitch could relax.

And right now, he had a whole hour before it was time to pick up the kids. Mitch shoved work out of his mind on the drive home, reminding himself that he had a much more interesting investigation to continue—the one to which his intriguing neighbor held the key.

He rolled down his window and didn't concern himself too much with the snarl of traffic. The sunshine was wonderful, the heat of it on his arm making him feel as though he'd spent too much time inside this week.

And not had nearly enough sleep.

Mitch cut through the university, circumnavigating the first moving vans of the year. In the next week, the campus would be crowded with first-time students moving into the dorms, jaded undergrads moving into the apartments and subdivided houses all around the university. In a week, it would be Labour Day weekend; in a week, Mitch would be in Kansas City; in a week, Andrea would be cruising the Caribbean.

In fact, she'd been delighted when he called this afternoon, declaring that she was going to rush right out and finish shopping for her cruise.

The thought of his stepmother led Mitch's thinking back to Lilith as surely as if he followed a line of bread crumbs home. He thought about the typed summary he had compiled, safely tucked into his briefcase, and decided it was time he went for broke in one corner of his life.

It was unbelievably reassuring that Lilith wasn't trying to hoodwink anyone. It left Mitch free to enjoy her company, instead of trying to unearth her subterfuge. It left Mitch free to make Lilith laugh, to talk to her, to help her fix whatever had gone so sadly wrong.

It let Mitch do his next best thing after investigative reporting. He could fix anything and he was going to fix this.

After all, you never knew what would be lurking around the next corner, never knew what kind of trouble would blindside you unexpectedly. If nothing else, this week had shown Mitch that things couldn't be taken for granted, that anything could change in the blink of an eye.

You had to take chances, risk going after what you really wanted or maybe lose the chance of ever having it at all.

Lilith had awakened something in Mitch that he had put aside a long time ago; she had dredged up all those romantic notions of a good life and a good partnership that he had been certain had nothing to do with him. Mitch didn't know whether he could have those dreams, whether he deserved them, whether he had earned them.

He was going to stretch out and reach for them.

And the first step on that path was seeing Lilith's trauma healed.

In the afternoon sunlight, Mitch decided that he was going to ask Lilith for the whole story of her immortality. It would only be then, when she voiced what had to be an illogical story, that he would be able to persuade her of the fallacy of her memories. She had a sharp mind, after all, and he knew she would see the flaw in her thinking.

And then, Mitch would do his damnedest to convince Lilith to go to one of the psychologists he had found. He'd help her in any way he could—but first, he had to persuade her to listen to his advice.

And that might not be very easy at all. Mitch guessed that people—especially bright people like Lilith—would not take well to being told that there was a fault in their wiring.

The discussion could go either way in Mitch's estimation, but he didn't think he had a lot of choice. It mattered a great deal to him that Lilith be healed—and it was more than worth taking a chance.

• • •

Opportunity presented itself sooner than expected. Mitch stepped out of the garage to find Cooley looking guilty and Lilith in the act of entering into his yard with a spade.

Mitch looked anxiously at the dog when Lilith smiled and waved. "Lilith, I don't think you should come in here like that," he said by way of greeting. "Not after Cooley growled at you last weekend."

"Oh, he's just fine now," she said with a breezy confidence Mitch had a hard time matching.

He looked at the wolfhound, whose expression immediately turned hopeful. That tail swept against the ground, but Mitch frowned.

"How can you be sure?"

"He's had another potion," Lilith confided. Mitch noticed suddenly that Cooley was looking quite damp. The dog stood up and shook himself, launching a volley of water.

Or something. The wolfhound smelled even worse than he usually did when Mitch finally hosed him down. "What happened?"

Lilith laughed. "Cooley came visiting. But he got an unexpected bath." Her explanation didn't exactly make everything crystal clear, but Lilith started shovelling dirt back into a hole that Mitch only just noticed.

Cooley wedged himself into the darkest shadow beside the garage and put his nose on his paws, his gaze fixed expectantly on Mitch.

Nothing like a couple of points getting together to make a line. Mitch suddenly had a very good idea how that hole had come to be.

He dropped his bag and crossed the yard with long steps to Lilith's side. "Let me do that," he insisted, taking the spade from her. "And you can explain all this to me again."

Lilith stepped back slightly—not enough to stop her perfume from assaulting Mitch and making his toes curl—and eyed him carefully. "You look tired," she said softly.

Mitch offered her a rueful smile. "Comes with the territory of putting a story to bed. Some of them wrestle like cranky three-year-olds."

She smiled, then watched Mitch shovel. "Do you do this often?"

Mitch glanced up and shrugged. "It happens." Lilith's eyes were shadowed with concern and Mitch's heart took a little leap at the sight. It had been a while since anyone had worried about him—that was *his* job—but Mitch liked the feeling just fine. He smiled, but Lilith didn't look particularly reassured.

Mitch knew only that he had to make her smile again. He adopted his best Foghorn Leghorn accent. "Fortunately, I keep my feathers numbered for just such an emergency."

To his relief, Lilith chuckled. The sun shone down on them, the yard was filled with the lazy sounds of a summer afternoon, and Mitch didn't want to go anywhere anytime soon. He realized that there was a tranquility to be found in Lilith's presence, a respite from the world and all its woes.

And he liked that just fine.

"The good news is that I have more flexibility these days," Mitch continued easily, enjoying the fact that he could discuss this with her. "I worked here the last couple of nights, after the kids were in bed. Thank God for laptops and modems." He smiled. "And Andrea, my nearly resident lifesaver."

Lilith's smile broadened. "You love it."

Mitch grinned at her. "Yeah, I do," he admitted. "As long as it doesn't happen all the time."

"I'll bet you're good at what you do," she suggested with a confidence in that fact that made Mitch's heart take off at a gallop. He stared at her, unable to remember when anyone other than his father had expressed such confidence in his abilities.

"You can judge for yourself in the morning," he said, less lightly than he might have hoped. "First edition, front page. That's my alibi for not cropping up over the last few days."

And Lilith smiled. "I was concerned," she confessed.

"Don't be. I don't take as many chances as I used to." They smiled at each other for a long, sultry moment, then Mitch turned back to the task at hand.

He shovelled the last of the dirt into the hole, well aware

of Lilith watching him. Mitch drove the spade into the ground, then rested his elbow on the handle to survey Lilith.

He wasn't in a huge hurry to leave. "So, 'fess up," he demanded with a smile. "What did happen here?"

Lilith turned to Cooley, who inched closer on his belly. The dog certainly didn't seem to have the same animosity toward Lilith he had shown before.

Which was pretty weird, come to think of it. What had gotten into the wolfhound lately?

Fortunately, Lilith was prepared to explain.

"After Cooley drank too much of that love antidote last weekend, he disliked me." Her voice was low and very easy to listen to. Mitch felt the last bit of tension ease out of his shoulders. "It wasn't his fault that he growled—the potion was too strong. Apparently, he took it upon himself to continue the hunt this week."

Before Mitch could ask, Lilith gestured to the hole.

"Fortunately, after some thinking, I came up with just the right potion."

Mitch sensed the story was being edited heavily. He wondered what the dog had done when he reached the other side today and suspected he would never know.

"I dumped it on him and it worked like"—Lilith grinned and snapped her fingers—"magick."

Despite his own skepticism, Mitch couldn't stop his own smile. "Magic, eh?"

"Absolutely. Just watch." Before Mitch could stop her, Lilith stretched out a hand and beckoned to the wolfhound. Cooley raced across the yard at this small encouragement, but there was no reason for Mitch to intervene.

The dog licked Lilith's fingers and wagged his tail so hard that he could hardly keep his balance.

Mitch tried to keep his mouth from falling open.

She couldn't be right. There was no such thing as magic, nothing remotely logical about potions. They were place-bos, at best, the belief that they worked being responsible for any results.

Which left the question of how Lilith could convince a dog that a potion worked.

Mitch couldn't reason that through, but knew it was only because he was tired. It was sleight of hand of some kind, and Lilith's belief in magic was just a necessity to protect her cover story.

"Aren't you glad?" Lilith asked.

"Oh, yeah." Mitch reached down and scratched the dog's ears. "Good to have you back to normal, ol' boy." Cooley nuzzled Mitch's knee and thumped his tail against Mitch's legs, his usual self in every way.

What was more important was how Mitch was going to raise the subject he really wanted to talk about.

"You seem distracted," Lilith commented when Mitch didn't say anything else. "Would you like to talk about it?"

It was the best opening he could have had. Mitch glanced at his watch, seeing that he didn't have long to get to the day care. He'd never get through this in five minutes!

"Well, it's a long story," he began, wondering whether they could meet after he got back.

But Lilith smiled outright. "And who has more time on their hands than an immortal, hmm?"

Mitch looked up in surprise. It was as though she had read his thoughts, but then it was hardly the first time he'd had that feeling with Lilith. Talk about cutting to the chase. Mitch decided not to look a gift horse in the mouth.

"You've got to admit that's a pretty uncommon claim," he said carefully.

Lilith nodded. "True. The secret of immortal life *is* carefully guarded. Do you know what would happen if the elixir fell into the wrong hands?"

Mitch declined to pursue that line of wild speculation. "So, how did you find it?"

Lilith shook her head with a smile. "Not *found*. I earned the right to a sip, after seven years in the tutelage of a company of sorcerers."

"This would be after you left the Gypsies?"

"Yes, I travelled west, as Dritta had counselled me." Lilith frowned, apparently in recollection. "She had heard of these people and told me to seek them, that my Gift would help me find them."

"Your gift of finding people's true loves?"

"No, no, not that. That came later. My Gift is the ability to see the future."

Mitch watched Cooley as he scratched the dog's ears, not wanting any hint of his rampant skepticism to throw this discussion off track.

Wherever the hell it was going.

The trick was just to keep asking questions.

"Well, how did it change?" he asked as mildly as he could.

"When I sipped the elixir, that changed my Gift. Maybe it honed it. I don't know, but from then on, it was focused and I could see destined loves right in people's eyes." Lilith shrugged and smiled. "Maybe it was because I had love in my mind when I drank."

"Right." Mitch couldn't hold her trusting gaze. "So, being able to see the future helped you find these sorcerers?"

Lilith's smile flashed unexpectedly. "At the time I thought it did, but maybe it was chance. Or maybe they found me."

Mitch couldn't help interjecting, "Maybe it was destiny?"

Lilith laughed merrily. "Maybe! I only know that I practically stumbled over them after I'd been alone for several years. They took me in, despite what they called the rawness of my skills, and began an apprenticeship."

She heaved a sigh of satisfaction and frowned slightly as she sobered. Her voice turned thoughtful. "It was the most challenging and rewarding thing I have ever done."

Mitch refused to think about military enlistment advertising campaigns. "How's that?"

"It was *hard*!" Lilith stared across the yard, a sure sign that she was thinking of something sensitive. Mitch dared to hope he was making progress. "There were times when I didn't think I'd survive," she admitted quietly.

Mitch's heart tightened. She had been through a lot, that much was for certain. And he was going to put everything to rights, if it was the last damn thing he did.

Lilith lifted her hand to halt Mitch's question before it came. "But don't ask me for details, I was sworn to secrecy and can't tell anything of what I witnessed among them or even of what I did."

A pledge of confidence was a pretty convenient little

trick, Mitch had to admit. No doubt it veiled some pretty painful memories—he'd leave uncovering that to the pros. "But you were there seven years?"

"Graduated with honors," Lilith confirmed with a small smile.

And she should be proud of herself. Even if she had worked up a complicated story to protect herself, Lilith had survived—and in Mitch's view that was worthy of honors.

But it was high time the mood lightened around here. *"Magnus cum laude?"* Mitch teased, wanting to see that smile widen.

But Lilith sobered. "Mitch, it was a very solemn event. Many adepts don't even survive the ceremony. The graduation and opening of the seventh seal is the final test. Only those who pass win a chance to sip the elixir of immortality."

Okay, she had headed to weird again. Mitch frowned and tried to think of a diplomatic way to make his point.

He couldn't, so he just laid it out. He managed to keep his tone thoughtful. "You would think that, over the centuries, there would end up being an awful lot of immortals in the world."

Lilith glanced up quickly. "And you're saying there aren't?"

"You're the first I've met."

She smiled. "You obviously travel in the wrong circles."

"Lilith!" This really wasn't working out as Mitch had intended. Lilith was sticking to her story like contact cement—and he was running out of time. "I'm serious."

"So am I," she said easily. "But the fact is that the vast majority of those who win the right to a sip *decline* the opportunity."

That unexpected comment gave Mitch pause. He eyed Lilith and his curiosity got the better of him. "Why would they do that?"

Lilith's expression turned sad. "Because the wisdom they have already gained has shown them that immortality can be a very lonely business."

"But you sipped?"

Her glance was bright. "I had no choice. I had only sought them out to win the chance for this sip. I *had* to have immortality—there was no other way I could have waited for you.''

Mitch frowned in concentration as he tried to find a question that would bring the truth to light, the truth he knew was hiding behind this fable. He not only had to find a hole in Lilith's logic, but show it to her to make her reconsider. ''But if I was going to be reincarnating, why couldn't you do the same?''

Lilith shook her head. ''In retrospect, it's clear that I could have. At the time, I thought we were just slightly out of synchronization. I didn't imagine it would take so very long. And by the time I realized the truth, I had already taken that sip. It was too late.''

Mitch tried not to sound skeptical, he really did. ''And you've been immortal ever since that sip?''

Lilith met his gaze with easy assurance. ''Yes. The elixir takes the one who imbibes it out of the stream of time. I stand still—like a rock in the river—while everything swirls around and past me.''

She shrugged as though this made perfect sense—which Mitch might have found difficult to argue if Lilith hadn't glanced back to Cooley's hole.

Because when she did, a single hair nearly buried in the dark tangle of her hair winked in the sunlight.

A single silver hair.

Mitch's heart leapt, but he tried to sound casual while he confirmed his suspicion. ''So, I guess you don't age, then?''

''Not since that moment. I'm eternally thirty-three years old.''

Mitch leaned on the shovel, trying to look nonchalant even when he sensed victory was nearly within his grasp. ''Sounds like a vain woman's dream. No wrinkles, no face-lifts.'' He paused significantly. ''No gray hairs.''

Lilith smiled sunnily. ''No, never a one in over five hundred years.''

''Then what's that?'' Mitch pointed to what he had just spotted.

Lilith raised one hand to her hair and frowned. ''What?''

''You can't see it because of the angle, but you *do* have a gray hair.''

Her eyes flashed. ''Impossible! I can't!''

"You certainly do," Mitch argued resolutely.

"I don't believe it."

"Then hold your breath and I'll show it to you." Mitch gently worked the offending hair free of the others around it, an easy task since it was of coarser texture than Lilith's silky tresses, and gave it a tiny yank.

She yelped, then her eyes widened when he presented it to her. The hair shone in the sunlight, unmistakably white, even as her fingertips massaged its source.

Lilith didn't seem to have anything to say; she just accepted the hair as though she couldn't believe it was real.

There was a glimmer in her eyes that made Mitch think that she was reconsidering everything she had told him, that maybe a few dots were teaming up to make a line.

This had to be a revelation of a kind. He could almost sense a door opening in her mind. Lilith was a smart lady, after all. Maybe all she needed was a moment to herself.

"It's not the end of the world," Mitch teased gently. "Let's hope three don't grow in its place."

Lilith stared up at him silently. She turned the hair in her fingers and stared at it again. "I don't understand," she said softly. "It's impossible."

"Clearly, it's not." Mitch touched her cheek with a gentle fingertip. "We're all getting older, Lilith," he said quietly. "I've pulled a few of those out myself."

"No! I'm not supposed to age," she insisted, her gaze fixed on the hair.

"Well, maybe something has changed," Mitch whispered. She looked up in alarm at this sentiment and Mitch smiled encouragingly. "It's not so bad. You'll see."

Lilith opened her mouth and closed it again. She frowned at the hair, then shook her head slightly. She looked so lost that Mitch wanted to gather her up and make everything better, but this was a hurdle she had to jump herself. Clearly, Lilith had some things to work through—and if her trauma had been as bad as Mitch feared, he had probably already pushed far enough.

He bent, unable to stop the tenderness flooding through him, and kissed her brow. "It's okay, Lilith," he said quietly. "I'll help you. You can come and talk about it anytime, whenever you're ready." She met his gaze, her own expression so vulnerable that Mitch's heart clenched. "Just say the word and I'll brew up some sangria," he promised, and was glad to see her fleeting smile.

"I just need to think," she said quietly.

"I know. Just remember that I'm here."

And then she really smiled, her eyes so warm that Mitch didn't want to leave her side at all. "I know," she said, stretching suddenly to press a quick kiss to his cheek. "And that's the best news of all."

She turned, hefted her spade, and strode back to her gate, that hair held before her like a trophy.

Admiration flooded through Mitch as he watched her go, admiration along with a certainty that Lilith would see her way through this. It wasn't easy to open doors that had been securely locked for a long time, but Mitch knew that Lilith would manage it.

She was really something special.

Lilith couldn't believe her own eyes. The silver hair waved in her grip as though it deliberately taunted her, as if its presence wasn't bad enough.

How could it be here?

Lilith didn't remember anything about the elixir wearing off over the years or any maintenance technicalities that she could have forgotten over the centuries. She put the hair down on her kitchen counter and stared at it.

This just wasn't right.

But the hair was here. And it was gray. And her scalp still hurt from where Mitch had evicted it. No doubt about it, it was her own.

What was it doing here?

Lilith frowned, then went into the living room and looked at the cards. The Wheel of Fortune was faceup now, right beside The Hermit. The first circle was complete, the first phase of Mitch's journey finished.

The challenge of the physical world had been met, but the confrontation with the spiritual world had only just begun. The seeker on the card descended into the underworld, seeking wisdom and abandoning himself to the illusion of controlling his fate. Great forces were in the wind when

The Wheel of Fortune appeared, powerful changes over which one had no direct influence.

Lilith sat down and looked at the card. The Wheel of Fortune whispered of taking chances, of throwing the dice, of betting it all, win or lose, of dancing a jig with the capricious partner named Dame Fortune.

A chance had been taken, or was in the act of being taken, a chance that could have long-reaching repercussions. Lilith thought about her gray hair, she thought about Mitch, she thought about him coming back to her.

He was right. Something *had* changed.

In fact, everything that mattered had changed. Mitch had returned to her—her one true love was right by her side.

Lilith's hand rose to her lips in delighted realization. She didn't need to wait anymore. She didn't need to be immortal anymore. In fact, life would be a whole lot easier if she and Mitch aged together, now that they had found each other again.

It looked as though her immortality was a thing of the past. And Lilith didn't have too many complaints about that. If anything, the gray hair was just a sign that they were solidly on the road to Happily Ever After.

But why the gray hair *now*? Had it been merrily growing, unbeknownst to Lilith, since Mitch's arrival?

Or was it new?

Lilith didn't know. When she looked down at the cards again, the next one had flipped over. Lilith had been sitting right there and she hadn't seen it move.

Yet all the same, Fortitude, number eleven, was turned up.

The Ferris Wheel of Fortune had completed its turn.

FORTITUDE

Fortitude was called Strength in one of Lilith's other decks, but the image upon it was essentially the same. Pictured on the card was a young woman in the act of prying open the jaws of a ferocious lion.

The card tells of conquering one's own shadow, of coming to terms with the conflict within one's own soul, of meeting a challenge with gentleness instead of brute force.

And reigning victorious, when the alternative might have been expected. The card indicates the power of inner strength, of conviction, of a fortitude born of belief in doing the right thing.

Mitch had an ample measure of that kind of fortitude, Lilith knew, and the realization made her smile.

She suddenly heard the children in the backyard and glanced up to find the shadows drawing long in the unlit house. Lilith didn't know how long she had sat there, meditating on the card, but it didn't matter.

Mitch would be where his children were, watching over them like a gruff guardian angel.

And Lilith knew exactly where she wanted to be.

Mitch sat on his back porch as the kids ran around the yard after dinner. He was perfectly content to let them burn off some steam before bed and was hoping that Lilith might make an appearance.

To his delight, she stepped out on her porch almost immediately. Mitch wondered whether Lilith could have been waiting for him and felt himself smile in welcome.

He liked how she smiled in response. The hinges creaked as Lilith let herself into the yard. Cooley trotted over to give her a sniff and collect a pat. The change in the dog's manner was amazing, but there had to be a reasonable explanation.

There had to be.

"Lillit!" The kids immediately ran for Lilith, their eyes shining as they told her all the stories they'd saved up since the weekend. She squatted down and listened to every word, asking perfect questions, sharing her attention between the two.

Mitch's smile returned as he watched. Jen and Jason really had taken to Lilith—and she seemed just as delighted to talk to them.

Jen's newest finger painting had been hung on the fridge—and Lilith waved on her way past Mitch as she was dragged into the kitchen to admire the handiwork.

She did and Jen beamed with pride. Mitch had a feeling that Lilith would soon have a masterpiece for her own fridge door.

"Have you noticed," Lilith asked the kids when they came back on the porch, "that the bats have been out these past few nights?"

Mitch was immediately beset by two children demanding approval to stay up late and watch for bats. He couldn't see why not, so he agreed and laughed when the kids cheered. He and Lilith dragged lawn chairs out into the middle of the yard as the sun sank below the line of houses behind. Mitch shut off the kitchen and porch lights and they sat in the twilight, waiting for darkness to fall.

When it did, the peculiar flying patterns of a trio of bats could be discerned against the night sky. Jason was entranced, but Jen nodded off to sleep in Mitch's lap. The bats circled, flying in a lopsided figure eight over and over again as they gobbled up mosquitos. They called to each other, a sound that was barely discernible by human ears, and one that would be missed by anyone not paying close attention.

Mitch hadn't known they could still be found in the city. Jason ran out of whispered questions and watched in wide-eyed silence. The rhythm of the bats' flight was soothing, the occasional flutter of their wings like a whisper in the night. Mitch leaned back in his chair to watch them fly the same course over and over again, letting the evening's quiet flood through him.

He hadn't felt so relaxed in years. It was wonderful, just sitting in darkness and silence, watching the stars come out, holding his sleeping daughter. Yet at the same time, there was a tingle of electricity running beneath Mitch's skin, a tingle fed by the occasional waft of jasmine, the glint of an alluring woman's smile, the knowledge that Lilith was just an arm's length away.

Tranquility, that's what Lilith shared with him.

Not to mention cats and toads and bats.

But then, she had said she was a witch, hadn't she? Mitch grinned to himself, glancing over at Jason and noting that he had also succumbed to the sandman. He was dozing against Lilith's shoulder, and she looked perfectly content to have him there.

Her gaze met Mitch's and she smiled, a warm, welcoming smile that made his toes curl. It was a smile that made Mitch think of all that old-fashioned stuff, all those things that he'd been sure would never come his way—cooking together and sitting on the porch, laughing and making love for a lifetime.

All that good stuff.

He impulsively reached over and caught Lilith's hand in his. When Mitch squeezed her fingers, she squeezed his back, then they both watched the bats fly until the moon rose.

The bats retired or sought their prey elsewhere—Mitch was sure they couldn't have eaten every mosquito in his yard—and he stretched, shifting Jen's weight.

"I should put these two to bed," he said softly, then got to his feet. He glanced down at Jen's dirty knees and grinned. "I guess there's more than one way to get out of taking a bath."

Lilith chuckled and sat forward a bit. "I think I'm trapped," she whispered just as Jason stirred.

"Come on, sport," Mitch cajoled and tousled his son's hair. "Time for bed."

But Jason snuggled against Lilith.

Mitch met her gaze, unable to stop his smile. "You are trapped."

"We could switch."

"You don't think Jen's too heavy for you?"

Lilith shook her head. "I can manage."

They did switch, Lilith following Mitch into the house and up the stairs, both of them carrying sleepy little burdens. Having Lilith's presence behind him felt perfectly natural. It made Mitch feel less alone, less responsible for every little thing, less burdened by the weight of the world. They were only putting his children to bed, but he had a tantalizing taste of being on a team.

He watched Lilith carry Jen and noted the protectiveness in the way she held his daughter, a gentleness in her fingertips and her voice when she laid the little girl on her bed. Mitch was humbled that Lilith could show such easy affection for children that were not even her own, children she didn't even know that well.

He could never imagine Janice this way.

Because Janice had never been as giving as Lilith.

The words resonated with truth. Mitch frowned in thought as he changed the children into their pajamas and then tucked them into their beds. He had always been sure that the fault in his failed marriage was his, that he had brought something out in Janice that otherwise would never have found voice, that his failure to love her enough or understand her intuitively or *something* he had done had been at the root of her lack of interest in their children.

Now, he wondered whether Lilith was right in her insistence that it wasn't all his fault.

Maybe he wasn't so bad at relationships, after all.

Mitch met Lilith at the top of the stairs, and was snared by the flash of her smile. He paused beside her, listening to the kids sleep behind, and stared into the shadows of her eyes.

He thought about kissing her and her smile quirked.

When Lilith reached out and touched his jaw, it was as though she read Mitch's thoughts. Or that their thoughts were as one. Either way, the tingle beneath his skin became a roar and he edged closer, unwilling to leave any distance between them.

"You were right, you know," Lilith whispered, her voice low and musical. She stepped closer, her breasts almost touching his chest, and the heat in the hall escalated.

Mitch let his hands fall on Lilith's waist; his fingers gripped her slenderness. He drew her minutely closer. "About what?"

"Something *did* change," Lilith admitted. Her eyes shone. "I'm not immortal and it's all because you're here."

Relief surged through Mitch, mingled with pride that Lilith was making such good progress in coming to terms with whatever demons haunted her. She had only to stretch toward him before he bent and met her halfway, his mouth closing over hers resolutely. He didn't care if she knew how much he wanted her, he didn't care if she guessed how he was feeling. This time he backed Lilith into the wall, loving how she responded to his touch.

There was no hesitation in her ardor, no strings on her passion, no negotiations necessary to win a single kiss. Mitch realized suddenly how Janice had cheated him with her constant complaints, her raw dislike of any show of affection.

He wondered suddenly whether she had even loved him.

Lilith insisted she did love him and gave of herself openly. Lilith never turned away, Lilith never snarled, Lilith gave and gave and gave.

And Mitch liked that very much. He knew that whatever this was between himself and Lilith was just the beginning of something very good, something that would improve with time, like fine wine.

But no sooner had Mitch lifted his lips from hers, than Lilith hauled the rug out from beneath him and challenged his conclusions once again.

He ought to be getting used to that by now, but he wasn't.

Not by a long shot.

"Maybe you *were* a sorcerer in one of your past lives," Lilith mused as she stared up at Mitch. Her heart was hammering in the wake of his kiss, but she was fighting her urge to drag him off and ravish him.

She had agreed to his terms, after all.

"What do you mean?"

Lilith slid her hands up the strength of Mitch's neck and let her fingers wind their way into his hair. "We certainly do make powerful magick between us," she teased. "It's worth sacrificing immortality, there's no doubt about it."

Mitch froze. "Sacrificing? I thought you had realized you were mortal?"

"I am *now*."

His gaze flickered, but otherwise Mitch was as still as a statue. His voice was very low. "Maybe you could run through that a little more slowly for me."

"I was immortal, for five hundred and"—Lilith did some quick math—"sixty-seven years, I guess it would be."

She smiled because Mitch looked suddenly so very grim. "But that's all right, because once my love was back by my side"—she stretched and gave him a quick kiss so he wouldn't have any confusion over who that individual was—"the elixir apparently wore off."

"Just like that?" Mitch asked dryly. He pulled back slightly and gave her a skeptical glance.

"Magick!!" Lilith declared and chuckled under her breath. "Honestly, I couldn't have planned it better myself. The great forces have given us the greatest gift of all."

Mitch looked somewhat less than convinced. But then, this was news to him while Lilith had been thinking it through for a few hours. He'd see it her way in a minute, Lilith knew. She linked her arm companionably through his and urged him toward the stairs.

"Just think about it, Mitch. It wouldn't be right if you aged and I didn't, and it would be very strange if neither of us aged at all. I can't even imagine how confusing it would be for Jen and Jason. And then, I would ultimately be left alone again, which could hardly be part of any divine plan." Lilith shook her head. "No, this is absolutely perfect."

Mitch looked a bit dazed.

Maybe he was tired. Yes, he must be exhausted after pulling that story together.

Maybe Lilith should make the sangria.

They were halfway down the stairs when a sudden

thought came to Lilith. "Oh!" She spun and locked her arms around Mitch's neck, treating him to a big kiss. "Mitch, maybe I could even have children now!"

Exasperation flitted across Mitch's brow. "Lilith, those kinds of things don't just change because people meet each other. . . ."

"Don't be silly, of course they do. I couldn't have children because my cycles stopped when I drank the elixir. But if I'm mortal, they'll start again!" Lilith nearly skipped down the remaining steps, knowing she had never been so enthused about receiving her monthly visitor in the past. "And all those hormones will get back to work! Ha! We *will* be able to have kids!"

She spun at the bottom of the stairs triumphantly and looked back at Mitch.

He remained on the third stair. He had his arms folded across his chest and looked markedly less delighted than Lilith about this news.

Oh, no. Lilith sobered. "You don't want more kids?" she asked quietly, hearing the disappointment in her tone. "I guess it doesn't really matter, and you do have two little darlings already. . . ."

"Lilith!" Mitch swore with soft eloquence, shoved a hand through his hair, and marched down the stairs. He caught Lilith's elbow in his hand and led her determinedly to the back porch. "We have to talk," he said grimly.

Lilith bit her lip, unable to contain her unhappiness. "I suppose that if you feel strongly about it . . ."

"Lilith!" Mitch spun her to face him when they reached the back porch and caught her shoulders in his hands. "I *love* kids. I could have twenty of them, as long as I could figure out how to feed them and send them to university. That's *not* the problem."

Hope fluttered in Lilith's heart. She felt her smile dawn anew. "Really?"

"Really." Mitch visibly gritted his teeth, then looked her dead in the eye. "But we are getting a bit ahead of things here."

Lilith folded her arms across her chest and stared up at him, not liking the sound of this at all. "I can't imagine what you mean. You're my true love, I'm yours—if nothing else, the loss of my immortality proves that we're destined to be together—''

"Stop!" Mitch interrupted before she could continue. "Let's just linger there for a moment. Think about what you call the loss of your immortality."

Mitch was so serious that Lilith did what he said. "Are you worried that I've not really become mortal?" she asked carefully.

Mitch's lips thinned. "Hardly that." He paused and looked into her eyes, his hesitation in choosing his words making Lilith brace herself for whatever he was going to say. "Lilith, were you ever really immortal at all?"

Lilith chuckled; she couldn't help it. He was so solemn—and his question was so ludicrous. "Of course I was! How else would I survive the better part of six centuries?" She shook her head at him. "People don't live that long, Mitch."

If she hadn't known better, she would have thought he ground his teeth. "But Lilith, how could it just change? How could it just go away?" Mitch flung out his hands. "How could this elixir keep you from aging for so long, then just stop working? How could it be cognizant of changes in your life? There's not a bit of it that makes sense."

Lilith smiled easily. "Magick makes perfect sense on its own terms."

"*Magic?*" Mitch paced the width of the porch. He rubbed his brow, muttered something about "making progress," then came back to face her again. His lips were drawn to a thin line, his eyes were devoid of a twinkle. "Lilith, it's time we got to the bottom of this. You have to know that there is no such thing as magic, that potions don't work, that no one can see the future."

Lilith blinked. Then she laughed. "I don't know any such thing!"

But Mitch didn't smile. He watched her and a sadness dawned in his eyes.

Lilith sobered as cold dread slithered down her spine. She took a step closer so she wouldn't miss any change in Mitch's eyes. "You're not serious?"

Mitch held her gaze unflinchingly. "That was my question."

Lilith gasped, the conviction in his golden eyes doing nothing to reassure her. Thank goodness she was still there in the shadows of his eyes!

But was her image getting smaller? Fainter?

How could Mitch not believe in magick? Lilith had to persuade him! "Of course there's such a thing as magick! The world is full of magick, everywhere you turn you catch another glimpse of the great forces at work."

Mitch looked decidedly unconvinced.

"What about Kurt?" Lilith demanded. "What about Those Men? What about Cooley?"

Mitch just shook his head. "There has to be another explanation. Potions and spells don't work, Lilith. There are no love spells, no antidotes, no great forces of magic at work. It's just the world, just life. It's just the way things are."

Lilith knew she looked skeptical now. "You aren't going to try and tell me that *life* isn't magickal, in and of itself?"

"Science—"

"Phooey on science!" Lilith interrupted sharply. "There isn't a scientist alive who can satisfactorily explain why those bean plants came out of those seeds." She pointed to the plants that had unfurled from the beans she and Jason had planted just a week before. "Or what makes a baby's heart start to pound, or why a child is formed of sperm and ovum some of the time and not others. Can you explain Jen and Jason with mathematics and theorems?"

"I can't," Mitch admitted uneasily. "But I'm sure that someone could."

"No one can," Lilith replied with heartfelt urgency. "Because there's something there beyond the cell division and the genetics, something that no one can put their finger right on. The whole reason *why* is beyond our comprehension. The impetus in the first place is unexplained, never mind the caprice of the same factors not always leading to the same result. It's magick, Mitch, it's magick as old as all the earth, which has a special kind of magick all its own."

"Lilith, the earth is just a great big rock. . . ."

"No. The earth is *magick*, right to its bones. There's magick in the air and in the ground and in the sea. No one can tell me why my roses grow bigger and redder when I talk to them, or how all of a plant—or even its blueprint—fits into a single tiny seed. No one can fully explain how the birds know when to go south or how they find their way to somewhere they've never been, or how my perennials know when it's really spring and not just a false start. It's magick, a magick that the creatures all around us understand and that we willingly deny."

Lilith waited. She hoped desperately that her argument was going to make some impact. She just couldn't imagine living with and loving a man who didn't believe in magick.

Especially given all they'd been through together. How could Mitch deny what had finally brought them back together again?

But much to Lilith's disappointment, deny it he did.

"Well, I don't believe in magic," Mitch declared with the definitive air of a man who has closed an argument, once and for all.

Lilith, however, was not prepared to let this go so easily. It was too important.

"Really?" She leaned closer and poked a finger into his chest. "Then how did I know you, and how did you know me? How did you end up living right beside me?"

"Lilith, we've been through all that. . . ."

"Clearly not, if you don't understand. This is *magick*, Mitch. There is something special between us that no scientific theorem can explain." She let her voice drop low and knew by the quick flick of Mitch's gaze that she had his attention. "Ask your scientists why my heart skips a beat when I see you."

Mitch glanced up suddenly at this admission and Lilith smiled right into his eyes. "It's not some textbook biological mating urge, because it doesn't happen when I see anyone else. It doesn't happen whenever a handsome healthy man crosses my path. Just *you*. It's magick, a magick that only applies to you and me."

Lilith framed Mitch's face in her hands and felt his conviction waver ever so slightly. He caught his breath as she moved closer. The velvet of the night seemed to press in

on them from all sides, and she knew she had to persuade
him of this one simple truth.

"Do you feel that tingle?" Lilith whispered, and when
Mitch looked into her eyes, she knew he had. There was a
fire in his gaze fueled by the very magick they made between them.

Lilith lifted Mitch's fingertips to the flutter of her pulse
at her throat. "What about that?" She brushed her own
fingertips across Mitch's chest and pressed her fingers
against the thump of his own increased heartbeat.

"That's not chemistry," she insisted softly, "it's magick. *Our* magick. It's recognition—despite an incredible
difference of time and place, despite the odds, despite even
the difference of the skin you're in. How can you imagine
that it's anything else?"

Mitch stared down at Lilith as though he couldn't look
away. She smiled up at him and eased to her toes, liking
how his eyes flashed and his arms slid around her.

He whispered her name, then bent and kissed her with
an ardor that made Lilith's heart sing. He might not be
persuaded completely, but she was definitely making progress.

When Mitch lifted his head tantalizingly long moments
later, his pulse was thundering in his ears. Lilith caught her
breath and smiled just for him. "Magick," she whispered
with delight, then ran a fingertip across his lips.

Her sure touch made him shiver, but Mitch stubbornly
attributed that to simple biology. All the same, it was clear
he wasn't going to make much headway against Lilith's
convictions, at least not tonight.

Maybe this was just another step in working toward an
acceptance of what had really happened to her in the past.
Mitch took a deep breath, looked into Lilith's glowing eyes,
and decided it was worth letting the lady chart her own
course. He supposed that someone who made a business of
telling fortunes would need to have at least a cursory faith
in magic.

Mitch conceded that he had finally met someone who not
only refused to follow his rules, but did it so enchantingly
that he was more than happy to let her continue.

That made Mitch smile.

In fact, predictability was starting to lose its allure in this woman's presence. It was time to go with the flow a bit. Mitch took a deep breath and deliberately changed the subject.

"So, what have you been up to this week?" he asked mildly. He caught Lilith's hand in his and led her to sit on the top step of the porch. Her shoulder bumped against his in a way that made him think of that kiss they had just shared and consider the merits of sharing another. "Make any more lovematches?"

Lilith shrugged and looked across the yard. "Oh, nothing particularly worthy of note," she said, but there was an undercurrent to her tone.

Mitch really liked that Lilith was as lousy of a liar as he was.

"Doesn't sound like it," he suggested.

Lilith smiled and shook her head. "It's not important."

But Mitch knew it was. He reached out and touched her chin, turning her to face him. In the light falling from the kitchen, he saw the shadow that had set up camp in Lilith's eyes.

Something *was* bothering her. Mitch had a sudden fear that his earlier comments hadn't been so readily absorbed as he had hoped. Dread rose in his chest and threatened to choke him. Had he pushed Lilith too far, too fast?

His voice sharpened. "What's wrong?"

Lilith started to shrug, but Mitch wanted to know the worst of whatever he had done.

"Tell me." He smiled encouragement and winked for her. "You can trust me, can't you?"

To Mitch's relief, Lilith smiled in turn. She even leaned her head against his shoulder. Mitch slipped his arm around her waist, liking the press of her warm curves against his side.

"A young man came to see me on Monday," Lilith admitted quietly. "He was *Rom*."

Mitch glanced down at her. "Gypsy?"

Lilith nodded but didn't continue. Mitch's imagination conjured up all sorts of possibilities as to why this would trouble Lilith, very few of which he liked.

"Did he bother you?"

She half-laughed. "Yes, but not in the way you mean." Lilith straightened and tossed back her hair, flicking a hesitant glance upward to Mitch. "He wanted me to visit his grandmother."

Mitch didn't understand the connection. "Why?"

"She won't speak English any more. She's in the hospital." Lilith frowned and Mitch knew she hadn't been unaffected by the young man's visit. "I think she's dying," she added quietly.

"What did he expect you to do?" Mitch wondered whether the visitor had expected some kind of mumbo jumbo healing ceremony with Lilith at the center of it all.

And Lilith taking the blame when magic didn't deliver the cure.

Well, Mitch wasn't going to let *that* happen. His protectiveness was just gearing up when Lilith's next words killed the engine.

"He wanted me to talk to her," she admitted softly. "In *Rom*. Translate, I guess."

That sounded pretty harmless. In fact, Mitch couldn't immediately discern what the trouble was. "What did you say?"

"I said no."

"You didn't want to get involved?"

"No." Lilith's lips set. "I am not *Rom* anymore." Her fingers were tightly knotted together, a sure sign that this wasn't an easy choice for her to make.

Mitch sensed that there was something important behind this assertion. Could Lilith be discarding select parts of her "cover story"? He reached out and ran one fingertip over her knuckles, wanting to help but not push. "Do you speak *Rom*?"

Lilith's answer didn't come immediately.

Mitch simply waited.

"I used to," she finally said.

"Then what's the harm in talking to her?"

Lilith's gaze swivelled and locked with his. "I am still *mahrime*. She won't talk to me."

Mitch had forgotten that part of the story. "Did you tell him that?"

"No. He wouldn't have understood."

Mitch studied Lilith's profile silently for a long moment. He knew the sound of fear when he heard it—and he also recognized something that might help Lilith deal with her past all by herself. It was so tantalizingly close—she could reach for this solution and Mitch would be right behind her.

"I have to admit," he said quietly, "that doesn't sound like you."

That got Lilith's attention. "What do you mean?"

"Do whatsoever you will but harm none," Mitch quoted quietly. "Don't you think your denial is hurting this woman? And what about her grandson?"

Lilith's eyes filled with sudden tears, but she didn't speak.

"I've never seen you turn away from anyone or anything, Lilith," Mitch added softly. "Although we haven't known each other long, I can see that you always give. Why not this time?"

But if Mitch was expecting his question to make a crack in the veneer of her elaborate story, he was destined to be disappointed.

Lilith's hands unclenched and she caught at Mitch's hand. "I'm afraid she'll reject me." Lilith took a shaking breath, surprising Mitch with this display of vulnerability. His protectiveness roared. "The way they did before. It was awful to see their eyes. . . ."

Mitch squeezed her fingertips and halted that painful story before she could get too far into it. "But what if she doesn't?" he dared to suggest. "What if she needs you just as much as you need her?"

Lilith turned and stared into Mitch's eyes. He didn't break her regard, and he didn't know what she saw, but after a few moments, she bowed her head.

She sighed. "I just don't know what to do."

But Mitch had a very distinct sense that this was important, that this was something Lilith needed to do. "Do you want me to go with you?"

That offer made her smile, her hand rise to Mitch's cheek. Lilith's thumb slid over his lip, her eyes shone slightly. "You'd do it, wouldn't you?" There was a thread of wonder in her voice that reminded Mitch of how self-reliant she'd had to become.

He smiled for her. "You bet."

That made Lilith ease closer. She brushed her lips across Mitch's so slowly that he felt a thrill run all the way down to his toes. "I think you know what it means to be a giving person," she murmured, her gaze roving over his features, "because you're a very giving man yourself."

Before Mitch could answer that, Lilith framed his face in her hands and kissed him deeply. He caught her against him, savoring the sweetness of her kiss, the delicacy of her waist beneath his hand.

Finally, Lilith pulled away, depositing a featherlight kiss on each corner of his mouth as though she couldn't resist him. "I'll think about it," she pledged.

Admiration flooded through Mitch that Lilith was working so steadily toward unravelling her past by herself. He was fiercely glad that he had been able to help her, even in such a small way.

"You look exhausted," she said softly, and Mitch had to nod concession.

"Two all-nighters have a way of getting to you." He yawned, then looked into her eyes. "You all right?"

"Fine." Lilith rose and strolled to the gate, waving her fingertips at him from her porch. "I think I could get used to having a champion around," she mused, then smiled. Mitch smiled as he got to his feet in turn.

"There's no rest for the wicked," he complained amiably. "See you tomorrow night?"

Much to Mitch's disappointment, Lilith shook her head. "I have readings booked every evening this week, but surely we'll see each other on the weekend."

"Kurt and I will probably end up waking you up."

"But the fence is done."

"This weekend, we're going to patch the roof."

"Is Andrea going to watch the children?"

Mitch grimaced. "I haven't asked her yet, after calling her at the last minute this week. I thought I'd give it a few days."

Lilith folded her arms across her chest, her gaze intent. "Let me watch them Saturday, Mitch. Andrea will be getting ready for her trip and we can have a little trial run while you're still around.''

"That's a great idea, although I'm sure Andrea will turn up at some point. Don't let us wake you up too early.''

Lilith smiled, then tilted her head abruptly, as though she was listening for something. Mitch listened, but couldn't hear anything at all. "I'll be up early on Saturday,'' she declared softly, her certainty catching Mitch's attention.

"You sound pretty sure of that.'' Mitch leaned against the pillar on his porch. Lilith's last luscious kiss was going to keep him from sleeping anytime soon, he knew that.

"There's something in the wind,'' she whispered mysteriously. "Something almost as special as finding you again.''

Before Mitch could ask, Lilith kissed her fingertips, then disappeared into her house.

It was very early on Saturday morning when Mitch thought he heard Jen stir. He rolled out of bed and crept into her room in the darkness, only to find her grimacing in her sleep. He knelt down beside her and tucked Bun safely back into the bed.

Mitch wondered what she was fretting about in her dreams. Jen frowned as though the weight of the world was on her tiny shoulders, fidgeted, and gripped Bun's well-worn ear tightly.

He hoped his unsettled week hadn't unsettled his daughter. Mitch knew well enough that kids had radar for these kinds of things, and didn't even need to be told.

Mitch brushed those blond curls back from her forehead, and murmured soothing nonsense to her. Slowly the rhythm of his touch seemed to ease Jen's anxiety. Her frown faded, her breathing deepened, and Bun's ear got a break.

Mitch squatted there and watched her sleep, his mind full of memories. He could still see the hospital waiting room where Janice had insisted he remain, he could still see the cheerful smile of the nurse who opened the door when he thought he couldn't stand waiting any longer and beckoned to him.

And he could still see Jen's tiny red face as the nurse passed his child into his arms. Jen's eyes had been squeezed

tightly shut, baby hair dark and damp against her brow. Her
tiny hands had been clenched into fists and she looked even
more like a little old man than Jason had.

She had been so small, so light, so precious. The nurse
had left him there, marveling at the bundle of flannelette,
while Janice slept beside him. Mitch had sat there all night,
transfixed by the way his daughter slept, amazed that she
even existed.

The second time that he held his own newly arrived child
had been no less of a marvel for Mitch.

The first light began to ease beneath the shade in Jen's
room, just as it had that morning over three years before.
It had awakened Janice that long-ago morning, and Mitch
deliberately stopped the replay of his memories without going any further down that particular path. He didn't want
to review Janice's shrill demands, he didn't want to relive
that hysterical fight.

Mitch straightened and winced at the kink in his legs,
glancing out the window before heading back to his own
bed.

But what he saw made him stop and stare.

Despite the earliness of the hour, Lilith sat in her garden,
so perfectly motionless that she could have been a statue.
She was sitting on a little stool, her hand outstretched, perfectly motionless. She was wearing a dress in shades of
gold, colors he had never seen on her before, and her dark
hair hung past her waist, its length wound with matching
ribbons.

The morning was perfectly silent—there wasn't even a
breath of wind—but Lilith's dress fluttered ever so slightly
all the same. Mitch watched surreptitiously as the sun rose
in the front of the houses, the shadows of the buildings
stretching long across their yards.

And still she sat there.

A band of sunlight painted the fence along the common
driveway in rosy hues, then moved closer to the houses like
a leisurely procession. Lilith didn't move. Mitch watched
the sunlight capture each sunflower along her far fence in
succession; he watched each blossom in Lilith's garden be
touched by the golden finger of the sun's light.

The garden stepped out of shadow, crossing the line from

night to morning, each plant after the other, each moment changing the view. Lilith's dress moved a little more, although there was something odd about its flutter.

When the sunlight finally fell across Lilith's still figure, Mitch abruptly realized what that oddity was. Her dress moved in sudden agitation beneath the heat of the sun, it fluttered and flowed, its color changed to vivid hues of orange and black.

And when the monarch butterflies—for that was what they were—absorbed enough of the sun's caress, they stopped stretching and quivering.

As one, they took flight in morning's first light.

Mitch had never seen anything like it. In a heartbeat, the air was filled with a cloud of sunlight and shadow, thousands of delicate butterflies simultaneously taking to wing. The sunlight glinted over the golden glory of their wings and the air filled with the faint rustle of their flight.

They rose from Lilith's garden in a swirling spiral, not so different from a migratory flock of birds. They danced higher and higher, their ranks swelled by even more butterflies hidden on the fence and in the trees, their presence unnoticed by Mitch until they took flight.

He stared in wonder until they began to disappear high up in the pale blue of the sky, then he looked back down to Lilith. She blew gently on one last monarch that lingered on her fingertip. The butterfly flapped, dipped, then chased his fellows as the sun illuminated Lilith's delighted smile.

She was wearing a sheer white sleeveless nightgown, its hem ruffled around her knees. Although it was not a magnificent gown wrought of golden butterflies, it was as feminine as the lady herself. Lilith's feet were bare and her hair was unbound, those ''ribbons'' having flown away. She stood, unaware of Mitch's presence, and waved farewell to the migrating butterflies.

They must stop here every year. Mitch knew monarchs migrated from Canada to Mexico and back every year, but he had never seen a butterfly flock take to the skies. He supposed he had never rolled out of bed early enough on the right August morning.

Mitch thought about Lilith's musings about magic. He thought about butterflies making their way over thousands of miles to a particular haven in Mexico, without ever having done it before.

He thought about a woman who could hear them coming, in the whisper of the wind.

And as he watched the last butterfly be absorbed by the endless blue of a summer sky, Mitch Davison wondered whether there really could be such a thing as magic, after all.

12

THE HANGED MAN

Kurt whistled as he flicked curled shingles free on Mitch's roof. It was a warm morning, sunny and clear, but not hot enough yet to make a guy regret getting up on a black roof without a tree in sight. Mitch was making short work of replacing the flashing on the chimney, and in reality there weren't that many bad shingles.

A couple of hours' work and Mitch could get another year or two without redoing the whole roof.

Kurt slanted a glance at his buddy and tried to think of a good way to bring up the suggestion that was kicking around in his mind. It was about time Mitch admitted that he was still alive, to Kurt's way of thinking. A man couldn't babysit and deny his basic urges forever.

It wasn't natural.

And there were dangerous signs that Mitch was reaching the end of his tether. The August 1976 issue of *National Geographic* had been on the kitchen table when Kurt arrived this morning, left open to an article on butterflies. *Butterflies!* That had to be a sign of desperation.

Kurt would think that a guy who wasn't getting anything would choose a more provocative kind of reading material.

One that he wouldn't leave lying around in the kitchen. But Kurt had peeked and hadn't found a single interesting thing.

He hoped it wasn't too late.

"Hey, Mitch," Kurt began as casually as he could manage. "You should see this chick I'm taking out tonight."

Mitch made a noncommittal sound in his throat and

frowned at the last end of the flashing. "Uh-huh."

"Vivienne," Kurt continued with enthusiasm. "What a knockout. French," he declared, with a significant glance to his clearly uninterested friend.

Things were much worse than Kurt had suspected, because Mitch showed no appreciation of this information.

He cleared his throat. "Major curves in all the right places. You know how those French women are. Dark hair and red lipstick, black lacy lingerie. Oh la la."

Mitch finished replacing the flashing on the chimney and sat back on his heels. He glanced over to the next roof and frowned. "Can you see what kind of shape Lilith's flashing is in from there?"

Kurt blinked. "Mitch, I'm talking about one hot woman here."

His friend shrugged. "And I'm talking about flashing."

Kurt frowned, and barely glanced at the neighbor's house. "What? You don't have enough to do around this place, without looking for extra work? It's not a sin to have some fun, you know."

"When were you last in church?" Mitch demanded with a grin. "Last time I looked, your kind of fun *was* a sin."

"Technicalities." Kurt waved off this argument. "You want me to see if Vivienne has a friend or not? We could make a foursome tonight. Andrea's coming, after all."

"Nope." There wasn't a flicker of interest in Mitch's expression or his tone. "Thanks, but no thanks."

"Mitch! You're divorced, not dead, you know!"

Mitch grinned. "Yeah, I know. It's okay—everything still works. Now look at that roof."

Kurt grumbled under his breath and looked. "Looks about as good as yours did half an hour ago."

Mitch eased his way across the steeply pitched roof to Kurt's side, shaded his eyes with his hand, and peered across the gap between the houses. "I think it needs to be replaced, too. And there's some extra flashing. We might as well fix it while we're up here."

"Watch out," Kurt said grumpily, not liking how quickly a plan he had seen as brilliant had been shot down. He pried another rotten shingle loose. "This could turn into a regular charity drive."

Mitch rolled his eyes and squatted down beside Kurt. "Hey, it'll take five minutes, it's probably not something she'd get around to doing herself. And besides, she's watching my kids."

Kurt's head snapped up and his eyes narrowed. "Wait a minute. Isn't that the fortune-teller's house?"

"Uh-huh."

Kurt squinted at his buddy. "You leave the kids with *her*?"

"Well, next weekend. I don't have a lot of choice." Mitch looked supremely unconcerned about all of this, which Kurt thought was pretty odd. He knew how protective Mitch was of those kids and he thought Mitch didn't like that babe. "I'm off to that conference next weekend and Andrea leaves for a cruise tomorrow."

"Why is she going away? Usually Andrea watches the kids."

"Something came up."

Kurt frowned. "Andrea doesn't usually do stuff like that."

But Mitch waved off the question. "It's a long story, but the good news is that the kids really like Lilith."

Kurt considered his friend for a moment. Slowly, he realized there could be something else causing Mitch's lack of interest in the possibility of Vivienne having a friend. "Yeah, and what about you?"

Mitch just smiled and headed for the ladder. "You coming down now? Or do you mind if I move the ladder over for a few minutes?"

"Wait a minute, wait a minute." Kurt quickly followed his friend, not in the least bit sure he liked the sound of this. "You're the one who warned me against her. You're the one who said she was a witch!"

But Mitch's grin just widened. "Sure, doc, I know, but aren't they all witches inside?" He wiggled his eyebrows and Kurt smiled despite himself, remembering the Bugs Bunny cartoon in question.

Then he sobered again. "But Mitch, you don't know what you're doing. There's something *weird* about your neighbor."

"Like what?" Mitch smiled crookedly. "She turned you down?"

"Well, that too." There wasn't anything funny about that. Kurt shoved a hand through his hair and flicked a glance at the woman's house. He dropped his voice. "But there's something about her eyes, the way they look right through you." He shivered despite the heat of the sun. "It's like she can see what you're thinking."

Mitch arched one brow. "Kurt, any woman with a brain can see what you're thinking."

"No, no, this is different. *She's* different."

Mitch smiled slowly. "I know. That's what I like about her." And he turned to descend the ladder.

"Mitch! Come out tonight with me and Vivienne." Kurt leaned over the edge of the roof as Mitch descended. "You'll have a great time, maybe get lucky, you never know."

He heard Mitch chuckle before he saw his smile. "Don't worry so much about it, Kurt. I've got all the luck I need right here."

Lilith was watching a pair of tanned and busy children splash in the pink pool on Saturday afternoon when Andrea popped out through the kitchen door.

There was a chorus of joyous greetings for Nana—who just happened to have picked up some licorice twisters in the course of her shopping—before the children dashed back to the pool. Andrea dropped down beside Lilith with a sigh of satisfaction, and poured herself a glass of pink lemonade.

"Mitch is on the roof," Lilith supplied.

Andrea rolled her eyes. "Honestly, he never stops."

Lilith smiled at the affection in the older woman's tone. "Are you all ready for your trip?"

Andrea smiled in turn. "Oh, yes. Ten o'clock tomorrow morning. I can hardly wait." She turned suddenly and looked steadily at Lilith. "I have to thank you, Lilith, both for reading my fortune and for agreeing to watch the children."

"I'm looking forward to it," Lilith confessed.

"I know." Andrea sipped her drink and wiped the faint

sheen of perspiration from her brow. "But Mitch trusts you, too. That's not a small thing after what he's been through." She put the glass down and turned it in the wet circle it made on the wood, her tone suspiciously idle. "I don't suppose he's told you much about it?"

Lilith's attention was effectively snared. "Just that Janice left when Jen was a baby."

Andrea shook her head. "And that's not half of it." She looked at Lilith again. "Am I wrong, or is this something you'd like to know?"

"I don't want to pry," Lilith said carefully.

Andrea grinned. "But you're itching to know—and you know as well as I do that getting the story out of Mitch will be like pulling teeth."

Lilith couldn't completely stop her smile. "He is a bit reticent."

"Gun-shy," Andrea affirmed, taking another long sip of lemonade. "And rightly so. But even if he won't talk about it, I will." She patted Lilith's hand. "You see, Lilith, I think this may help you understand him a bit better. I may not have your gift for seeing lovematches, but I still have eyes in my head. And you're the first woman that Mitch has taken notice of in a long time. That can't be insignificant."

Lilith smiled, hugging the details to herself. It was true love, no doubt about it.

Andrea took a deep breath. "Now, I have to admit that I never liked Janice. Not from the first moment I met her. There was something calculating about that girl, something that got my back up. I don't care for vanity, frankly. But no one else saw it, and since I was new to the family, I kept my mouth shut."

"New to the family?"

"Well, Mitch is my stepson. I don't have any children of my own. Mitch's father, Nate, was my third husband and oh, what a man he was! But I'm getting out of order here. You see, first there was Bernard, a perfectly wonderful man. He was so trim and athletic, so clever and handsome. I moved to Toronto from Montreal to marry him. We were very happy, but he died quite young. A skiing accident, which was fairly rare in those days."

"I'm sorry, Andrea."

The older woman smiled. "So was I. We had such good fun." She shook her head. "It took me a long time to get out in the world again. By the time I met Walter, it was too late for me to have children. And Walter, well, he was so perfectly elegant, it was hard to imagine that he could have fit children into his life anyway." Andrea shrugged. "Walter was a lawyer, and we knew Nate and Eliza as vague social acquaintances. We'd pass at parties and so forth. Pleasant people, I was always struck by how much in love they obviously were."

"It was about a year after Walter died when I heard through the grapevine that Eliza had died of an aneurism. It was disappointing news—they were such a happy couple that I had a hard time imagining Nate on his own, even though I didn't know him that well. They were always so inseparable, you know?"

Lilith nodded.

"I found out later that Nate had a nearly impossible time with the concept himself. I'm sure he blamed himself more than he ever admitted to me. Nate believed he could fix anything, that an ounce of prevention was worth a pound of cure. It must have appalled him to have the love of his life swept away from him so suddenly and irrevocably. He missed her terribly."

"Yet you married him."

Andrea patted Lilith's hand again. "Oh, don't be getting misty-eyed for me. I loved Nate and he loved me, but it's different each time. The part of his heart that he had given to Eliza was hers forever—the part he shared with me was something she had probably never seen. It might have been a part of him that came to light only when he lost her."

Andrea shrugged. "He could probably say the same thing about me. But if we didn't change over the course of our lives, well, we wouldn't be learning much from life, would we?"

She paused for a moment, then frowned slightly. "It shakes your universe to lose a great love, and I saw evidence of that in Nate. He was determined to live for the moment, to savor every bite the world offered. It was three years after Eliza's death that we crossed paths at a charity dance and it is some commentary on the man's charm that I didn't dance one dance that night.''

"You said you love to dance," Lilith said with a chuckle, and Andrea grinned.

"Oh, Lilith, it was absolutely wonderful. Like it was destined to be. Nate made me laugh at some silly joke, I looked into his eyes and I saw the way they twinkled. Something happened in that moment, something magical, and I knew before we said another word that I was going to see a lot of Nate Davison from that point on.'' She smiled into her lemonade. "He had a way of making you feel as though you were the very center of the universe, or at least of his universe, that you were the sun and the moon and the stars.''

Lilith could certainly see the same tendencies in Nate's son.

"And I liked him very much." Andrea licked her lips and studied her glass. "I have to admit that there were times when I wished I had met Nate sooner, but then, neither of us would have been the people we were at that ball on that night." She shrugged. "And maybe then, there would have been no spark. I don't know.''

Andrea took a deep breath. "I do know that I loved Nate right through to the bone, that we could talk and talk about nothing or about everything. I loved how we had champagne in bed just because it was Tuesday, how we made love anywhere we felt like it." She grinned in recollection and Lilith smiled with her.

"I loved how he brought flowers and never really stopped courting me. You see," Andrea smiled sadly, "I had learned how fleeting the good moments can be, too. We took every single moment we had and made them count, we lived those five years with an intensity that most people don't match in the sum of their whole lives.''

"It sounds wonderful.''

Andrea sobered, her gaze on the children. "It *was*.''

Then she swallowed a gulp of lemonade and Lilith let Andrea take a minute to compose herself.

"I'm telling you this, Lilith, so you understand the world Mitch was raised in. He knew nothing but love and harmony as a child, of giving and laughing, of perfect partnership and love everlasting. Nate and Eliza were smitten on sight, as the story went, and were together virtually from that moment on. They were *happy*. Mitch grew up believing that was how all marriages were—he never knew any different. He never realized that he was used to a Rolls-Royce until he found himself in a much more basic model.''

''With Janice?''

''With Janice.'' Andrea looked as grim as Mitch could. ''I have no doubt that Mitch swept her off her feet, that she felt like she was the center of the universe. Mitch is a great deal like his father and he had learned so much of love and giving in that household. The difference was that Janice only *took* and Mitch only *gave*.

''Over time, the deficit starts to get difficult to manage. It's like buying everything with credit cards and never paying the balance, just the minimum payment. The debt mounts and mounts, until your whole life collapses around you like a house of cards.''

Andrea looked Lilith in the eye. ''Love shouldn't be that way and neither should marriage.''

She sipped her lemonade. ''I find it hard to believe that Nate never saw the truth, but maybe he just didn't want to notice it. Or maybe he didn't want to comment on it. He was a tremendously loyal man—it would be like him to believe that since marriage was forever, that time would put the balance back in Mitch's marriage.''

Andrea frowned. ''But I never believed it and I never liked that Janice. You could see the hunger in her eyes— she'd gobble up the whole world for herself given half a chance. And by the time I came along, she was getting miserable. The Queen of the May did not have the exclusive attention of her courtier and she didn't like it one bit. But she wasn't overt about it—maybe only another woman would see the signs. And Mitch, of course—she made sure he never missed it.''

Now Lilith was intrigued. ''What do you mean?''

''I remember a dinner party thrown for an old friend of Mitch's—a friend who just happened to be a woman. Charming girl, you could see at a glance that she and Mitch would never be more than friends. She was going to Europe for some plum job, destined to be gone for a decade. Her parents were great friends of Nate's, but had moved to a condo and didn't have the space, so we hosted a black-tie farewell party.

"Well! Janice came in a dress that nearly spilled her breasts onto the table. They were fine enough breasts, but we all really didn't want to see them. But she couldn't risk sharing Mitch's attention, even for an hour. And that wasn't the worst of it.

"Janice was so jealous that Mitch might pay attention to someone other than herself, that she never left him alone that night. She ran her hands all over him, she pinched his butt when we went in to dinner, she was hanging on him every minute. It was terribly embarrassing. I spread a rumor that she was drunk." Andrea shrugged. "What else was I going to do? People were noticing.

"I sat them opposite each other at dinner, to deliberately give Mitch a bit of breathing room, and his friend by his side so they would have *some* chance to talk. Yet during the meal I couldn't help but notice that Mitch was looking particularly uncomfortable. He was very quiet and he had that beleaguered look."

Lilith smiled. "I know that one."

Andrea nodded sagely. "So I went to check on dessert—completely unnecessarily, of course, we had excellent staff—and just happened to walk down that side of the table." She straightened indignantly. "Janice had her toes in Mitch's lap! I could see his napkin moving, as no doubt did everyone else on that side of the table. I could have smacked her silly! And do you know what happened later?"

Lilith shook her head.

"They stayed the night. Of course, we had plenty of room, and gave them the spare room with en suite. I *thought* they were going to need some privacy, after that performance! I thought I heard arguing, but then remembered what it was like being young and hot to trot." Andrea smiled. "I shut the door to our suite and didn't pay much attention." Her smile faded. "But in the morning, Mitch was asleep in his father's study, still in his tux."

Andrea looked Lilith in the eye. "She didn't *want* him. She was only teasing him to keep him from giving his attention to somebody else. That's just how she was. Mitch never knew I saw him there, for he took pains to slip back upstairs and emerge as though he had been in that bedroom all night." Andrea grimaced. "Loyal to the end. Janice might have been pulling his chain, but he wasn't going to give anyone any reason to malign her." She took a swig of lemonade. "I never told Nate."

"Why not? Maybe he would have talked to Mitch."

Andrea shook her head. "You think Mitch is reticent about emotional matters, you should have seen Nate. And Nate was a consummate family man, too. Divorce really wasn't in his personal vocabulary, even though he was a lawyer. It would have broken his heart to know what was going on there—and even I only had a glimpse of it."

She stared into her glass and smiled slightly. "But you have to wonder if there is some kind of divine plan. You see, Nate died while Janice was pregnant with Jason. He was very pleased about the pregnancy, with the prospect of a grandchild. And Mitch was relieved and excited, too. People have this great faith that the presence of children alone can mend gaping rifts in relationships, but it just isn't so." Andrea sipped. "If things are bad, the arrival of a bundle of joy makes things worse."

"What do you mean?"

"It's not easy having little ones underfoot. They're demanding, they don't sleep for nice eight-hour stretches, they can't do anything for themselves. They're a lot of work, particularly at the beginning, and when couples get frazzled and tired, even the most healthy relationship will show strains."

Andrea sighed. "I'm glad that Nate missed all of that—I wish Mitch could have. Even the last trimester after Nate died was rotten business. It would have broken Nate's heart to hear Janice's tirades about how fat she was getting, never mind her refusal to eat properly for the sake of the baby. She nearly made Mitch crazy, but then, she had his undivided attention that way, which was probably the only thing she wanted."

"That's hardly fair to the baby," Lilith said softly, thinking of how Mitch would have worried.

"No, it's not. I fret myself silly. Yet someone somewhere blessed them with a perfect little boy, despite all the foolish things Janice had done during those nine months. She was very lucky, but she didn't see it that way. Not at all. When I visited at the hospital, I watched Janice.'' Andrea swallowed. ''I saw her malice when Mitch showed us his son, there's nothing else you could call it. Mitch was so delighted, so tickled with this perfect little baby—and fairly so!—that he never saw Janice's expression when she realized she was always going to have to share. I was very afraid that there was going to be trouble.''

''Was she cruel to Jason?''

''No.'' Andrea frowned. ''Surprisingly not.'' She smiled. ''For some reason, Janice was an exemplary mother, if rather an unaffectionate one—maybe that was her tack to get Mitch's approval for those couple of years. I don't know, but everything really did seem to settle down. When she got pregnant again and they said it would be a girl, she seemed pleased. I thought she might bond better with a girl, so when Jen was born, I took Jason for a few weeks.''

Andrea smiled. ''I think every pot in my kitchen had a spin around the floor, he worked every clasp and figured out every baby-proof device in the place. Tupperware fascinated him—I can still hear his chortles when he managed to make it close with a burp. We were having quite a lot of fun, Jason and I, until Janice pulled her stunt.''

Andrea's lips drew to a thin line. ''Clearly, things were much worse than I had ever imagined.''

She cleared her throat. ''You see, Janice was a taker of the first order. She never understood the golden rule, that everything you give comes back to you a hundredfold. The great irony of all of this is that if she had given just a tiny bit to Mitch, she would have been showered with more love and attention than even she could have handled.''

Andrea met Lilith's gaze. ''She truly would have been the center of his universe for all time, because if nothing else, Nate taught Mitch how a man should love his wife. But Janice only saw what was in it for her, and she missed the greatest prize of all.''

Andrea shook her head abruptly. ''I'm still angry with her,'' she confessed. ''I'm still angry that she hurt Mitch so badly, that she left him believing that it was his fault.

I'm not proud of that, but it's unfair that Mitch blames himself for her selfishness. It's unfair that he gives and gives to his kids, but doesn't dare expect anything for himself. Janice taught Mitch that—and it's a lot less than he deserves. She's *still* got him all trussed up, and oh! It makes me furious!''

Andrea reached out suddenly and squeezed Lilith's hand. She took a deep breath and obviously tried to blink away the sheen of tears in her eyes. ''But you're undoing the lesson, Lilith, as I never imagined anyone could.'' She bit her lip. ''Don't stop. Don't give up on him.''

''I won't,'' Lilith pledged, surprised when Andrea gave her a big hug.

''I know,'' Andrea whispered. ''That's what I like about you. You're almost as stubborn as I am. You're going to fit right in to this family and don't let anyone tell you different.''

Lilith grinned and hugged Andrea back, wiping away a tear of her own. She looked up to find Mitch lingering at the gate, his gaze warm. He smiled at her and Lilith smiled back.

''Okay?'' he mouthed and she nodded.

Mitch slammed the gate as though he was just arriving and the kids raced to meet him. Andrea straightened and wiped away the last of her tears, summoning a quick smile.

''Is there a nice cool swimming pool back here?'' Mitch demanded. ''I need a swim.''

''Me too!'' Kurt declared, following Mitch into the yard.

''Here, Daddy, here!'' Jen cried, running to catch at Mitch's hand when he made a great show of not being able to find the pool. He collapsed into it finally, almost overwhelming it. Jen jumped on top of him, Cooley barked, and Jason got the hose and turned it on Kurt. The yard soon became grounds for a big, boisterous water fight that left them all soaked.

Mitch shook out his hair the way Cooley did and grinned up at Lilith. ''I had this idea,'' he said to no one in particular, his gaze fixed upon hers. ''How about we take Nana to the airport tomorrow, then go to the zoo?'' This idea was greeted with great approval, but Mitch was watching Lilith closely. "Join us?" he asked, the tentative edge to his words making her smile.

"I'd love to," Lilith replied warmly. Andrea hummed approval but Lilith was much more interested in Mitch's flashing grin.

"Good!" he said, leaving no doubt of his feelings about the matter and Lilith felt her heart begin to pound.

"Lillit!" A bedraggled Jen tugged on Lilith's skirt. "Can we take Dartaggin? He can visit the big kitties."

Jen looked so hopeful that Lilith didn't immediately have a good answer for that. "I don't think so, Jen."

"Why not?"

Andrea started to chuckle. "Get used to that one," she murmured, then ducked into the kitchen. Mitch winked, then insisted on seeing the state of Jason's garden, the two of them soon talking about all manner of bugs and crawly things. Kurt waved and departed for his big date.

"Why not, Lillit?" Jen demanded again and Lilith knew she had to think of something quick.

Talk about trial by fire.

When Lilith went home that evening, the next card had turned itself over.

She picked up The Hanged Man and studied the card. Pictured was a man, hung upside down. A rope bound his one ankle to the bough of a tree, a noose on the wrong end, like the Norse god Odin swinging from the World Tree for nine days and nights in search of illumination.

Number twelve in the higher arcana, The Hanged Man was a clear reference to Sebastian's untimely demise. It also symbolized Mitch Davison after Janice got through with him.

On a third level, it could be Mitch today. Lilith sank into a chair and thought about it. The Hanged Man has the courage to challenge what he knows is true, to put aside the pain of his own experience, and to trust that taking a chance will win him results. The Hanged Man trusts in what he cannot see, what he does not really know to be true but *believes* is true. The Hanged Man sacrifices what he holds dear, counting on forces he can't explain to take him to a new plateau of understanding.

Lilith fingered the card. Clearly, Janice had shaken Mitch's faith in love and given him a radically different experience of marriage than the one he had expected. And just as clearly, Mitch was slowly putting the "lessons" Janice had taught him aside. Lilith could feel him letting down his guard, trusting her, showing her more and more of who he was. The way his gaze clung to hers, the way he worked to make her smile were the mark of a man preparing to come courting.

Lilith smiled with the realization that Mitch was taking a chance on love, despite what he had experienced before, no doubt in the hope that he and Lilith would find a magickal love well worth that risk. He had to be facing one of his great fears—for Lilith knew how tender broken hearts could be—but Mitch faced the challenge squarely. She had to admire his steady progress and his determination.

But then, they were destined to be together, after all.

Lilith put down the card thoughtfully. She considered that Mitch had something to teach her. Her own refusal to visit this elderly *Rom* woman looked childish in comparison to his resolve.

Lilith wasn't taking any chances. Lilith believed in a lot of things that couldn't be seen, but she hadn't been prepared to risk anything beyond that.

She was acting like a coward. The realization did not sit well.

But as Lilith sat there and considered that, Mitch's conviction in the merit of taking a chance fueled her own. She felt his faith well up inside her and heard again the echo of conviction in his suggestion that this grandmother might need Lilith as much as Lilith needed her.

He might be right.

He might be wrong, but there was only one way to find the truth. And there was only one way to prove that she wasn't a coward. Lilith was still afraid of what might happen, but she had to face her fear.

When she stood to go to bed, Lilith knew that she would go to the hospital.

Mitch was a very happy camper. They'd had a great time at the zoo, just like a family. The kids were so comfortable with Lilith that he knew he had nothing to worry about on that score, and she was so clear-thinking and sensible that he knew she'd take exemplary care of them.

Of course, he'd still worry, but he'd worry less.

On Tuesday, the hardware store called to say that Lilith's new storm door was in. Mitch picked it up on the way home and installed it that evening, keeping one eye on the kids as they played. He could hear Lilith reading fortunes in the front of her house and shamelessly eavesdropped.

Her advice, without fail, was positive, caring, and compassionate. Even if she had some strange preconceptions, it was clear that there was no maliciousness or opportunism in Lilith Romano.

For once in his life, Mitch was very glad to be wrong.

On the following Thursday afternoon, Lilith took a deep breath and dressed carefully, then walked down to the subway, a scrawled slip of paper in her hand. It was high time she shook hands with her destiny and confronted the legacy in her veins.

Even if the prospect made something tremble in her belly.

The hospital was bustling with activity, the emergency ward filled to the brim with the first onslaught of holiday weekend accidents. Lilith worked her way through the throng to the main reception and discovered, to her relief, that she hadn't come too late.

The smell of death, or more accurately the sense of its presence, grew stronger in the elevator, and stronger again when Lilith walked down the long, pale corridor. Nurses brushed past her with efficient smiles, but as she drew near the end of the hall—and closer to the room number she had been given—the activity slowed noticeably.

And the tang in the air grew stronger. Lilith realized that no one else could sense it, no one without her Gift, but to her, it was as tangible as the sting of freshly cut onions.

It was the last room in the hall that bore the right number, the same room from which the whisper of death emanated. Lilith tapped on the door and, when there was no answer, she nudged it open.

An elderly woman sat staring out the window, as though

she would make sense of the rush of traffic on the highway below. She didn't even look up when Lilith stepped into the room, but Lilith knew she was in the right place. The woman's cheeks were hollow, her gaze distracted, a knowledge in her very pose of her own inescapable fate.

Not to mention its proximity.

And Lilith knew from the hook of the woman's nose, the squint of her eyes, the determination of her posture, that this was the *Rom* grandmother she sought. Although she wore the standard hospital issue backless gown, her feet were shoved into slippers rich with colorful embroidery. Gold hoops hung from her ears, and a floral shawl was cast over her bony shoulders.

Lilith paused and stared, suddenly awash in recollections. This could have been Dritta, it could have been a dozen women Lilith had known.

It could have been herself if she hadn't drunk the elixir. Lilith swallowed hard. The prevalence of white in the room even made Lilith shiver, the scent of disinfectant and laundered sheets so far from the fresh breeze of the outside air.

Lilith bit her lip, recalled the grandson's dismay, and considered that this grandmother was in no small pain herself. It was clear she had no interest in who came to her door, her manner much like that of Dritta in a temper. Lilith remembered how she had coaxed Dritta from a foul mood with compliments, and decided it was worth a try.

She had come all this way, after all.

"Good afternoon, *phuri bibi*," Lilith said softly from the doorway in *Rom*. She used the term *phuri bibi*, literally "old aunt," but its import was noble, more like "great lady."

The woman stiffened and turned, her eyes narrowed as she surveyed Lilith. Her lip curled. *"Poshrat!"* she charged.

Half-blood.

Lilith swallowed, certain her expectation of rejection would soon be proven right. But she shook her head. The *Rom* had little use for half-breeds, and the woman was obviously using that as an excuse to get rid of Lilith.

How like Dritta that was!

"Tacho rat," Lilith corrected softly. Full blood.

The older woman's eyes widened. She turned slightly in her chair and her gaze sharpened like that of an inquisitive bird. When she spoke in full sentences, Lilith knew she had made progress.

"But you say words like they do not belong on your tongue," the woman charged in rhythmic *Rom*. "You cannot be of us."

Lilith advanced into the room and paused, not far from the woman's bright gaze. "I have not spoken *Rom* for a long time," she admitted. There was no point in lying, even if the truth gave this woman the excuse she needed to send Lilith away.

"Why not?"

Lilith looked into those dark eyes so like her own, took a breath and confessed. "I was called *mahrime*."

The woman's lips pursed, but she did not pull away. "Why?"

"I loved a *gadjo*."

The woman snorted and fussed with her gown. "No *Rom* man was good enough for you?"

"No *Rom* man was my soulmate."

The older woman looked up at that. "You have him still?" she asked with a coyness so unexpected that Lilith almost smiled. Instead she nodded and her companion's resulting smile spread slowly.

Then the older woman abruptly looked across the room. "I had a soulmate until they stole him from me."

Lilith didn't know what to say to that, so she waited.

The other woman finally bit her lip and looked back to Lilith, her tone brisk once more. "Are you a good *Rom* girl? How did my grandson find you?"

"I am a *drabarni*," Lilith admitted. A fortune-teller. An herbalist. A healer. For the *Rom*, they were all one and the same.

The woman's eyes gleamed approval. "He is a clever boy in his moments." She reached up and pinched Lilith's cheek. "And are you a good *drabarni*? Do you have the Sight?"

Lilith nodded, unable to deny how the woman reminded her of Dritta.

She nodded approval of that. "You make your man a

good wife, whether he is *gadjo* or no. After all, *shuk chi hal pe la royasa.*"

~~Beauty cannot be eaten with a spoon.~~

It was a favorite old *Rom* proverb and good to hear on another tongue. The very sound of it reassured Lilith that she had done the right thing in coming here.

"But I am *mahrime*," she felt compelled to remind the woman. Contact with her could taint this woman. "Does it not trouble you?"

The older woman blew through her lips like an old horse. "We are not so many that we can stand apart on such things," she said regally. "I am too old to care. You are here. You speak *Rom* to me. It is enough."

The relief that flooded through Lilith left her feeling weak in its wake. She blinked back unexpected tears, seeing now how foolish she had been to be afraid. Mitch had given her this, Mitch had given her the gift of confidence to face her past.

She was going to have to make sure the man was rewarded.

Lilith's characteristic determination to set matters to rights was rising to the fore again. "Your grandson said you had something to tell him," she suggested gently.

The woman clicked her teeth in agitation. "I must tell him in *Rom*. It is not a tale for *gadje* words." She seemed to get much more upset suddenly and stirred in her chair. "This wicked *gadje* place, I do not like it, with all its white and bad luck and death. It is wrong, it is evil, it is not where I should be!"

The grandmother struggled now to get up, as though she would walk right out of there, but she was obviously too frail to do so. She railed against her weakness and made a sound of frustration in the back of her throat, cursing the *gadje* with unexpected vigor. Lilith reached out to reassure her, and the woman grasped her hand with surprising strength.

At the move, the older woman's bright shawl fell back and Lilith saw the blue tattooed number on the woman's forearm. A shiver ran over her own flesh at the sight, then she looked up to meet the woman's eyes.

"You see it," the elderly woman whispered with triumph, her voice less even than it was just a moment before. "You *do* know without knowing."

Before Lilith could agree, or dismiss the dark images that crawled into her mind, the older woman's fingers tightened around Lilith's like a claw. "I think you know what it is to be hunted."

That Lilith did. Her mouth went dry, her gaze strayed again to the tattoo. She heard the dogs, she felt the ground tremble, she smelled fear.

The woman leaned closer, the shimmer of a tear in her bright eyes, anxiety in her words. "But tell me, child, tell me. Your *gadjo* is not such a man as these were, is he?"

"No." Lilith shook her head vigorously. She had seen pictures of the Holocaust, she had heard of the trials faced there. But she had not considered that her own people had suffered.

"They said they came to study us, but that was not enough for them." The old woman straightened with a snort. "We called it the *porraimos*."

The Devouring. Lilith closed her eyes as a cold hand clenched inside her. Like most words the Rom reapplied to situations for which their language had no words, it was more than apt.

She felt foolish now that she had never guessed what was happening within a Germany run by people so concerned with the purity of bloodlines. Though she had lived through those years, Lilith had never known, never imagined that the *Rom* had suffered. She wondered what she would have done if she had known. Lilith wondered whether she, like so many others, would have believed that there was nothing she could do to help.

It was only now that she saw the weakness of not even trying.

"How many?" she whispered, knowing that even one was too many.

"Half a million, maybe more, maybe less." A tear worked its way down the elderly woman's leathered cheek. "He must know the story," she said urgently. "He must understand. You must help me."

"Yes," Lilith agreed without hesitation.

It was late, too late for those half a million souls, but

Lilith would do what she could to help. This woman's acceptance of Lilith despite her *mahrime* status undermined all of Lilith's own rejections. She was *Rom*, her legacy coursed through her veins, just as Dritta had declared it always would.

Mitch had been right. This woman did need Lilith's abilities, just as Lilith had needed her acceptance.

There had been absolutely no reason to be afraid.

And now, now Lilith could help this woman, could do some healing, could set some matters to rights. Mitch had given her this gift, for Lilith wouldn't have been here without his example and his encouragement.

They were going to make a good team. Just thinking that made her smile, but Lilith had work to do. "What will you tell your grandson?" she asked softly.

"He must know of my soulmate. He must know of the grandfather he never knew. He must know what it means to be hunted, what is the price of trusting foolishly. He must know the legacy that comes to him in blood."

The woman's voice faltered. "I must tell him in *Rom*, but he does not understand it. And I, I am forgetting what little *gadje* that I did know." She shook her head. "I think it is a vengeance of my tongue, or maybe the *mulo* of my love does not want to hear me speak thus. I hear him in the wind now, he is close."

The two women looked into each other's eyes and Lilith saw that this one task left undone was all that gave the woman before her the will to continue.

They would have to hurry, to see it finished in time. Lilith was suddenly very glad that she had come.

And she was humbled that she held the key to grant this woman her one desire.

Lilith smiled and squeezed the older woman's hand. "Then we shall teach him, you and I. And then he will know both your story and your tongue. It is a fitting legacy for your only grandson." Lilith leaned closer, easily remembering the *Rom* superstition of naming those who have passed on. "And he will know of the one we cannot name. He will know not only what it is to be hunted, but what it is to be loved."

With that soft pledge, the older woman began to weep silently.

She didn't bow her head, she didn't sniffle or wipe at her tears. She simply let them flow, looking every bit as proud and determined as she had when Lilith had entered the room. She clutched Lilith's hand, though, her own a withered shadow of what it once must have been. Lilith sat silently beside her, watching the tears roll and shed one or two of her own.

"Grandmother?" A young man's voice carried from the doorway.

Lilith looked up to find a familiar young man hesitating on the threshold, fresh flowers clutched in his hands. The woman stiffened and sniffled.

"*Puri daj,*" Lilith corrected softly. "That's *Rom* for 'grandmother.' "

The concern eased from the grandson's features, relief brightened his eyes as he stepped into the room. "*Puri dej,*" he repeated carefully. His gaze flicked to Lilith, then back to his grandmother. "Are you all right?"

"*Ov yilo isi?*" Lilith supplied. He looked to her questioningly. "Is it okay?" she whispered, blinking back her own tears. "Or literally, is your heart still there?"

The young man bent to kiss his grandmother's cheek. "*Ov yilo isi?*" he said with slow precision.

And she smiled. She clasped the flowers to her chest and clutched at his hand, reaching up to kiss his cheek in return. Then she tapped her heart and wiped away a tear. "Such a good boy," she whispered in *Rom*, then rapped Lilith on the knee with sudden severity. "You will find him a nice *Rom* girl, a *drabarni* like you."

Lilith smiled and glanced to the mystified man before her. "I will try."

"Try!" The woman snorted disdain. She rallied and snapped her fingers under Lilith's nose, once again the grand and proud lady in command of her domain. "If your *gadjo* is not smart, my grandson will steal away your heart to make it his own!"

There wasn't much chance of that happening, which suited Lilith just fine.

13

DEATH

Mitch walked up the street on Thursday night, kids in tow, and found himself whistling under his breath. His pulse leapt when he spotted Lilith lingering on her porch, then Jen broke free and ran.

"Lillit! I made you a picture!"

Lilith stepped from her porch and scooped up Jen with easy familiarity, the two having bonded something fierce in the last few days. The picture was duly admired, Lilith's dark gaze dancing repeatedly to meet Mitch's while the children shared their news with her.

For the first time in his entire career, Mitch was not looking forward to attending this annual conference. It was a huge meet and greet, a terrific networking opportunity, but he didn't want to pack up and leave in the morning.

He wanted to have another weekend just like the last one. He wanted to go to the zoo, and laugh with his kids, and lose himself in the sparkle of Lilith's dark eyes. The kids climbed Lilith's porch, Jason opening her door and Jen looking for D'Artagnan, which left Mitch and Lilith momentarily alone.

Lilith threw her arms around Mitch's neck and kissed him as though there was no tomorrow. He was more than happy to enjoy the moment, to cradle the sweet weight of her against him.

When she finally pulled away, he couldn't help but smile. "What was that all about?"

"I went to the hospital," she confessed breathlessly, her smile telling Mitch all he needed to know about what had happened. "And I want to thank you in every way I can imagine." She stretched to her toes and would have kissed him again, if Mitch hadn't landed a thumb against her lips.

He grinned. "How about some ways *I can* imagine?"

Mitch felt her lips curve under his thumb. "Just how imaginative are journalists, anyway?" she teased.

"You might be surprised. We're very creative people." Mitch chuckled and let his fingertips slide along her jawline. He felt her shiver and considered several very interesting possibilities before voicing the one he had in mind.

"But I want to spend tonight with you and the kids," he confessed quietly. "Tell me all about the magic you've made this week."

Lilith tilted her head to look up at him. "I thought you didn't believe in magick."

Mitch smiled wryly. "I saw you with the butterflies last weekend," he confessed, "and I think I feel a conversion coming on." Mitch sobered as he watched his fingertip slide across the fullness of her lips. "I have to leave at five in the morning, Lilith. I want to have this evening to replay all weekend long."

Tonight he needed a little sample of Lilith's tranquility to take along with him.

And he saw in her eyes that she understood.

But the twinkle that immediately appeared told Mitch that she was going to give him a hard time about it anyway.

Of course, Lilith always gave him a hard time, in more ways than one. She challenged everything—not the least of which was Mitch's self-control.

Maybe that was why she so thoroughly captured his attention.

Lilith slipped her fingers into his hair, her touch featherlight, then brushed her lips against his. Mitch felt an ember begin to glow deep inside him. Then Lilith's eyes flashed and she pivoted, tossing a flirtatious glance over her shoulder.

"All this delay," she said archly. "I'm going to start thinking that you're not interested after all."

There was an opening that couldn't be refused!

Lilith barely made it into the foyer before Mitch caught her in his arms. She laughed throatily as he held her close, and returned his kiss hungrily. He only stopped when they were both in need of a deep breath.

"That should clear up any doubts," he growled, deliberately letting her feel the indicator of her effect upon him.

"Tease!" Lilith charged with a playful wrinkle of her nose. Then she spun out of his embrace and danced toward the kitchen, the flash of her bare feet making his chinos tight.

"Me?!" Mitch demanded in astonishment. But Lilith laughed unrepentantly and ran for the sanctuary of the kitchen.

And Mitch, ready to follow, paused and looked around Lilith's house for the first time. It was strikingly cozy, welcoming, and comfortable. He felt at ease just crossing the threshold. He fought his smile as he followed her to the kitchen, not surprised to find his kids already bumming cookies.

"What would you say to sharing a bit of your decorating advice?" he asked, unable to forget Andrea's early suggestion. Lilith turned with a smile that told Mitch he already had her agreement. "I could definitely use your help."

It was when she went home to pick up a few things Friday morning that Lilith found the Death card.

She had come home humming from taking the children to day care, memories of the evening before making her smile. She had dumped an armload of groceries on Mitch's counter and was happier than she could ever remember being. She had just come home for a few things and saw the card waiting for her.

Lilith's heart stopped at the sight of it, then began to race. She stared at the card from the threshold of the living room, reluctant to draw any closer to it, and felt the blood drain from her face.

An Italian village square, its corners haunted with the shadows of twilight, loomed in her mind with sudden clarity.

Lilith thought about plane crashes, car accidents, hotel bombings, and elevators dropping like stones. Flukes of nature, and earthquakes and rivers rising, jumped into her mind. She thought about noble-minded men dashing into burning buildings to save children, and pedestrians being mowed down by drunk drivers just for stepping off the curb.

Lilith's stomach rolled at the realization that there were a wealth of nasty possibilities that could keep Mitch from ever coming back again.

But she couldn't lose her true love again! It wouldn't be fair, it wouldn't be right. Mitch couldn't be stolen away from her, not after all this time, not after all she had done, not after all the hurdles they had leapt together. They were close, tantalizingly close to making a commitment to each other—the Fates couldn't cheat Lilith again.

Or at least she wouldn't just stand by and watch.

Lilith stormed into the room and tried to pick up the card. She tried to turn it over and make it go away.

But she couldn't get a grip on the card. It seemed to be stuck to the table, and clung there with a force she couldn't undermine. Lilith couldn't lift it from the table—she couldn't even slide her nail underneath it.

Its stubbornness made her panic. Lilith scrabbled at the card, then turned her attention to the next one. She tried to force things to move on, understanding that there was much more at stake here than the inexplicable flipping of cards.

But she couldn't turn over the next one either.

Lilith sat down with a thump, pressed her fingertips to her temples, and took a trio of deep breaths. She sternly told herself to get a grip.

She focused on the card. It didn't always mean death literally and Lilith knew that, as little consolation as that was.

The Death card could mean transformation, change, a shift in viewpoint. It could mean metamorphosis. She tried the cards one more time but they were all apparently sealed in place.

And Lilith knew there was only one way to make them move.

Something had to happen.

Something had to *change*.

Okay. If there had to be transformation for the cards to move on, then Lilith would engineer some changes around here. She was a can-do kind of witch, after all. She would short-circuit the cards, whatever their intent might be.

A feline yowl carried from the yard in that moment, followed by a wolfhound's low bark. Lilith straightened and looked to the kitchen. She could take a hint, she thought with a smile, and knew exactly what her first change was going to be.

If D'Artagnan wondered why he was being given his very favorite salmon at a strange time of the morning and for no obvious reason at all, he didn't show it. In fact, he practically inhaled the unscheduled meal, then sat back, burped inelegantly, and began to clean himself with satisfaction.

Lilith smiled, knowing he hadn't even tasted her little amendment. She waited until his eyes started to droop, then scooped him up and headed next door.

D'Artagnan squirmed drowsily at the sight of Mitch's back gate, evidently guessing where Lilith was going but not having the fight in him to do much about it. She could get used to him being mellow like this, but knew the herbal addition to his meal would wear off quickly.

For the moment, D'Artagnan was uncharacteristically placid, which was exactly what Lilith needed.

Cooley wagged his tail when Lilith opened the gate, his gaze sharpening when he spied the cat. He sniffed with enthusiasm and Lilith put D'Artagnan down right under his nose. She held her breath, hoping that familiarity would breed a lack of interest.

The cat wobbled slightly and shook his head. Cooley sniffed on full power, circling the dazed cat with evident fascination. He drew near warily, ducking and weaving until he was certain he wouldn't be clawed. When the dog sniffed D'Artagnan's ears, always a sensitive spot, the cat half-heartedly tried to bat the dog's nose away.

The move made D'Artagnan lose his balance. He sat down with a thump and hissed at the dog, though the gesture lacked its usual vehemence. His tail was already starting to flick with displeasure.

But Cooley's curiosity was apparently satisfied. He considered the cat only a moment longer before wandering off to explore more interesting matters in the garden. D'Artagnan straightened clumsily and stared after the dog.

His tail waved like a banner, his ears stood up, he mewed loudly. Lilith had the distinct impression that he was insulted to have lost the dog's attention.

D'Artagnan yowled but Cooley barely even looked back. The cat ran a few uneven steps, puffed out his tail, and hissed in a more typical manner. The dog crashed against the back porch, stunningly indifferent, and nosed out something that had gotten into his paw.

D'Artagnan glanced accusingly at Lilith and she could only smile. Just as she had hoped, Cooley had only wanted a good sniff. Now that he had had one, there was no curiosity to satisfy. The cat tiptoed closer and boldly batted the dog on the nose, as though challenging him back to the chase. D'Artagnan ran a few uneven steps, then glanced back in consternation when he was not pursued.

Cooley wagged his tail, then dropped his chin to his paws with a noisy sigh and started to snore.

The cat's tail dropped. He seemed so uncertain as to what to do that Lilith laughed aloud.

One change made with resounding success. Lilith let herself into the kitchen and began a quick survey of the house, considering all the while what could be done.

Then she headed to the paint store, more than ready to make a little transformation of her own.

Mitch had asked for her help, after all.

Jen awakened in the night with the dreadful certainty that her daddy wasn't there. She clutched Bun to her chest and felt her little heart go pit-a-pat.

She was alone.

Jen bit her lip, she blinked back her tears. She had promised Daddy that she would be a big girl, that she wouldn't get scared, that she would be good for Lillit.

But it was hard to do in the middle of the night. The shadows loomed large around Jen's bed; the darkness in the corners were deep enough to hide any kind of spooky thing. She was suddenly quite sure that there was a monster under the bed. Jen rolled into a little ball and felt the first tear slide down her cheek.

She was all alone.

It was really scary, yet she couldn't help straining her

ears. Jen hoped she wouldn't hear that monster breathing, she didn't want to know for sure he was there, didn't want to suspect that he was hungry. But she listened all the same.

And that was when Jen heard the music.

It was coming from the kitchen.

The kitchen, where Lillit was.

And Lillit, Jen knew, would know what to do about monsters.

Jen grabbed Bun tight, afraid he would be eaten if she left him behind. She jumped as far out of the bed as she could, almost certain the monster would reach out and grab her as soon as her feet hit the floor.

He was too slow, though, that monster. Jen made it to the door, her breathing fast, and bolted for the stairs. To her relief, she could see the golden light spilling from the kitchen at the bottom of the stairs.

Light and music, Lillit and safety.

Jen hoped she could get there before the monster snatched her up.

The Beatles were singing that all you needed was love and Lilith was painting up a storm. She couldn't go to sleep without being certain that Mitch was safe, she couldn't stray from the phone and risk missing a call. She certainly couldn't turn off the radio and not hear the news every hour. So she painted and she sang.

It was just past two o'clock, the darkness was pressing against the windows, and the streets were silent, when Lilith turned around to find a very distraught little girl in the kitchen doorway. There were tears on Jen's cheeks and Bun was caught in a headlock.

Lilith immediately dropped to her knees beside Jen, surprised when the little girl cast herself into her arms without hesitation.

"I was all alone!" Jen wailed, but Lilith held her close. She felt a little heart fluttering in fear.

"You weren't alone," Lilith whispered. "I'm right here." Jen sniffled, apparently encouraged by that, and Lilith made Bun dance a little bit. "And you had Bun to keep you company."

"He's scared of monsters, too."

"Monsters?" Lilith let her eyes widen, knowing exactly the demon that Jen was fighting tonight. "There's no monsters here. Your daddy kicked them all out of the house."

Jen eyed her solemnly. "There's a big one, right under my bed. He came back 'cause Daddy's gone."

"Well, we can't have that!" Lilith said firmly. "We're going to go up there and tell that monster to get right out from under your bed and go home to his own."

Jen bit her lip and frowned. "But he'll eat you up."

"No he won't." Lilith dropped her voice to a whisper. "Because I know a secret about monsters."

Jen's eyes went round and she whispered back, "A secret?"

Lilith nodded. "Monsters are *scared* of love. You see, when you love someone, or they love you, you're never alone. And monsters can't get you."

Jen thought about this, too busy thinking to remember to cry. "I love Bun," she offered.

"Oh, that must be why you're safe." Lilith heaved a sigh of relief. "And your daddy loves you, and your nana loves you, too. Why, that monster hasn't got a chance! Once he knows about all that love, he'll just disappear." Lilith snapped her fingers. "Poof!"

Jen visibly brightened at this news. "We could sing him the Barney song," she suggested. "That's about love." Lilith's confusion must have shown because Jen patted her hand. "Don't you know the Barney song?"

Lilith had to admit she didn't.

Jen scrambled to her feet with purpose and took Lilith's hand, as though Lilith was the one who had come running in tears. It really was funny how many of Andrea's gestures the little girl mimicked. She dragged Lilith toward the stairs. "I'll teach you and we can sing it together."

Fortunately, the Barney song was not overly complicated. By the time they reached Jen's bedroom the pair of them were singing it together. As they sat on the bed and sang it three more times, Lilith noticed that they weren't alone.

D'Artagnan had trailed behind them. He jumped onto the end of Jen's bed, kneaded the cover to his satisfaction, then curled up to sleep.

He threw Lilith a glance that dared her to comment on his choice and she knew better than to say anything. By the time Lilith turned out the light and left Jen slumbering, it was clear that the little girl had a bright-eyed champion more than ready to defend her from any monster fool enough to slide under the bed.

Another change, credited to Jen's charming of the crusty D'Artagnan. Who would have guessed that the independent cat would melt for a little girl?

Lilith paused in the hall to listen and heard Jen's breathing slow. Maybe Jen could get over being afraid to be alone. That would make another change. Lilith decided to mix up some Monster Repellant to let Jen mix into the paint when they did her room the next day, just to help things along.

Because Lilith knew the mystical power of threes. She had made two transformations, but her Gift warned her that there was going to be a third.

She hoped it could be the conquering of Jen's fear. Lilith returned to her painting, keeping one ear tuned to the news, and hoped that Mitch would come home safely.

Until then, all she could do was keep busy. Fortunately, she wasn't likely to run out of painting anytime soon.

This was one transformation that was going to take a while.

Mitch felt like hell.

Three days of lectures and networking and being away from home had beat the stuffing out of him. His mind was swimming with possibilities and trends, opportunities and considerations. All he wanted was a little peace and quiet to sort them out. And he wanted to know how everyone was doing at home.

Oh, he had called a couple of times, smiled at the kids' stories, and warmed to the sound of Lilith's voice, but tonight a phone call just wouldn't do. When a group of old cronies settled in to drink on Sunday afternoon, Mitch decided enough was enough. He blew off the last day of meetings, called the airline, and changed his flight.

Eight hours later—after an excruciating wait at O'Hare that he roundly deserved for changing his flight schedule—

he was scooping up his garment bag at Pearson and jingling his keys as he headed for the Honda.

Home.

And Lilith.

Mitch couldn't get there fast enough.

The house was quiet when he unlocked the kitchen door, although the light was still on in the kitchen. It smelled like paint and there was a can of flat ceiling latex open on the counter. The radio was on at a low volume, some sixties ballad echoing softly through the house. Cooley yawned and stretched before getting up to wander across the kitchen to greet Mitch, tail wagging sleepily.

Mitch scratched the dog's ears with a grin. "Some killer watchdog," he teased. "You didn't even wake up until I was in the house."

He put the lid on the paint while Cooley took a pause outside. Mitch locked the kitchen door, turned out the light, and left his bags in the hall. He heard the wolfhound collapse under the kitchen table as he climbed the stairs.

The smell of paint was stronger up here, though the windows were all open. He looked in first on Jen and smiled when he found her smiling in her sleep. D'Artagnan, surprisingly, was curled on the end of Jen's bed. He lifted his head and treated Mitch to a cold glare as Mitch entered the room.

"It's okay, tiger," Mitch whispered, biting back a smile at the cat's protectiveness. "I'm just going to say hello."

D'Artagnan, unconvinced, kept a wary eye on him all the same.

Mitch noticed Bun was abandoned on the other side of the room for the first time since they had moved in. It was a good sign, but Mitch scooped up the stuffed toy and tucked it into the bed beside his daughter just in case.

Her room seemed slightly different, even in the moonlight. Mitch realized that it had been painted, although he couldn't clearly discern the new colors. There was a wallpaper border about waist high around the room. Plump unicorns pranced through rainbows upon it, daisies scattering to all sides.

The room felt different, too, Mitch noticed, and it was

more than the paint and the border and the sheer curtains wafting in the cool evening breeze.

Jen's room felt *safe*. As secure as a little cocoon. Mitch shook his head, knowing full well who was responsible and wondering whether she would blame it on another spell.

That made his smile widen. Lilith's magic was more than welcome around here.

Mitch kissed Jen's temple, and D'Artagnan only dropped his chin after Mitch left the room.

Mitch silently continued to Jason's room. The little boy was snuggled deep beneath his sheets, his fair hair tousled. It had been painted in here too, some shade that seemed to glow faintly. The room seemed cleaner and brighter; Jason's indestructible furniture in primary colors looked right at home. There was a book on his desk that Mitch hadn't noticed before. *Insects A–Z.*

He opened the flap and found an inscription in an elegant feminine hand. *From the library of Lilith Romano.*

"Lilith lent it to me," Jason confessed quietly, his voice thick with sleep. Mitch looked down to find his son's eyes open. "There were bugs in the garden like lights. Lilith said they were fairies, but when I caught one, it was a bug." He yawned.

"Lilith let you catch a bug?"

"Only for a minute so I could see. Then we looked in her book for its picture. It's a firefly, not a fairy."

Jason snuggled deeper as Mitch sat on the side of his bed. "And what did Lilith say about that?"

Jason smiled sleepily. "That fairies don't like to be caught and that it changed just to fool me. She said they're like that."

Mitch grinned and hunkered down beside his son. "But the book doesn't say anything about fairies?"

Jason shook his head. "Nope. I think she made it up, just for Jen. Like the radio." His eyes drifted closed.

"The radio?"

"In the kitchen. Lilith left it on at night when she painted, so Jen would know she was there."

Mitch's heart warmed at Lilith's concern. No wonder Jen was sleeping so contentedly. Mitch brushed the hair back from Jason's brow as the boy's breathing deepened. "Sleep well," he whispered. "It looks as though you've all been busy."

"Mostly Lilith," Jason murmured, then he rolled onto his back and smiled. His eyes opened slightly, the serious gleam there catching Mitch's attention. "I like her, Dad." He smiled and pointed past Mitch's head. "And she gave us the stars."

Mitch followed his son's finger to find the ceiling covered with luminescent stars. There were even a couple of planets glowing softly in the darkness. The sight of them and Jason's choice of words made Mitch smile.

Lilith giving his children the stars. Mitch liked the sound of that. And he liked very much the kind of magic a certain witch was spreading around his house. She harmed no one and she certainly made a lot of people happy.

Mitch could live with that.

In fact, he really wanted to.

He kissed an already slumbering Jason and crossed the hall to his own room. The lady who had haunted Mitch's own dreams was curled up on his bed, her feet bare, her hair loosened like a dark cloud behind her. Mitch's heart skipped at just the sight of her there and he hesitated on the threshold, not wanting this moment to end too quickly.

He could stand here and imagine that he really came home to Lilith, that she really was waiting for him, that they really were making a household together. As long as he stood here, he could imagine that she would awaken with a smile and beckon him to bed, that she would curl against him and whisper to him of what had happened in his absence. That he could tell her everything he had learned, everything that troubled him. That they could make love slowly and thoroughly, that together they could make the marriage Mitch had always wanted to have.

It was there, standing in the doorway of his own bedroom, watching a beautiful woman sleep, that Mitch Davison realized that he was in love.

And he was in love with the most unlikely woman of all. A winsome witch who only believed in things she couldn't see, an imaginative and delightful woman who spread fairy dust throughout his house, a generous and giving soul who asked for nothing but his love in return.

He was ready to give it to her. Because Mitch loved Lilith, as he had never imagined he would love a woman.

For a long time, Mitch had believed that he would never find love, that he would never take a chance again, that it just hadn't been worth it. But Lilith had challenged his preconceptions, she had made Mitch rethink all those conclusions that he'd thought were set in concrete for all time.

Now, Mitch couldn't imagine his life without her. He couldn't imagine his heart not doing this goofy little jump every time she smiled at him, or her image popping up in his mind unexpectedly. Never to hear that low voice again, or hear the tinkle of her laughter, or see her dark eyes dance was completely unthinkable.

Mitch felt as though he had always loved Lilith, though he smiled at that echo of her own conviction. She was starting to infect his nice, orderly thinking with her crazy ideas.

And oddly enough, he didn't mind in the least.

Mitch stepped into the room, not intending to wake her, but Lilith stirred as though she had been waiting for him. Her eyes opened slowly, her gaze fixed on him, and she smiled so warmly that Mitch tingled from head to toe.

"You're home!" she murmured, with a delight that made Mitch's heart do that goofy jump. "I thought you weren't coming back until tomorrow," she whispered, her pleasure at his change of plans undisguised.

It felt damned good to be missed.

"Couldn't stay away," Mitch admitted huskily. "You've been busy."

Lilith stretched, her toes pointing then curling contentedly. She nestled into his pillow and smiled sleepily. "I wanted to surprise you. I would have finished the ceilings by tomorrow."

"Well, now you'll have to deal with inexperienced help underfoot." When Lilith chuckled, Mitch came and sat on the edge of the bed, unable to resist the urge to brush her hair back over her shoulder. "And you have surprised me," he said gently. "Both kids' rooms done already is a pretty impressive feat. Especially with them around."

Lilith smiled. "All you need is a little creativity."

Mitch smiled back. "No magic?"

Lilith wrinkled her nose, her gaze warm. "It can't hurt."

Her hair was as soft as silk beneath his hand. Mitch ran his fingers over it, the dark tendrils curling around his fingers as though they would snare his hand in their softness. He didn't want this moment to end. "So, what colors are they? I couldn't see in the darkness."

"Mmm, mauve and aqua and mint, nice safe colors for Jen. A sea-washed haven for her. And a crisp yellow for our intrepid explorer." Mitch caught his breath at the easy way she said "our" but Lilith didn't notice. "You'll be amazed how much bigger and brighter the house looks, just with the ceilings repainted."

Lilith nestled closer, her hand landing on his. Her fingers were warm and soft. Mitch turned his hand over and held hers tight.

"What are you going to do in here?" he asked, mostly because he didn't want her to stop talking. She could do anything she wanted with his bedroom, as far as Mitch was concerned.

Lilith smiled. "True blue," she confessed as she met his gaze warmly. "And maybe some silvery stardust to keep things interesting."

Mitch grinned. "I like the stars in the kids' rooms."

Lilith rolled to her back and stretched. "Jason had to have planets too, but I refused to lay them out according to the star map enclosed."

"You'll never live that down."

"I know." Lilith sighed and squeezed Mitch's fingers. "Maybe you can fix them for him."

Mitch really liked her implication that they were in this together. Lilith eased back, making room for another on the mattress without slipping free of his hand. She smiled, her voice dropped low. "Get naked and come to bed, Mitch. I want to touch you and know you're really home."

The invitation was everything Mitch could have hoped for. He certainly didn't need a second request. He peeled off his shirt and dropped his trousers, leaving them in a pile with his socks and shoes. Now that he was down to his Jockeys, he slipped between the sheets with a sigh of contentment and reached for Lilith.

But she hooked a finger in the elastic of his briefs.

"Everything," she insisted, the mischievous twinkle in her eye making Mitch's heart pound.

"I thought it was too late."

"Definitely too late for *talking*," Lilith confirmed, then winked.

There was no doubt what she meant.

Mitch's mouth went dry. "You sure?"

Her smile broadened. "I missed you. Besides, you're the one who had to make up your mind," she teased. "Are *you* sure?"

Mitch was.

Without a doubt.

But things still weren't simple.

He frowned. "Lilith, I wasn't planning this. I don't have any condoms."

She seemed untroubled by this confession. "So?"

Mitch might have shed a lot of preconceptions, but he hadn't lost all his practicality. He knew he was as clean as a whistle, but he didn't want Lilith worrying about anything later.

"Lilith, it is the nineties. Aren't you worried about little biological souvenirs?"

She laughed then and tapped a fingertip on the end of his nose. "The only man I've ever been with, one way or the other, is you. And we didn't have any condoms those other times either."

There really was no arguing with her on that. And she had been supremely unconcerned so far, even though they had done it without protection once.

Of course, there was one other issue, but Mitch wasn't going to raise that question again. In fact, he couldn't think of anything more wonderful than Lilith conceiving his child. She'd be a terrific mother.

And he'd have another point in his favor when he proposed.

Let the lovemaking begin.

Mitch stripped off his Jockeys and cast them across the room with a flourish. He grinned at Lilith's whistle of admiration, then flicked a finger at the sleeve of her dress. "And what about you?" he challenged softly.

Without another word, Lilith sat up, then climbed to her

feet. She held his gaze while she unbuttoned her dress with theatrical leisure, bared one shoulder as though dancing to a band only she could hear, then covered it up and playfully bared the other.

"Tease," Mitch charged, and Lilith laughed sensually.

"You're the one determined to take things slowly." She turned her back on him and shook her shoulders so her dress fell down her back. She tipped back her head and laughed at Mitch when he made a great show of trying to see some flesh behind the curtain of her hair.

When she spun back to face him, her dress was back on her shoulders but open the whole way down the front. Mitch glimpsed her matching lingerie, the smooth creaminess of her belly. Her legs flashed and he realized he'd never seen them before.

"You always wear dresses," he mused.

"It's my *Rom* roots showing," she confessed with a smile and an easiness that surprised him. "We'd rather show our breasts than our knees."

With that, she flicked back her hair, wriggled the dress off her shoulders, and bared her breasts. The dress fell around her ankles in a floral swirl, then Lilith stepped out of it, like Botticelli's Aphrodite stepping off her seashell.

Mitch's mouth went dry. Her skin glowed like sun-kissed sandalwood in the pale light. She was smooth and curved like a goddess. She was wearing a feminine froth of a brassiere, the open work of the white lace etched against the golden hue of her skin. Lilith was achingly feminine, lusciously curved. In those lace-edged panties, she was a sight infinitely better than any skinny model in a lingerie catalog.

When Lilith knelt on the bed beside him and reached to unfasten her bra, Mitch captured her hands.

"Let me," he whispered. Her eyes shone as she lifted her hands away and Mitch ended up with her breasts in his palms. They fit perfectly as though she was made for him to love, or the other way around. Mitch grinned at the whimsy of that thought.

"What?"

"Perfect fit." He arched a brow and met her gaze. "Must be destiny."

Lilith smiled in turn, her lips brushing against his.

''Mmm, kismet indeed,'' she breathed. Her perfume swallowed Mitch like a cloud.

His thumbs slid across her nipples and despite the gossamer layer of silk covering them, Lilith gasped at his touch. Mitch felt her nipples bead, then he bent and kissed her lips more thoroughly. Lilith sighed and leaned against him, as warm and as soft as she always was in his thoughts.

Mitch closed his eyes and tasted her skin, smelled her scent. He let his hands run over her curves, let his lips wander across her collarbone, down her throat, across those full breasts. He bracketed her waist with his hands and suckled her through the bra. She cried out and clutched at his hair.

Mitch eased Lilith back onto the bed and let his questing lips wander lower. He traced the length of each rib with his kisses, he twisted his tongue into her navel, he revelled in the love thundering through him. He wanted to savor this woman, he wanted to pleasure her, he wanted to wipe everything out of her universe except his own touch.

He wanted to do to her what she so readily did to him.

Mitch pulled down her panties with his teeth, his hands roving endlessly over her, his tongue making her cry out with delight. He cast off her underwear and slipped himself between her thighs, he cupped her buttocks in his hands, he set to work coaxing her response. Lilith moaned, she twisted, she writhed, she whispered his name, she arched her back off the bed.

And she was wetter than wet. Mitch thought he would explode at the evidence of her arousal. He gave her no respite, he teased until she shivered and then he teased some more. He wanted this to be a night to remember. Lilith reached for him, but he caught at her hands and interlocked their fingers.

Lilith gasped. Mitch could almost feel the heat rising beneath her skin. His own erection was enormous, made more so with every hint of her own rising passion. She came with a cry of victory, her back arched high, and he thought he couldn't last.

When she mumbled in contentment, Mitch slid up the length of her, nibbling her flesh all the way so that she shivered anew. Their fingers were still entwined when he braced himself above her, her breathing was rapid, her eyes shone.

"Okay?"

"Wonderful." Lilith smiled in a way that made Mitch's heart clench, then expand. He bent and captured her lips with his. They kissed hungrily, lingeringly, slowly bringing Lilith's desire to a simmer once again. Without breaking their kiss, she wrapped her legs around Mitch in silent demand. Mitch eased himself into her, his own eyes closing at the way her warmth closed securely around him.

Again, a perfect fit.

"Kismet," he whispered against the perfumed softness of her throat. Lilith's low laughter fanned his ear.

And then, she rolled her hips beneath him.

Mitch caught his breath at the surge of desire that fired through him. His blood pounded in his ears. Lilith smiled and did it again. Mitch braced himself on his elbows, then moved within her with slow deliberation. Lilith's hands locked on his shoulders and she writhed beneath him so beguilingly that he knew he wouldn't last.

He couldn't last.

But this wouldn't be the only time. They had decided to make love, and by God, they were going to make love until they couldn't make love any more. Lilith was going to know what she did to Mitch, she was going to understand how much he cared for her, and Mitch didn't care whether it took all night or all year.

Or even all of his life.

He moved with powerful strokes, aware of nothing but the woman gasping beneath him. Mitch slipped his hand between them, his thumb found the spot he sought and Lilith arched her back with a little cry. He bent and swallowed the sound, kissing her, touching her, filling her.

Again, the sight of her rising passion drove him on to greater and greater heights. Lilith's ripe lips parted, she writhed in the dark tangle of her hair, her fingers gripped his shoulders, the softness of that lacy brassiere brushed against Mitch's chest.

Suddenly, Lilith's eyes widened, she stared at Mitch and she cried out in pleasure. He barely saw the flush race over her features before his own orgasm thundered through him.

For that incredible moment, time stretched out to infinity and Mitch touched the stars.

Slowly, Mitch tumbled spent into the arms of his equally exhausted lady. He ran his fingertip along the edge of her bra and smiled when she shivered. "We didn't even finish the job," he mused.

Lilith curled up against his side, all softness and femininity, her legs tangled around his. "Next time," she whispered.

Mitch grinned at the thought. He enfolded her in his arms and rolled to his back, more than content with the place in which he found himself. Opening his heart to this woman had changed more than his perspectives—it had changed Mitch himself.

Mitch was a new man, and he liked that just fine.

"I love you, Lilith," he whispered, his eyes drifting closed before he saw Lilith's answering smile.

Mitch was asleep by the time she stretched and kissed his brow.

He never did see her take off that bra. When he awakened hours later it was gone, although its absence was no impediment to their lovemaking the second time.

Or the time after that.

14

· TEMPERANCE

Lilith awakened when the first ray of sunlight poked through the bedroom window. She sighed and snuggled closer to Mitch's warmth, then wrinkled her nose at the earthy aroma they emanated.

Something had to be done.

Lilith gave Mitch a friendly poke. "Wake up," she whispered urgently. "We need to have a shower."

Mitch opened one eye and smiled lazily, a decidedly amorous gleam in that gold eye. "I like a woman who isn't afraid to say what she wants," he teased, then kissed her leisurely.

Lilith sighed with contentment. The man was thorough, she would willingly give him that.

And just about anything else he wanted from her. Lilith was tired in all the right places, and filled with a certainty that they had only just begun to explore something truly wonderful.

But despite the gleam in Mitch's eye, another bout wasn't exactly what she meant. "The kids will be awake soon," she whispered when he lifted his lips from hers.

But Mitch rolled over and pulled Lilith purposefully against his side. He nuzzled her neck enough to make her toes curl. "I don't care if they find us together," he mumbled, then kissed that tingly spot right under Lilith's ear.

His words made a little glow launch around her heart. His kiss made numerous other—equally good—things happen.

"No, not that," she protested weakly. Mitch kissed her

neck, his fingers sliding around her breast. "And not that!" she added breathlessly.

Mitch lifted his head and met her gaze. "Then what?"

Lilith sniffed and grimaced again. "It just smells a bit earthy in here, if you know what I mean."

Mitch deliberately sniffed in turn and made a comical face. "Phew! What's been going on in this bed?" He grinned, then bounded from the bed. Lilith only had a moment to admire Mitch's muscled legs and bare butt before he pivoted and scooped her into his arms. In a heartbeat, he was headed for the bathroom. "I did mention that I have a weakness for clever women, didn't I?"

Lilith tapped him on the shoulder. "You only get to have a weakness for *one* woman now."

Mitch grinned, obviously untroubled by that. "Fair enough. As long as we're both playing by the same rules."

"Of course."

Mitch kicked the bathroom door shut behind them, pulling Lilith close and landing a bone-melting kiss on her. When she was certain she couldn't even stand up on her own, he lifted his head.

The twinkle in his eye should have warned her.

But Lilith found herself dumped into the shower before she could protest. Mitch turned on the water, she sputtered, but he turned back to lock the door.

"We don't went any little eyes or cold noses investigating," he confided as he climbed into the tub beside her. After the initial cold spurt, the hot water had come and the shower was becoming quite cozy.

Intent shone in Mitch's eyes, and one glance further south confirmed to Lilith exactly what he had in mind. His hands roved over her, starting little fires everywhere they touched.

"Now then," Mitch purred as he backed Lilith into the tile wall. His chest hair tickled against her breasts, the warmth of his smile made Lilith's heart pound in anticipation. He quirked one chestnut brow. "How about some good clean fun?"

Lilith had only a moment to laugh before Mitch's lips closed demandingly over hers. He caught her around the waist, his hands nearly encircling her, and lifted her so that her toes dangled off the ground. He imprisoned her against the wall and Lilith couldn't imagine a better place to be. The water drummed down on his shoulders and Lilith closed her eyes with contentment.

Mitch loved her.

She loved him, they were together. That was the only thing Lilith had ever wanted and she had it right in her hands. Her heart sang and she knew she would treasure Mitch's whispered confession for the rest of her days.

She ran her toes up the back of his legs, giggling when he growled. Lilith locked her knees around his waist, more than ready to repeat their earlier activities. Mitch's hands slid lower and he cupped her buttocks, a very wicked gleam lighting the amber of her eyes.

"Why don't you put your feet on the edge of the tub," he suggested in a low growl. Mitch gripped her cheeks tighter when Lilith followed his suggestion. "And don't worry," he breathed against her neck. "I'm not going to let you fall." His erection pressed against her softness, his lips moved in her ear.

And Lilith knew right then and there that they were going to run the hot water tank dry.

"Daddy's home!" Jen exploded into the bedroom and bounced on the bed with delight, just half an hour after the shower to end all showers.

"You're still asleep, naked lady," Mitch mumbled in Lilith's ear. Then he sat up with a gasp of surprise for Jen's benefit, acting as though he had just awakened. Lilith followed orders and feigned sleep. Jason was right behind Jen and the mattress was soon bouncing with a different kind of excitement than it had the night before.

Lilith had to wonder what kind of person they thought she was, expecting her to slumber right through this kind of ruckus. That made her smile even more.

To Lilith's relief, no one seemed surprised to find her curled up in bed with Mitch. She snuggled lower, hiding her bare shoulders beneath the sheet.

"Shhhh!" he said loud enough to wake the dead. "Lilith's still sleeping." Lilith bit back a chuckle. The children shushed each other so loudly that Lilith nearly blew her cover. Whispers abounded, then the mattress moved as they eased from the bed.

To Lilith's astonishment, she earned two surreptitious and slightly sticky kisses. She only barely hid her surprise, and had to bite her lip when Mitch whispered in her ear. "Hmmm, I had no idea you could be so sneaky," he teased, then kissed her lightly. "I'm going to have to watch my step."

Lilith knew he saw her unwilling smile.

Down in the kitchen, Cooley barked, obviously feeling left out of things.

"Daddy, you have to see!" Jen dragged Mitch off to see her room, her explanation filled with a tangled story of Lilith's Monster Repellant. He then admired Jason's room, suggesting a bookshelf for all of the books that were being acquired.

"Did you have fun?" Mitch asked in the hall. A chorus of assent answered his question and Lilith smiled against her pillow.

"Lillit scared away the monsters for good," Jen announced.

"Did she? And she painted the house too."

"And she sang with me," Jen contributed solemnly.

"We found some tadpoles in the creek and they had legs already," Jason contributed. "We're going to go back today to see how much they've grown."

"Wow," Mitch mused. "It sounds as though Lilith worked pretty hard." He dropped his voice to that loud whisper that Lilith was almost certainly supposed to hear. "Maybe we should make her breakfast."

"We could make pancakes!" Jason suggested.

"And fruit salad with lots of grapes."

Mitch chuckled. "Whose favorite food is this supposed to be?" he asked and Lilith guessed the answer to that. "What do you think *Lilith* would like?"

"Pancakes!"

"And fruit salad with lots of grapes."

Lilith couldn't stop her laughter. She tried to muffle it in the pillow and was glad to hear Mitch's chuckle echo more loudly at the same time.

"All right, I give up," he confessed. "Pancakes and fruit salad it is."

Jen squealed, Jason cheered, Cooley barked with determination.

"*Shhh!*" Mitch counselled, and they all shushed. "Be vewy vewy quiet," he added in quite a good imitation of Elmer Fudd. "We are huntin' bweakfast."

Jason mimicked the cartoon character's distinctive laugh and the sound of their giggles moved toward the stairs.

"Gee," Mitch said with sudden loudness. "I really hope Lilith sleeps long enough that we have time to finish making our surprise."

Lilith rolled to her back and grinned, knowing full well that she was supposed to hear that. She stretched and considered the ceiling. It looked much better white, even if it did still need another coat to cover that horrible green completely. The room looked cleaner and brighter already and Lilith couldn't wait to finish transforming this house.

It was a challenge of the first order. Her house hadn't been nearly so bad when she'd moved in. Lilith wiggled her toes in the sheets, quite content to linger and daydream about paint and carpets and perfect furniture for each corner.

Lilith had no doubt that Mitch would loudly wonder where she was when it was time for her to make an appearance.

Lilith surveyed the room, trying to decide what particular shade of blue would be rich but not too dark. The corner of a piece of paper hung out of the top closed drawer of Mitch's dresser. She had noticed it the other day and meant to stuff it back in. If anything else, it was hanging out further than Lilith remembered.

It was the only thing in the room that looked sloppy, besides the rumpled bed. Sometime during the night, Mitch had even hung up his trousers.

Lilith's lips quirked with the realization that she was getting a man who was already trained.

She eyed the piece of paper, unable to decide why that dangling corner bothered her as much as it did. Lilith wasn't that much of a neat freak, after all.

She looked away and tried to forget it, but when she looked back, it seemed to be hanging out even further. It was almost wiggling at her, daring her to come and stuff it back into the drawer before it fell right on the floor.

That was enough!

Lilith rolled out of bed and crossed the room. She pulled open the drawer, meaning just to stuff the paper further in, but it fluttered to the floor. And when she bent to pick it up, the first few words jumped out at her.

Lilith hadn't meant to read it; she certainly didn't intend to pry. But why did Mitch have a list of psychologists in his drawer? And why was this doctor specializing in emotional trauma circled?

Lilith sat down on the edge of the bed with a thump. Was Jen more scarred by Janice's departure than Mitch had already admitted?

What could she do to help?

Mitch was in a rip-roaring good mood. In fact, he couldn't remember feeling so incredible in the morning, or having such anticipation of the day ahead.

Hell, of the *life* ahead.

He popped his favorite cartoon tape into the VCR and set to work dicing fruit as Michigan Frog was discovered in a box outside a construction site. He didn't mind the kids watching cartoons but one morning with Jason in front of the television had convinced Mitch that you never knew what kids were going to see these days. Warner Brothers' work hadn't hurt Mitch any, so he'd gone out and bought a posse of tapes.

They were the only things the kids were allowed to watch on their own, although there were no complaints. Jen and Jason loved Bugs Bunny and all the other characters, even though they practically had the tapes memorized.

Jason ran to turn up the volume, then came back to perch on a stool and wash fruit.

"Wash it really well," Mitch counselled.

"Can you say fat-soluble pesticides?" Jason parroted Mitch's usual advice, clearly without any understanding of what it meant. They said it again using Sylvester the cat's characteristic lisp and laughed together at their own silliness.

Mitch scooped up Jen and perched her on the counter,

giving her a job, too. She picked the green grapes off their stems once they were clean and made more than a few of them disappear.

Cooley waited, eternally patient, for something to fall.

And when the frog started to sing, they all knew the words. Both kids kicked their feet in a rendition of the frog's dancing, and they belted out the tune, two sopranos and a baritone.

Mitch tossed a grape into the air and caught it in his mouth. The kids immediately had to try this, too, and Cooley soon had more grapes than even he wanted.

In the midst of all of this, Lilith cleared her throat from the doorway. Mitch spun and grinned at her, catching a grape with a flourish.

It was only then that Mitch noticed that Lilith wasn't smiling. She turned a piece of paper, a worried frown drawing her brows together. A question lurked in her eyes and Mitch looked again to the paper she held.

When Mitch recognized it, he had a very bad feeling.

Damage control time.

"Can you peel this orange?" Mitch said almost absently to Jason, then crossed the room with quick strides. "Let's talk in the other room," he suggested, capturing Lilith's elbow in one smooth move and turning her away from the children.

Mitch knew he had to talk fast if he was going to save this situation.

Let alone his butt.

Too bad he didn't have a clue how to start.

"Mitch, why do you have this list of psychologists? And this trauma specialist?" Lilith asked with obvious concern. "Is it Jen? Is she more upset than you told me?"

"No, not Jen." Mitch swallowed, hating that words chose this moment to desert him.

"Who, then?" She clutched at his arm. "Not Jason?"

"No, Lilith, no." Mitch frowned. "Lilith, it's not for the kids."

"Andrea?"

"No. Andrea's about the most well-adjusted person I've ever met."

Lilith leaned closer, her eyes wide with concern. "Has something happened to you?"

"No." Mitch shoved a hand through his hair, knowing that at this rate, she was going to get to the truth before he could come up with a reasonable explanation.

Lilith drew back slightly and frowned at him. "I don't understand, then."

There was no easy way to say this. Mitch took a deep breath and plunged right in. "Lilith, I researched the list for you."

His words seemed to stun her. "Me? But why?"

"Well, yeah. You see, when you told me about the whole Gypsy thing and being an outcast and your true lover leaving you, I thought the story might be a way of dealing with a trauma in your life."

Lilith straightened, her expression puzzled. "The trauma in my life was seeing you killed." Her tone was frosty and Mitch knew he was on shaky ground. He gripped her upper arms, unable to quell a sense that she was poised to flee, and tried to explain himself.

Fast.

"But you do know, Lilith, that people don't live for six hundred years? It just isn't possible—in fact, you mentioned as much yourself."

"I told you I was immortal. . . ."

Mitch spoke gently. "Lilith, there aren't any immortals and we both know that." He looked deeply into her eyes and saw disbelief dawn there in the same moment that she gasped. "Now, it doesn't matter. . . ."

"It certainly does matter," she interrupted and pulled her arms out of his grip. "You think I lied to you!"

But Mitch was still trying to save the situation. His words came fast and low, his tone as gentle he could make it. "Not exactly a lie, Lilith. I think you're trying to protect yourself, that the mind does incredible things to deal with trauma, but . . ."

Lilith backed away, her eyes snapping angrily. "You don't believe me! You think I lied to you!"

"Well . . ." Mitch couldn't think of a good way to explain himself nearly fast enough.

"You think I made it all up!" Lilith spun and marched

to the other side of the room, pivoting only at the window.

Then she stared at him, consideration bright in her eyes. "But wait—if you don't believe me, then how could you have remembered *anything* about being Sebastian? If you remembered, you'd know I was telling the truth."

"I never said I remembered!"

Lilith strode across the room, determination in her every step. She waved a finger under Mitch's nose. "You said you didn't remember nearly enough. I remember that quite clearly."

Caught! He *had* said that, although Mitch couldn't exactly remember why it had seemed like a good idea at the time. He looked at his feet and frowned when no ready explanation came to his lips.

"You implied," Lilith continued coldly, "that you remembered something and that you wanted to remember more."

Mitch heaved a sigh. "Lilith, I'm sorry. I made a mistake. I was concerned for Andrea."

"So you lied to me." Lilith's eyes flashed. "You pretended that you did remember something when you didn't. And you think the fact that you believed I was a criminal preying on other people makes that all right!"

"Lilith, I was just trying to help. . . ."

But Lilith poked a finger hard into Mitch's chest. There was a dangerous glint in her eyes. "I don't need to be helped. I don't need to be *fixed*." Her voice rose slightly and Mitch realized that she was very, very angry.

So, maybe he hadn't handled this too well. If only she would give him a chance to explain. "But Lilith, I wasn't going to give you the list! I don't care whether you ever sort all that out."

She snorted, clearly unimpressed. "How gracious of you to accept damaged goods!" She pointed her finger at Mitch's chest. "But there's not a single thing wrong with me, Mitch Davison, except that I'm different from you. I'm starting to think that's an awfully good thing!"

"Lilith! Can we just talk about this?"

"There's nothing to talk about. If you really loved me, you'd accept me as I am. You'd *believe* what I told you, and you wouldn't lie to me."

"But Lilith . . ."

"Mitch, this has not been easy!" Lilith drew in a sharp breath and straightened to her full height. "You've fought me and destiny every step of the way here. I understand that things haven't always been easy for you, and I've tried to be understanding, but I'm tired of doing all the work! Do you remember being Sebastian or not?"

Mitch heaved a sigh. "No."

Lilith's lips tightened and she turned away.

"But I love you. I'm not lying about that."

Lilith looked Mitch right in the eye. "That doesn't give you the right to hurt me," she said softly. "And it doesn't give you the right to assume you know best." Lilith licked her lips, her words falling quickly. "You've got to do some thinking, you've got to make some choices, and you've got to come to terms with the truth."

And with that, she turned and walked away.

Mitch blinked. He couldn't believe she was leaving.

He couldn't believe that no one had thrown dishes, or had a showy tantrum, or made enormous demands.

Lilith just asked for his faith, told him what she wanted, and walked away. It was so completely different from how things had been with Janice that Mitch was momentarily stunned.

By the time he acknowledged how different Lilith was, she was gone.

But Mitch couldn't let this argument end here. He couldn't let Lilith walk out. She was right—he would have called his kids on the carpet for even an almost-lie like the one he had made.

Mitch had to apologize—he had to fix this. He told the kids he'd be back in two and raced out the back door. The gate was swinging and Mitch leapt through it, catching the flick of Lilith's skirts from her front porch.

"Lilith! Wait!" Mitch raced down the path between the houses, vaulted onto her porch, and tried the door.

It was already closed and locked.

Mitch rang the bell, but no one answered. It didn't take him long to realize that Lilith wasn't going to answer anytime soon.

Screwed up again, Davison, Mitch congratulated himself.

He shoved his hands into his pockets and glared at the door, not yet ready to take no for an answer.

He might not be a star at relationships, but he was damn well going to give this his best shot before he gave up trying. There had to be a way to work through all their various hurts and misconceptions and get back to the place where they had been last night.

Mitch wasn't afraid to work for it.

15

THE DEVIL

Lilith came home at lightning speed, ripped open her front door, and slammed it shut behind her, still seething. She heard Mitch behind her but was too disappointed to face him now.

How could he have lied to her?

And how dare he not believe their story? It was such a stunning breach of faith that Lilith wouldn't have believed it possible, if she hadn't heard it from Mitch's own lips.

He thought she was traumatized and making up stories! She wanted to fling her hands toward the sky and scream. *Men!* Lilith was so irked with Mitch that she wouldn't have been surprised to find smoke curling out of her ears.

What she did find was an unfamiliar man lounging in her living room, toying with her tarot cards.

Lilith froze in the hall and stared. She had locked the door, she knew it. How had he gotten in here? And why was he sitting so calmly in her living room? The intruder had dark hair and dark eyes and dressed with a flamboyance that made her Gift whisper in the back of her mind.

Before Lilith could summon a word, he looked up and grinned. "Lilith!" Her heart hammered that he knew her name. "Took you long enough, baby. How about a kiss for an old friend?"

And he flicked a card from his fingertips to land on the floor at her feet.

It was The Fool, from Lilith's own deck.

"Sebastian?" she whispered, barely daring to believe.

Lilith sank into a chair, so shocked that she was certain her legs wouldn't continue to support her.

"The very same," he confirmed and grinned, clearing enjoying her surprise. "Miss me?"

Lilith stared at him and fought against the truth. Her destined lover was the man sitting right in front of her.

Not the one banging on her door, demanding admission.

Uh-oh.

16

~

THE FALLING TOWER

Suddenly Mitch's confusion made a whole lot more sense to Lilith. Because Mitch wasn't her destiny, after all. Lilith exhaled weakly and tried to wrap her mind around the concept.

No wonder Mitch had been so stunned when she jumped on him. He hadn't understood the import of their entwined fates, because their fates *weren't* entwined.

Lilith's destiny was sitting right in front of her, grinning smugly. There was something about Sebastian's smile that made Lilith want to slap it right off his face, and she certainly didn't like being called "baby" by anyone.

Surely they had just gotten off on the wrong foot.

Lilith glanced from Sebastian to the door Mitch was pounding on and knew there was no point in delaying the inevitable. However disappointing the truth might be, Lilith knew she couldn't challenge destiny.

It simply wasn't done.

She had to tell Mitch the truth.

Lilith opened the door just as Mitch let loose an eloquent stream of cursing. He stopped as soon as he saw her, his eyes widened, and he lifted his hands in a plea for truce.

"Lilith! Just give me five minutes to explain. . . ."

"You don't have to explain," Lilith said flatly. She ran a hand over her brow, feeling suddenly very tired. She couldn't help it—finding her destined lover wasn't as wonderful as anticipated, since it meant giving up Mitch. "There's nothing to explain. I was wrong about everything.

I know it now. Good-bye, Mitch. I'm sorry that you got tangled up in all of this.''

Mitch's eyes narrowed. ''Excuse me?''

''I'm sorry.'' Lilith didn't know what else to say.

Mitch frowned. He looked to his house, then back to Lilith, uncertainty in his eyes. ''Did I miss something here? Correct me if I'm wrong, but didn't we just spend an awesome night, not to mention make a very promising start to the morning? Aren't we making up from an argument?''

''No, Mitch.'' Lilith heard the defeat in her tone. ''We're ending whatever we had begun.''

Oh, she had his attention now. ''What?''

''We aren't destined to be together after all.'' Lilith tried to shut the door and turn away, the whole conversation making her want to cry.

But Mitch's eyes flashed gold and his hand snapped up to stop the progress of the door. ''What the hell do you mean? Okay, okay, I was wrong, but come on, Lilith, give me a chance!''

Lilith shook her head despondently, wishing she could give him a different answer than the one she had to give. ''It's no good, Mitch.''

Mitch folded his arms across his chest, planted his feet in her foyer, and looked about as ready to move as the Rock of Gibraltar. ''What exactly changed in the last five seconds?'' he demanded, his voice dangerously low. ''Give me one good reason why I should walk out this door.''

''Everything has changed.''

''We had a misunderstanding,'' Mitch insisted stubbornly. ''It changes nothing.''

''No, you just don't understand.'' Once Lilith realized that she wasn't going to get by with a quick explanation, she stepped back and gestured to the foyer. ''Come in and you'll see. You have a right to know the truth.''

Mitch's lips tightened. ''I can't leave the kids. Why don't you come back and have breakfast?''

''Because what you have to see is right here,'' Lilith said softly. She managed a half-smile for him. ''This won't take long. Soon you'll see exactly what I mean.''

''Lilith,'' Mitch said her name softly and hesitated, his gaze lingering on her as though he would find the truth in her eyes. Lilith averted her gaze, not wanting him to see the misery surging through her, not wanting him to guess that she wasn't finding it easy to do the right thing.

Because Lilith knew that they didn't have a choice.

Mitch made a frustrated noise in his throat, then strode further into the house. There was purpose in his step and a part of Lilith was pleased that he was not ready to surrender their relationship.

Even if she didn't dare savor that thrill for long.

Without a word, Lilith indicated the living room. Mitch evidently thought she was inviting him to sit down and headed immediately in that direction, looking as though he was preparing to argue a court case.

One that he had no intention of losing.

But Mitch froze on the threshold of the room and stared, in an unconscious echo of Lilith's return home just moments before.

"Who the hell are you?" he demanded of the man Lilith knew was lounging there. "And what are you doing in Lilith's house?"

Sebastian smiled wolfishly just as Lilith entered the room behind Mitch. "I'm Sebastian, come to claim my one true love."

"What's he talking about?" Mitch turned and frowned at Lilith. "I thought *I* was Sebastian!"

"So did I," Lilith conceded. She shrugged sadly and tried to hide her tears from Mitch's perceptive eye. "I guess we were both wrong."

But Mitch shoved a hand through his hair impatiently and scowled at the newcomer. "How long has this guy been here? Has he been bothering you all weekend?"

"Bothering her?" Sebastian swept to his feet. "I've returned to my destined love because she summoned me." His eyes flashed. "And it seems that I've arrived just in time!"

"Don't worry, Sebastian, Mitch always does the right thing."

Mitch swivelled to meet her gaze. "Which would be what?"

"Leaving," Lilith said simply, then laid a hand on Mitch's arm, wishing she could make this easier for him.

Never mind easier for herself.

"Go home, Mitch," she urged gently. "Go home to your kids."

But Mitch's eyes flashed. "You can't be serious about ending this!"

"We don't have a choice."

"The hell we don't!" Mitch gripped her shoulders when Lilith didn't say anything more, as though he wanted to give her a shake. Instead, his voice dropped low. "Lilith, listen to what you're saying! I'm sorry, I made a mistake, but let's talk about it. There's something good growing between us, don't just throw it away."

But Lilith knew better. She dropped her voice and looked into Mitch's eyes, even managing to smile although her heart was aching. "Mitch, you don't understand. . . ."

He spun away from her, clearly seeing that he was making no progress. "No! I don't!" Mitch retorted in frustration, then gestured angrily at Sebastian. "This guy just shows up and that's good enough for you? You had, what, one night together some six hundred years ago? What about us? What about the time we've spent together? What about last night?" Mitch's gaze clung to hers, all amber intensity, and he didn't have to give voice to his real question.

What about his confession of love?

Lilith knew it hadn't been easy for Mitch to let himself care about her, but maybe that was all part of some divine plan. Maybe she was hurting him now so that he could go on to find his one true love. Maybe he had to hurt to learn to love again. Lilith didn't know and right now she didn't care to figure it out.

But she had to do what was right. There was no point in trying to cheat Dame Fortune.

Because the Fates could be vengeful.

"Mitch, we can't fight destiny. . . ."

"Why the hell not?" Mitch leaned closer, his gaze dangerously compelling. "What happened to you, Lilith? What happened to fighting for what you wanted, what happened to not surrendering regardless of the odds? It isn't like you just let something go, particularly something very special."

Mitch took a deep breath and slid his thumbs across her

shoulders. She shivered despite herself, unable to keep herself from responding when a smile tugged at his lips and his voice dropped low. "Lilith, it isn't like you to ignore *magick*."

Lilith's heart skipped a beat as she stared wordlessly back at him. Mitch's determination, as well as his acknowledgement of the magick between them, made Lilith want to throw her arms around his neck and surrender.

But she didn't. Instead, she took a deep breath and looked into his eyes.

But the light was wrong. It was too dim in the room to see whether anyone lurked in the depths of Mitch's eyes or not, though Lilith's Gift whispered to her of the truth.

They weren't a perfect lovematch, at least not anymore. She didn't have to see to know. Sebastian's return had changed everything.

Lilith knew that the future is a constantly changing array of possibilities, a world of options that changes with every choice that each person makes. It didn't make her feel any better that somehow her choices, or Mitch's choices, had led to a fork in the path they walked together, a fork that would compel them each to walk in different directions.

But Lilith couldn't summon the words to explain all of that before Sebastian unfolded himself like a large version of D'Artagnan and strolled across the floor. He halted right in front of Mitch, and poked a finger in that man's chest.

"Beat it, pal. We've got destiny on our side." Sebastian smiled coldly. "And three is a crowd."

"Lilith?" Mitch made one last appeal.

"I'm sorry, Mitch." Lilith swallowed, the words not tasting good in her mouth. "This is how it has to be."

Mitch swore, pivoted, and stalked out the door.

And Lilith felt suddenly as though she had lost everything that had ever mattered to her, even knowing that her destined lover had returned to her embrace.

Surely she and Sebastian had merely had a rough start. Surely once they were alone together the passion that had united them once would flicker to life again.

Surely Lilith couldn't have made as big of a mistake as she felt quite definitely she had.

• • •

Mitch couldn't believe it. He was furious with Lilith for refusing to see the truth. For a woman who talked about destiny and love all the time, she was really missing the road signs on this one.

He loved her. And Mitch knew she loved him.

He wished he could say something that would convince her of the truth. But Mitch had laid out his best arguments, to no discernible effect. And he knew that Lilith wasn't easily persuaded to abandon whatever whimsy she took to heart.

Maybe she hadn't taken him as close to heart as Mitch had thought.

That thought stung, but Mitch knew better. He'd been following his gut instincts long enough to know a reliable lead when he found one. Lilith was the woman for him, Mitch knew it in every fiber of his being.

All he had to do was convince her of the truth. It was hard to walk away from her, doubly hard to leave her in the company of the wretch who had kept her waiting for so long, but Mitch knew an argument that couldn't be won when he saw one.

And he wasn't going to persuade Lilith of anything today.

Mitch took a deep breath as he reached his own back porch, and fought to compose himself. He'd need answers for the kids, reasons for Lilith's quick departure and for her inevitable absence.

Because she wasn't going to be out of his life for long. No way. Mitch had taken one look at this Sebastian and recognized a man of Kurt's ilk. Sebastian wasn't the man for Lilith.

Mitch was.

She'd see the truth soon enough. The guy had some hold on her, that link in the past, but Lilith would see her way through that. This was something she had to work through, like his reassessment of his former marriage. Mitch respected Lilith's intellect and knew she'd make the right choice. And when she did, Mitch would be waiting.

He didn't care how long it took.

And then Mitch would start wooing Lilith in earnest. After all, the lady had appointed Mitch her champion and that was a role he took pretty seriously. It was a role he was damn good at.

It was a role he wasn't going to surrender without a fight.

Lilith sat down weakly in the closest chair and stared at Sebastian, unable to get things into any kind of order in her mind. The strange thing was that the sight of Sebastian did absolutely nothing to her pulse rate.

In fact, the man before her didn't appear to be her type at all. He looked very slick and more than a little unreliable. He didn't even look the way Sebastian had looked all those years ago. And there was a decided absence of magick in the air since Mitch had left. If Sebastian hadn't known about the card, Lilith would have thought he was a complete stranger.

She still felt as though he was.

Of course, nearly six hundred years was a long time. People grew in their own ways. It wouldn't be easy just to pick up where they left off.

And destiny really was on her side this time. Lilith pushed the sight of Mitch's hurt out of her thoughts, deliberately stomped down on the ache of her own heart, and focused on the issue at hand.

As reunions went, this one hadn't been particularly celebratory so far. Maybe she could get them back on the right track.

"So, you are Sebastian," Lilith said deliberately, as though stating his name would make everything make sense.

It didn't. His name didn't even linger deliciously on her tongue the way it had for many centuries.

Lilith frowned and told herself not to fight things she couldn't change.

"Yeah, that's me." Sebastian grinned and preened, clearly expecting Lilith to admire his physique. He did have the build of a legendary Latin lover, bedroom eyes, golden skin, and ruffled dark hair.

But the sight of him did absolutely nothing for Lilith.

"A little upgrade, you know," Sebastian confided. "I wanted a slicker package this time, something with some *serious* style." He flashed a very white smile. "Like it?"

Lilith swallowed, not having it in her to lie and knowing he wouldn't appreciate the truth. "How did you get in here?"

Sebastian's smile broadened. "I hate to be the one to tell you this, baby, but you've got a seriously inferior grade of lock on your door. It was like picking my teeth."

Lilith swallowed her gasp of outrage. "You broke into my house?"

"I didn't break anything," he retorted. "I'm a pro!"

Her destined love was a professional criminal. Lilith pressed her fingertips to her temples. This was getting better and better.

What had she done to deserve such a fate?

"I thought you would have shown up sooner," she commented quietly. "Where have you been?"

"All over the place," Sebastian confessed with a vague wave of his hand. "Spreading the wealth, you know. I've got to tell you that I've had *action* in this life, like you wouldn't believe. Yet there are women everywhere who haven't yet made my delightful acquaintance." He examined his nails with a gleeful smile. "I do what I can to set things to rights."

"What?" His confession brought Lilith to attention with a snap. "You've been with other women?"

"Hundreds of them, baby." Sebastian smiled and shrugged. "Maybe even thousands. Over the years, I've lost count."

Lilith sputtered in her indignation. "But you're supposed to be my one true love!"

Sebastian rolled his eyes. "Women and the stuff they come up with," he mumbled, then smiled engagingly once more. "Sure, Lilith baby, whatever you think is fair."

Lilith leaned forward on her chair. "Don't you think we're destined lovers?"

Sebastian shrugged. "Well, that's what the crowd said when they interrupted a truly perfect seduction scene a week back." His eyes gleamed. "It was on the Riviera, you know, in this great little hotel, all the amenities, if you know what I mean. And I had met this blonde with hooters out to tomorrow. . . ."

"What crowd?" Lilith shook her head. "What are you talking about?"

Sebastian blinked as he found the thread of his story that had caught Lilith's interest—it took him a moment, because it was not the thread that interested him. "The crowd? Oh, yeah, this whole party burst into my room." He snapped his fingers. "Just like they came out of nowhere. It was weird, truly weird."

Lilith's mouth went dry, her Gift sparkled like starlight, and gave her a definite nudge in the direction of a conclusion. "Who were they?" she asked, suspecting she already knew the answer.

"Some council, they said. Pretty hoity-toity name, I don't remember, but they had some really fancy tricks."

"The Grand Consulting Council of Immortals," Lilith whispered reverently, awed that they had taken an interest in her plight.

"Could have been." Sebastian shook a finger at her, more than ready to get back to his story. "Now, this blonde was wearing a bikini, or actually *not* wearing it. . . ."

But Lilith wasn't interested in the blonde. "What did they say to you?"

"Huh? Oh, that I had some obligation from a past life or something equally weird. Freaked out the blonde, which didn't thrill me particularly, I have to say. After she took off, they laid a lot of goofy doom and gloom on the table. I didn't know what they went on about until one of them touched my forehead. I suddenly remembered all these past lives. It was pretty bizarre."

"So you didn't remember anything before that?" Lilith asked, wondering why she didn't find that very reassuring.

"No, but then, it was all right there. Just to make matters more strange, they insisted that I had to come here, that you were waiting." Sebastian leaned closer, no doubt turning what was his best smile on Lilith. "If I'd known you were such a looker, baby I wouldn't have argued as much as I did."

A sick feeling coiled in Lilith's belly. Her voice was tight. "You mean you didn't want to come?"

"Naw! I mean I remembered the other time, but it was hardly anything to chase after, no offense. You were just a skinny kid, not bad looking, but the blonde had you beat hands down. And you couldn't touch her in terms of experience.'' His lips quirked in a smile. ''Nothing personal, baby, but I've got to keep my eye out for myself.''

Lilith forced her words past the lump in her throat, knowing she had to have everything perfectly clear. ''So, you do remember being Sebastian before?''

''Well, now, yeah.'' He shrugged. ''Kind of a gruesome way to go, but that's life. At least I got to come back a few dozen times. And since those council types visited me, I can remember all those babes!'' He winked confidently. ''Pretty neat that my name is the same this time, don't you think? Just like *destiny* or something.''

He'd reincarnated dozens of times, yet he hadn't come looking for her. He'd been too busy spreading ''the wealth,'' as it was.

Lilith didn't like this at all.

She folded her hands together carefully and held Sebastian's gaze. ''Tell me—if you hadn't been arrested all those years ago, would you really have come back to me?''

He smiled coolly and Lilith knew the truth.

No. He'd never cared for her. He'd only wanted to seduce her. Her uncle had been right—and Lilith had been foolish enough to believe otherwise for much longer than she should have.

Her blood ran cold at the realization that this man was still her destined companion for the rest of her days.

''But see, baby, there wasn't a lot of chance of my coming back, anyway.''

Lilith blinked, almost having forgotten where they were. ''What do you mean?''

''Well, I was caught red-handed, as they say.'' Sebastian tapped his temple. ''I remember it all now.''

Red-handed? A lump of horror rose in Lilith's throat as she saw the truth in his eyes. ''You *did* kill that widow!''

Sebastian shrugged. ''Hey, it was an accident. I didn't mean to kill her, but you know, she liked it a bit rough.'' He winked. ''If you know what I mean. Things got a little out of control that night.'' He shrugged easily, supremely unconcerned. ''Happens.''

Lilith could barely choke back her anger. It was bad

enough that Sebastian had taken her virginity, made her all sorts of promises, then gone to another woman's bed—never mind that he had killed that widow and didn't feel a pang of remorse.

He was worse than pond scum!

Oh, she had been an idiot to believe his lies!

The worst part was that she had pined for this pathetic excuse for a man for almost six centuries! Mitch, now there was a man worth pining for.

But he wasn't the man for her.

Lilith decided right then and there that destiny sucked.

"Hey, Lilith, baby, you look like you could use some cheering up." Sebastian leaned closer, his eyes gleaming. "And I've got just the medicine you need. What do you say to a healthy dose of Sebastian for breakfast?"

"No!" Lilith bounded to her feet.

Sebastian's eyes flashed before he smiled with smooth charm. "Hey, you called me. I sure wouldn't have come to this city all on my own. There's nothing going here." His eyes narrowed. "Besides, I heard that you said you were going to make it worth my while."

It didn't help that he was exactly right.

But Lilith still didn't want to keep her word. She rose from her chair, intending just to slide out the door. But Sebastian lunged to his feet, clearly not willing to let her go.

Lilith fled, ripping down the hall to lock herself into the kitchen. Sebastian's footsteps echoed behind. Lilith closed her eyes tightly and chanted a spell to make the lock hold, her heart nearly stopping when Sebastian jiggled the knob forcefully.

The knob stopped moving and Lilith took a wary step back.

"You can't resist my charm forever, Lilith baby," Sebastian whispered through the keyhole. "After all, it's *destiny*."

But Lilith was already hauling her cauldron toward the stove, determined to conjure up an eviction spell. She had been such a fool—somehow there had to be a way to make things come out right.

Lilith flicked on the radio so she wouldn't have to hear

Sebastian breathing on the other side of the door. She was encouraged to hear Gladys Knight singing about her lover taking the midnight train to Georgia. With every "he's leaving" that the Pips echoed, Lilith tossed another pinch into the pot.

She couldn't conjure quickly enough.

Sebastian could have broken the lock, he was sure he could pick it, but clearly Lilith needed a moment to think. Women were like that. But they always came around.

Besides, a little pause in the action wasn't such a bad idea.

Because this wasn't the way Sebastian had seen this deal, not at all. Nobody had said anything about fighting off competition. Of course, that council hadn't been prepared to listen much to Sebastian's point of view, but he was sure that there was a little bit of something curvy in this deal for him.

And that it would be easy pickings.

Clearly, though, Lilith was holding out on him. And she was going to keep doing so. Since that was completely contrary to her passionate response of several centuries ago, Sebastian guessed that the fault lay outside her character.

It was that guy next door. He'd been playing in Sebastian's pond while Sebastian was otherwise occupied. It wasn't pertinent that Sebastian had had no intention of seeking out Lilith before the council intervened.

He was here now—an entire ocean away from civilization as he knew it—and if nothing else, Sebastian wanted what he had come all this unholy way to get.

He'd give Lilith a little time to calm down, then come back and win her over with a healthy measure of his undeniable charm. Sebastian grinned to himself.

She'd forget that jerk next door in nothing flat.

Sebastian slipped out of the house with a whistle on his lips, confident that no matter how Lilith tried to barricade against his return, he could get back into that house.

Guaranteed.

17

THE STAR

Andrea couldn't hide from the fact that she was disappointed. Eight days into her cruise and she still hadn't met anyone even remotely interesting.

Could Lilith have been wrong?

The worst thing about that would be that it would prove Mitch's skepticism right.

She hated proving Mitch right—mostly because it happened too often.

Andrea sighed and took her new swirly blue dress from the tiny closet. She held it up to herself and smiled for her reflection. Tonight was the night Andrea was to sit at the captain's table, although she really wasn't excited about the prospect.

She was tired of old women and men who couldn't dance, honeymooners staring into each other's eyes, and children bored to death after days at sea. She was tired of bingo and skeet shooting and buffets that only seemed to be cleared to make way for another lavish meal. She didn't want to sunbathe anymore, or learn to play shuffleboard, or be marched through an island village in a convoy of tourists. She didn't even want to languish on a perfectly white endless beach.

Andrea wanted to dance. She flicked the hem of the skirt and considered the prospect of having her toes trodden upon yet again. She hadn't seen a single man on this ship who seemed to have a talent for dancing, much less one as interesting as Lilith had promised.

And Andrea had had a good look. She pouted at the

possibility that Lilith had been mistaken, the reflected gesture reminding her so much of Jen that she laughed aloud.

That made Andrea feel better. She'd do some shopping for the kids tomorrow—as though they needed more souvenirs of her trip than she had already acquired. Watching Mitch growl about them getting spoiled would mitigate the disappointment of seeing him proven right again.

Andrea chuckled to herself at the prospect. "If you don't play, you can't win," she informed her mirror image sternly and hung the dress on the bathroom door with purpose. Andrea hadn't gotten this far in life by sitting in a corner and feeling sorry for herself, and she wasn't going to start now.

And she was going to go out with a bang. Partner or no partner, tonight Andrea was going to dance—and dammit, she was going to *sparkle*.

Andrea swept into the dining room with every bit of her usual style and grace. She smiled at the maitre d' and accepted his arm, her chin held high as she was led to her seat. It was a perfect evening for romance, the chandeliers glittered like starlight, the band was playing marvelous music. The crystal tinkled, and there was a low murmur of conversation.

Despite herself, Andrea felt her anticipation rise. She was reminded of nights spent dancing to big band music at Casa Loma with her second husband—well, not actually with him. Walter had always escorted her, then sat with a drink and watched others twirl Andrea around the floor. Walter knew she loved to dance and had been quite philosophical about his own inabilities.

The memory made Andrea smile.

She thought then of her first husband, Bernard, and the way he compelled the younger partners in his law firm to waltz with her at least once at every Christmas party. Those were *parties*! Glittering fêtes at the Park Plaza or the Royal York, either hotel more than competent at elegant little canapés and conjuring the perfect festive mood.

Like the one tonight.

Andrea took her seat and thought of Nate. Now, there was a man who had stolen the key to her heart and never surrendered it again. He had been the only one who wouldn't encourage others to dance with her, a regular old bear when it came to keeping Andrea by his side. She had loved him so much, she just didn't mind. On a night like this, he would have ordered champagne, commandeered a table in the corner, and bent his attention on making her laugh.

Yes, Nate had been a wonderful man.

Andrea blinked back her tears and smiled at her dinner companions as they exchanged introductions. Directly opposite her was a very handsome man about her age, one whom Andrea had not seen about the ship yet. His green eyes twinkled, seeming to hint at a joke only he could discern. An equally handsome wife sat at his side, turning her wedding band around and around her finger as she leaned against her husband and whispered anxiously in his ear.

A pair of elderly sisters from Paducah sat beside them, a besotted young couple beside the sisters stirred themselves long enough to confess that they had just been married on the last island. A retired librarian named Ethel, whom Andrea had already met and whose wry jokes she quite enjoyed, slid into the seat beside Andrea with a smile.

"Lovely, isn't it?" Ethel asked.

"Wonderful," Andrea agreed, consciously masking her disappointment.

Because the captain himself greeted them all from behind his chair, his presence finished the seating. Ethel had already confided that the captain was happily married, that his wife would be joining him for the next circuit of the cruise.

Andrea stared at her salad plate and recalled Lilith's assertion that she would not immediately recognize her soulmate, that he would seem unavailable. Well, barring the possibility that Ethel was hiding her true sexual identity, or that the captain had a liking for women twice his age and was prepared to risk his wife's opinions on the matter, or that the British woman would suddenly drown in her lobster bisque, it didn't appear that Andrea's destined lover had troubled to show.

Well, Ethel was good company.

Andrea turned to the friend she had already made on this trip and—quite deliberately, very defiantly—sparkled.

Andrea was in the act of declining another waltz with a man who seemed to have a rare gift for stepping hard on her toes, when a smooth British accent interjected.

"Perhaps I might have the honor of this dance?"

Andrea turned to find the man from her table with the sparkling green eyes. "Nigel Farnsworth," he reminded her, with a slow smile. "I've made it my personal duty to dance with every lovely lady from our table this evening. Would you indulge me?"

Andrea's gaze flicked back to the table. "Your wife won't mind?"

Nigel's lips quirked. "She might if I had one, but I don't."

Andrea frowned. "But you were sitting—"

"With my sister. Widowed a year ago and moping ever since." He glanced back to the table himself and the twinkle faltered. "I was hoping this cruise might cheer her up a bit, but so far, no luck. She's spent most of the cruise sulking in the cabin and insisting I remain with her." He looked back to Andrea, his expression rueful. "I had no idea the cabins would be quite so small."

Andrea giggled despite herself. "You've managed to escape."

"And only just." Nigel smiled, his eyes twinkled, and Andrea's heart skipped a beat. "One must make the most of one's opportunities. Shall we?"

"Of course," Andrea said and took his hand. The band struck up a waltz and Nigel swung Andrea out onto the floor with the grace of a man who had been dancing from the cradle.

Andrea sighed with delight. "You can dance," she murmured.

Nigel chuckled. "Let me guess—your toes thank me."

Andrea smiled at him. "Every single one of them is charmed."

Not to mention a good part of the rest of Andrea. He was a devastatingly good dancer, guiding her effortlessly through the throng of inexperienced dancers, leaving the perfect distance between them, moving so gracefully and so in tune with Andrea that she felt as though they'd been dancing together forever.

And he wore a very sexy cologne.

"I must confess," Nigel murmured moments later, "that I've been shamelessly eavesdropping on your conversation with your friend." His voice dropped low, his accent making Andrea's bones melt. "You must tell me where the most intriguing woman on this ship has managed to hide for an entire week."

Andrea laughed at his compliment. "Not in my cabin."

"Nor in mine, clearly." The corner of Nigel's lips tweaked. "It seemed I missed more than the shuffleboard tournament."

Andrea looked into the twinkle of his very green eyes and couldn't quite catch her breath.

Everything froze around her as she studied Nigel's smile and realized belatedly that everything was just as Lilith had said. Andrea hadn't guessed that Nigel was available, although she had noticed him first. And he could dance, there was absolutely no doubt about that. She liked the glint of humor in his eyes, she liked how trim he was, she liked the stylish cut of his tux and the tang of his cologne. She liked that he was worried about his sister.

And she liked that he had finally put his foot down.

Andrea stared up at Nigel and her heart seemed to have stopped beating. It suddenly felt as though someone had tied a great big ribbon around her heart and knotted it tight.

It felt as though, one more time, a man had stolen the key to her heart while she wasn't watching. There was a glint of determination in those green eyes and Andrea knew with complete certainty that Nigel wouldn't give that key back without a fight.

And that suited her just fine.

The music changed and Andrea arched a brow at her partner. "Dare I hope that you can tango?" she asked, fully certain of what the answer would be.

Nigel feigned an aristocratic scoff. "What man of substance cannot?" Then he winked, flicked Andrea into a perfect spin, and they danced.

They merengued and they waltzed and they polkaed until

Andrea was sure there were holes in the soles of her shoes. They laughed and they talked and they didn't even notice that nearly everyone was wandering off to bed.

Because they danced some more.

When the band finally called it quits in the wee hours of the morning, Andrea peeled off her shoes and Nigel cast off his jacket. He snagged a bottle of champagne from the maître d' along with a pair of flutes and they laughed as they escaped into the moonlight like naughty children. The bubbles were delectable, the conversation was lively, his puns were horrible.

When the sun painted the horizon pink, Nigel and Andrea were still slow-dancing barefoot on the upper deck. The tingle of champagne bubbles lingered on their tongues, Nigel hummed the "Blue Danube" into her ear. As she watched the last star fade into the morning sky, Andrea knew there was nowhere else she wanted to be.

And that was before Nigel kissed her.

18

THE MOON

Lilith leaned against the hall door to listen.

Nothing.

She turned the key carefully and eased open the door to the foyer, half expecting Sebastian to pounce on her.

Still nothing.

She strained her ears and couldn't hear a thing.

"Sebastian?" Lilith waited and called again. She could feel the house breathing all around her, hear distant sounds of children playing outside.

But she felt no hint of her unwelcome guest. She couldn't even sense his presence, and she had before, as soon as she had stepped into the house.

Could Sebastian have left, *without* imbibing of her special brew?

That would be almost too good to be true. Lilith picked up The Fool card from the floor and peered into the living room. Relief surged through her at its emptiness. She ran upstairs, checking every corner, but already certain what she would find.

He was gone.

For now. Lilith wasn't about to believe that he had abandoned her for good, not as easily as this.

And there was no telling when he would come back. Lilith stepped into the living room and made to put the card back in its place, chiding herself for being so unwelcoming to her destined lover. Sebastian must have *some* good qualities.

It looked as though she was going to have lots of time to find them. Lilith grimaced, then froze when she noticed how many of the cards had turned over during her stay at Mitch's house.

The Death card was the last one she had seen turned up, and much to Lilith's relief, they had clearly moved beyond that point. She pulled up a chair and stared at the cards, hoping for a guiding light of some kind.

Temperance was the card after Death. The woman on that card was in the act of mixing water and wine, of combining two vastly different elements to create something new. Temperance didn't always herald the creation of something good, Lilith knew. There were many different issues to be balanced when this card appeared, volatile elements to be combined, and the result could tip either to wine or vinegar.

That made her think of the argument she and Mitch had had this morning. There was more to that story, Lilith guessed, but things certainly hadn't fallen from their lips in any sort of coherent manner. Hurt was like that—it tipped the scales in favor of misunderstanding.

Lilith pursed her lips and eyed the next card, not even interested in touching it. The Devil. She could make a pretty good guess whose arrival that card heralded. And it was a card that indicated physical temptation, an all-too-evident reminder of how all of this had started so many years ago.

The Falling Tower was the next card and Lilith wrinkled her nose at the sight of it. All of her preconceptions certainly had come tumbling down this morning—a bolt from the blue, just like the lightning bolt on the card, had struck right at the foundation of everything Lilith believed. The house of cards that was her conviction that she and Mitch belonged together had tumbled, not to mention that their entire relationship lay in ruins.

A more apt card to describe this day could not have been found in the deck.

The Star was next, a card of destiny fulfilled, of finding a guiding light, of hanging your hat on a moonbeam and sliding into happiness. Lilith couldn't figure out what the heck that had to do with anything.

Was *that* what she was supposed to do with Sebastian? Was his return that ray of moonlight? Although Lilith might once have expected as much, Sebastian's return to her life— and Mitch's departure from it—had left her feeling less than enthused about the match. Eternal happiness seemed rather an unlikely prospect, given what she had already learned about Sebastian.

He was thief and a womanizer. Maybe this was the lesson of her life—to learn how to love anyone, or how to discriminate between suitable loves.

Lilith half-wished she'd died and gone the cockroach route to atone for her sins instead.

Finally, the Moon card was faceup. It was a portent of a crisis of faith, which was something Lilith could really relate to right now. The Moon was a card that hinted at the need to feel your way forward through the darkness, to find the true path with insufficient light.

Well, it was true that Lilith didn't know what to do. She knew that you couldn't fight destiny, she knew that the right choice was to cleave her path to Sebastian's.

But she didn't like him. Not at all. And she liked what he had done even less. She folded her arms across her chest, sat back, and stared at the cards. Lilith's intuition—solidly within the realm of the Moon, she realized suddenly— urged her to reconcile with Mitch.

But the very thought of defying destiny made Lilith dread the consequences. This wasn't paltry stuff. She knew the Fates couldn't be challenged, for if they were, they took a toll of their own invention.

The truth was that Lilith wouldn't be afraid of paying any price herself. She was pretty sure the Fates would know that.

Which meant that Dame Fortune would take her toll for Lilith's crime in the one place that would hurt Lilith the most. And Lilith knew where her vulnerability lay in all of this—it lay where she had entrusted her heart.

Lilith feared for Mitch.

The simple fact was that she loved him, regardless of what the cards or his eyes or even destiny had to say about it all. She didn't want to see him hurt, or his fortune take a turn for the worse, or anything at all to happen to those darling children.

No doubt about it—as much as Lilith would have liked otherwise, indulging her own desire to be with Mitch couldn't lead anywhere good.

Lilith was just going to have to get over it.

She couldn't help it if that prospect was less than inviting.

It was very early in the morning when a faint sound awakened Lilith. She had fallen asleep on the sofa, both waiting for and dreading the return of Sebastian. Lilith was momentarily disoriented to find herself still in the living room. She just had enough time to wonder what had awakened her before the answer landed square on top of her.

Sebastian!

He pounced with deadly accuracy, his weight knocking the breath out of her as he pinned her to the sofa. Sebastian snatched at her wrists when Lilith started to fight him and kissed her hard. He stank of cigarette smoke, his touch was rough and unwelcome.

"Hey, baby, I'm home," he rumbled in her ear, loosing a stench of beer. The faint undertone of Shalimar clung to him and Lilith had a very good idea how Sebastian had whiled away the hours he was away.

She fought him, but he wasn't going to take no for an answer.

"Easy, baby, you know you want me." Sebastian held Lilith's wrists and leaned his full weight on top of her. She was crushed, she was captured and cornered, and she didn't like it one bit.

Lilith decided in that moment that she'd live out her life alone—however long it might prove to be—rather than put up with having this man underfoot.

Or overtop.

He landed a wet kiss on her, clamping his lips down hard when Lilith tried to turn away. Sebastian slipped his tongue between her teeth and a repulsed Lilith bit it hard. At the same moment, she drove her knee up into his crotch.

Sebastian yowled, Lilith shoved his weight off of her,

knowing that she had only succeeded in tumbling him to the floor because he was shocked.

Lilith bounced to her feet and wiped Sebastian's saliva from her lips with disgust. She wanted to scrub every inch of herself to get rid of his filthy touch.

But first she had to get rid of him. Her wrists still hurt from Sebastian's cruel grip on them and she knew she'd be bruised.

She was lucky to have no greater scars.

Sebastian rolled into a ball on the floor and howled, a response that might have been comical if Lilith hadn't been so mad.

"My tongue! Baby, I think you took the end off it!" He glared lethally at her. "It's your loss, baby. This tongue is worth its weight in gold."

Lilith spat at him and backed away. Sebastian's eyes flashed, he bounded to his feet, and lunged after her. He was bigger than her, he was stronger, he was drunk, and he was mad.

And he wanted one thing from her that Lilith didn't want to give.

There was only one thing she could do to defend herself. Before she could change her mind, Lilith called down a hex. Sebastian snatched at her as she started to chant, his handsome features contorted by a menacing snarl.

Lilith danced back, and she sang out the last line of the curse. She felt the power coil within her, she felt the heat of it seeking a direction. Sebastian swore and jumped as Lilith pointed her finger directly at him.

No sooner had the last word crossed her lips than Sebastian froze.

Lilith sank against the doorframe in relief, hearing her heart race. Her hands were shaking.

Just in time.

Sebastian was locked in the act of leaping after her. His hands were outstretched, his fingers distended, and Lilith knew that in another heartbeat, they would have been locked around her neck. His features were dark with fury, his nostrils were even slightly flared.

And he wasn't breathing. Lilith listened carefully just to make sure. He wasn't dead, he was just . . . stopped. He wasn't hurt, or dead, or even uncomfortable.

Sebastian was just stuck in one particular second of his life.

Lilith liked him much better this way.

She exhaled shakily once she knew for sure that her spell had worked. Although he was hardly the most tasteful sculpture she'd ever seen, in this state, Sebastian was no threat to her.

At least for the moment.

But Lilith still didn't know what she was going to do. The hex would last for maybe a day. She couldn't put this spell on Sebastian indefinitely and she knew that he wasn't going to be a good sport about this when he was back to his usual self.

She didn't even want to look at him.

Lilith didn't know what sort of repercussions would come from her casting a hex. Although technically she hadn't harmed Sebastian, he was mightily inconvenienced. The Rule of Three did say that all a witch cast out into the world would come back upon her threefold.

It was a fairly serious motivational tool. Lilith had a habit of doing only good—her first curse, even for the sake of saving herself, left her very uncertain of the ultimate result.

Would she be trapped similarly for three days, in exchange for every day Sebastian spent this way? Or would the Fates toy with her in another way?

Before Lilith could think any further, the doorbell rang.

19

THE SUN

Mitch had had enough.

A day and a night hadn't improved his mood over Lilith taking on this Sebastian guy and he figured he'd already given her plenty of time to think things over. There was no way he was going to get anything done at work today with this hanging over his head. Mitch bit the bullet, shoved his pride into cold storage, left the kids sleeping, and took a chance.

He went and rang Lilith's bell.

She answered really quickly, the shadows underneath her eyes encouraging Mitch that he hadn't been the only one to miss a night's sleep over this. Relief washed over her features when she found him on her doorstep. Mitch's heart skipped a beat at this sign that he had done the right thing.

"Lilith, we have to talk," was all he managed to say before Lilith grabbed his hand and hauled him into her foyer. It put Mitch in mind of their first meeting, an encounter he wouldn't mind replaying if it could all end more happily.

But Lilith clearly had other things in mind today.

"Look!" she urged and pointed him toward her living room.

Mitch peeked into the room, and jumped in shock to find himself about to be attacked.

Then he realized that Sebastian wasn't moving.

In fact, Sebastian didn't look like he *could* move.

It was as though he was frozen. Curious despite himself, Mitch wandered into the living room and circled Sebastian.

He even touched the man's clawing hand and found the skin still warm.

The hair rose on the back of Mitch's neck. Sebastian didn't even blink, but Mitch had the distinct sense that his rival was *in there.*

And bloody mad about the whole thing.

Mitch stepped back and glanced at Lilith, suddenly having a very clear idea how Sebastian had gotten this way. It seemed that Mitch's ideas about spells were doomed to follow the same path as his certainty about magic.

He cleared his throat, and decided that wasn't so bad.

It was only then that he noticed how Lilith hung back in the foyer, her hesitation decidedly uncharacteristic.

Mitch frowned. "What exactly happened here?"

Lilith bit her lip, her gaze flicking to Sebastian with uncharacteristic nervousness. "He jumped me," she confessed quietly.

What? Mitch saw suddenly that there were bruises already forming around Lilith's wrists. He stepped closer and took Lilith's hand, examining the marks with a frown. An anger rose within him, a fury that any man could treat any woman with such disrespect, that this man had abused this woman this way.

"He was gone all night, he must have been drinking." Lilith's words fell hastily. "I fell asleep on the sofa and he seemed to think I wanted something he had."

Mitch met her gaze. "Did he hurt you?"

Lilith's tears welled, then she shook her head and blinked them away. "He frightened me," she admitted, then glanced at the motionless Sebastian as though she didn't trust him to stay put. Lilith took a deep breath. "I've never cursed anyone before."

Mitch took a long look at Sebastian's pose, at the fury in his expression, and slipped one arm around Lilith's shoulders. "You didn't have a choice," he said softly, pleased when she turned into his embrace.

Mitch held Lilith closer when he felt her trembling, his gaze running over her would-be attacker. He would not think about what this excuse for a man had wanted to do to her.

"I wish every woman could cast a spell like this one."

Lilith looked up at him questioningly. "I thought you didn't believe in spells."

Mitch smiled crookedly. "So, you've convinced me."

But Lilith didn't smile. She eyed Sebastian from the haven of Mitch's embrace and frowned. "It won't last a day."

"Then, what are we going to do before that day is up?" Mitch asked.

Lilith blinked. "We?"

"Yes, *we*." Mitch was resolute. "Lilith, I meant everything I said yesterday. I love you and I think you love me. We make a hell of a team and I'm not prepared to let it all go just because this jerk showed up."

Lilith frowned and avoided his gaze, her move feeding Mitch's certainty that she was less certain of her path than she would have liked to be. He bent his will on persuading her to his side. "You can't spend your life with this guy, and you can't keep hexing him like this."

"No," Lilith admitted.

"Lilith," Mitch said softly, tipping her chin up with his fingertip so that she met his gaze. Her eyes were wide and dark, wondrous eyes that Mitch could willingly gaze into for the rest of his days. "I love you," he insisted, "and I don't intend to stop."

Her smile was fleeting, her frown returning when she glanced again at Sebastian. "But he's my destined lover."

There was less certainty in her tone than there had been originally and Mitch dared to be encouraged.

But he'd have to argue on her terms.

"Says who? You're the one who saw all sorts of meaning in my buying the house next to you. Don't you think that events—not to mention a dog and a cat—have conspired to throw you and me together? Who's to say *that's* not destiny?"

Lilith nibbled her bottom lip. "But, Mitch, it doesn't count. My destiny was sealed before I met you. We can't defy destiny."

"Why not?"

"Because we can't." Lilith's lips set stubbornly.

Mitch gripped her shoulders, sensing that the tide had turned against him again. "Why the hell not? We just do it, we just get rid of this loser—we'll FedEx him to Kashmir, if we have to—then we'll live happily ever after. It's not that complicated!''

But Lilith shook her head. "No, it doesn't work like that." Something flickered in the depths of her gaze when she looked up at him and Mitch thought it might be fear. He caught at her chin, but Lilith danced out of his grip, refusing to look into his eyes.

"What are you afraid of?" Mitch demanded. "What can go wrong? What do you know that you aren't telling me?"

Lilith's lips tightened, then she folded her arms across her chest, and she looked hard at Mitch. "Why do I have this impression that you're not going to leave without an answer?"

Mitch grinned. "Because I'm not." He sobered, his gaze locked with hers. "There are things," he said softly, "that are worth fighting for, and this is one of them."

Lilith held his gaze for what might have been an eternity and Mitch could almost hear the wheels turning in her mind.

Then the defiance melted out of the set of her shoulders. "Challenging destiny comes with a price," she said quietly.

"What kind of price?"

"I don't know." Lilith licked her lips as though choosing her words carefully. "I'm not afraid of paying any toll the Fates charge. I'm afraid that they'll hold me responsible, if you and I decide to challenge their edict, because I should have known better. I'm afraid that they'll bring misfortune down upon you to teach me a lesson."

Lilith was refusing Mitch to ensure his own future. He was humbled by her concern—even though he was certain it was misguided. He stepped back to her side.

"But Lilith," Mitch argued with quiet conviction, "if we're together, we can face anything the Fates toss our way. I don't want to be lucky if it means being without you."

Tears welled in her eyes and Mitch took a step closer. "Be with me, Lilith and we'll surmount any obstacle before us."

"I love you," Lilith confessed softly. "I love you in a way I never imagined I could love anyone. I was wrong about Sebastian—I saw what I wanted in him instead of what was really there.''

Mitch smiled. "Been there, done that," he acknowledged. "It's not fatal. Besides, I'm starting to think that the only people who never make mistakes are people who never take chances." Mitch offered Lilith his hand and his voice dropped to an urgent whisper. "Let's take a chance on happiness, Lilith."

And Lilith smiled fully, for the first time since Sebastian had arrived. She stepped forward with glowing eyes and put her hand into Mitch's palm. "There's no gamble between us," she declared, "just in what the Fates cast our way."

"Absolutely," Mitch concurred as he drew her into his embrace. "Now, do I get a kiss to celebrate this happy ending?"

Lilith smiled fully and just had time to slide her arms around Mitch's neck before there was a thunderclap loud enough to pop an eardrum.

It seemed to come from the living room.

They both jumped at the sound and turned as one. Mitch had no doubt that he wasn't the only one suspecting Sebastian had broken free.

But Sebastian remained exactly as he had been.

It was the assembled multitude behind him that made Mitch's eyes widen. Clearly the room had been magically enhanced to hold this entire auditorium of guests. More than one steely gaze returned his glance and Mitch had a very definite impression of disapproval.

No doubt about it, Mitch had a sudden certainty that their happy ending was far from assured.

"The Grand Consulting Council of Immortals," Lilith breathed.

Mitch looked to her in mingled confusion and alarm. "What?"

Lilith met his gaze, her own expression troubled. "Sort of a supreme court for destiny," she said ruefully. "It looks as though we've already attracted attention."

20

JUDGMENT

The Grand Council chamber hadn't changed much in the past few centuries. It was still a circular and massive auditorium, with tiers of seating for its membership.

It had been here that Lilith was granted the elixir, beneath the watchful eye of several thousand council members, each outfitted in their finest. They were a varied group, including Merlinesque old wizards with their long gray beards and glinting eyes, witchy old hags who cackled when they laughed, the lithesome young beauties with ancient eyes.

There were shamans of every persuasion and shape-shifters who could not be relied upon to remain still, let alone the same, or the duration of a single session. There were fauns and fairies, leprechauns and nymphs, the stuff of mortal legends in the flesh. Unicorns and centaurs, griffins and dragons—in general, all manner of mythical beasts crowded the hall.

The less predictable immortals included ballpoint pens that always seemed to go missing, single socks that found escape through the dryer vents throughout the world, washers that had abandoned the screws they had been made to fit, and thumbtacks that dropped, rolled, and were never seen again. Much more sentient than mortals believed, these creatures had escaped what they saw as the slavery of the material world, crept through wormholes in the space-time continuum, and earned their immortality through tests as arduous as Lilith's own had been.

Mitch had been right—there were a lot of immortals. They just stuck to their own kind.

The floor of the chambers still took Lilith's breath away—the brilliant lapis lazuli inlaid with golden zodiac signs so beautifully wrought that she didn't want to step on it at all. The ceiling arched high, so much like a starlit sky that she still couldn't tell where it ended, if indeed it did.

For the chambers had been constructed in a dimension beyond the three of usual human perception, or even the fourth suspected by many mathematicians. Lilith had heard rumors that it was firmly lodged in the seventh dimension, but could not say for certain.

Physics had never been her strong suit.

One thing was clear—the way to the council was obscured to all except those that were specifically summoned.

The presence of Lilith's living room table, her tarot cards still laid out as she had left them, showed the link to the world she knew best. And Sebastian, of course, had apparently been summoned as well, although he was still frozen in that pose.

An older woman leaned over Lilith's table, a bright floral shawl wrapped over her hair, her bony finger poking at the cards. Lilith saw that the cycle was nearly complete, The Sun having turned faceup after The Moon.

The Sun, which hinted at refuge after facing adversity. The Sun, which told of finding a haven, a garden, a place of repose. The card told that the journey was nearing its end and hinted that all would go well.

The Sun could only signify Mitch's determination that they should be together, whatever the odds.

But Lilith knew what the next card was and it was no small obstacle. As though hearing her thoughts, the elderly woman picked up the next card and deliberately turned it over, snapping it against the table.

Judgment.

Lilith's mouth went dry. Then the crone looked up, letting Lilith see her face for the first time, and smiled knowingly.

"Dritta!" Lilith exclaimed with delight.

The older woman chuckled and shook a finger at Lilith.

"You did not think I would abandon you?" she demanded archly. "Child of my child, holder of the Gift, I could not let you wander alone."

Her gaze wandered over Mitch, no doubt noting the way he held Lilith's hand, then lingered upon Sebastian. Dritta's lips were drawn into a stern line when she looked at Lilith again. "Even if you have made some unconventional choices."

Dritta spun in a flurry of skirts and held up her hands to the council. "I called this meeting for the sake of my own grandchild," she declared. "It is a breach of our code, I know it well, but blood calls."

"What of this one?" demanded a shaman garbed in bone and hide. He stood up to open the discussion and pointed to Sebastian. "He was her destined lover, he pledged to her on the gallows that he would return."

Lilith had no chance to respond before a pale green fairy sparkled on the back of her seat, determined to have her say. "And she swore to love him forever," she squeaked.

It was hard to argue your case in a court like this one, where anyone could voice a concern and everyone could hear your resulting thoughts. Lilith had found it chaotic the last time she was here—and then the council members had already been fairly unanimous about her winning the sip of the elixir.

This time, they were so unsettled that they made her head hurt.

"She *summoned* him," intoned a graybeard with obvious disapproval. "That is no small thing."

The council members stirred at this, a ripple of anxiety rolled through their ranks. Lilith knew she didn't imagine that their gazes turned sharper.

She lifted her chin. "I summoned my lover true," Lilith corrected, lifting the hand that was still entangled with Mitch's. She smiled just for him, hoping this exhibition didn't challenge his newfound faith in things beyond the material world. "And he came."

"You didn't keep your word!" cried a mauve unicorn.

"Not for lack of trying!" Mitch retorted with his usual loyalty. He pointed to Sebastian. "Lilith waited almost six centuries for this jerk. And he had *no* intention of keeping his word!''

Chatter broke out in the seating and more than one argument could be heard as everyone had his or her say. Dritta lifted her hands in a bid for silence, then whistled sharply when she didn't get it.

The council members settled restlessly.

''Lilith has made choices I would not have condoned, but her intentions are pure.''

''She has to pay a price!'' demanded the graybeard.

''She has already lost her immortality,'' snapped Dritta, raising her hands when they started to mutter again. ''Lilith meant no harm, she did no harm, she made a mistake, but found love all the same. Who among you can say whether this was a grand scheme to help these two find each other?'' She straightened and eyed the assembly. ''Why else would the elixir fail her now? It's never happened before!''

The arguments erupted again and grew more heated.

''She believed herself that Sebastian was her destined lover!'' squeaked the fairy.

''But I was wrong!'' Lilith cried. ''How many times has he reincarnated? He never returned to me, not even once.''

''So, you hexed him for vengeance?'' demanded the graybeard who clearly thought little of Lilith's case.

''I hexed him to keep him from raping me.'' Lilith folded her arms as the council clicked their tongues.

''It's true, I was watching,'' affirmed one.

''And he was with three other women during the night.'' There was a lot of tsk-tsking in the group.

''Hardly a lover true.''

''Hardly a man worth waiting for.''

It seemed that every member turned simultaneously to examine Mitch. He straightened behind Lilith, his grip sure on her hand, and she welcomed his strength of conviction.

''He loves her.''

''She loves him.''

''He defends her.''

''He believes in magick now, too.'' That was greeted with a murmur of pleasure.

Dritta smiled approvingly at Lilith and Mitch, a wealth of affection in her eyes. ''And he was willing to defy us just to have her by his side. That is a love worthy of indulgence."

Approval swept through the ranks and Lilith dared to feel encouraged.

"I ask you only to bless their match," Dritta continued, her tone turning authoritative once more. "And to forgo any retaliation for defying destiny, given the extenuating circumstances in this case.

"Even I was wrong about that one." And she gave Sebastian a dark glance.

The council nodded, they closed their eyes. Dritta closed her fist and Lilith held her breath. She gripped Mitch's hand tightly, knowing that whichever way the vote went, there could not be another man for her.

"What's happening?" he asked in an undertone.

"They're voting. Their thoughts will conjure a ball in Dritta's hand that shows the majority." Lilith met Mitch's concerned gaze. "White is the one we want."

"Is there any appeal?" he asked, ever the practical one.

Lilith shook her head. "The council stands by their decisions, for all eternity."

Mitch frowned, heaved a sigh, and frowned again. "I don't suppose you could come up with a little spell?"

"Not here. We've already done all the magick we can do."

In that moment, Dritta turned, her clenched fist held high. "It is done," she declared, then faced Lilith and Mitch. Lilith held her breath and Mitch's fingers tightened over hers.

When Dritta slowly opened her hand, the result of the vote was cradled in her palm.

It was a white ball.

Lilith gasped with delight, then pivoted to fling her arms around Mitch's neck. "They said yes!" she cried, and Mitch swung her into his arms, laughing as he caught her against him. He kissed Lilith on the end of the nose, then put her down and inclined his head to both Dritta and the council.

"I thank you all for this," he said simply. "But we still have one problem." And Mitch indicated the frozen Sebastian.

"The spell won't last long," murmured Dritta. "It fades even now."

"We'll have to decide what to do with him."

"Definitely a penance is due." The graybeard seemed to think everyone should pay for something.

An elegant young witch slipped out of her seat and crossed the floor, circling Sebastian as she gave him a thorough appraisal.

"But he has a certain roguish appeal," she conceded with a wicked smile. "I could make something of him."

"More toads," murmured the graybeard wearily.

The witch fired a glance across the hall so hot that it flashed like a laser and bore right into the arm of the graybeard's seat. He flinched as steam rose from the resulting hole. The graybeard took a deep breath and seemed to grow in place, but Dritta lifted her hands.

"Enough of your bickering! Save your thunderbolts for later." The wizard slumped reluctantly, muttering audibly to his neighbor that Dritta was not being fair.

The witch tossed her hair and patted Sebastian's rump proprietarily. "I'll take him."

"Not yet," Dritta counselled. "He must pay for his failure to keep his word before he becomes your toy." She pursed her lips. "He must learn about love, because that is what he disrespected the most."

Mitch cleared his throat and all eyes turned on him. "If you don't mind the input of a mortal, I have an idea."

Dritta's eyes gleamed, and the council leaned forward. "Tell us!" they cried.

Mitch did, his idea so brilliant that Lilith couldn't stop her laughter from bubbling forth. It was just too perfect— and passed council approval with ease.

A vivid blue brew was bubbling and ready when Dritta finally snapped her fingers under Sebastian's nose. He blinked, flexed his muscles, and relaxed his posture. He looked around, then rolled his eyes with a groan.

"Oh, no," he muttered. "Not again."

"Oh, yes," Dritta declared and gripped the back of his neck. The lovely young witch sidled up beside Sebastian and gave him a thorough kiss. When she stepped back, he tried to follow her, but Dritta's grip prevented that.

"Hurry back," the witch purred, then lifted the blue potion.

Sebastian's nose twitched. He seemed to guess what she intended to do with the noxious-looking liquid. He tried to retreat, but Dritta held him firmly in place. He grimaced when he got a whiff of the brew, but the witch firmly pinched his nose shut.

She tipped the long vial, and Sebastian struggled mightily.

He held his breath, he closed his eyes.

He took a sip.

And he disappeared in a blinding flash of orange light.

Kurt nearly drove his truck into the ditch when this guy just appeared in the passenger seat beside him.

Okay, it was early, he'd been out drinking the night before and had spent most of the night entangled in some redhead's legs. He hadn't had that much sleep.

But this tall, foreign-looking guy in macho leather definitely hadn't been invited into Kurt's truck.

And his sudden appearance nearly made Kurt swerve off the highway. "Jesus Christ!"

The man shook his head, then grabbed the wheel to steady it. "No," he said tightly. "You've got me confused with someone else."

But Kurt was still rattled. "How did you get in here? I'm doing a hundred and twenty klicks here!"

"Get used to it," the man said grimly.

"Get the hell out of my truck!"

The man shook his head. "Won't help. You're stuck with me, Kurt MacEwen, although neither one of us has to like it."

The way this guy knew his name was even more creepy. Man, what had he been drinking? "What the hell are you talking about?"

"I'm talking about love."

"No offense, but you're hardly my type." Kurt looked the intruder in the eye. "I'm a straight shooter, all the way."

"You and me both," the other man agreed with a sudden smile. "But then, they said we'd think exactly the same."

"They?"

"The people who sent me here. Don't even ask for details, you won't believe it." The man straightened. "Hell, I didn't believe it until I saw them myself."

A wacko. He had a wacko in his truck. "So, do you always see people that other people can't see?" Kurt demanded skeptically as he took his exit. "Or do you just hear them?"

To his surprise, the intruder snatched at his collar and once again nearly compelled him off the road. "Listen," the man hissed. "I've got a job to do here and I don't want to do it any more than you want to be a part of it. But no one's giving us a choice." He gave Kurt's collar a shake, then released him, sitting back in his seat like a big ruffled cat. "You want to get rid of me—you just get the job done."

"What job?" The light at the end of the ramp had turned green and somebody was honking behind him, but Kurt didn't drive on. He was staring at this guy, unable to shake the sense that this was really important.

The guy's lips tweaked as though he had just thought of a private joke. "You've got to learn to fall in love. You've got to make a commitment to one woman for the rest of your life."

"Yeah, right." Kurt snorted and stepped on the gas. "You're wasting your time, man. That's never going to happen."

"Oh, I say it will," the man murmured silkily. "Because I don't get out of this until you do just that, and I'm not feeling inclined to take no for an answer."

But Kurt had had enough. He pulled over to the curb, slammed the truck into park, leaned across the guy, and opened the door. "Get your ass out of my truck."

But the man smiled coldly and showed no intention of moving. He was a big guy, tall and lean, probably even stronger than he looked. And there was a determination in his eyes that made even Kurt think twice about crossing him.

Kurt, after all, was a lover, not a fighter.

"I don't think that's a good idea," the intruder said smoothly, his eyes narrowing. "You see, I'm going to find you, no matter where you go.'' He calmly recited Kurt's address and phone number, and Kurt felt a sudden chill. ''And don't worry, I can outsmart any lock. The fact is, if I'm not in a good mood about things, well, you might not like the results.''

''You're threatening me!''

''No, I'm *promising* you. I want this done and I want it done soon, and if you're going to buck me on it, well''—the man's cold smile broadened—''I might get vengeful.'' He poked a finger in Kurt's chest.

Kurt sat back in his seat with a thump. He shoved a hand through his hair and looked sidelong at his companion. ''So, you just show up in my truck, threaten me, and insist you're going to plant yourself in my life . . . unless I fall in love?''

''That would be it.'' The man closed the door and offered Kurt his hand. ''Sebastian. I suggest we keep this short and simple.''

Kurt shook it, not certain what else to do. ''I just have to fall in love with a woman to get rid of you.''

''Exactly.''

Kurt pursed his lips. ''I hate to be the one to break this to you, but you don't just pick some babe up off the street and fall in love with her. Or maybe you would, I don't know, but it's not my style.''

''Your style is get in and get out, I know that,'' Sebastian snapped. ''And there's no need to worry about the woman in question.'' He pulled a slip of paper out of his pocket. ''I just happen to have Isabel's name and address right here.''

''What?''

''Just drive,'' Sebastian instructed. ''I understand this Isabel thinks about men in the same way we think about women. It could be quite interesting. *She* could be quite interesting.'' He smiled again. ''I just might give you a run for your money.''

Kurt floored it and the truck leapt back into the stream of traffic. He was always ready for a challenge.

''She'd better be cute,'' he said grimly.

''On the contrary,'' Sebastian countered with poorly concealed amusement. ''You'd better hope that she thinks *you're* cute.'' He stretched his legs, looking long and lean and very masculine, then smiled that smug smile that made Kurt want to deck him.

That settled it. Kurt was going to beat this bastard at his own game, one way or the other.

Even if he had to fall in love with some Isabel to do it.

As soon as Sebastian was gone, Dritta led Mitch and Lilith before the council. They turned to face each other, right hand clasping right, left clasping left, the crossing of their arms making the same figure eight that Lilith had made with her cards.

The mark of infinity, the sign of a timeless love circling back over and over again. This was her destiny, this was her fate, this was the man she'd find time and again. Lilith smiled into Mitch's eyes as they pledged their love to each other before a multitude of witnesses.

''And now,'' Dritta said, ''you may kiss the bride.''

Mitch did exactly that.

When Lilith opened her eyes, they were standing alone in her living room. Although Sebastian was gone, the sky was the same hue of early-morning gray.

It was as though they had never been gone at all.

Except there was an envelope on the mantle that hadn't been there before. Lilith crossed the room, and tore open the envelope, smiling when she saw its contents.

It was the last card of the higher arcana.

''Mitch, they've given us The World!''

He grinned and strode in pursuit, taking the card from her hands and flicking it back onto her table. ''No,'' Mitch said, his eyes bright with intent and his voice low. ''They're telling us that we already have it.''

And this time, without an audience, he really kissed her.

Lilith was only too happy to kiss him back.

21

THE WORLD

New Year's Eve

It was going to be a beautiful wedding.

Andrea had clearly spared no expense on the black-tie fête planned to mark her fourth taking of marital vows. Nigel, to his credit, insisted that this would be Andrea's last trip to the altar and Lilith loved how the older woman giggled at that.

In fact, they were quite the couple, obviously completely taken with each other and bent on making each other happy. Nigel was a perfect gentleman, dapper and diplomatic, always ready with a word to make everyone smile. He could dance like a dream and Andrea just glowed in his presence. This shipboard romance showed no signs of limping back to port.

Even Mitch conceded that he couldn't have picked a better man for Andrea himself.

To the astonishment of everyone—except Mitch and Lilith—Kurt and the intern Isabel from Mitch's paper had become a devoted couple. They were so smitten with each other that Andrea had invited them to the wedding, making more than one comment about Kurt finally finding his match. There were rumors of a ring being in the offing for Valentine's Day.

Jen would be the only flower girl for her nana's wedding, a role that delighted her to no end. Lilith had picked up the rose petals after three practice sessions, then declared that enough was enough and stored the basket high. Jason had marched up and down the living room with the lacy pillow for the rings until Lilith pronounced his pacing right, although he had yet to be trusted with the jewelry itself. Mitch had the rings in safekeeping.

Jen looked like a little angel in her pink taffeta dress. There were clusters of silk ribbon roses in myriad shades of pink stitched along the bodice, chosen to match the real flowers ordered for the wedding. A lace-edged petticoat held out the full skirt and Jen was so smitten with that frilly petticoat that she willingly showed it to anyone.

Mitch had rolled his eyes the first time Jen did this and called it a bad omen of the future.

Jason was less thrilled with his miniature tuxedo and its emerald jacquard vest. He made a great show of sticking out his tongue as though he were asphyxiating when Mitch knotted the tie. They both looked cute as could be, though, and ought to be able to stay that way at least until the end of the ceremony.

The wind was sending snowflakes against the windows and the children were downstairs when Mitch's reflection loomed behind Lilith's own in their bedroom mirror. He was perfectly turned out in his tux, his wavy hair combed to some sort of order, a smile curving his firm lips.

Lilith's heart made the little flutter at the sight of Mitch that she sincerely hoped would never stop. "Need help with that zipper?" he asked, and Lilith nodded mutely. The black and white of his tux complemented the deep ruby red of her evening dress, the garnet rose on Mitch's lapel marking them as a couple.

Lilith liked that.

"You'll outshine the bride," Mitch teased in a low voice, taking his time with the zipper, then running a leisurely fingertip across her bare shoulders. His golden eyes gleamed when Lilith caught her breath, the warmth of his fingertip meandered down her spine. "Have I mentioned that this is a very sexy dress, Mrs. Davison?"

"About forty times," Lilith admitted with a smile. "Today."

"Then, let's make it forty-one," Mitch breathed. "I like your hair up—it leaves lots of neck free for nibbling." He caught her shoulders in the strength of his hands and, as

Lilith watched in the mirror, bent to kiss her nape.

His breath and the gentleness of his touch made Lilith shiver, but she straightened deliberately. "If you're going to do that all night, I'll have to wear a jacket."

"Mmm, then I'll have to behave," Mitch murmured, showing no immediate intention of doing so. His hands slid around her waist, his kisses meandered closer to her earlobe. Lilith was trapped between his hips and the dresser and didn't really want to escape. "Is it all right with you if I fantasize about the matron of honor during the ceremonies?"

Lilith laughed. "Fair enough. I'll be thinking about taking off the best man's tux."

Mitch's eyes glinted with mischief as he met her gaze in the mirror. "With your teeth?"

Lilith pivoted in his embrace and looped her arms around his neck. "It could be arranged," she whispered, then stretched to kiss him.

Mitch was every bit as delicious as he had been that very first time. Lilith loved the taste of him and the smell of him, she loved going to sleep in his arms and waking up with their legs tangled together. She loved living together and laughing together, cooking together and raising the kids together. They had sold her house, Lilith more than ready for the challenge of rescuing another, and Mitch good-naturedly lugged paint and stripped ancient wallpaper at her command.

Maybe one day they'd have more children, or maybe that wasn't destined to be. Lilith didn't care. She was happy and she knew from the light in his eyes that Mitch was happy, too.

It was more than enough. All that good stuff, Mitch had once called it—and this certainly was good.

Long moments later, Mitch lifted his head and stepped away. "Ready?"

"This is as good as it gets," Lilith said with a smile. She touched up her lipstick and dropped it into her evening bag, then turned to find that Mitch had conjured a small blue gift box tied with a white satin ribbon.

"Maybe you need just one more thing," he suggested softly.

Lilith looked from the box to him. "What's that?"

Mitch shrugged. "You'll have to open it to find out."

Clearly he wasn't going to give her any hints. Curious, Lilith accepted the box and untied the ribbon. She opened the lid to find two matched gold rings—one big, one smaller—nestled in the deep blue velvet lining.

"They look like wedding rings, old ones." Lilith looked questioningly to Mitch, who stepped closer.

With gentle fingers, he lifted the pair of rings from the box and his smile faded. "They were my parents' rings," he admitted, his voice unusually husky. "Andrea gave them to me the other day."

"She must have thought you'd want them as a memento," Lilith suggested, not expecting Mitch to look up so quickly.

"I do," he affirmed, then lifted the smaller one between his finger and thumb. "But I don't want to tuck this box away somewhere, as though they're just more things to store." Mitch took a deep breath and Lilith knew whatever he was going to say was important to him. "And I thought that this might be the perfect night to show them to you."

"Since we're going to a wedding?" Lilith asked with a smile.

"Exactly." Mitch returned her smile, then frowned down at the ring he was rolling between his finger and thumb. "I'd like these to be *our* wedding rings, Lilith," he said quietly. "I'm not superstitious, but I think it would be good luck."

Mitch glanced up, his expression somber, a question lurking in his eyes. "Lilith, would you wear my mother's ring?"

Lilith saw the memory of his parents' love shining in those golden eyes, as well as that tiny reflection of herself waving back. "Are you sure? They're quite precious to have. I wouldn't want them to be damaged."

Mitch nodded firmly. "They'd be pleased, both that we've found each other and that we're wearing their rings. And they're already broken in."

Lilith could only smile. "You sound as though you don't think your parents know about us."

Mitch's gaze flicked to hers, then his lips curved in a

slow smile. "Maybe they do," he conceded, clearly liking that possibility.

Lilith put her hand on his. "I'd be honored to wear your mother's ring, Mitch. Andrea told me that they had a wonderful marriage."

"A love for all time," Mitch said as he slipped the smaller ring onto her finger and Lilith wasn't sure whether that was an agreement or a pledge.

It suited her either way.

When the ring was at the base of Lilith's finger, Mitch looked into her eyes. "Perfect fit," he mused.

Lilith picked up the other ring and slid it onto Mitch's ring finger. It also fit as though it had been made for him. She stretched up to brush her lips across his.

"Kismet," she whispered, her heart singing when Mitch kissed her soundly.

Because that was exactly what it was.

TIME PASSAGES

__CRYSTAL MEMORIES *Ginny Aiken*	0-515-12159-2
__A DANCE THROUGH TIME *Lynn Kurland*	
	0-515-11927-X
__ECHOES OF TOMORROW *Jenny Lykins*	0-515-12079-0
__LOST YESTERDAY *Jenny Lykins*	0-515-12013-8
__MY LADY IN TIME *Angie Ray*	0-515-12227-0
__NICK OF TIME *Casey Claybourne*	0-515-12189-4
__REMEMBER LOVE *Susan Plunkett*	0-515-11980-6
__SILVER TOMORROWS *Susan Plunkett*	0-515-12047-2
__THIS TIME TOGETHER *Susan Leslie Liepitz*	
	0-515-11981-4
__WAITING FOR YESTERDAY *Jenny Lykins*	
	0-515-12129-0
__HEAVEN'S TIME *Susan Plunkett*	0-515-12287-4
__THE LAST HIGHLANDER *Claire Cross*	0-515-12337-4
__A TIME FOR US *Christine Holden*	0-515-12375-7

Prices slightly higher in Canada   **All books $5.99**

Payable in U.S funds only. No cash/COD accepted. Postage & handling: U S./CAN $2.75 for one book, $1.00 for each additional, not to exceed $6.75; Int'l $5.00 for one book, $1 00 each additional. We accept Visa, Amex, MC ($10.00 min), checks ($15.00 fee for returned checks) and money orders. Call 800-788-6262 or 201-933-9292, fax 201-896-8569; refer to ad # 680 (4/99)

Penguin Putnam Inc.   Bill my: ☐ Visa ☐ MasterCard ☐ Amex _____ (expires)
P.O. Box 12289, Dept. B   Card#_____
Newark, NJ 07101-5289
Please allow 4-6 weeks for delivery.   Signature_____

Foreign and Canadian delivery 6-8 weeks

Bill to:
Name_____
Address_____ City_____
State/ZIP_____
Daytime Phone #_____

Ship to:
Name_____	Book Total	$_____
Address_____	Applicable Sales Tax	$_____
City_____	Postage & Handling	$_____
State/ZIP_____	Total Amount Due	$_____

This offer subject to change without notice.